Burning Heir

KELSEY FORSTER

For the daydreamers, the wanderers of worlds unseen—may you forever lose yourself in stories and find yourself in the magic between the pages.

For Onagh, who never got the chance to read this dedication.

THE SERPENT ACADEMY
WINTER
WALL OF CRIMSON
AUTUMN
DRAGON FIELDS
THE ACADEMY
DAY
DOC
SERPENT ESTATE

NIGHT
SPRING
GRIFFIN FIELDS
TRIAL GROUNDS
SUMMER

LEADERS ARE NOT BORN. THEY ARE MADE.

The Serpent Academy was established by Cleminore Herring after the totalitarian rule of her snake-wielding bloodline. All Seekers have been killed off, and the Forgotten have fled. Yet, more lands become barren as the attacks on Verdonia continue.

The Malvoria guards will reap the dropouts of the Serpent Academy. Die for your claim or die for your land.

It began with six—six Gods whose blood fell like rain, carving the borders of frost, where the winds of Autumn carried the voices of the lost. Heat was silenced, transformed into lush groves, and the ocean's salt became a breath of Spring's toxins, seeping into the land. And then, daylight shattered—stolen, forced to barter for the sun's very essence. Realms were severed between six. No ruler could wield all the powers, so they created the Academy and various thrones for heirs to claim.

Chapter 1

My father once told me I could one day rule our iced kingdom. I never believed him—not with four older brothers, each spouting their own version of that political gospel. It seemed more like a distant dream than a reality, one I was never meant to inherit.

But then one failed. The other died. The remaining two were never even invited. That's when I began to understand the weight of my father's words, as one by one, the Serpent Academy slipped past them, and Father's wards weakened with each passing year.

For the first time, I realized the true power of his vision when his only daughter was called to claim his throne.

The air was thick, charged with inevitability. It was the calm before a storm. Beyond the peaks, griffins stirred restlessly, their wings beating against the still air. Whether it was fear—or something rarer, something darker—I couldn't say.

No one ventured into the iced lands anymore. No one came back.

I hated the cold. But I hated visitors more. Not since Klaus's death had I dreaded a knock more than I dreaded this one.

Father had warned me my letter was coming—but not during the thawing of the land. When the mail carrier arrived, I barely looked at him as he handed over three letters. But only one mattered—mine.

These letters didn't just deliver news. They chose us. If I was worthy, I would go to the Serpent Academy. If not, I'd likely be married off to a ruler, forced into a loveless marriage.

Out of five siblings, I was the last one left. The last to be chosen.

Cully, the second-oldest Blanche, noticed the letters. "Is that the mail?" he asked, his voice low. He already knew what he was getting—a routine assignment from Valscribe to journal somewhere on the Continent.

Knox, a year older than me, stood beside him and smirked. "Let's open them on three, yeah? Then maybe I'll have time to run before Charles drags me off to Malvoria to become a guard."

Knox had aged out of the possibility of becoming our father's heir, so it was only a matter of time before he was forced to protect our borders as a guard.

Cully grinned, gesturing toward the fireplace. "We could always burn them. Who'd know?"

Knox shook his head. "Right, because throwing them into the fire is totally going to work when Father's wards fall apart with no heir. Severyn was invited. We all know it."

Cully stared at Knox's golden letter, his rounded glasses catching the light from the overhead lantern. "That doesn't look like a Malvoria invitation. A golden letter? That's from the Capital."

Knox shrugged, snatching the letter before Cully could investigate further. "Let's get this over with," he muttered. "I don't care where they're sending me."

Cully hesitated. "On the count of three. One…" he began.

"Two," Knox interrupted, already tearing into his envelope.

"Three," I whispered, barely able to breathe as I tore open mine. Iridescent scales flickered beneath my touch, shimmering like magic. "Serpent," I whispered. The sleek, geometric snake crest of the elite Serpent Academy stared back at me, its design almost hypnotic.

Cully frowned. "Well, shit. I've been posted to journal on the prisons again."

I felt sick. Fear, mixed with something like freedom but too dangerous to be real. I had never stepped foot outside of our iced barriers, and now... I would be surrounded by civilians from every realm.

Cully nudged Knox in the ribs. "Why are you smiling like an idiot at your letter? Let me see it."

"I… got Serpent as well," he said. "I've been chosen to compete for Father's title against Severyn."

"But you aged out last year," I protested. I couldn't face Knox in a battle for the throne. I couldn't—I wouldn't survive. Not against him and his six-foot frame, which took after our father.

Cully's gaze flicked between Knox and me, his lips tight. This was blood against blood. Father had always said it would come down to one of us, but if he had his way, neither of us would be chosen. It should've been Charles, our eldest brother. Hell, even Klaus would've been better off than us. Yet Knox wasn't even looking at us anymore. His mind was already calculating how he would rule this kingdom. We all knew the academy favored the bloodborne legacies, yet no one had the courage to challenge that.

The front door creaked open, and winter air rushed in with the sound of heavy boots. Charles stepped inside, his presence filling the room even before I saw his face. He had always been the one we measured ourselves against, even in his absence. His gaze swept over us, unreadable, before settling on me with quiet intensity. In that moment, I knew—this wasn't just another visit.

This was my future. And Charles was here to ensure one of us would claim Father's title.

Gods, why was he here now, after disappearing with the guards for nearly two years after Klaus's death?

He shrugged off his coat and hung it on the serpent-shaped hook by the stairs, his movements deliberate. Mother rushed to greet him, her voice a little too high-pitched. "Charlie! My goodness," she trilled, half-hugging his waist. "I'm so thankful you could come and celebrate with your siblings. Two prosperous heirs chosen, my dear."

Charles didn't acknowledge her cheerfulness. Instead, his gaze moved over the table, lingering on the torn envelopes Knox and I had left behind. Then, with a heavy sigh, he met my gaze.

"Well," he said, his voice smooth, cutting through the tension, "let me be the first to congratulate you both. Given Father's health, I pulled a few strings and secured Knox a chance at the Serpent Academy."

My breath caught, sharp and cold. "Most students don't survive their first year at the Serpent Academy. What do you expect to happen between us when we are pinned against the other?"

Charles smirked. "Lovely as ever, Severyn." He turned to Cully, eyeing his letter. "They're sending you to journal at the prison again?"

I'd almost forgotten about Cully, but as his shoulders slumped forward and he tossed the letter at Charles, I knew something was wrong. "I still haven't had an article published in the Serpent Press. I expected this. It's like Valscribe wants me to fail."

Most noble children attended the Serpent Academy, but anyone could, provided they had the courage to be greater than their rival. Leaders weren't born—they were forged, stripped to the bone until something stronger emerged.

But I was still sifting through the pieces of myself since Klaus's death. This would be my death, just as it had been his.

In another life, I might have had a choice. Life. Death. To live. But here? Herding sheep was out of the question, and ruling a land felt as impossible as flying without wings.

I was good at talking—spinning words into shields, daggers, or distractions. But fear had stolen my voice. All that remained was anger, guilt, and grief, ever since Klaus died at the same academy Knox and I had been invited to.

We'd become strangers in our own home. Awkward banter and forced smiles were the only things that remained between the elite Blanche family. Father locked himself away in his study, obsessively researching ways to strengthen his shields, as though they could protect him from the past. He never told us why his shields were weakening, or why the threat of barren lands was whispered in hushed conversations between Fallon, my mother, and him.

"How soon until the Academy expects us?" I asked, my gaze lingering on Mother as she ladled garlic and evertree soup into bowls. A North Colindale traditional meal.

Charles shrugged off the last of the snow from his hair, his expression distant. "Three days. Lorna and I will escort you both."

"Three days?" I repeated. "That's too soon."

Charles slammed his hand on the table, rattling the dishes. "It's a two-day trek. You don't have a choice, Severyn. Our land's survival depends on one of you claiming Father's title."

I scoffed. "Well, perhaps the letter could have arrived earlier."

Cully spoke quietly, "Learn the academy grounds, Severyn. The library will be your greatest ally. At least you won't have to write in a dungeon for three months."

"Words won't keep me alive," I muttered. I needed to claim this for Klaus. I knew I had no choice.

Charles's grin returned as he unsheathed two frost-tinted daggers, handing one to each of us. "The handles are carved from the glaciers of our lake. They're warded never to melt. Father gave Mother her first dagger at the Academy. I hope this will be a tradition for years to come when your children are called to claim the throne of our iced land."

The blade was cold as Charles placed it in my hand. "I won't survive a week there. Let's not pretend this isn't an invitation to my death."

"You will survive," Charles said. "You don't have a choice, Sev. This is your calling."

"And was it Klaus's calling to be murdered in cold blood?" I hissed, my voice sharp with the old wound. "Or have we forgotten the fifth Blanche who never returned?"

Even speaking his name felt forbidden. Mother's voice cut through the silence. "Don't be ungrateful, child. People would die to be in your place. You're a legacy."

I wasn't like most legacies. They'd ventured to other realms, attended Serpent Balls, mingled in distant worlds I had never even seen. I had no experience in the outside world. No choice but to follow the path laid before me.

For Klaus. I would do it for Klaus.

* * *

The hours between the letters and the never-ending fear seemed skewed. I remembered tasting the garlic in the evertree soup, the clunk and whirl of metal scraping against the bottom of our bowls.

Mother's words still lingered in the air, cutting through the heavy silence of the live-edge dining table: *"Your father is the last iced Serpent to bear an heir. We don't need some scavenger coming onto our lands and taking the title from under our feet."*

Knox and I exchanged a quiet, awkward glance, the weight of her words settling between us. Most legacies had grand celebrations, but in the isolated North, we ate dinner in silence. The absence of joy hung heavier than any conversation.

Afterward, Mother lit a candle in honor of Klaus. This week, he was citrine and cinnamon. But I was out of hellebores for his grave. Father always made sure we had seeds come Thaw, the petals—sometimes purplish with pink streaks—being the only splash of color in our land.

This year, they wouldn't grow. I wouldn't be here. Father, Andri, attended the yearly Serpent Bid, where all the rulers of Verdonia gathered. Every year, he only asked for seeds as he bet on the future heir who would claim the next title.

The day Klaus died felt like this: suffocating, inescapable, and cruelly familiar. Maybe that's why I'd always hated blue eyes. For the poison I'd heard spill beneath them. Every time a visitor came, my heart shattered.

I said my goodnights as Charles regaled Mother with tales of his latest travels. I passed Father's study, where he was buried in a book about Winter shields. He'd made it clear long ago he wasn't to be disturbed. None of us ever disturbed him. I wondered if he even cared how fearful I was of becoming his heir.

Hours turned into a restless night. The nightmares of the academy kept me awake until iced swirls cracked against my window. It wasn't the fading sun that startled me, but the sound of caws and heaves from golden wings as Charles's griffin prepared for flight.

I made my way to the kitchen, bracing for another argument over breakfast about how ungrateful I was about possibly dying.

Instead, I found silence. Mother wasn't in her usual spot by the fireplace with her mug.

Knox tugged my arm. "We're going to be late for Father's speech," he said, opening the iron door.

"A speech?" I asked. "For whom?" A cold gust dragged through my lips as we hurried down the mountainside.

"The civilians. Father must announce us for the run to become the next leader here," he said, adjusting his sleeves.

"I don't remember Klaus having one," I muttered, the memory of that snowy morning still fresh. He had left with only a limp bag and a smile. He never knew he would die.

Knox and I stood at the edge of the frozen lake. Frail figures gathered around, standing before the Seventh Frozen Valley of North Colindale. "What is happening?" I asked. Were the civilians always so… gaunt?

Knox shushed me, his hands clasped behind his back.

Father's trembling arm rose before the crowd. "My children have been called to claim their right. Yet only one will lead our nation. The Blanches have ruled North Colindale for over a hundred years, and I do not doubt my children will endure the sacrifices and strength to maintain that standing." His hand lowered, resting on Knox's shoulder. "My heir will save our land. I promise my child's blood on it."

Not even a tree rustled a branch.

I never imagined Knox would become my rival. But as he nodded and smiled at the civilians, my heart sank.

"If chosen as heir, I vow to protect my people," Knox declared. "I promise to carry on our legacy."

I waited for Father's calloused grip to fall onto my shoulder, but it never came. They said blood was thicker than water, but desire was unyielding.

Knox's chin was steady, his gaze unblinking as he stared beyond the peaks. Our hair matched, down to the white streak in our bangs and the birthmarks brushing three lashes on our left sides. Even our lips curled the same. But Knox was calculating, a tower of Blanche bravery coursing through his veins, driven by an insatiable need to prove himself.

Title children, or legacies, had no understanding of the civilians' struggles—their hunger. Yet when three voices chanted Knox's name, I bit my tongue. The last son of the Seventh Frozen Valley would claim Father's heir.

I whispered just low enough for Father and Knox to hear. "They want you to win the title, Knox. Not me."

I was the daughter destined for a political marriage, a trade deal pawn. Even though I didn't care about becoming a ruler, this was supposed to be my turn.

The ceremony ended, and I took the long way home.

The frozen railway tracks groaned in the distance. The train, laden with seeds, should have been hauled across the frozen land, but the tracks remained iced over. Sivil, our aide, could use my plot for whatever she desired. She'd need it to keep her family fed.

The hard ground meant life or death. I was too young to remember the famine—the starved villagers pleading for anything to feed their families when the sun began to fade.

A snowflake landed on my forehead, melting into my cheek as I stared at the dusted sky. It was a soft tug of dreams, a land I had no choice but to love and accept. My heart ached for these frozen streets. The sun faded yearly, as though the captive rays froze with the harsh winters long past.

People would die. My people would die if the cold didn't relent. Farmers dug their hearts out, sweat dripping down their overalls as their shovels cut through the hard dirt.

We needed sunlight.

Father needed an heir to hold his shields high.

My laces dragged through the fresh powder beneath me. The steel gate screeched open, and two griffins snapped their beaks, rattling the chains tied to their leather reins.

Charles waited beside Setrephia, his bonded griffin, while Father stared at the sun, silent, with Mother at his side. Knox leaned against the fence lining our estate, wearing a new leather jacket with our family name etched near the collar.

"Did you wish every snowflake goodbye?" he snickered. "Seriously, you'll permanently engrave a frown on your face. Lighten up, we're finally escaping this cold hell."

Mother stepped toward me, her embrace sudden and warm. "Remember, you will always be Winter's children. Be proud of your roots, my dear." Her strange, pitted-black eyes held me together for a moment, and I saw her pain—the mother who had lost a child, sending two away to the same fate, all for the sake of a legacy.

I nodded. "Soon enough, I'll be able to create snow like Father." I had always loved watching his iced powers, how he twirled perfect crystals between his fingers. Our ice was our legacy.

She hesitated before touching my shoulder. "Just keep it away from the North for a while. I'm a bit weary of the frost not melting."

Mother seldom hugged. I believed the last time we embraced was when we learned Klaus had died. Perhaps death and fear burrowed the same pain. Father held me with an awkward half-hug. That affection was nearly as rare as an all-purple hellebore sprout.

A misted breath hovered in the air. Each word tumbled from his ashen beard, soft but firm. "You will always be my warmth, Severyn. Save our land."

It felt like a funeral. They were preparing for my death, I could feel it in the air. But I leaned into the moment as if it were my last. "I'll miss you," I whispered, pressing my fingers against the smooth velvet of his coat.

It would be years before I came home—if I survived.

Charles cleared his throat, cutting through the silence. "I'll take Severyn. Knox, you'll ride with Lorna and Jullian."

And with that, the fear returned. I hated griffins. Well, griffins hated me. Especially Setrephia, who never let me near her when Charles first bonded with her at the academy.

"You expect me to fly on that bird?" I asked, turning to face Charles, who was untying her reins.

His lips tightened, his expression giving nothing away. It was clear—flying on the griffin wasn't open for discussion. "I told her to be on her best behavior." He rummaged through his bag, pulling out a hunter-green cloak and draping it over my shoulders. "Father gave Knox his riding jacket from his academy days… this one was Klaus's. Keep it."

I fisted the soft, fur-lined inner lining, trying to swallow the lump in my throat. "Thank you. I needed something to remind me of him."

"I kept it safe for you." His voice softened as he placed a hand on my shoulder. "Now, would you please get on Setrephia before we're late for your first day, little sister?"

I waved a final goodbye to my home—the icy fortress that had cradled me for all these years. My last glance at it before I fought to claim it as its next ruler.

Chapter 2

We stopped for the night at a Serpent hostel in Otin, a nomadic land that had once been a vibrant town decades ago. Now, nothing stretched across the village for miles except for the bunker where we'd spend the night.

The setting sun dimmed low, but the slivered orb above our country grew with each mile we flew. It seemed odd, like a shield of iced winds barred the light from cracking through the clouds.

Some Serpents bartered seeds; others offered stars in the night sky, giving hope to dreamers. Otin, however, lay in ruin, waiting for its collapse until they did. No one needed ice, which was probably why Father seldom made barters with other realms.

A barren land meant the worst had happened. Blood once stained these grounds. Now, only starved trees and parched plants rustled in the wind. People had lived here once.

I wondered how a land froze over, how the wind carried a different kind of sorrow. They said it began with six after the Forgotten fled.

Dust choked my lungs as we stumbled into the brick building, seeking refuge from the lightning storms gathering in the distance. Inside were six bunk beds, each with gray sheets and worn blankets. A stove sat beside a rusted sink, a kettle rimmed with burnt debris atop it.

"This can't be a protected Serpent bunker," I muttered. "I thought Serpents lived lavishly. Is it safe?"

Charles pulled a fern leaf from his pocket, scribbling "North Colindale" before pinning it alongside the palm leaves on the wall. A tradition while staying in a Serpent Bunker.

"This is a barren land. Have some respect," Charles said. "This could become our home if Father has no heir this year. Not everyone lives like you."

The wind rattled the metal door. "I'm just asking. Why couldn't the neighboring countries help?" Otin had fallen before Charles was born. My grandfather ruled then, but my father never explained why.

"Ask Father when you're his heir," Charles said, tightening the latch. "Lots of politics."

Lorna sprawled across a bed, tying back her short blonde hair. She glanced at me, eyes hard. "Don't let those assholes get to you. There aren't enough female Serpents," she whispered, nodding toward Knox. "No offense, but given your family's history—"

I cut her off. "I won't let anyone get to me." I fell back onto the stiff mattress, groaning.

"Good. The Iced Valley's kids of Winborrow are cutthroat. Your father is the only ruler without an heir. They won't hesitate to kill you, Severyn," she said, her voice quieter. "Charles rose the ranks slowly, working directly under the king. If you don't make Serpent, Malvoria will find you a place as a guard. He's worried about you."

"I'll find a way to stay alive." I yawned.

Lorna wasn't graceful. Her lips didn't curve upward at a man's glance. Instead, she flashed a dagger, then a sharp grin. Her parents were both guards. She grew up in Malvoria, born in Winborrow. Charles once said they wouldn't work out—her parents wanted her to marry a Serpent.

Charles crossed the narrow rug towards the bunk beds. He extinguished the lantern before heading to bed. "You've got a long day tomorrow, Sev," he said, slinging his sword over his shoulder. "Rest before you forget what it feels like to close your eyes willingly."

Knox was already asleep, unfazed by the world. I envied his ability to sleep through anything.

That night, I tossed and turned, sweat soaking my skin. The air was thick, stifling. I woke an hour before dawn. The mattress groaned as I got up to shower before the others. Ice-cold, cloudy water sputtered from the taps. I braided my neval streak into my hair, knotting the end to keep it in place.

I knew my birthmark was different. Mother always claimed it was a slip of her paintbrush, but it never faded, no matter how hard I scrubbed. Klaus had one, too, though I was starting to forget his face as time passed.

Voices echoed in my ears as I splashed cold water on my face. After changing into a beige sweater Mother had knitted for special occasions, I left the bathroom to join the others outside. We prepared for the final flight to Serpent Academy.

A perfect circular sun rose high, warming the land with its radiant heat. Cully once told me the sun was meant to breathe. Ours, though, only warmed the land for three months a year. He said ours was borrowed. I never understood.

I shoved the cloak into my bag, determined not to feel the sun's harsh rays later as we climbed higher into the sky.

Charles joined me for breakfast, tossing a few bites of oats to Setrephia and Julian as I stared at the chipped bowl in front of me.

"Big day today, little sister," he said, a thin grin playing at the corner of his mouth.

I dropped my spoon, my hands suddenly unsteady. "I'm going to die, Charles. I'm scared."

"I was scared once," he replied, his tone quiet but firm.

Knox mounted Julian with an eager tap on the griffin's mane. "The wind's not getting any younger. Let's go."

"How much longer?" I asked, voice tight, as Charles slammed the bunker's hatch shut.

With a grunt, Charles helped me onto Setrephia. Once in the air, he stole a glance toward the distant peaks. "About six hours."

The wind had settled overnight, but knots twisted in my stomach as we flew over three smaller countries. The air grew warmer with each passing mile, and the heat beat against my scalp as we crossed the rolling dunes of Ravensla. There was endless hills and ponds, dragon-shaped sand sculptures rising from the vibrant city below.

Ravensla, the closest port to the academy, would be where the flightless travelers left. I wondered what it would be like to grow up under a bright sun, to never fear the cold.

Charles pointed to a group of cloaked figures. "Those are scavengers. They have no quells. More or less, they're nomads roaming Verdonia. Stay away from them if you leave the academy."

Trinkets hung from their frail bodies as they dragged their feet through the sand. They looked withered, nearly skin and bone.

A sour feeling twisted in my chest. "Is that what Mother is?" Her quell had dimmed two decades ago—no amount of Cully's scriptures could explain it.

Charles' tone snapped. "Mother was stripped of her quell at the academy. Don't speak of her like that."

"Stripped?"

Charles shuddered. "I'm warded against speaking about a lot of things, Severyn. I'd rather not risk us falling to our deaths. Let's just say she was gifted a quell that wasn't allowed."

"I don't understand."

Charles kept his gaze fixed on the cloudless sky. "It's rare. Mother was stripped the year Father claimed the Serpent title." A vein twitched in his forehead as he closed his eyes. "I wasn't supposed to tell you. Please don't tell Mother I did."

A forbidden quell. My mother had a forbidden quell? How had I not known? "Charles, what was her quell?"

He hesitated, clearly weighing his words. "Severyn, a quell doesn't define a person. I can wield ice, but I'm not Father's heir. It's better if I don't tell you. All you need to know is that Mother is not... one of those street rats. The land we stayed in last night was attacked by a powerful force, and the scavengers are the civilians left behind."

"What powerful force?"

His tone lowered. "I can't speak of them."

The silence stretched between us. I thought of the Seekers— those whose written prophecies once foretold the future. They'd been wiped out by the Herring family nearly three decades ago. My mother couldn't even predict her own children's moods. How could she have written the future? Surely... it had to be something far worse.

"Her eyes," I stuttered. "They're black."

"Don't let it consume you, Sev," Charles said firmly. "Our family has secrets—many. I've protected you from most of them, even in my daily work."

During last year's harvest break, Cully had told me about the dangers of forbidden quells. Most quells were tied to one's realm—Winter's being ice or some form of snow-wielding. But unnatural quells existed, born from darkness too potent for any one person to hold.

It started with six, they said. Six who defeated the Forgotten. Six Gods for each Season, including the shadows and light. Clearly, Charles couldn't speak of the Forgotten who killed the original title winners of the Serpent Academy.

Charles had sworn an oath to safeguard Verdonia as a guard, yet I didn't realize how deceptive that promise was. I was his sister, but he still treated me like I was seven.

Setrephia glided over the ocean, her wings casting shadows on the dark waters below. Her claws skimmed the sea before she tucked her wings and soared upward. I raised my hand, feeling the breeze curl through my fingers. A yell broke free, part joy, part terror. For a moment, freedom felt boundless.

Charles yanked me back, his elbow digging into my ribs. "You're distracting her."

I turned to face him, wind tousling his hair, sand sticking to his temples. "Do you ever have fun, Charles? Have you ever lived a day without being tense?"

Charles, always the golden child, shook his head. It was hard to imagine him laughing. His voice softened. "Lorna and I enjoy moonshine once a month."

The thought of Charles being drunk was strange. "Will you and Lorna ever marry?" I asked. They'd been bonded griffin riders for years, it seemed inevitable.

Setrephia cried out, almost in agreement. Charles chuckled. "My life's too busy for marriage. Besides, her father wants her to marry a Serpent, not someone like me." Lorna spun around. Apparently, their rider bond was open. He added, "Our thoughts are connected, Sev. Let's talk about something else."

"Do you regret not staying at the academy?" I asked.

Charles had been a perfect fit for Serpent. Bold, loyal with an asshole authoritative personality.

"No," he replied. "I did what was right for Verdonia. I still work closely with Saani, who won Serpent the year I attended. You'll meet her today. She's a mentor now, keeping me updated on the dropouts. The title system places you where you belong. Most years, no title is earned."

His guard demeanor shifted as Galthyn came into view, the island was shrouded in a layer of smog.

I knew Charles wanted to lead. Being a royal guard eased that desire, but it never satisfied him. Even Mother's stripped quell was more than a family secret—it was a lie.

A faint electric hum thrummed through my chest as the academy's ward came into view. I tightened my grip on Setrephia's reins. The island stretched before us: towering forests, crystalline peaks, and griffins landing on the beaches below. The island was shaped like a hexagon, divided into six distinct realms—one in constant shadow, the other drenched in sunlight.

Charles veered sharply. "Hold on, Severyn!"

A dragon's scaled wing grazed Setrephia, and I caught sight of it. A large vermilion creature released a sharp snarl.

"Dragon," I breathed. I had never seen a dragon before.

"Yeah, stay away from dragon riders. Conceited assholes, all of them," Charles yelled over the wind. "Better yet, stay away from the male gaze until your first year ends."

Setrephia's golden wings stretched wide as we descended.

"I'll keep that in mind," I muttered.

Charles's voice faded as we neared the academy. "Welcome to the Serpent Academy, Severyn. Our legacy was born here."

Fear gripped my chest at the waves below, white stripes of fury breaking against the rotted docks. I turned to Charles one last time. "I take it back. I'll go to Malvoria with you!"

Charles chuckled, but there was sadness in his tone. "Mother would disown me if I let you do that. She's more worried than Father."

We landed at the docks, where a dozen first-years waited. Knox had already dismounted Julian, scanning the academy grounds. Lorna wiped the sweat from her brow, pouring water into Julian's beak.

"We made it," Lorna said.

Setrephia cawed, her talons gripping the wooden dock. She dipped her head low, allowing me to dismount. My boots hit the planks unsteadily as waves pushed beneath us.

"Put your cloak on," Charles said, pulling the hood from my bag and placing it over my head. "Neval hair isn't common around Verdonia."

"It's a birthmark," I muttered.

"It's a mark, Severyn. Now, go find Knox."

I said one last thing to my eldest brother, "I promise one of us will win," I said, "but I can't promise we'll both return."

He nodded silently, his face unreadable.

Knox stood at the golden gates, the faint sound of combat clashing beyond the stone walls. "Did you see that dragon?" I asked breathlessly.

Knox nodded. "Take a good look while you can. Dragon riders wouldn't be caught dead talking to us. We're just pigeon riders to them. Weak."

I always assumed the northern winds were strong. "That can't be true," I said. "Father would have told us."

"Face it, Sev. We know nothing outside of North Colindale. You think a bird is more powerful than a dragon? We were isolated." Knox scoffed.

Behind golden fences, the Serpent Academy loomed. Sculpted hedges formed poised creatures along slick, onyx stone, reflecting like black water. Ships docked as creatures of all kinds flew in, their feathered wings sweeping above. Hundreds of students moved through the courtyard, their quells rippling from open palms, relics and marks etched into their skin.

The senior students stood out in dark green blazers, each adorned with the academy emblem—a geometric snake. Some wore sweater vests, others leather vests slashed by claws and combat. Not to mention the daggers strapped to every limb.

A hazel-eyed male met my gaze from the path ahead, a fleck of blood crusted on his dimpled chin. His smile slowly curled towards me.

Was it a requirement to be attractive here? *Because... shit.*

I reminded myself that they could kill with one single glance, most students were already masters of their quells.

"Charles said we should hide our hair," I whispered. "Do you have a cloak?" I glanced at Knox's rucksack—worn from years of hunting trips with Father and Charles. It seemed unlikely he'd packed many clothes.

Knox scoffed. "They say our birthmark's a curse—oh, shit."

He froze, eyes fixed on a three-headed hydra. A blonde woman steered it down the path, her hair tangling in the wind. The dragon spread its scaled wings and landed gracefully before the doors.

"That's... Malachi Herring," Knox whispered. "*The* Malachi Herring."

Herring. A name among the most elite in Verdonia, meaning she was either related to or married into King Norvin's family. Her cloak glinted with golden stars, revealing muscular legs beneath a pale lace dress. The wind seemed to follow her, flurrying around her pristine combat boots. A bejeweled dagger hung at her ribs.

"Is she a student?" I asked.

Her amber eyes swept over the crowd before she glided past us, leaving a trail of vanilla scent in the air. She draped a sheer lace cloak over her head, the wind nudging her heel, stirring debris. She didn't look back, her gaze fixed ahead as she approached the ancient stone steps.

"Looks like it," Knox muttered. "The king's granddaughter definitely rides dragons."

The king's granddaughter had come to face trial. I never realized someone with her authority would need to attend the academy.

We passed beneath a silver-and-gold-scaled archway, like dragon wings were dipped in metal to form an entrance to the black-stone castle. Vines snapped at the approaching students; even the plants were deadly. I was in over my head.

At the castle's edge, a black-glass snake coiled around the southern end, its head frozen in mid-attack. Trees bordered the campus, flanking six narrow trails. One was slicked with frost— Winter's trail. Another, likely Spring, burst with lilies and sunflowers. A faint electric hum buzzed from the entrances, the ward trapping heat and cold behind it.

Guards stood at the gates, assessing every student. They dismissed Malachi with a simple nod. Their snakeskin cloaks swayed as swords glinted at their spines.

One guard raised his sword, nearly slicing me as he yanked my hood down. "Conceal," he muttered, his copper eyes piercing. I feared he might strike, but he lowered his blade, allowing us to pass.

I clung to Knox's arm, nearly tripping on the pearl rug. Whispers rippled among the first-years as warmth pulled us into the academy's grand hall.

Light filtered through stained-glass windows, casting scales and shattered light. A grandfather clock ticked by the podium. Two staircases forked ahead—one marked with a sun symbol, the other with a blue thunbergia, symbol of Spring. The castle groaned with age as students crowded around.

Knox nudged me, his gaze flicking to six figures near the podium, each marked with intricate serpent tattoos.

A woman with dark skin stood with arms crossed, braids cascading over her shoulders. Her upturned nose seemed to smell the fear in the room. That must be Saani. A whip of flame curled around her wrist as embers crackled in the air. To her left stood a tall man with olive-toned skin, muscles straining beneath his white, tailored shirt. Violet buttons ran down his broad chest, each one barely holding against his frame. His sharp blue eyes swept the crowd, as did the serpent tattoo coiling around his neck.

I couldn't help but wonder why Father's serpent mark was on his arm—and why he always kept it hidden from us—

Then recognition hit me like a blow to the chest.

The man beside Saani—I knew him.

"That's Archer Lynch," I whispered, breathless. "He won the title the same year Klaus attended. I bet he killed him. That's why he came that day to deliver the news of Klaus's death."

Father had sent him away with a slam of our iron door, nearly shattering the wards with how angry he was.

Knox met my eyes, his sharp chin dipping in a curt nod. "Don't get too worked up, Sev. Someone like him will never know your name. But I've got to admit, the shadow realm is pretty badass."

"But why—" I shook my head, the words sticking in my throat. "He had no reason to know Klaus. I overheard Charles talking to Father after Klaus died. Archer was the last student to see him alive, Knox."

Knox shrugged. "Klaus failed our family, Sev. I know that's hard to accept."

That Serpent had wormed his way into our home. His smile and voice lingered in the portrait plastered on the Serpent press for weeks after his crowning. I'd never seen Father so furious— never knew parchment could burn twice. Father fed the flames every time the mail arrived, bearing Archer's iced eyes.

I needed a distraction. I needed anything to convince myself that my brother's killer wasn't a fucking mentor here.

My reflection caught in the lanterns strung along the hall. I was not doing well. I was not even thinking straight. I couldn't meet Archer's eyes again. Not after they wilted me, like a beetroot left to rot in last season's harvest.

Silence fell as a cloaked figure entered.

The man I assumed was the headmaster strode forward, standing beside the six Serpents. He raised a curled fist, his cape billowing. Yellow eyes glinted like polished glass, sweeping over the new students. His black curls framed his pale, nearly translucent skin, hard lines marking his expression. Every eye turned to him, including mine, though my focus wavered, torn between the headmaster and the storm of Archer's gaze.

His voice rasped as he spoke. "The Serpent Academy welcomes you for another year to earn your title. I am Professor Mundair, your headmaster as you begin your journey to leadership."

A hiss carried each word. "Six Serpents will mentor you. They'll hand-pick you based on tests and trials over the next three days. A map will be placed in your dorms. There are aides to care for, cook, and mend you. When the lanterns turn on, it's lights out. You may not enter other trails or realms without permission.

Leave campus without it being a holiday, and you'll be expelled. Now, I'll introduce the Serpents who volunteered their time to mentor you. Do not disturb them unless they approach you."

They were beasts in my eyes, untamed wild snakes, sensing blood and fear as all six flicked their gazes among us.

The headmaster gestured. "Monty Garcia, Serpent of Bright Day." A male stepped forward, black hair slicked to show off his angular jaw. He waved with a smirk, bowing smugly.

Monty's name was plastered in the papers every other week. Last year alone, three mistresses.

"Jenessa Link, Serpent of ice Winter." My heart skipped as Jenessa stepped forward. Her dark complexion glinted in the lantern light, her skin as smooth as ice. She looked around Charles's age, possibly the Serpent of Winborrow.

"Saani Kaur, Serpent of Summer." Saani didn't step forward, but brushed a pin-straight strand of black hair behind her ear, the tail end of her whip slashing the stone. She was draped in gold: hoops, bangles, and a golden cape that swayed with her slender frame.

"Tydon Braie, Serpent of Autumn." A fire-headed male bowed, one hand behind him.

"Archer Lynch, Serpent of the last standing Night." Archer furrowed his brow, a cocky grin forming on his lips. Dark hair shaved at the sides, with a wave swooping above his brow. Tall, fearsome, cruel—a man rarely seen in the press, even when we needed more cinder.

"Levisly Bloom, Serpent of Spring." A pixie-like woman twirled forward, vines wrapping around her petite figure. Her fingers curled into a wave.

The headmaster let the room settle, waiting for the students to stop whispering about Archer and Monty and how… attractive they were. Even Knox's lips parted in awe—hard to believe it came from him.

"Some of you may not survive your first night. Leaders are not born. Half of those who received letters will die or be sentenced to the Malvoria Institute before the year ends," he continued. "So, I ask you all: Who does not wish to be here?"

The room stirred as students turned to watch for those brave enough to raise their hands.

Knox pinned my wrist down, eyes forward. "Don't you dare think about raising your fucking hand," he hissed.

A shuffle went through the crowd as a dozen raised their hands. Then, a familiar voice cleared his throat, stepping out of the shadows. "Malvoria welcomes you. You'll all make great guards." Charles stood beside a black column, his Malvoria suit pressed perfectly.

He didn't fly us here out of kindness. He came to recruit the dropouts. He knew better than to glance our way. He knew all he'd see was the pulsing anger in his youngest sibling's eyes. Perhaps he knew his vow of protection to the Continent was more than clipped words—it was entrapment.

What happened next was more or less a nightmare.

Screams echoed. A girl fell to her knees, dragged towards Charles by a guard gripping her hair and wrist. Her hands flailed like a griffin caught in a trap. Six more students walked over, knowing their fate as they whimpered in fear.

A few tried to barter with the headmaster. "It was a mistake, sir. I want to continue with the academy." Tears stained the stone as their cries consumed the air.

I whispered to Knox, "They should have known there's only one way out of here."

"There's always death," he said. Surprisingly, I didn't shudder at his words, but an awful ache rolled in my chest, knowing those twelve wouldn't make it a year in Malvoria until they were left with half a soul and a crippled body.

The last of the twelve bold enough to question their journey at the Serpent Academy raised a shaking hand above his heart. "Forgive me," he whispered, eyes on my eldest brother.

Professor Mundair offered no remorse. "There are no second chances. Your heart does not lie with Galthyn, but you will spend the rest of your life protecting our land."

Distorted shrieks sounded from that male student. His hands bent, palms flat as he collapsed to his knees.

"What is that sound?" I asked Knox, wincing in pain from the screech.

"It's a screamer quell," he said with a grunt. "Rare but deadly."

A few ears bled, silenced to their knees. Charles closed his eyes and walked towards the male, then wrapped his hands around the boy's neck. "Enough!" Charles grunted before snapping it.

I stifled a scream as a deafening crack echoed through the hall when the man's body hit the stone.

Charles... how could he?

How could he?

Part of me had never believed cruelty could take root in him. But perhaps power and protection were molds, slowly growing until they infected his mind.

I buried my face in Knox's leather jacket. "Is it over?" I asked, feeling Knox nod. "Knox? Charles... he…" I gripped his elbow, but he shrugged me off.

"You look weak, Severyn. Control it," he snapped, his gaze fixed on the still body below Charles. "We can't let anyone see us as weak."

A silver-haired first-year snickered beside us, her eyes identical to the smog outside. "That's why they teach you to control your quell here. He never would have made it, even in Malvoria. Screamers aren't someone you want near you. Their voices are deadly, but there's no sense when everyone around you is in pain—guards, too."

And he was killed without even possessing a forbidden quell. Charles killed someone. He killed a student. In front of me. Us.

Chapter 3

"A mark of the six realms will appear on your palm," the headmaster said. "Those with the same mark will be both allies and rivals in your journey to greatness. The academy chooses based on bloodline—here, heirs are made. Pain is temporary, but legacy lasts. Who will rise to become the first in their generation for the throne?"

He continued, "A student mentor will guide you to the trial grounds, where, in the next two nights, you will discover your quell and your enigma if you do not already have one."

Knox leaned over in pain, clenching his fist until his knuckles whitened.

"Shit, it burns," he hissed, his lip curled as thick, purple veins jutted from his neck and arms.

Groans and shallow breaths filled the air as first-years writhed in their stance. But I felt… nothing. No power rushing through me. No sharp pain like Knox's.

"Let me see," I said, my voice tight.

Knox uncurled his fist, revealing a glowing circle etched into his palm, bright as the sun sinking beneath the horizon. It looked raw, like bone and skin had fused beneath the surface.

"Is this some kind of joke?" His voice cracked slightly as he glanced around, like someone might leap out to laugh at him. "Severyn, I didn't get Winter. This is Day's mark."

I hadn't looked at my own palm yet. "How is that even possible?" I asked, slow and deliberate. "Knox, you're a Winter. We're Winter."

Knox's calm composure barely slipped, but when his gaze flicked to Monty Garcia, the Serpent of Day, his shoulders stiffened. "This is bullshit," he muttered.

I ran my fingers lightly over the circular mark on his palm, where golden rays broke through the lines of his calloused skin from years of hunting and camping. I closed my eyes, half-expecting the same light to spill from my own flesh, but terrified that it wouldn't. Terrified that I'd be left—what? Alone?

"I can't look. What's mine?" I let my wrist dangle, Knox pulling my fingers apart like I wasn't in control of my own hand.

"You don't have one," he said, voice low. "You don't have a mark, Sev."

"What?" I yanked my arm back, my pulse thudding in my ears. "How can I not have a mark? How can you be called to Day? This makes no sense."

Around me, everyone seemed oddly calm. Knox had the same circle as the others called to Day—suns, snowflakes, flowers, moons—each person marked. But not me. Not a thing on my palm.

Markless. I was markless.

Knox leaned in closer, his whisper barely a breath. "Maybe it takes a day to show up?"

I didn't buy it. "I need to talk to Professor Mundair."

The room filled with the sharp ring of a bell as I pushed through the crowd, only to meet the cold, unblinking stare of the headmaster. His bright yellow eyes pierced through me, as if he already knew what was wrong.

Was he… Day-blooded?

Curls framed his face, his translucent skin glowing unnaturally under the chandeliers. He took me in, head to toe. "Ah, Fallon's daughter," he said, nodding. "I knew this year would be… difficult. It's always an eventful year when a Blanche child faces trial. But two…" His gaze flicked to me with a hint of curiosity.

"Nice to meet you," I forced out, my voice tight. "I think my mark isn't showing."

"What do you mean, dear?" His expression softened slightly, though I knew he must have a truth quell—one capable of detecting lies. Headmasters and professors typically had invasive powers like that.

I opened my fists. "I have no mark, sir."

He patted my palm with a sharp nod. "It seems the academy believes they made a mistake inviting you. No realm has called to you." His gaze flicked to where Charles stood, and my blood iced. "They'll treat you well in Malvoria, given your eldest brother's ranking. I'm sorry you traveled this far."

"No, I need to stay! There must be a mistake." It wasn't entirely a lie, so maybe his truth quell wouldn't detect it or maybe he didn't have one.

"What is this?" A voice demanded, cutting through the tension.

Blonde hair brushed my shoulder as another student shoved past me. "I've been marked with the Unknown. Fix this now."

It took a moment to recognize Malachi Herring, her expression pinched as she spread her palms. Her hands were unnervingly smooth, as though bathed in golden goat's milk.

"Me too," I said, showing her my empty palm. "There's nothing."

"Interesting." The headmaster said. "Well, there must be an explanation. Don't worry, Miss Herring, we'll sort this out."

"Let me see." The voice came from behind—one that had haunted my dreams for the past two years.

Archer Lynch stood in a pool of violet shadows, reaching for Malachi's wrist. "The academy doesn't know where to place them because their bloodline is torn between realms," he said.

Malachi yanked her arm away, her white boots clicking sharply against the stone. "Send me to Autumn," she hissed. "The king wants me there. It's where our family has roots."

I hesitated. "How can I be torn between two realms? My father is the Serpent of North Colindale."

Archer kept his focus on Malachi but answered anyway. "What about your mother's blood?"

"My mother…" I faltered. I'd always assumed she was Winter, but I'd never asked.

"I know exactly what her mother is." The headmaster's voice snapped like a whip. "The Serpent Academy doesn't entertain forbidden quells. Your mother was a death curser. I see that mark in your hair. I know what you are. Perhaps we'll send you to Malvoria before you tear the school down, just like she did."

Archer crossed his arms. "If you send them to Malvoria, they'll be executed on arrival, just like that student was. The mark of the Unknown shows in many forms."

Could Charles kill me? I wanted to believe his loyalties lay with family.

"Let us live," I said, my voice shaking. "Put us through whatever trial you have, but don't send me to Malvoria." I was the only one left to claim my father's heir. I couldn't be expelled.

Malachi scoffed loudly. "Good luck executing the king's granddaughter," she drawled, dragging a finger down Archer's shirt. "Although I'm sure Archer would appreciate it. One step closer to stealing my grandfather's crown."

The headmaster's yellow eyes flicked between us. If it were just me, I'd have been thrown out by now. But Malachi's name held too much power to ignore.

The headmaster clamped my fingers shut. "You don't speak a word about this. Not to anyone. Blanche, you will stay in Winter. Herring, I will send you to Autumn. Perhaps your quells will manifest into something tamable in a familiar environment."

Archer's brows lifted like he recognized my name but couldn't place it. His eyes lingered briefly before turning away, leaving me no choice but to remain silent.

I kept my head low, flexing my fingers as pain flared across my knuckles. Blood pooled between them, forming a snowflake carving. Phantom shudders rippled down my spine, too cold to ignore. The mark mirrored Father's and Charles's.

I exhaled slowly, relief threading through me. My father's title was safe—for now. But questions swirled like smoke. Was Day the realm where my mother had grown? Why would the academy place Knox somewhere foreign to us, a realm that offered no comfort, no familiarity? Knox would be sheltered in light, while North Colindale—our home—desperately needed that.

The students were divided into six realms: Night, Day, Summer, Winter, Autumn, and Spring. Knox's group departed first, led by a tall brunette named Everett Kilian. His confident strides and sharp jawline commanded attention, drawing glances from the crowd. Each year, a student mentor was chosen to lead, though it only mattered if you were thrown into the final trial.

I didn't want to think about who was in the lead to claim my father's title.

Malachi darted towards the Autumn section, her cloak billowing behind her like a storm cloud. I stepped towards the Winter section, where thirty-one first-year students waited. The air here felt colder, almost biting against my skin, as though the ward separating the realms had seeped through the academy's iron doors.

Some students were pale and gaunt, their hollow cheeks betraying their hardships. Others—the Winborrow natives Lorna had warned me about—were easy to spot, clean-cut with thick muscles rippling beneath fur-lined cuffs. Some realms were better off, while Winter countries had it the worst.

I counted thirty-one students, all competing for my father's title. And that didn't even include the second- and third-years who were already far ahead in their training. It all came down to me now.

I knew Knox would abandon me as the days wore on. He was Day, and ice never dared to touch golden light. The weight of our hundred-year legacy rested on my shoulders.

Great.

As I joined the group, a curly-haired woman caught my eye. Her dark locks were gathered into a chunky braid, tied at the end with a silver bead. She nervously bit her nails, her deep-brown skin framed by a pale wool cloak. For a moment, her gaze locked with mine. "I've heard our student leader is ruthless," she whispered. "Bridger Thorne. Just be prepared for three days of hell." She let out an exasperated breath as she glanced around.

"Thanks for the warning," I whispered back.

Frost peeled the onyx stone, spiraling like spider's webs. Swallowing my hesitation, I shifted my weight as a white-haired man stalked through the grand hall's double doors and took his place before our group. His cloak dragged beneath his slender frame, the same shade as obsidian.

"Disappointing," he muttered, before lacing his iced palms behind him.

Thorne. It was a Colindale surname—I knew him.

His parents were the same age as mine and had lived under my father's reign as civilians. He was one of the few children born and raised in our village. His father was a farmer, and his mother—a teacher—had come to our home every Tuesday.

He was ordinary. Not a legacy, not even a rival trying to claim his throne back. He was… a civilian and he was the one person I needed to beat.

I held my breath as his eyes swayed to meet mine. It had been years since I'd seen him. Most Colindale males had the same golden hair and plain features that never turned heads twice. His mother had fallen ill when I was eight, and after she stopped her visits, she was replaced in a day—another faceless servant to my family.

Shit. He'd kill me if he recognized me.

I tightened my cloak around my shoulders as we followed silently behind him towards the main courtyard.

He arched his neck, walking backward. A green-handled sword was sheathed tight against his spine, and several daggers were strapped to his limbs.

"Come along," he said. "I'm Bridger, third-year and your Winter student leader. Once a year, the Serpents choose their leader for the crown during the year-end Bid, and I've never lost that title. Jenessa, the Serpent mentor, left the Rite to me. I'll decide if you stay or go."

He flashed a grin, one that lingered longer than the cold biting my exposed knuckles as we neared the frozen trails.

"Malvoria's a kinder sentence than pissing me off. If you cry, your face will freeze. The forests harbor deadly beasts, so stay on the trails unless you want to die. Any questions?" He paused, clapping his gloved hands. "Great."

"My name's Myla," the curly-haired girl whispered. "Myla Reinhart. I'm from Ravensla."

He was too close. I couldn't risk saying my name.

"Sev," I whispered back. "Nice to meet you."

But her words hit me only after. "Ravensla? Isn't that a heated realm?"

She nodded. "I'll explain later."

Had my father been a tyrant during the famine? Had the rations been enough to feed our village? He was lower class, barely above the poverty line, but his family had roots.

A frosted wind scurried from the trail, dancing like cotton. I'd spent two days under the sun, just long enough for the cold draft to nip at my skin as I stepped through the ward. Snow's bite was deeper than any beast—more like venom slipping through my veins, burrowing into my bones. I wiped my dripping nose, shoving my hands under my armpits for warmth.

Another student nudged a male beside him. "Which one do you think is her?"

He sighed, pointing to Myla. "Not her. Her eyes are too dark to be from an iced valley."

Who were they talking about?

Bridger, daringly walking backward, slicked his hair to the side of his forehead. "I hear we have the Serpent's daughter with us. What a wonderful surprise."

It was me they were talking about. I could probably pretend—

"Severyn Blanche, what does one do if they get frostbite?"

Dread settled in my stomach. Golden eyes latched onto me from all directions. "Check for hypothermia and seek help," I said.

Myla's eyes widened as she clipped her breath. "Oh, shit. Your father's the Serpent?"

A student behind me hissed, "Looks like first-blood to me. Easy target. They seem to favor the legacies here."

Bridger cocked his head. "Who will help? I sure as hell am not stepping in. Say you are alone in the forest, the temperature drops, and there is no chance of warmth. What do you do?" He bit his glove, pulling it off and showing us his fingers where the tips of two were missing, concealed with a nasty stitch. "I stitched my hand up after I lost the top bit from frostbite."

Myla breathed loudly, "That's... badass."

Guilt washed over me.

"I do not know, sir." I needed to play nice, perhaps a bit dumb. I became increasingly aware that everyone wanted me dead. To know I was hated for simply having a last name felt heavy. I didn't know them, but they knew me.

I continued, "I would pray to Soliath. Hope he spared me until the sun came up."

"And if no God answered your call, you would accept death?" A smile curled up his lips. "Severyn Blanche is a prime example of why the title is earned and not given through blood. Now, I understand the passion to claim, but killing her will not make you a leader."

Snide remarks simmered from the other students.

Our title was passed through generations of Blanches. Bridger couldn't steal that from our heritage. But could he? My family needed a Serpent to carry on our legacy. We would lose everything without one.

The slow venom of coldness ripped and scratched through my skin. Grinding my teeth, I kept on. Golden eyes locked onto me as if I were nothing more than a privileged daughter of titles. I refused to let the whispers around me linger.

I refused to die because of my last name.

Mistletoe grew along the swaying trees, bulbous red berries dangling above. The narrow, tight trail forced most of us to step onto the icy mulch. Bridger's lantern swayed, its light the only source as it creaked side to side. We walked in silence for a while. Caws and hisses echoed along the path. The dagger Charles gave me was tucked between my slacks, the sleek metal pressing against my hipbone.

Bridger suddenly thrust out his hand.

The trail dipped sharply into a pool of black ice, leading to a guttered ledge. Crystals protruded from the cliff like makeshift handles. Snowflakes swirled through the misted veil, catching on the cliff's jagged edge.

Bridger gestured downward, yelling over the unruly snowstorm, "You've all been selected to reign over Verdonia's frozen valleys. Each of you was chosen because the academy believes you will be the next Serpent for these lands. Only one heir is yet to be claimed, and the Serpent's daughter stands with us. Do what you must, but use integrity." He arched a brow at me, then continued, "Scale this wall, and you'll officially be initiated into the running for Serpent."

A blonde male wearing a fur coat cocked his brow. "They call this the wall of crimson for a reason." He took a barreling step towards the edge. "Don't mind if I go first. Not all is fair in the title." He sank to his knees, crawling down with a grin.

Bridger brought us up one by one. Most used the same technique: legs first, straight down, bleary-eyed on their boots. I stifled my breath as I heard the first crack—the screams that followed as the ice broke away.

Three more fell, their voices echoing for the next hour, carried by the shuffle of limbs and heavy sighs. Bridger would save me for last, but he'd be the first to take me.

And these slacks barely kept me warm. I took another step forward every twenty minutes once the student either fell or made it down the Crimson Wall, and from the screams, about half were gone, broken-limbed, waiting at the bottom.

This was a nightmare, a cold, deranged nightmare.

Myla was next. She glanced at me, tightening her lips. Her one hand slipped as she stared below, yelping.

"Your hands can hold you up if you lose balance. The bluer the ice, the older it is," I said.

Bridger scorned me, "Don't help her, Blanche. Myla's father was born in Icillian. She can tap into her distant blood."

Ravensla was the hottest country in Verdonia. It was beyond cruel to allow Myla to face this, to be called to become a Winter Serpent.

No screams sounded after the first few moments. A half-hour passed. Then Bridger nodded at me.

"Let's see if all those years of hiding like the little princess you are if you have it in you to know what real Winter is like."

Scoffing, I said, "I can handle it." I was the last to go down, but Bridger forced me to wait even as I took one final step towards the ice wall.

His fist went up with a slow shake of his head. "Patience, Severyn."

"You're going to kill me, Bridger," I hissed through my chattering teeth. But I'd allowed him to see me crumble as frozen tears clung to my cheek.

His neck rolled. "I have every right to kill you, Severyn." I didn't know a grin could stretch that far as he hissed, "But I won't ruin my image around the academy. I'll instead let the cold kill you as it nearly did to me. First, your fingers will turn black before they die off. But your mind begins to stray before that."

He reached for my trembling jaw, hands tight around my chin. "Tell me, has your mind gone yet?" Hooded silver eyes crept through me, colder than the ice rattling my bones.

It took everything in me not to tear his hands off my skin. But I leaned desperately into his cruel warmth, salvaging whatever heat escaped him.

Numbness crept up my joints, leaving the slow hammer in my chest a fighting chance. Bridger dropped his hand as I hissed, "My mind is fine."

He scoffed as I stumbled past him, my stiff legs betraying me. Each bend of my knees shot sharp pain through my body, and my fingers scraped across the ice. I lowered myself, belly down, dragging my body across the frozen surface. Bridger stood above me, his white hair fluttering in the snow flurries. He reveled in my struggle, relishing the pain in my eyes as I fought not to fall. My fingers clenched, desperate to hold on.

"I waited two years for the last of the Blanches to arrive," he said, his voice dripping with malice. "I think I'll enjoy this."

His lip curled into a mocking pout. "Shame your brother couldn't join us. He gets to live another day, unlike you."

I clenched my jaw, willing myself not to lose my footing. My fingers felt like brittle glass with every slow, calculated movement, and the ice was slicker than ever from the last thirty-one hands that had touched it. I shouldn't have glanced up, but the fury in Bridger's eyes above me was worse than the dark, swirling pit below, where five bodies had already been swallowed by the growing snow.

They had come here to prove themselves—to become my father's heir. The rest were struggling to stay warm, some running in place, others blowing into their palms. Only Myla's eyes were on me, sharp and unblinking.

"Prove you're worthy, Severyn," he yelled down at me. "Prove to me you're better."

The cry that escaped my chapped lips betrayed me. "I am worthy."

Bridger laughed. "I would never stoop as low as your father. Instead, I'll watch you slip and fall to your death. It's time a new leader took over the North. His wards are already failing. If he wasn't screwing that neval mother of yours, maybe he would've learned more about shields at the academy."

Bridger would break me.

He would claim our family's title. The ache in my lungs tempted me to give in.

"My father is a great Serpent. The frozen lands are known for their extreme climates. You can't change that." The wind gusted again, and I clung to the wall, my cloak snagged on the ice.

The tip of his boots edged forward, spiteful and unwavering. "I won't allow another Blanche to destroy my home. For twenty-one years, I bowed to him. I begged for food, for medicine. Your family is an infestation!"

I didn't know what to think. Maybe I did, but everything felt tangled now.

I was a quarter of the way down, and Bridger's eyes hadn't left my hands. If I fell now, best case, I'd break my legs. Worst case, my neck. Or maybe that was the other way around. Perhaps death would be kinder than staying under Bridger's watch.

I needed to jump. A broken arm, maybe a rib—if I managed to roll—could be survived. I tried to kick a hole into the ice, but it barely budged. Frustrated, I grabbed the dagger at my hip, jamming my knee against a sharp rock.

My foot slipped, and the ice crumbled beneath me. Pain jolted through my hips as I hit the ground. I rolled to my side with a grunt, gripping the button of my cloak.

Then Myla's hand appeared above me, framed by the swirling snowstorm. Her gaze, soft and brown, pulled me through the haze of cold. I reached up, grateful.

"Thank you," I muttered, breathless.

I survived the wall.

"At least there's plenty of ice to soothe that welt you'll have after that fall." She warmed me with her slight touch, pulling me against her side.

I tried my best not to imagine the bodies beneath me.

Desperate for any distraction from the shooting pain, I kept talking to Myla. "How do you enjoy the cold?"

"I've never even seen snow before," Myla said, a hint of pride lacing her voice. "I'm quite proud of myself for scaling down that mountain."

"Why were you chosen for Winter?" I asked.

"My father was the Serpent for Icillian for thirty years before he died. I had no idea. The surprise on my face when he shipped me my inheritance, a whole sword collection from the Forgotten days," she said. "We're called children of offering—where a Serpent has children with another realm in hopes of enhancing their bloodline. Turns out, I was his only child."

"You never knew?"

"No," she said, stretching with a groan. "It makes sense why I was placed in Winter now. Makes me feel connected to him in a way. My mother, on the other hand, is a seamstress. She made gowns for the Serpent of my country during her earlier years."

"My brother got placed in Day. I thought Winter was my entire bloodline until three hours ago."

"My guess is you were part of the offering bid they had. I'm sure a lot of students here are mixed. It's going to cause for some interesting trial days."

I shivered, and Myla wrapped her arms around my shoulders again. "My parents met here, actually," I whispered into her wool cloak. "I don't imagine we get much free time here?"

The same student who went first crossed his arms over his chest. "We should keep walking the trail. I'm Hunter. Born in Winborrow," he said. "I'm not usually a dick, but, hey, first impressions matter."

Myla and I nodded. Walking seemed better than waiting for death to find us. Bridger was just another like him—trying to be the first in his bloodline to win a title.

Amid the murmurs, I learned that only Myla and I were born of Serpents. Some of the others had distant grandfathers who'd worn the title decades ago, and now they were trying to earn it back. More than half of the students here wanted to kill me. They wanted what I had.

But how could I explain how sheltered I'd been? How I'd felt the sun for the first time just yesterday? How I felt weak—entitled even—to believe I deserved to be called Serpent?

Knox didn't carry the weight of a hundred-year legacy on his shoulders.

In a clearing, six cabins lined the ocean of slushed ice. The beach, littered with frozen sea urchins and starfish, clung to the rocks. It felt wrong—this frozen ocean, the black abyss of shadows creeping with each wave. The wind died slowly against the trees, and I was thankful for the brief relief.

I knew I wouldn't make it to the Serpent Rite without resting my aching joints, but I also knew Bridger wouldn't let me make it that far.

I wondered what Knox was doing. Was he enjoying the Daylight realm? I couldn't imagine anything worse than scaling down a frozen wall. What kind of initiation had he endured? Had he, too, begged for his life to be spared tonight?

The academy will break you. Had my innocent gaze cried enough ice to prove my worth as I thought of those grey corpses?

Chapter 4

I collapsed onto a cot with Myla lying next to me. She'd draped her cloak over both of us, and I thanked her through my trembling jaw, knowing I'd be dead by dawn without her help.

On day two of initiation, my body screamed in protest. Every muscle ached as I limped to the cabin door, stepping into the biting flurries of dawn. Snowcapped mountains framed the clearing, and moss-flecked boulders, long deprived of sunlight, jutted along the horizon. The waves crashed against the frozen shore, the sound of congealed ice curling with each tide. The ringing in my ears faded, but the crunch of bones I'd dreamed of all night lingered, haunting me.

Bridger stood by the fire, freshly showered, while Myla sat on a carved log, eating porridge. Forcing a grin, I flattened my palms near the flame, trying to warm them.

"I'm starving," I muttered, sitting beside her.

She passed me the bowl of porridge. "Take the rest. I didn't realize there'd only be enough to feed ten of us."

Ten. Only ten could eat.

I hesitated. "I can't take your food, Myla." She'd already done enough for me, and I owed her my life.

Bridger scoffed, his voice dripping with derision. "How long can someone survive without food, Severyn?" He spat my name like venom, legs spread as he basked in the fire's warmth.

I forced a sharp smile. "Careful, Bridger, you might warm your cold heart if you get too close to the flame." I took a spoonful of the oats. Myla nudged the bowl towards me, her eyes urging me to have more.

"Thank you, Myla," I said earnestly. Every word of gratitude I'd uttered to her that cold night had been genuine—even my apologies for my chattering teeth.

Eleven more students joined us over the next half hour. Bridger scooped the last of the porridge into his bowl, licking his fingers clean. When the remaining cabin doors creaked open, I closed my eyes as those students realized the food was gone.

Bridger stood, brushing crumbs from his coat. "Those who are hungry should've woken up earlier. If you beg, you will never thrive."

His words weren't for the group—they were a direct jab at my father. I knew exactly what he thought of me.

"For day two of Winter," Bridger announced, "your quells should be waking up. Some of you may have ice manipulation or a variation. There are two types of quells: the one you're born with, and the one passed through your enigma. Focus on your mark. Feel its strength."

He raised his palm, revealing the faded snowflake etched into his skin. An icicle hovered above it, its point sharp enough to kill. Without warning, he hurled the spear at me. It grazed my ear, drawing blood.

I gasped, clutching my shoulder as blood rolled down.

Myla leaned in. "Are you okay?" she whispered.

I nodded, though my hands trembled.

Death may stare you down, may laugh and offer a hand of bone, but I would not fray. I recited passages from Cully's Fables to steady my heart. *The Bones of Love* was my favorite. Death, disguised as a friend, a lover—greedy for a single breath, a glimpse of my soul.

Cully loved writing fables and poems. If he saw me now, I imagined he'd write about the daughter of ice forced to climb the ranks. But I wasn't ready to know the ending. I longed for the days when I was young and naïve.

Everyone extended their palms. Hunter was the first to summon a snowflake, pride glowing on his face. A vein pulsed on Myla's forehead as her eyes fixed on her mark. I raised my palm to the sky, willing the ice to break through, desperate to prove to Bridger that I was Winter's daughter.

"Shit," Myla breathed as icy tendrils spiraled around her fingers. The storm grew until Bridger clamped her hand shut.

"Your professor can train you," he said tightly. "For now, let's not kill us all. Your father was skilled with ice powers—I expected nothing less from you."

I couldn't hold back. "Are you even qualified to open our quells? You're a senior and still haven't claimed the title. Why is that?"

The group stilled, and Bridger's face darkened. "I don't see your quell, Severyn. A Serpent's daughter should've caused the ground to shake by now. I am… disappointed." His tongue clicked twice.

Hunter frowned at me. "Open your palm wider."

I obeyed, holding both hands out, but nothing happened. Tears burned my eyes as I stared at the falling snow. Father always made it look so easy. I clenched my fists, trying to summon anything—ice, frost, even a chill. Nothing.

Bridger smirked. "Good luck at the Rite tomorrow, Blanche. Jenessa was hopeful for you—it'll be a shame when I tell her you're falling behind."

A few others laughed. I clenched my fists against my ribs, trying to drown out their mocking voices as the rest practiced their powers. I stared at my scarred palm. *Please, give me something.*

Leaning into the crackling fire, I felt a hand on my shoulder. Myla's voice was soft. "You'll get it. Give it a few days."

Before I could respond, a shorter girl with pinned-back dark hair overheard and interrupted. "There aren't days—only hours left to prove ourselves. Only twelve will make it on." She gave a small nod. "I'm Chanvin. I was born in Icillian. Your father was a great man, Myla."

At least someone's father had kind words spoken about them.

Delwyn and Aspen, cousins from Autumn who had been placed in Winter, walked past, their fingers stained red as they popped berries into their mouths.

"What are you eating?" I asked, desperate for a distraction.

"The berries from that vine," one said, pointing to the mistletoe.

I shot to my feet, nearly knocking the berries from their hands. "Those are poisonous! Spit them out!"

Their eyes widened. "We were starving. We couldn't help it."

I stormed toward Bridger. "Two of them ate mistletoe. They're starving! We're starving! You've tortured us enough!"

Bridger's silver eyes flared with rage. "You don't get a say in how I lead, Blanche. This is Winter. Food is sparse in most regions, and people die. This is your first test to know if you belong, which, from the looks of it, you don't."

I bit back my anger. "What about those who fell off the wall? Will their bodies be returned home?"

"Most students who die here don't get letters sent to their parents. The academy won't waste resources dragging bodies out of the ground. People die here—it's nothing new," Bridger said coldly. He waved dismissively at Aspen and Delwyn, who clutched their stomachs. "They'll live. Besides, mistletoe is the most invasive species in the North—after the Blanches."

"I am not your enemy, Bridger."

"I saved your life on that slope."

"Not kicking me off isn't heroic."

Bridger's jaw tightened. "Do you know why your father's wards are failing?"

"He needs an heir to lean on," I said.

Bridger smiled cruelly. "You have no idea, do you? Your father bartered something he couldn't uphold."

The weight of his words settled in my chest like ice. "Over my dead body will the Blanche name leave the North."

"That'll be easy," Bridger sneered, his silver eyes piercing mine. Ice crept into my throat as he raised his hand, choking me until I couldn't breathe. "You are weak and don't deserve to become a ruler. Misspeak again, and I'll freeze your tongue until it snaps."

He released me, and my tongue felt like a stone in my mouth. Bridger stared at the sun dipping past the horizon. "Everybody rise. It's time for your enigma bonding. The younger the creature, the stronger your bond will be. We have griffin eggs that should hatch in a few weeks, but the egg will choose you." He unsheathed a knife from his inner thigh. "Can someone tell me what type of creature will bond with us?"

Myla spoke first. "In Ravensla, we have dragons and wyverns."

Bridger's smile twisted. "You're not wrong, but a dragon won't choose you. There are other bonded creatures for the Frozen Valleys—griffins, hippogriffs, rocs, phoenixes, and wolves."

Hunter's eyes flashed at Bridger. "I want to fly. A wolf can't fly, and a phoenix is a small bird."

"You don't get a choice. If a creature doesn't bond with you, you're out," he said. "I was lucky—bonded to three wolf pups my first week. And a griffin."

The bushes rustled, deep growls cutting through the air. Two yellow eyes stalked, a grey coat flickering through the frosted trees. The other was midnight black.

"Where's the third?" Myla asked.

"I prefer her to keep an eye on my parents," Bridger replied, gesturing sharply. The wolves vanished into the trees. "It's against academy law to kill another student's enigma in your first year. The bond strengthens over time."

Chanvin asked, "What about rider bonds? My sister formed a pack during her year. She could speak to her best friend from halls away."

"Bonding with other riders is forbidden until year three," Bridger said, voice flat.

Hunter frowned. "Why? I have nothing to hide."

Bridger shrugged. "Hormones. No sense in bonding with someone who might be your rival. Rider bonds tie you to one mind. Being indebted to someone for the rest of your life when you're still figuring things out? Foolish."

We entered the forest, evergreen trees swaying in the wind. The low tide revealed three small caves along the mountain's edge, their entrances submerged beneath icy water.

"Who wants to go first?" Bridger's eyes locked onto the black waves, daring someone to step forward.

A male named Robi shook his head. "The water's freezing. We'll drown if we get stuck inside."

Even Hunter stayed at the water's edge, unwilling to step closer.

Bridger folded his arms over his chest. "Then you drown. If you want your enigma to give its existence to you, you must earn that trust. Nothing will be handed to you—especially not a title." His gaze flickered to me. "Severyn, since you went last down the mountain, why don't you go first this time? I wouldn't want anyone to think I was treating you differently."

"Myla can come with me," I said, my voice tight. She nodded, casting a quick look at Bridger, waiting for his approval.

"Sure," he hissed. "You'll need the protection, I suppose."

The first step into the water was brutal, a shock of ice that numbed my legs instantly. The second step felt like walking through daggers. By the sixth, the cold bit at my hips, and I waded deeper until the water was up to my ribs.

Panic surged. My mind screamed at me to turn back.

Deep breath in. Release through your nose. Fight the burn. Fight the numbness.

Myla shivered, now chin-deep in cold water. "Do you often swim in ice back home? Is this… normal?"

"No," I said. "Bridger is trying to kill us."

The water level sloped to a drop, and my head fell under the black seawater. Exasperated, I gasped to the surface as I cut through the ice crystals with my fist.

Myla huffed, a sign that she was okay. My boots weighed me down like two boulders tied to my soles. I swam towards the mountain, below it a jagged entrance, sucking the water in and spitting it back out.

"I always thought I'd ride a dragon. What are griffins like?"

Gripping the cave walls, a wave slammed me forward and up. "They'll peck your eyes out if you touch a feather wrong," I said, hoisting myself atop the frosted algae of slime and into the tight cave.

"I see why we bond with eggs," she said.

Rock pressed against my ribs, forcing my breath into shallow inhales. We crawled on our hands and knees, our noses skimming the water as it choked and dripped into our lungs. The passage seemed to grow tighter with every movement.

"I can hardly breathe," I gasped, ribs flattened against the crushing rock. Even she was barely visible once I took a narrow turn and eased my limbs to drag on.

Salt burned my stinging hand, where a rock sliced my thumb on another squirm through. This seemed to be the last moment where only my mind could scream.

"Keep going. I—I see the light," she cried. "Keep going, we'll make it."

I would die here.

I believed the cave would squeeze me until I was pulp. I willed the desire to lay here, to suffice my body to melt to the rock as my elbow jammed against my knee on that final drag.

Light cracked, and Myla eased her feet into a groan beside me as the stone widened into a hollow core. We had no time to admire the jutted crystals prodding through the rock. In another moment, I might have called it beautiful.

Through the darkness, her finger pointed towards a ledge. "I see them," Myla yelled. "There's four eggs."

Grey-wired fur protruded and twined to create a makeshift nest. I wondered what beast's fur had been plucked and if a creature worse than Bridger waited beyond the cave.

"Grab one, and let's get out of here," I said as the water sloshed near our boots, rising higher every second.

Dimmed sun rays broke through the cavern walls, stretching on for miles. I had no intention of finding the end.

Myla reached, skimming the golden and blue eggs with her nails. "I can't reach them."

I leaned against a rock in screaming pain. Fighting every desire to faint, to leave. To give up. "Can you—climb up?"

Myla raised her boot, sliding down the ledge with a thud. "It's too slippery." Her voice echoed back. "Get on my shoulders, and you can grab them."

"Okay," I said as Myla lowered her neck.

I climbed her shoulders, wobbling as I skimmed the jutted rock ledge. Myla tipped back, and I clung, using my last bit of energy. I reached towards the eggs, sliding my hand over the gritted surface. The blue one was the size of a griffin egg, and the golden one, I couldn't tell from this far away what it was. It was smaller than the rest, with a glossy film covering the slicked shell.

A low hiss sounded close to my fingers. Then, two slivered red eyes blinked with scales.

I screamed, "Snake, snake… snake!" Myla stumbled back, nearly taking me down with her. It snapped forward, curling its tail around the eggs in a protective stance.

"Grab the eggs before the snake eats my enigma!"

"Myla, I don't think I can." Another snap of its fangs, this time inches from my hand. "Myla, can you try to freeze the snake from where you're standing?"

"I can try—I can't see past my fingertips. You'll have to tell me where to aim."

Lifting four shaking fingers, her breath fell into a different rhythm as a swirl of snow pushed from each tip.

It wasn't strong enough. She needed to get closer.

"Higher, it's on the left!" I yelled as another hiss and snap came from the beast. Iced flurries shot forward, twirling faster around her index finger. I grabbed her elbow as frost coated the air, forming a labyrinth of cracked ice along the walls.

The snake's tail whipped the blue egg forward. Myla caught it before it smashed into the ground. "I got it!" she cried and began to lower.

I quickly snatched the cold and waxy golden egg as the snake rose for another attack. It was a griffin egg, probably identical to Setrephia's golden feathers from the color of its shell.

I knew next to nothing about bonding. But I knew it would call to you before. I knew that time would stop, and I'd feel what those folktales spoke about when one finds their creature. I placed the egg in the nape of my velvet-lined hood before Myla could see. We returned to the cave's mouth and those gurgled waves of ice.

My feet touched the water again. I stared breathlessly at Myla, skimming over that baby-blue egg in her clutched arms. "Looks like a hippogriff, maybe even a roc egg," I said.

"I'll name it Haziel, after my father's last name." She ran a hand down the egg, her eyes wide and dancing over every speckle. "Did you grab one? Did it call? I swore I heard it whisper my name."

"None of them called to me," I said.

We retraced our steps, back through the tight, rib-crushing cave. I kept my head high, hoping my hood wouldn't graze the cold waters. Myla swam one-handed, the other proudly holding the blue egg flush against her palm. A few students cheered. Bridger patted her back, his hand lingering at her waist.

He looked at me, his eyes cold. "Perhaps you're not cut out for the Serpent Academy. All but two eggs have been claimed." He started to turn but sighed, adding, "The boat will pick you up tomorrow. We don't have time for failures."

Myla quickly corrected him. "There are three eggs left in the cave."

I didn't know what compelled me to speak, but I regretted it immediately. "No, one was eaten. The snake got to it." I kept my back to the waters, careful Bridger wouldn't see the lump in my hood.

Bridger stiffened his shoulders. "I see."

Two others held eggs. One was a pale white, shimmering like an opal stone. Robi had found a hatchling, a meaty, featherless bird, shrieking by his feet. Two rocs perched on the branches above, their eyes fixed on three students below. Slices marred the branches where their claws had torn, their seven-foot tawny feathers flaring. The branches cracked as they took flight into the grey sky.

None of them called to me—or to anyone else.

I walked over to Robi, chuckling at the barbed bird below him. Being friendly was my best shot at surviving another night. "Congratulations on fatherhood," I said.

He eyed the shrieking bird. "You think the ladies will enjoy this new look?" He flashed a grin, his lanky arms bending to graze the bird's bony spine.

I was about to laugh, but Hunter diving into the water caught my attention.

The sea barely hit his calves as his fist slashed through the ice. He gripped the cave walls and hurled himself forward. Moments passed in pure silence. Even the thrashing waves dulled.

"Snake," he yelled. "Help me! I'm stuck!"

I jerked towards the water, but Bridger pulled me back hard. "You can't interrupt. This is part of the bonding process."

"Like hell. He needs help." I ripped my arm away, and Bridger whistled.

Two wolves lunged at my chest, pinning me down with one paw on either side of my waist. Jaws snapped, dripping hot drool onto my forehead. One sniffed close to my hood, whimpering.

Bridger stared down. "Nothing beats a bond like Lucy and Niagra. Elmira got a taste of blood two years back. I couldn't have her on campus anymore after that, but all three are so connected it's almost as if they can smell whose blood she tasted."

"Your mut attacked my brother?" Of course, Bridger was a third-year. He knew Klaus.

His eyes hardened. "Perhaps." He called the wolves off, and they darted back into the woods with a howl.

"Did you kill him?" I asked. "Tell me… how he died?"

"Wouldn't you love to know? I find poison and honesty taste the same."

And a voice, so slight and tender, whistled a melancholy tune through the forest, *"Severyn. Find him. You must."* I glanced at where I thought the voice came from. Scattered sounds rustled the bushes, but it was just Bridger's wolves.

"Find who?" I asked Bridger.

He clicked his tongue. "You have lost your mind."

I glanced through the misted veil before lowering my eyes to my drenched boots. "Nothing. I—I heard a voice."

"We don't need another mad heir or Serpent. Thank the Gods your title is out of your hands."

No Serpent would choose me at the Rite. Not if they knew I'd lose my mind before the night ended.

"Find him," it called once more. *"He waits in slumber."*

Chapter 5

Bridger led us through the Autumn woods towards the academy. Vibrant leaves danced between life and death, the crisp air biting my cheeks in the warmest way I'd felt in two days. Scaling the ice wall had been strenuous, but the two-hour hike through peaks and sprawling grass was even more exhausting. Unmarred blue skies stretched overhead, the awakening I needed for the Rite.

All first-years were organized by last name. Myla stood further back, her egg secured with a sling to her hip. Robi's hatchling had grown overnight, now the size of a house cat, its white feathers fluffed out. I tried petting it earlier, but it nearly bit my finger off.

I repelled griffins.

The crowd seemed smaller than the first day. Exhaustion brimmed in the students' wide eyes. Lacerations marked their arms and cheeks. We all struggled to survive during those initial days, which perhaps humbled me.

The six Serpents stepped into the entrance of the academy hall. Archer was the last to join. He wore a long-sleeved dress shirt tucked into dark pants. The serpent on his neck clenched, its two sets of daggered eyes wavering. He looked bored, as if this Rite was the last thing he wanted to attend. Monty gave a sly grin with a hand perched beneath his chin. I kept sight of Jenessa, pleading she'd cast a glance at me.

Bridger gave us the rundown of the Rite as we traveled back to the academy. Jenessa, the Serpent of Winborow—the fifth Frozen Valley in Verdonia—chose Bridger to decide who went on. My odds were unfavorable. Time slipped away as I stared at the ticking grandfather clock across the hall. Knox stood beside me, silent as if Day had stripped more than just his voice and beard. I hardly recognized him without the pubescent wires clung to his jawbone.

If I weren't chosen today, I would be sent to Malvoria, and my family would lose everything.

I whispered to Knox beside me, "I need you to kill Bridger Thorne if I don't make it."

He darted his eyes at me. "We're supposed to stay quiet, Sev."

Monty Garcia was the first Serpent to call names forward. His black hair appeared almost blue-hued under the lanterns, but daylight rippled along the bends and curves of his knuckles as he read his chosen twelve names off a scroll. "Gwen Sidhu, Novely Hastings, Knox Blanche…"

I stopped listening once I heard Knox's name. He gave a shuttered sigh, taking his place behind Monty.

The headmaster shook each hand enthusiastically. I figured he favored Day from the shattered prisms I'd seen in his eyes as he smiled at them.

Knox was safe. Yet, his group had started with nearly the same amount as us, and only three weren't chosen.

Bile rose in my throat as I saw what initiation Knox had gone through. Blood cracked the beds of his nails, marring his dirtied tunic. Day's initiation was not a wall of ice but a leap of cruelty—the blood of another in return for power.

My bleak thoughts simmered as Levisly stepped forward, vines lacing her smooth, porcelain skin as her fingers gripped a rolled scroll.

Spring had come and gone. Eleven were no longer students but products of Malvoria as they were dragged by their arms out of the estate. Dewed lashes blinked, surrendering with a final stare at Levisly. Summer was more cutthroat. Saani spared no grins for the crowd of eager students as only ten names were called from her list.

A male thrashed his arms as a guard hauled him back. "My father will demand my return," he screamed, spitting a crimson brine on the onyx stone. "To hell with you all."

Autumn's choices left nothing but questions as he called those twelve names one by one, and not a whisper of Herring sounded from his lips. Margaret and Cormac, two of Autumn's newest initiations, gave Malachi a silent weep as they left her behind.

Jenessa stepped forward. I watched her lips, her every breath as she glanced at the parchment in her hands that Bridger had slipped her moments before.

"Myla Reinhart… Robi Wills, Chanvin Lynn." She said nine more names, but none were mine.

My knees buckled. What do I do?

Nothing. I could do absolutely nothing but grieve my failures as those twelve chosen to become my father's heir stepped past me.

Bridger shifted through the crowd towards me. Myla's boots echoed past before taking her place behind Jenessa. Her eyes wandered around the room, the slight of the unchosen and Night staring back. She knew I would leave—knew her warrants of unselfish warmth were for nothing.

Half of those who received letters would be sent to Malvoria.

The grandfather clock ticked three times, my heart seven.

Bridger grabbed my wrist tight. "Wouldn't want you to be late for the boat to Malvoria," he hissed, lips against my ear. "You'd be dead in a week anyway."

I ripped from his grasp, but he locked his other hand around me. "Get off me," I hissed.

A throat cleared from where the Serpents stood. "What are you doing with my student, Thorne?" My eyes slipped up, distorted from the tears masking my vision. The voice was Archer Lynch's.

Bridger dropped his hand. "I am escorting her out, sir. Jenessa has not chosen her." He chuckled hoarsely. "She's nearly lost her mind. She rambles in her sleep. Best to take her outside before she causes a scene."

Archer glanced down for a second. "Her name is on my scroll." He flashed the curled piece of paper where my name was last on the list, written in darker ink.

A few quiet murmurs sounded in the room. "Sir, you have thirteen names on that list," Bridger said. "The maximum is twelve first-year students."

Humor beamed in Archer's blue eyes. "Do you have an issue with my decision?" he asked. "Do I need to remind you who I am?"

"Severyn Blanche is a Winter. That girl will not survive under Night's leadership. You are only delaying her death."

The room silenced. "Is there anything else, Thorne? I suggest you step away from Miss Blanche."

Bridger shook his head with a huff.

Archer read the names from his scroll. "Malachi Herring… Jace Lorangail, Alaric Nite…. Antonia Welsch." My brain was mush by the eleventh name, and I swore when he said Severyn Blanche, I nearly dropped to the stone ground.

The headmaster cleared his throat. "Walk forward, Severyn Blanche."

Heart stuttering, I walked toward the chosen students, thankful the attention had turned towards Malachi, strutting a few steps behind me.

Sixty or so students remained unpicked, now the property of Malvoria. Guards escorted them out, bounding them with some type of invisible tether. They went not without struggle, not without curses and thrashing hands.

A soft voice trilled behind me, then a double tap on my shoulder. "You can be my roommate for now," said a voice. Malachi. "There are only twelve rooms available, and you don't want to bunk with any of the others here. Trust me." Her amber eyes wavered across the other eleven students of Night.

"Roommates?" I whispered. "You want to be my roommate?" I took in her blonde waves, the freckles on her cheeks, and the single dimple on her chin. She was soft, nearly radiating, and I assumed her to be cruel.

"Yes. We seem to be living the same life." She uncurled her fist, and a ripple of wind circled each finger. Her eyes went up and down my bruised frame. "I'm a tad less injured, I suppose."

Nothing seemed real. I locked eyes with Bridger. I knew he wouldn't stop until I was dead.

Archer spoke to the headmaster and a senior female student. The tips of her shifting fingers were chrome-colored like she'd dipped her arm in liquid iron. Her long, braided blonde hair was tied with a golden ribbon.

Malachi nudged me, noticing my blatant stare. "That's Delair Sorpine. She's in line to become Archer's heir. Stay away from her. She wields metal, and her daggers are sharper than needles."

She wore the same metal snake pin as Bridger. "She's… intimidating," I said.

"As I said, most Night students lack sunlight. Their minds are nearly as dark-willed as their powers."

"Why—why us? We stand no chance with us being under another ruler's mentorship."

She smiled wide. "Perhaps to stir the game. This is all a ploy of kill or be killed. Win or lose. If someone saves your life, expect their demand for retribution. I give great advice. I suggest listening to it."

Archer's attention slipped to the onyx stone, and I swept behind the other students, hoping to thank him… hoping to demand why he'd chosen me, why he traveled three days to perform a sudden death to my parents when most students never received a simple letter. Shadows dripped from his perfectly tailored shirt, and I swore I nearly broke my nose, smashing into a shield.

Black and white speckled my vision. I recognized Alaric as one of the chosen Night students who ripped me back. "What do you think you are doing?" His pointed features hid beneath a shadow with eyes resembling a midnight storm wavering up and down.

I choked on my breath. "I was going to talk to Archer."

Antonia crossed her arms, her mousy features scrunching as her pale eyes—like the silver dagger Charles gave me—contrasted sharply against her black hair. Both sides of her nose were pierced, connected by a silver chain.

"You don't just speak to a Serpent without getting called on. You are lucky his shield didn't kill you." She took me in—the snow burns on my dried, flaking skin. The Night students didn't seem half as traumatized as Jenessa's initiations.

"A shield," I muttered.

Antonia pursed her lips. "Now, what does the bitch of the Continent and a snowflake have to do in Night?"

Malachi stood beside me again. "Antonia, no need to be hostile. We have no intention of becoming the heir of Night. Archer and I go way back."

Antonia scoffed. "Try not to keep me up when you scream at night. We all know you are a walking target, Herring."

* * *

The Night corridors were up a golden-railed spiral staircase on the second floor, beneath a crescent moon relic hanging over the arched entrance. Cold drafts pelted the halls as candles flickered in the hanging lanterns. Shadows crawled up the walls, brittle like branches, casting slender flames high and low. The rooms were small—barely enough space to move after Malachi forced the guards to bring in a second bed and two of everything else.

I quickly slid the griffin egg beneath my bed, tucking it safely into a makeshift nest I'd fashioned from the cloak Charles had given me. My closet was already stocked with the academy's uniforms—Serpent green, as deep as pine forests. Evening suits hung neatly alongside thick sweaters for colder days, and plaid skirts emblazoned with the academy's crest. The oval stained-glass windows painted a constellation of stars across the stone walls, the fading sunlight igniting them in hues of amber and violet.

After a long, hot shower, I stretched out on the mattress—a welcome relief compared to cabin bunks, where every twist and turn met the jab of a rebellious spring. I sighed into the softness, savoring the moment.

Malachi, however, didn't share my appreciation for rest. When she finally emerged, she was dressed in a plaid skirt and a white polo, unbuttoned just enough to reveal a hint of cleavage. Her blonde curls bounced just above her collarbone, still damp from the shower.

She stopped short when she saw me sprawled across the bed. "*What* are you doing?" she asked, her tone hovering between curiosity and shock.

"I'm resting," I said, leaning on the wooden frame. "You look nice." She smelled of that same rich vanilla scent from before.

"Tonight, we celebrate. It's our first official night at the Serpent Academy. So, get up," Malachi said with a grin.

"Malachi," I began, my voice heavy with exhaustion. "I'm grateful you got another bed put in. Really, I am. But I just survived the most brutal nights of my life. And I don't even have my quell, let alone my enigma."

She stared at me as if I'd sprouted horns. "You are Fallon's daughter, are you not?"

Her words hit like a misfired arrow. I returned her stare, confusion knitting my brow. "My mother?"

"She's a legend around here," Malachi said, the grin widening as if she couldn't believe my ignorance. "Won Skyfall two years in a row with her wyvern. Managed to keep her forbidden quell hidden, too. First student ever to be publicly stripped of it. I read all about her before the Rite."

"My mother was a dragon rider?" I echoed, blankly staring at her, trying to reconcile this version of my mother with the woman I'd known.

"Well, technically, she rode a wyvern. The difference is in the legs. But yeah, every academy student is journaled—their quell, house, and enigma. You can look up anyone's records in the library. My family rides dragons, too. I mean, we have to— because of my grandfather. A griffin? Cute, but not much help in a fight. No offense." She grinned, radiating self-assurance, as if she were too delicate to be lethal—despite the glint in her eyes that said otherwise.

"That dragon you rode in on—is that yours? The one with three heads?" I asked, shifting the subject with ease.

"Tors?" She shook her head. "I used him to train my entire life, but he's not my enigma. Dragon bonding isn't as simple as just finding an egg. Dragons have roots, and I'm not in the mood to give a history lesson right now."

"I don't want any distractions. My family is depending on me."

"Well, lucky for you, you'll have plenty of time to figure it out." She grabbed a matching academy uniform from the closet and shoved the plaid skirt against my chest. "Now, get dressed. We're going to enjoy the party. And that Bridger guy? He definitely had his eye on you. Keeping close to student mentors isn't just smart—it's survival."

"Bridger wants to kill me and steal my father's title. Of course, he had his eyes on me."

Malachi hummed a soft tune. "Are you going to let him?"

"No," I said, pulling the shirt over my head and tucking it into the patterned skirt. "What exactly is this *party*?"

Surely, I looked like a swollen doll from the welts marring my legs and arms.

"This party is to get to know your fellow students and the Serpents. Just because we are under Archer's watch doesn't mean you can't learn from the others. Take Monty. He can teach you how light affects your quell." She gave me a subtle wink. "Second and third-years will be there."

"What is that wink for?"

She stretched her arm over my shoulder. "I meant that Monty Garcia is hot and offered to teach me special classes. It doesn't hurt to flirt your way to power."

Flirt my way to power. I scoffed. Malachi was flawless, with a sheer grace of cunning. It terrified me that someone could be so bold. I suppose she was the king's granddaughter.

"You're courting with the Serpent of Day?" I asked. We stepped into the hallway. I wouldn't mention how many mistresses I had read about. Malachi, of all people, would know.

Malachi pressed her finger on my lips, shushing me. Her hands trailed down my neck toward the buttons and undid two. "Not courting. I have no intention of marriage anytime soon." Her features pinched. "Or ever, for that matter. But you must admit Monty is gorgeous."

"Oh, I suppose," I muttered. "Shouldn't we focus on our quells and studies? My father's title rests in my hands. I don't want… distractions."

"You won't survive here if you don't find your alliances. Your enemies should be your friends—Monty wants me dead. And it doesn't hurt to have a little fun."

"So, you're planning on *hooking up* with the man who wants to kill you?"

She chuckled, and the smile she gave was something I hadn't expected, given her following words. "Everyone wants to kill me. Perhaps even you someday."

So, Antonia wasn't kidding when she mentioned Malachi's screams would wake her from doors away.

Every lantern lit the halls with shattered light. Swallowing that curling shadowed brick. We passed the library at the grand entrance, arching into a black windowed door. I needed to visit it tomorrow to read what Malachi learned about my family.

"The headmaster said we should be in our rooms when the lanterns turn on."

She laughed. "The professors will be drunker than us by the time we arrive. It's only a threat. No one enforces rules here.

They trap the most powerful students and expect us to obey?" She raised a brow.

I asked, "What did the professor mean when he said my mother was a death curser?"

"Fallon could wield death with only a single touch. But her wyvern gave her the quell of sound. She could hear things from behind doors."

Death. My mother had the death quell.

"Did it say anything about Klaus? He was my older brother."

Malachi pushed the double-wide doors open. Night took us into the shadows of grey clouds. A gust sprang up, glinted with gold and lavender speckles.

Dare I say, I felt bold stepping outside without a jacket.

"Flame," she whispered a beat later. "Klaus was placed in Summer."

My gaze probed the approaching night, grappling with the words Malachi had fed me before they coalesced into meaning. Klaus was a fire wielder. I knew Father would have disowned him the moment that knowledge trickled down the line of Serpents, discovering that a son of Winter melted the land he was born in.

"I never knew," I said softly, fighting the urge to be pissed at Klaus but knowing I had no right. At least Knox was alive, and I could curse him for betraying our family and leaving it all up to me. "I come from a long line of ice powers. This makes no sense," I added.

"The academy takes your most potent traits and places you where you will be the most powerful. You must be born with Summer in your blood for Klaus to wield flame. That is why you were markless during initiation. Your mother was more powerful than your father."

"I am a Winter." I stifled my breath as we walked down a narrow, shaded path to the backside of the castle. Silver and black fences guided us to a clearing, where fifty people gathered around a fire pit.

The gnawing sea hurled in the distance. Canopies hung low, adorned with crystal and golden teardrops. Flowers budded from the ground, curling around the fence separating the ocean from the cobblestone path.

Malachi looped her arm within mine, vanilla ripping through my tightened lungs as she leaned closer. "Winters are known to be shy. Don't worry, I'll break you before the academy can."

I muttered back, "You can't break broken."

"We all have more room to break."

She was right. I feared the pieces left inside of me. I couldn't focus on Klaus. I couldn't be this empty soul anymore.

A flurry of ash rippled through the air, carried by the soft crackle of the fire. A dozen students mingled around it, their green-and-black uniforms blending into the night. I scanned the crowd for Knox, but he disappeared into the sea of identical blazers.

The sounds of voices bouncing off waves filled the space—clipped conversations, bursts of laughter, and the occasional crack of kindling. The night should have felt alive, but anger, guilt, and grief churned within me, threatening to drown the moment.

Archer Lynch caught my eye, lounging on a log with a blonde girl perched in his lap. Her veins shimmered like twisting vines, and tiny flowers bloomed from her hair, each strand adorned with delicate beads. She had to be from Spring—her presence radiated a dangerous allure.

Beside me, Malachi spotted Monty Garcia and locked eyes with him, a grin already spreading across her face. She turned to me. "The more people you know here, the better. Find some alliances tonight—maybe even your enemies." She shrugged, then added with a teasing lilt, "But if you kiss someone, I want *all* the details."

"I'd rather not make enemies," I called after her, but she was already striding towards Monty, his arms outstretched as if he'd been waiting for her all night. She melted into him effortlessly, leaving me alone to fend for myself.

I sighed and turned back to the crowd. Knox. He stood behind Monty, hands tucked awkwardly into his trousers, the hem of his cotton blazer brushing his hips. He looked out of place, his quiet presence stark against the lively chatter of the Day students around him. I started towards him, softly uttering his name.

Before he could hear me, a hand grabbed my shoulder. I spun around, ready to scold. "Bridger, I swear to god—"

But it wasn't Bridger. Hazel eyes met mine, sharp and unreadable, framed by short, dark locks. His skin was sun-kissed, his jawline strong and clean-shaven, with a single dimple pressed into his left cheek. Handsome, in a way no North Colindale man had ever been.

"Who is Bridger?" he asked.

I crossed my arms, staring at the hand still on my shoulder. "A student."

His eyes stroked me down, not shying away from my breasts. "Neval hair, and you're hanging out with Malachi Herring. You must be quite interesting." He passed me a darkened bottle of liquor he'd already drunk a quarter of.

I shook my head. "No thanks. I prefer to be coherent for my first classes tomorrow."

"Docile as well." He flashed a quick smile. "My name is Damien. Second-year, Summer."

"Severyn." I quickly noticed that a last name held power around here, and from how many death wishes I had upon me, I couldn't admit more. "First-year, Winter."

He took the bottle back, holding the rim against his lower lip. "A Winter student. Now, that would be my last guess."

"And why is that?" I asked.

He glanced at Myla and the four other Winters walking toward the fire. A Serpent relic pinned to his shirt caught my eye. Damien was in the lead to claim the next title.

"Because Archer chose you for his roster—it's unheard of for students not to be placed under the house of their called realm," Damien said. "The Serpent Press will have a field day if the headmaster allows this information to spread."

"Winter is not a weak realm. Just because we don't ride dragons doesn't mean we aren't strong," I shot back.

Damien raised his hands defensively, his palms calloused. For a moment, I found myself counting the scars on his chest, visible through the V-neck of his tunic. "I'm the last person who'd want to get stuck in a snowstorm," he said. "I admire it, honestly. Winter's quite alluring. Who doesn't love dry skin and goosebumps?"

"I think you're insulting me," I said. "And... I think you winked at me two days later if I recall correctly."

More scars lined his forearm, jagged cuts that lacked any discernible pattern. I wasn't sure I wanted to ask about them.

"I prefer brutal honesty and yes, that was me."

I glanced at Malachi, who was sitting on Monty's lap now. "Tell me about Malachi. Brutal honesty."

"Shall I add demanding to that list?" He tilted his chin. "One drink equals one answer." He shoved the glass bottle into my chest again, his lip pouting slightly.

"Fine." I took a heavy sip. It was tangy, with hints of orange. But it was definitely booze. "Now, tell me about Malachi."

His smile turned smug. "The king had five grandchildren, and each one died at the academy because they were the heir of Verdonia. But since Malachi is the last living grandchild. A

Serpent will take the throne if Malachi dies after the king passes. There is this game the students play each year a Herring attends the academy called, 'Who can Kill the Herring First.' The six Serpents this year are the Continent's youngest rulers, so the king chose them to mentor this year as the runners to claim his title."

He narrowed his eyes. "Archer saved Malachi tonight because she would have been killed if placed under Tydon's mentorship. Why do you think he hasn't taken his eyes off her?"

A beautiful blonde student was sitting on his lap, giggling, but his eyes were on Malachi. She even had his leather jacket draped over her vined shoulders.

"So, Archer loves Malachi?" I breathed. This was… *deadly* gossip.

Damien snorted. "No. Not like that. Archer vowed to keep Malachi safe. Something about her brother being his friend when he was a student."

There seemed to be secrets everywhere. My mother's mystery of her wielding death and being publicly stripped of her quell. The unknown Day blood that gurgled through my veins—our veins—Klaus's placement in Summer. Nothing made sense.

I shifted my weight, changing the topic. "What is your quell?"

A disapproving tsk sounded from his mouth. "You don't just ask someone their quell. Where are your manners, Severyn? I've told you four things. Tell me something about you."

I pointed to Knox. "That's my brother, Knox. My eldest brother Charles is a guard for Malvoria." I didn't mention Klaus. I knew once death was brought up—he'd linger. Linger in the sigh Damien would give me, followed by his words of condolence. I learned how to respond, having done it repeatedly.

Damien rolled his eyes. "That's common knowledge. Tell me something I can't find in the library, and don't give me some scripted response."

I pressed my lips together. No one had ever drawn interest in me, and thinking back on my life, I was rather dull. "I'm terrified of birds and am forced to bond with one for the rest of my life."

He waved a hand in the air. "Tell me a secret. We are fighting for our lives, more or less a title. I'm pretty good at listening. You might die tomorrow. We all could."

I grabbed the bottle from his hands and took another sip. The slow ache in my body dulled as the liquor settled in my stomach. "I'm an open book. Really, I have no secrets."

He flicked my neval streak. "I doubt that."

My breaths shortened. "I didn't realize a quell was private."

"I prefer to keep my quell private until I know someone isn't my enemy. But seeing as most of your camp either got their quell or their enigma, I'd say you are the least of my worries."

"You can trust me." I gave him a shy grin.

Was this considered flirting?

"If I were you, once a Winter student dies, I would see if Jenessa will take you in. Archer won't be able to mentor you. Shadow and ice are very different."

"What if I'm not meant to be in the North? Has that… ever happened before?"

"Then you already have more enemies than you think."

The blood drained from my face.

I listened to the cheers as a crowd surrounded Monty. His fingers danced in the air, shredding light through the star-flecked night. His serpent mark illuminated as if a string of lights were buried under his skin.

Perhaps he was gorgeous. Perhaps the male beside me, even more so. *Damnit*. I couldn't get distracted.

I exhaled. "And what's Archer's quell? Shadows, I assume?"

"Archer controls the dark. Shadows are his eyes. Monty controls light. If he wanted to, he could blind all of us with a wave of his hand."

I understood why Malachi wanted to keep Monty close.

Malachi gently twirled her hand, creating a flurry of wind around him. Then, his lips were on her neck. She arched back, and the air stilled.

"Wind could be powerful," I said.

"Air is powerful," he corrected. "Malachi must become a Serpent before she can take her grandfather's throne. As you two are roommates, I'd be careful—she can hear through the wind. Every quell has its limits. Wind becomes air as light becomes blinding."

"And how deadly can darkness be?"

"Archer is wounded right now. He's hardly a threat."

"Why is that?"

Damien glanced at the bottle in my hand. "That answer requires another drink."

I slammed the liquor, shaking my head as the burn traveled down. "Go on."

"His enigma is gone."

"Gone, as in dead?"

"Missing."

That was hardly worth the sting in my stomach. "You know a lot about the people here." If Damien was willing to tell me all of this over a slosh of cheap booze, I knew I couldn't trust him.

"My brother is the Serpent of Shadows. I know a lot about people. Especially ones who share my blood."

My mind went blank as his words whirled around. "Your name is Damien Lynch?" My stomach dropped, and I took another willing sip of the swirling liquor.

"And you are Severyn Blanche." He struck his hand out for me to shake. "Nice to meet you finally."

My lips parted as cool fingers curled around mine. "Yes."

"Let me know if you need someone to show you around campus. Your senior mentor doesn't seem to have your best interests at heart." His eyes flickered to Bridger. "Good luck tomorrow."

"You knew—" But Damien was gone before I could finish. Scattered dust flurried in the moonlight, and my fingers tightened around the near-empty glass bottle.

And shit, I was drunk.

* * *

That night, I wrote a letter to my parents. I told them about the griffin I bonded with on the first day, my quell, and the frost that surged through my veins. I could afford to break, but my father's wards were near shattering, and I feared his entire fortress would crumble if I told them the truth.

Chapter 6

We left for the Winter forests by the crack of dawn.

Ice crusted my hair on the first step down the ice wall. Robi and Chanvin joined us, hoping to find their enigma.

"My mother found her griffin egg before she joined the academy, how lucky," said Chanvin as she made her way down the Crimson Wall.

Robi shook his head. "I just hope it's not a wolf. No offense to Bridger."

Surprisingly, today was an easier climb. Although, My joints hadn't healed from yesterday's hike, and I still hadn't found my quell or creature as we searched the frosted woods for two hours. I didn't dare step inside that cave—the tide was too high, and I'd risk drowning.

My mind drifted to Hunter. Was he still in there? Had his bones frozen in the cave? His voice, trapped in a sphere of ice, crystallizing as the snake devoured him.

Bridger's words lingered. "You're going to wish that Serpent never chose you," he had hissed before we parted ways.

Malachi and I walked to our first class that afternoon. My palms were blistered, swollen, and my lips cracked. As I glanced down at my reflection in the stone beneath my feet, I realized I felt worse than I looked.

The school sprawled before us, disorienting in its size and structure. Warding class was on the eastern side, the realms divided by dorms. There weren't many professors, and the first-year focus seemed to be mainly on building strength. The seniors, I'd heard, had an etiquette class. To the south, the griffin fields stretched across the land; to the north, dragons roamed. Last night, I'd studied the map, committing every path, every hallway to memory. Students were granted only eight days off a year: four for the Harvest Festival, which was in a few months, and the rest for Winter Solstice.

Professor Cain taught warding. I'd watched my father's hands tremble while working on shields over the years, so I didn't know what to expect. Warding protected our lands; shielding defended us. Those with quells were encouraged to combine them with their shields. For Malachi, a soft wind spiraled around her, forming a dome-like frenzy as she outstretched her hand. The hum of dozens of quells vibrated faintly in the air.

The first day was for first-year students only; second-years would join us later. Quells were quick to learn, but mastering the advanced techniques would take years. My father could create avalanches, not that he ever used that power.

Professor Cain's voice sliced through the shuffle of restless students. "Raise your palm and feel your shield around you. There are mind reader quells at the academy, so it's best to master protecting yourself—and your family's secrets," he instructed, his tone sharp despite the squeak in his voice.

He adjusted the rim of his square glasses, his short, greying hair catching the dim light. His muted grey robes were frayed at the hems—a detail I couldn't help but focus on as he shuffled down the rows of long wooden desks.

Mind readers. The thought sent a shiver down my spine. I'd heard of mental quells before—powers that ventured far beyond the ordinary.

Malachi sat to my left, Knox to my right. Across from us, Malachi's allies, Margaret and Cormac, stared at their hands, amber-hued, foxlike eyes intent on summoning their wind quells.

Myla entered the class, spotting me. "You should've come over last night," Myla said, sliding into the seat beside Margaret. "The Winter dorms are beautiful. The columns are made of crystals and diamonds."

She was describing my home.

I gave her a curt nod. "Sounds beautiful," I said. Nor did I have any interest in mingling with students eager to make me their first blood.

Malachi raised her hand. "Professor Cain, could you explain how mind reading isn't a forbidden quell?"

Cain paused, narrowing his gaze on her. "Normally, we don't discuss forbidden quells on the first day, Miss Herring. But to clarify, a forbidden quell is any power capable of permanently altering something, or one stronger than most. Mind reading doesn't kill—it simply observes."

His deep brown eyes scanned the room, lingering briefly on each of us. "Most of you will possess two quells: one natural to your bloodline, and one inherited from your enigma, provided the creature was mature at the time of bonding. You'll find a warding book on your desk, which covers all types of shields."

I glanced down at the worn leather-bound book in front of me, its edges frayed from years of use. A shield, the professor said.

But what kind of shield could protect against the chaos already brewing within these walls?

Antonia raised her hand from a few seats back. "Forgive me, professor, but you seem to be missing one: antecedent quells."

Professor Cain pursed his lips. "It's quite rare, but your enigma can absorb a quell from a fallen past rider and pass it on to you. Like a family heirloom—those quells date back hundreds of years, to the Forgotten days."

I was listening to the professor, but I couldn't ignore the way Myla glanced back at the other Winter students. I wondered if she regretted not sitting with them.

"Malachi, this is Myla and Knox," I said, sensing her aversion.

Malachi pursed her lips. "Icillian blood, right?"

Myla opened her palm, dusting snow across the wooden desk. "Yes. Should I say you're golden-blooded?"

Knox thumped his leg a mile a minute. "I know who Malachi is, Severyn," he hissed.

"I thought we could all form alliances," I whispered, holding out my hand. "We're less likely to kill each other if we're not fighting for the same title."

But as I spoke, a sharp burn tore through my forearm. Knox seemed to be struggling too. Myla nearly perfected her shield as an impenetrable ice barrier formed around her.

Malachi snickered. "We can still kill each other. Blood doesn't define our morals."

"Blanches, are you even trying?" the professor groaned. "I don't feel any repel."

I shot Knox a look, my eyes wide.

"Drag your shield from the inner depth of your body. Think of protecting your homeland. Think of every cruel beast that dares to cross over!"

He could yell all he wanted, but no shield would form. Sweat broke across my forehead, and I felt my arm give out in protest. "I can't, professor," I gasped, breathless.

Cain clicked his tongue. "You might have a block. It's not uncommon. I'd recommend seeing a healer when you can. But remember, you'll need those shields strong to fend off the snow beasts."

I sighed. Malvoria seemed closer every day.

Malachi leaned in. "You'll get it. Don't worry. Cormac's a late bloomer too." She shot a mischievous look at her auburn-haired male alliance.

"Shut up, Malachi. I know too many of your secrets to be hearing this," Cormac shot back.

She twirled wind around her index finger. "Not another Serpent Press scandal," she chuckled.

Margaret laughed. "Everyone saw you with Monty Garcia. I'm sure there's already a story in the works surrounding the both of you. A Princess and a Serpent sounds like a folktale."

I listened to their conversations, trying my hardest to form a shield, to form ice. Yet an hour passed, and the first class was over.

The next class was combat—thankfully, the first-years were only to observe the senior students. My muscles thanked me as Malachi and I stood on the sidelines.

Bridger and Damien were among the mix, shirtless, with sweat glistening on their bodies as they sparred. I couldn't take my eyes off Damien's steady flex of each muscle and the way he smiled at me across the combat ring.

"Can you fight?" I asked Malachi.

"I learned how to duel before walking," she replied. "You?"

"Same. But I stopped training for two years."

I yelped as two glass daggers appeared in Damien's fists with a quick raise of his arms. "North, I hope blood doesn't scare you," he yelled from the sparring ground. "The first class can get a bit brutal."

North. I didn't despise that nickname.

Malachi scoffed. "Of course, Damien fucking Lynch is here."

"I met him last night," I said. "He seems nice."

She twirled the wind around her middle finger ever so slightly in his direction. "I can only imagine the dread he must feel being the heartthrob of the Continent's brother. And Damien is not nice, let's get that straight."

Damien and Everett were dueling each other. Day's student mentor unsheathed a dagger from around his wide thigh, ripping it past Damien's left eye—missing by a hair. Damien's arms wound around Everett's waist, slamming him into the grass as blood dripped from his nose.

He was… strong and quick.

"Everyone here looks like a heartbreaker," I said, more honesty in those words than I let on.

Metal clashed against metal, the sharp echoes filling the training grounds. Students' lungs heaved as they fought, sweat dripping from their brows. I stood back, watching silently while shadows crept along the grass, leeching life from the greenery.

Then Archer emerged from the haze, his presence commanding as he joined the combat instructor, Professor Knight. Knight had a balding head, deep lines carved across his forehead, and a jagged mark running from his temple down his neck.

Archer's voice cut through the metallic din. "How are the first-years supposed to learn by watching?"

Myla nudged me in the ribs, her eyes fixed on Archer. "That's your Serpent leader? He's…" Her voice tightened as she stared. "Intimidating."

Two students over, Margaret added with a smirk, "And hot."

Knight glanced at Archer. "Very well. But if one of them dies, their blood is on your hands."

Archer had a voice I would never forget. Even if he had saved me, I still couldn't trust him. My thoughts seemed to drift to him at the worst times, like now, when Antonia reached him first. Her shadow quell danced around her feet, subtle yet deliberate, as she batted her liquid silver eyes at him. He brushed off her flirtation without a word, his gaze sliding past her and landing briefly on Malachi.

He must prefer blondes, I thought bitterly. Spring students were absent. Rumors swirled about their private classes and special wards. Apparently, they were too poisonous to be around the others.

It seemed everyone was willing to lose themselves to impress the Serpents as more approached them. It's not like swooning would win them a title.

Knight's gravelly voice broke the tension. "Do any first-years wish to spar today? Five daggers win you a sword. We rotate realms against realms." His gaze shifted to Damien. "Summer might be our champion this year. You'll have to beat your own record from last year, eh?"

Damien grinned. "Thank you, sir."

Knight's tone grew stern. "But, let me lay down a few house rules. Quells are prohibited until your second year during combat. The more daggers you claim from other realms, the more eyes you'll draw at the Bid. Combat builds strength—and alliances, should you win your title or graduate as a Griffin in the event you do not claim the title as heir."

I gripped the hilt of my dagger instinctively, the words sinking in. Titles, alliances, survival—it all came down to blood and blade.

Margaret went to raise a hand, but Knox beat her to it. "Severyn Blanche will fight."

I shot my brother a look of death. I knew he'd done it to ensure our legacy stayed within, but I couldn't help the silent curses I threw at him. "No, I won't," I said loudly enough that nearly every student turned to face me. I hated attention and I wouldn't be the first student of the year to fight.

"Severyn, go." Knox shoved me forward. "You can fight. Remember what Father and Charles taught you."

Malachi stepped into the circle, tying her hair back. "I'll go against Severyn."

"Okay. Fine," I muttered. We were handed daggers of equal length, their handles marked with intricate carvings. The wood was from the Spring realm, decorated with flowers, while the copper-stained metal ensured no blade was sharper than the other.

We both bowed, the formal gesture before a fight.

She struck first, faster than I anticipated, slicing across my right leg. I retaliated, our blades clashing with a sharp ring. She grunted, her aim darting for my neck. I dove, rolling over my shoulder, and barely managed to spring to my feet. She was quick—her every move calculated, the result of years of training.

"You're fast," she said between breaths. "But you haven't landed a single hit on me."

"Perhaps I am learning you," I yelled, dodging a second blow.

My blade hit her shoulder, she swung out of the way, and I took my moment to pounce and pin her chest down, elbow lodged into her throat as I held the blade against her neck.

"I also have four brothers," I hissed.

She could have countered me, could have kicked her legs up and into my stomach, but she didn't. She let me win, and for whatever reason? To show her weakness to others? For Monty to watch and curl his finger under his chin as all eyes were on me now.

"You won," she breathed, gripping the blade's sharp end.

I helped her up. Then Bridger ripped the dagger from Malachi's grasp. "You let her win." He stole the words right from my bitten tongue. "Let's see—you against me, Colindale. Perhaps that's what you need to gain your quell."

I stared desperately at Professor Knight for him to interject, but he seemed just as interested in seeing the daughter of the Serpent and the lead to take North Colindale fight.

I caught my breath, keeping that dagger tight in my fist. "Fine," I hissed.

Bridger didn't bow or take the respectful three steps back. He swung right away, landing a blow on my shoulder and twisting. I screamed in pain as he dragged the blade under my shoulder— and something inside me tore. His leg came up, kicking the dagger from my sweaty hands as it flew behind me.

"You can't do that," I grunted, reaching for the dagger— fingers skimming the bare stone.

A boot pinned my chest down. My heart thumped as a rib popped, heat swelling in my cheeks. Then, it was only silver eyes peering at me. A valley of cruel ice consumed my sight as he leaned over, blade pressed against my throat.

Bridger said, cold and bored, "Lesson one of combat, Blanche, never take your eyes off your opponent." His boot shifted, and the sound of bones crunched in my wrist as Bridger stomped hard.

I gasped in pain. Sheer pain I'd never felt before.

The groans spewed in a stream of curses laced in my breath. My palm lay flat, flushed red, swelling as I gazed up. Cruel didn't do his features justice.

"You broke my wrist," I hissed, forcing back tears. I wouldn't cry, not in front of the entire academy.

But pain gripped me—had me nearly crouched to my knees as I hurled forward. Pain. Had I ever felt pain like this? I stared at his severed fingers.

I was the daughter of the man he hated. The man he was forced to worship when his pain was silenced.

Knox ran to me, grabbing my elbow carefully. "You're okay, Sev. We'll take you to the healer." Then, I swore he lit up like lightning struck his core. "What the hell, man? It's her first day of combat."

Bridger raised his hands. "If she wants to be my ruler, she must earn that right."

"Well, let me teach you a fucking lesson on hierarchy." Knox barreled forward, punching him in the jaw, nose, and lips until blood splattered from Bridger's face. "If you touch her again, I will force you into a permanent bow." And it took all but one Serpent, a professor, and two other males to pull Knox off Bridger's body.

He wasn't dead, but I was sure Knox would have killed him if he hadn't been stopped. We bled the same shade. He and I were not so different. Knox jerked as Monty and Damien held him back.

I might have blacked out while leaning on Malachi's arm as she brought me to the infirmary. My wrist dangled, limp at my side. The pain radiated through me—a raw, searing agony that demanded restraint to keep from screaming.

She laid me down on one of the twelve beds in the wing. Blazing lanterns hung overhead, their flickering light casting uneven shadows. Citrine and rust lingered in the air. Cracked white walls closed in around me as Malachi sat at the foot of the bed.

"Now, do you trust me?" she asked.

"Trust you?" I repeated, my cheek pressed against the rough cotton sheet, my free hand raised slightly in question.

"I heard you talking to Damien Lynch about me last night."

Her words rang in my ears, muddled by the relentless pounding of my thoughts. How had she overheard that conversation? The pain was too unbearable to dwell on it. "I was curious who you were. I should have asked you."

She signaled for an aide. "Damien's hot. Go for it, but he's got issues. I've known the brothers since I was young. We met at Serpent gatherings."

Through clenched teeth, I said, "We were just talking, Malachi." I cursed under my breath, biting back the waves of agony. "My wrist is broken, isn't it?"

"Yes. Someone like Bridger has never tasted freedom and won't stop until he gets it," she said. "Don't let him win."

The aide, a short woman with a curvy frame, approached briskly. "Oh dear, the first broken bone of the semester," she hummed. "My name is Estella, and you are?" She smiled warmly, a few gray strands peeking above her ears.

"Severyn Blanche," I muttered. The sound of my last name seemed to stretch her smile into wide-eyed recognition. Clawing panic churned in my gut as she lifted my arm and gave it a squeeze. My legs curled toward my chest instinctively, tight and protective.

Malachi rambled on, her tone as casual as if we were discussing the weather. "Monty will kill me when I let my guard down. My best chance is seducing him, so he feels just a little guilt before slicing my throat. Trust me, Severyn, everyone wants to kill me. Some just to say they did." She fisted the white linen sheets.

I nodded faintly, my focus split between her words and the sharp throbs of pain. "He's not that impressive."

"How many Blanche children are in that family of yours?" Estella asked. "Charles was lovely, such a handsome young man."

She lifted my arm again, and I screamed. "There's five of us," I managed to choke out.

"Broken," she confirmed, sighing softly. "There isn't much I can do besides wrap it, dear. I'll give you some pain medication to reduce the swelling, but it'll be at least a week before the healer arrives. Do you think you can manage until then?"

"I can try," I whispered.

"Severyn, speaking of Monty, I told him I'd meet him after combat," Malachi said abruptly. "I feel like such an asshole leaving you, but Estella is wonderful, and she will poison Bridger if he tries to hurt you tonight." She placed a hand on Estella's shoulder with a grin. "Isn't that right?"

Estella rolled her eyes. "I'm waiting for the poisons to arrive."

"I'll see you back in the room," I said, giving Malachi a quick smile as she left. The heavy doors slammed closed. A window facing the dragon grounds rippled as her taps echoed through the hall.

"Remind me of your other siblings' names." Estella's nose crinkled as she uncapped an orange bubbling liquid, dabbing it on a cloth.

"Only Charles and Klaus were students before. Knox is here with me. Cully, the second oldest, aged out three years ago. He attends Valscribe as a journalist."

She ran the cloth over my shoulder. My blood congealed like gelatin, sliding down my arm.

A vile beside the table shuddered as a wing struck the building. Dragon riding class must be starting.

"Fallon was one of my closest friends during my student days here. Your father was so smitten with her. Seeing you makes me feel younger."

"You knew my parents?" I asked.

"I should have suspected, you look just like her."

"Can I ask you something?"

She sucked a breath in, throwing the bloodied cloth into a bin. "Of course."

"I've never known what color her eyes were. Do you remember what they looked like?"

She fumbled with the lid of the ointment. "There once was a man who picked every leaf he could find for one that matched those eyes of green. He went through every land in Verdonia, searching high and low. Unbeknownst, his daughter would have the same eyes."

"I have my mother's eyes?" Father had always described them as lovely, not the ferns near our lake or the color of algae once the light hits. He never had a way with words. "What happened to her?" I asked. "It seems everyone has something to say about Fallon."

"Something you'll face, but the Blanche blood has always been strong. Fallon was top of our class for the most part… she skipped class, which I will not tolerate."

I stared at my wrist. "I'll be dead in a week."

"You have her eyes, and I know damn well you will have her cunning mind." She brushed a grey strand behind her ear. "I remember when your mother was pregnant with Charles, and she was still kicking ass during combat."

"*My mother?* Are you sure you have the right Blanche?"

"Yes. Your mother was pregnant during her second year here. It seems like only yesterday we were fighting in combat and surviving the academy."

The doors flew open, and two bloodied students walked in. Estella gave me a silent nod as she rushed to attend to the two males. My arm was bandaged up and slung with a brace. It was not the fiercest look, but I could handle a week before the healer could fix my bone.

The males were in worse shape than me. Jace had a broken nose, while Alaric's collarbone jutted out unnaturally. "You were so close to landing that fall," the blonde male exclaimed. "A wild wyvern threw us overboard during flight, ma'am."

Estella shot a disapproving, motherly glance at the two males. "You can't tame a wild wyvern, you idiots. Dragons choose their riders."

"Half of the first-years have found their dragons already. It isn't fair. Archer is going to be so pissed when we tell him we haven't found our enigma yet," Jace said to Alaric, wincing in pain.

I left before I passed out, recoiling at the sight of blood dripping from Jace's nose. Tomorrow, Bridger would drag me to the Winter forests, and I'd have to scale down that wall with one hand.

Wandering out the back towards the dragon training grounds, I observed three large dragons soaring in the sky, their scales boasting various shades. Some lounged on the grass in scaled rays of brilliance, spikes lining their spines in a fierce and deadly gesture, their necks rolling. It was hard to imagine my mother riding one, let alone Klaus. Dragons lived for hundreds of years, sometimes having multiple riders throughout their lifetime.

I wondered why half of my history was hidden under a veil of weakness. Why I'd never known my bloodline was tainted with flame and light.

"Pigeon riders," I scoffed.

One yellow one heaved its wings, releasing a cry through the air. I'd never been close enough to see their snouts growl as their talons shredded through the dirt. The creature's elongated neck arched gracefully, crowned with a regal crest that gleamed in metallic gold. Fierce, intelligent eyes surveyed the fields, pupils narrowing to slits as they observed the students. Its snout, adorned with intricately carved patterns, swallowed a bout of air.

I stood on the cobblestone pathway of the castle, watching every stroke of wings against the clouds. The riders flew high, bodies swallowed with leather and muscle. I'd be scorched if they knew a bird rider was here… if I could even call myself that. I couldn't slip my stare as I leaned against the stone wall.

Everything reminded me of Klaus, yet I had never seen him stand on that field. Had he run laps like the others had? Was I secretly searching for the golden tone of his dragon, not knowing it was the same color as the academy arches like my father searched for my mother's eyes for all those years? Missing someone hurt, but losing someone wilted the core. Not knowing someone seemed worse. I knew nothing about Klaus and if he'd stood in the same spot as me, with his hand shielding his eyes from the sun along the horizon.

"Your brother has anger issues." A voice said, startling me. "And standing there is a sure way to get hit."

I jolted. Archer leaned on the same wall beside me, standing in a single shadow. How long had he been there? I raised my injured wrist. "He has a right to be angry," I hissed. "I was leaving the infirmary when I saw the field. I'm leaving now." I looked down, afraid to meet his eyes. Afraid to question him.

The sound of his knock still rattled me. My eggshell-colored gown clung to my legs as I stood frozen. It was autumn, and the fields stretched wide with roots, nearly ready for the second harvest. Visitors were rare, except on Thursdays when the post arrived. But this was Friday, and noon seemed to hold a foreboding weight in my chest. The wind chimes shuddered as his shadowed fingers curled against the door. He said no more than three words before the door slammed shut behind him.

"Klaus is dead."

Bones could heal, but a bruised heart never beat the same— never regained its color as grief stained the blood grey. And he died for a title that bore no likeness to him. I clipped my thoughts short, swallowing the rising ache. Archer stood before me, his eyes heavy with the same truth they'd carried when he first spoke those words.

He had no idea who I was.

"Your wrist doesn't look reset to me. Your bone is protruding out." He narrowed his eyes over my injury.

And it wasn't fear I felt, but a roll in my gut as I stared at the row of thick lashes lining those cruel blue eyes.

Death crept toward me one final time, and I mistook his bones for beauty. That was the end of Cully's poem. Archer was beautiful in a way I wanted to hate every cell in his body. But I didn't understand why he'd delivered the burden. Why him, of all people?

Everything about him set something on fire in my stomach. I'd make a fool if I dared to part my lips, but I did anyway. He was a Serpent, *my* Serpent, and if Alaric and Jace had broken bones to prove themselves to him, then what was I?

"Estella couldn't do much until the healer comes in a week. Since this is my last few days, I might as well explore the grounds."

"Are you always this insufferable?" he asked, shading me with his tall figure. "No one will pity a frown."

I slid my gaze to meet his. "I haven't found my quell nor my enigma. I—I understand if you're upset." I felt like a begging dog seeking approval.

I swore his face fell as I did it. "You're expected to find your quell by the end of the week, Blanche. Don't make me regret allowing you to stay under my house."

"Why did you?" I asked softly. "Why—why did you come to my house that day?" He knew what I meant as a single brow cocked for a second.

"I don't have to explain myself to you. If you do not reset your wrist, it will heal broken, and you surely won't make it very far."

"Too painful." I shuddered.

He blew a deep sigh. "I'll reset it for you."

"No." I pressed my spine against the stone wall as he angled his knee, trapping me.

He forced a grin. "As your mentor, I insist. It would look quite bad on my part if one of my first-years could not defend themselves during the trials. You'll need to win, and your tears will not help. People will not take pity on you. Everyone here has lost someone. You aren't special."

My heart stopped for a second as he lifted my sleeve and held my forearm between his hands. "This is an order. Let me help you."

Burning. I was burning from his touch. I swallowed my dry spit and nodded, knowing nothing I said mattered. "Please be quick."

"Look into my eyes and take a deep breath."

And so, I did. I saw the depths of the sea whirl in those eyes, my startled reflection captured within their storm. His thumb brushed over the tender part of my arm, sending an involuntary shiver up my spine. My heart beat embarrassingly fast as he hovered over my pulse. "One… two," he said. "Why do I make you nervous?"

Perhaps I was mesmerized by his cruelty. My gaze lingered on the violet buttons of his coat, each thread meticulously looped. Then my eyes drifted to the hissing snake tattoo curling up his neck. "You—don't," I said, though my voice betrayed me.

On the second breath, I was on my knees—falling forward as a sharp snap echoed in my ears. My vision spun, my body betrayed by the searing pain. But Archer's arms caught me before my nose could meet the unforgiving pathway. He held me firm, his shoulders carrying the scent of dirt and leather, his presence heavy and grounding. His arms hovered over my spine, as though afraid to fully touch me, while the darkness creeping at the edges of my sight blurred everything.

Or perhaps it wasn't the pain, but his shadow quell slithering up my back, cold and invasive, seeping into the cracks of my will.

His voice muffled, but I heard his last insulting whisper, *"She's weak, Ciaran."*

* * *

I sucked in a sharp breath, staring at the lantern flickering on the side table in my dorm. Malachi was fast asleep in her bed. My clothes from the day before were neatly folded at the end of mine, and I realized—he had undressed me. He had carried me back.

No. Warmth crept up my face at the thought of dangling limply in those strong arms, but it was quickly overtaken by a boiling rage. How dare he rummage through my belongings? How dare he undress me?

How dare he speak of Klaus's death so casually.

My wrist throbbed, though the bone no longer jutted outward. I flexed my fingers, wincing as pain shot down my forearm. Tolerable pain. I imagined clinging to the ice wall again in less than an hour, sliding helplessly when my grip failed.

A week ago, I had begged to see the sun. Now, I wished dawn would slow.

I showered and dressed in field attire, layering an undershirt for warmth. The cold would claw at me the moment I stepped onto the trails. Climbing the wall again would be grueling, but it was unavoidable.

With my hair tied back, I headed out.

Dawn crept slowly over the mountains. Golden splinters of light broke through the dark, inching higher with every passing moment. I stood at the edge of the Winter trails, my socks already soaked from the dew. My gaze drifted to the Spring borders, where enchanted forests spread like a storybook come to life.

Vines twisted along the fence, and I imagined those students living out their fairytales.

Cully used to read me fables about princes saving princesses. But those heroic tales never breached the confines of ink. Here, there was no one to save me. I had to save myself. I needed to find my quell—at the very least, my bonded creature.

Did I even belong here? Was the false mark on my palm a scar of my failure?

'No realm has called to you.'

My gaze shifted between the winding trails and the imposing black iron door of the academy. Where was Bridger? Dusk had fully settled, yet he was nowhere to be seen.

Moments later, Damien emerged. He wore fewer layers than I did, as though the cold didn't dare bother him. He nodded toward the Summer trails, a playful smirk tugging at his lips.

"You're coming with me today," he said, his tone leaving little room for argument. "Bridger's recovering. Besides, trust me— you don't want to be in Winter today."

"What happened to Bridger?" I asked.

"Knox broke his nose in that fistfight yesterday. Luckily for you, I have two others who have not found their quell, so you get to join me in Summer today. You might need the heat to find the ice in you."

"Is that allowed?"

Damien glanced around. "I don't see anyone stopping us. You'll be happy to know Bridger is worse off than you are. Knox packs quite a punch. Remind me never to piss *him* off."

"He's protective," I whispered—only realizing a half-beat later he'd invited me to join him in *Summer*. "And you think the heat will help me find my quell?"

Damien motioned for me to follow him, staring at the Summer trails where waves bounced off like a kaleidoscope of wings. "It's worth a shot. Klaus was a Summer. Perhaps that mark of Unknown got it wrong." A hazel eye winked at me.

"Who—who told you?"

"Secrets don't last long around here." He flashed a crooked grin, nearly the same as two nights before at the fire. "I'm quite fascinated by you, Sev. Do you prefer me to call you Sev?"

I stumbled towards him. A brow, already slicked with a sticky condensation, raised. I pulled two layers off, tying my sweater around a tree. "Call me Sev, call me Severyn. I find the shortened version is only dire when people want my full attention."

"I like North, it's cute." He laughed. "I was a bit worried your saliva was poisonous when I carried you home last night. Thankfully, only a stained shirt."

My throat tightened. "*You* took me home and undressed me." We walked through the trails, and two students followed behind nervously.

Damien put his hands up defensively. "Malachi took over once I dropped you on your bed. She nearly winded me out. Quite literally."

"Thanks. He's quite… intimidating—your brother. He reset my wrist."

"Don't take it personally. Serpents don't care about first-years, and it's not the best look carrying a lifeless girl across campus. Especially for a Serpent."

I nodded in response, trying to rid last night's memory forever.

Cosmos of all shades of pink and purple lined the heated trails. I didn't know what to expect, but it wasn't a zip line with a shabby hook and no restraints as Summer's initiation. I stopped near the cliff, watching pebbles fall into the ocean below.

"A zip line?" I asked. "I can't hold myself up with one hand."

He rolled his eyes. "Make it work," he said, pulling the handle back. "If you fall in, it's only a mile-long swim to shore. Hook your elbow over the top and hold on with your other hand."

"I'm not a strong swimmer," I protested. "Need I remind you, most lakes in the North are frozen?"

The sling snapped against the metal pole. "Too bad. You're up first."

I sighed, gripping the crescent-shaped handle with my unbroken hand as I pulled my armpit over the bar. I grunted, jostling forward as my feet raised to the tips, testing the strength of my arm. It would hold me for a bit. I stepped back before running forward, and my feet dangled in the air with a heave.

It was like flying, that moment of freedom as nothing was below your feet. Sweat simmered on my brow as a rush of hot wind swept through my limbs. The ocean snapped against the brittle rocks, sloshing between the ten-foot gap that separated the trails.

I toppled over, the handles slamming into the metal stopper. Damien pulled the line back, and the students followed behind. He landed gracefully a moment later, handing me a dagger.

Gliding my hand over the metal shaft, I asked. "Should I be worried why you are giving me a dagger?"

"Each season, we face trial. I'm expecting one to happen while we are here. Don't be alarmed if you see students from other realms here," he said. "The academy loves the element of surprise."

"What kind of trials?" I asked.

Strange howls and chirps echoed through the trees, weaving an unsettling melody into the air. The peaks were flecked with moss, curling vines rounding every corner of the path. Dust and sand swirled low to the ground. It was almost impossible to fathom that mere steps away lay a land of perpetual snow.

"It could be mental or physical," Damien said. "The academy tests us on certain skills. For example, how we handle loss, how well we can navigate, and if we can lead. The first one is usually easy, but the Serpents observe how we react. Mind games can be just as deadly as combat. And sometimes, the trials are personal. You might not know you're in one."

I tightened my grip on the dagger in my hand. A deep, mournful cry echoed from within the forest. Suddenly, thrashing wings and talons tore through the shielded trail.

"Are there beasts in the forests?" I asked, my voice quieter than intended. "I never saw any in the Winter trails."

"The worst kinds," Damien replied grimly. "Trapped and starved. I wouldn't plan on having a cozy campfire anytime soon."

"He is alive," that same voice hissed low. The one I heard back at the initiation.

Scattering sounded from the bushes. Then, a scream. "Did you hear that?" I asked, eyes blaring.

Damien cocked his head. "Hear *what*?"

"I heard someone hiss just a second ago… then a scream." I went toward the forest, brushing a few branches out of the way. "I think we're being watched."

"He is alive. Find him," that same voice said once again. It was feminine, with an assertive sweetness humming each word. I shook my head. Klaus was the only person I knew to be dead, and Damien's warning of the beasts ravaged my mind, but not enough to dull my terrified curiosity.

"He calls to you in water," it sang. *"His name, etched beside a thumping heart, cascading between bones. He slumbers, awaiting his savior."*

"It's the trial, North," Damien said. "Ignore it."

I pricked my index finger on a thorn, peeking through the lush. "It sounds… lost." I stepped over the path, heat vibrating against my skin.

"He is not dead, Severyn. Find him. Now, before it is too late."

It was enough for me to run towards the voice.

"Stay out of the forests. We are only protected on the trails," he yelled after me, but I didn't listen. Not if Klaus was somewhere out there. Had he been trapped in the forests for two years? If the wards could separate frost from warmth, perhaps they could also imprison someone.

The thought drove me forward, ignoring Damien's curses as he chased after me. Hisses echoed from every direction, the sound growing sharper as I ran. Thorns scored my arms, curling around them like starved leeches, their sharp edges biting into my skin.

I clutched the dagger Damien had given me with raw desperation. Every tree looked identical, the swirling patterns in their bark merging into a dizzying blur. Pain flared as a cloud of yellow gnats swarmed me, their tiny jaws nipping at my exposed legs and arms.

Dawn pierced through the swaying branches, its light weak against the dense canopy. I tightened my grip on the dagger, trying to ignore the agony burning through my legs. The thorns had to be laced with poison—red welts pulsed angrily on my arms and legs, each heartbeat sending fresh waves of pain through me.

I kept running—that voice drew closer, screaming in my mind, *"FIND HIM."*

I came to a lake hidden behind trees in the middle of the forest, a narrow bridge gaping over the ledge. Rotted wood floated along the brimmed surface. A rush of pins and needles coursed my senses. My palms burned and pulsed as I stared at the swamp.

"At the bottom of the lake, you will find your answer. Die trying, and you will never know." My boots were nearly halfway off the ledge, hand gaped out—

Damien yanked me back. "What the hell are you doing? You'll get yourself killed or skinned out here," he said with such demand I knew he was next in line to become a Summer heir.

"There's something down there," I whispered, eyeing over his tensed shoulder. "It wants me to find it."

"Severyn, it's a lake." Damien furrowed his brows, and a silent plea dangled on his parted lips. "There is nothing in those waters. There are dark forces within the forests. They can mimic people you know. If anything, you'll drown the moment you step inside."

I choked out a loud breath as we got further from the lake. "I don't know what happened."

Damien shoved me aside as a faceless grey creature swiped at us with three long talons. Purple veins struck through its core, crackling like lightning behind dense smog. A visible, beating heart pulsed in its chest as it struck again. Two more beasts lunged out from the forest, their movements erratic and lethal. Damien unsheathed his sword, driving it straight into one of their cores.

Winged bones fluttered wildly. Rows of jagged fangs snapped inches from his face before black fluid spilled onto the ground. A guttural hiss escaped from the creature's gaping mouth as it collapsed. Damien turned sharply, slicing into the second beast.

"We—we should run!" I screamed, my voice cracking.

Damien shot me a sideways glance, his silver sword poised. "When I said you fascinated me, Sev—I didn't mean this."

"I'm happy to disappoint you," I retorted, taking a shaky step back. My eyes locked on Damien as he swung his blade again, slashing at the relentless beasts. "Now, let's get the hell out of here!"

The creatures dropped to all fours, hissing as they hurled themselves towards us. We sprinted onto the trail, their wrinkled torsos slamming into the barrier like rain against a glass window, unable to breach the enchanted divide.

I collided with Damien's chest, winded and disoriented. Staggering back, his hand shot out, gripping my shoulders to steady me as I trembled.

"What the hell were those things?" I yelled, breathless.

He dropped his hand, annoyance flashing across his face. "Damnit, what were you thinking? Rule one: never enter the forests unless you know you can defend yourself. A small dagger wouldn't even scratch a death dweller's skin." His gaze flicked back toward the beasts, now retreating into the shadows.

"I heard a voice in my head," I whispered, my throat tight. "It lured me there."

"Not everything your mind hears is real," he said, sheathing his sword with a sharp motion. "I'm not sure what you Winters do, but in Summer, we fear beasts like that."

As we caught our breath, we continued walking along the trail. "It—it sounded real," I muttered, my cheeks flushing with heat. The voice lingered in my mind, a raw and desperate whisper I couldn't shake.

"You'll have a nasty rash wherever those vines grabbed you," Damien said, his tone casual, though his eyes scanned the trail ahead. "I bet plants don't try to kill you in Winter?" He chuckled dryly.

"I think the cold would kill them before they grew limbs." My voice wavered with unease as I noticed the weapons strapped to the other students passing by—daggers, swords, even spears. Nervousness prickled my skin. "That's a lot of weapons," I murmured under my breath.

We reached the base camp for Summer, where twelve cabins stood in a clearing. Palm trees swayed gently in the warm breeze. The camp bustled with activity, students moving in groups. Some bore Spring marks on their palms, while others carried Autumn leaves etched into their skin.

"On trial and test days, there aren't any rules about barriers," Damien explained. "Just don't wander into other trails alone. Most prefer their first kill to be from another realm—it eases the guilt."

"Are you going to kill me?" I asked. "I'm too exhausted to run anymore."

"Yes, Severyn. I risked my life to save you just so I could kill you moments later," he said, his tone laced with dry sarcasm.

Malachi stepped into the campground. Two daggers sheathed around her slim ribcage, another around her calf. She grinned, waving me over. "I didn't think you'd be in Summer today. How is your wrist?" she asked.

"Bridger is worse off than me." I wiggled my fingers. "It feels better," I said. "Also, avoid the forests, we were nearly just eaten."

"Are you ready for your first trial?" she asked.

I was never good at lying. "No. I haven't a clue what to expect."

"Try to stay low profile. There is no sense in drawing attention to yourself when you can't use your quell. The first trial is usually a lesson or riddle we must solve before the year ends. Don't worry—you shouldn't lose any blood today."

Damien gestured to Malachi. "Hey, Mal. Long time no see."

Malachi strummed her fingers across her arm. "I didn't expect to see *you* here. How was boarding school? I see they let you out early."

Damien scoffed. "Good behavior. I see you got your enigma, a silver Daigthorn. I didn't take you as a wyvern girl."

"She is quite the creature." Malachi tensed. "Severyn, any luck on finding yours?"

But Damien didn't let me talk. "How interesting that Severyn's mother used to ride that same wyvern, and now you are roommates."

"I was going to tell you, Sev—" Malachi began, but her words were swallowed by a sudden commotion. A dozen students turned their gazes skyward towards the glaring sun.

"The trial is starting," she whispered, tension lacing her voice.

Malachi bonded with my mother's wyvern? The revelation struck me, but the chaotic energy of the trial distracted me before I could demand answers. Above us, the clouds parted, and a dozen folded scrolls rained down like fluttering origami dragons.

"This trial pissed me off last year," Damien muttered, reaching up to snatch a golden-edged scroll mid-air. "Took me nearly a year to figure it out."

Students scrambled, their hands darting to catch the delicate parchments before they touched the ground. The red ink shimmered under the harsh sunlight as I lunged forward, grabbing one for myself.

Malachi opened hers first. "What the hell," she hissed, quickly folding the paper and shoving it into her boot.

If hers was that bad, I couldn't imagine what mine read. I uncurled the note. *A failed bargain for your freedom leaves the Winter throne without sunlight. Betray them before they destroy you.*

I shuddered.

My freedom? "Are these supposed to be cryptic?" I slid the paper into my pocket, turning toward Malachi. "Are you okay?"

But she left before the words reached her.

Damien stayed still, reading over his scroll word for word a few times. I'd heard the clang of metal and assumed paranoia's passion crept into some students' minds. Friends would turn on friends. And it'd become a blood bath if it already hadn't. I knew this trial was to stir us, to poison our minds slowly.

To test us. I needed to find out who this was about.

Father's wards *were* shattering, and the sun had dimmed over the years. Was it my fault?

I reached for Damien's arm. "Damien," I stuttered. "We—we should head back."

But he stayed locked on that scroll. "Go, Severyn. Go back to the castle." A flash of rage stormed across his features. White knuckles flushed as he crumbed the golden-edged paper. "I need a moment alone."

I took off for the academy. I was in no shape to stay as students fought. I ran through the trails, stopping at the guttered cliff.

The zip line had snagged in the middle.

The waves rippled, curling with blackened clenches. I pulled on the rope, heaving it back, but it wouldn't budge. I needed to get my leg up and around.

I jumped, grabbing the wire with one hand as I hoisted my knee over. The wire dipped low, curving into an outstretched *C* as I crawled across, my hair sprawling over the rapids below. The wire bit into my palm, a few strands snagging and pulling me down. Pain tore through me as I screamed, gripping the wire with my injured hand.

Reaching for the bar, I nearly slipped, swinging to the left and tipping sideways. My elbow caught the edge, and I gasped as my sore wrist took the brunt of my weight.

Moisture speckled my brow as waves crashed into the rocks below, each pull dragging me closer. The trail opened ahead, speckled leaves ricocheting off the buzzing ward.

With one final swing, I released the wire. Air shredded through my hair, and I barely skimmed the ground before rolling onto my spine.

Summer had spit me out.

I stumbled along the slicked stone pathway toward the academy. Cold air rushed over my heated cheeks as I collapsed onto the floor beside the library doors, inspecting the welts on my arms and brushing the dust off my knees.

From that voice in the forests to the scroll—my mind was a tumble of skewed thoughts. *Failed bargain. Find him. He's alive. He's alive.*

Was Klaus alive? Or was it simply a beast luring me into the woods?

"You were smart to run," a voice rang behind me. "The test of sanity is a sure way to decipher who has the mental ability to look beyond words."

Archer. He was leaving the library with a concealed book tucked under his arm. The words on the cover were smudged as if the ink had rubbed off. Numbness crawled along my nerves as I stared up.

I said, "I would hardly call that a trial. What am I supposed to do with a cryptic note?"

Those blue eyes beamed with slight amusement. He crossed his arms over his chest, stroking silver hooks over my swollen skin. "You figure it out. The academy sees things beyond us. This trial is meant to help you." He paused. "Were you in the forests? If you wish to end your life, I know of easier ways than getting eaten alive."

"I wasn't trying to die—I was…" I couldn't tell *him* about the voice. I changed the topic. "Leaving me unconscious in front of a dragon field is another way to die." My curiosity about him boiled. "Sir," I corrected with a hiss.

"I reset your wrist. I didn't say I would tuck you in and read you a bedtime story. If someone wishes to finish you off, that is not on me."

"Thankfully, your brother found me. He's very noble."

Archer chuckled, snugging the book tight against his ribs. "Damien will sleep with any girl who bats her eyes at him. Perhaps you should focus on your studies and not those of the male gaze." Not entirely a demand, but I heard the unsteadiness in his voice.

"I have no intentions of dating anyone here." My voice lowered as heads turned.

"Good. Because my brother will break your heart, I'm saying this as your mentor to try and focus on gaining strength and finding your damn quell before you do *anything*. The first year is about surviving. You eat, sleep, and fight."

Archer and Charles would be great friends. "I heard you're wounded. Doesn't that make you seem weak to the students?" I whispered.

Within a blink, Archer grabbed my steady wrist, pressing it against my chest as he leaned in. "Don't you dare speak to me like that. I *selflessly* saved you by allowing you under my mentorship. Every sound that escapes your lips belongs to me. If I want to break you, I will." I couldn't meet his eyes or release the air trapped in my lungs. "I expect you to be there tomorrow at sunrise with Bridger to find your damn quell before you embarrass me any further."

Heavy tears brimmed my bottom lids, and I conjured up the most genuine grin. "Yes, *Serpent*. Do you have any more demands of me?"

"Stop crying. The salt will only burn your wounds more." He let go and walked away.

I drowned out the sharp rhythm of his black boots tapping against the ground. My knees met the cold, unyielding stone. I tried to brace against the void curling within me.

The terror of a promised tomorrow echoed in their frozen depths, louder than any words he could have spoken.

Chapter 7

Malachi focused on strengthening her shield during warding that next day. But that whirlpool of wind she created was nearly deadly as it blew her hair in a frenzy. Something dimmed in her eyes as she watched the air around her spin as if she saw her life spiraling inside. I didn't ask if she was okay.

I figured Malachi was the kind of person who didn't share too many details about her life.

I managed to find a faint shield, nearly rupturing a dozen blood vessels. But the breath knocked from my lungs as Knox leaned across the table towards me. "I think I got my quell yesterday. It's not useful, but I started feeling people's emotions," he said. "Right now, you are anxious." He closed one eye, hand slightly raised. "Perhaps it's anger."

"What gave it away?" I muttered.

"I read about this quell. If I keep working on it, I can alter people's emotions. There are certain levels to each quell." Knox raised a brow toward Malachi. "I'll bet she can make tornadoes if she keeps up with it. She could be a literal beautiful disaster."

I sneered quietly, "Does someone have a crush on the heir of Verdonia?"

"No. Not Malachi," he answered, a smug grin pressing at the corners of his mouth.

Knox never dated anyone, not that I knew of. And the Colindale selection had few options, especially with our name.

I prodded his shoulder. "Knox has a crush?"

"Everett," he admitted in a whisper. "We've been talking during Day outings. He's... different."

"Isn't Everett your rival and student mentor? Won't that end... badly?"

He thumbed the spine of his warding book, slamming it shut. "Possibly. Forget it, Severyn."

"There's only one Day realm, Knox. Only one heir." There used to be more, but Father mentioned there were wars between Night and Day decades before.

"I—I know, Sev. We're allowed to feel something besides pain here." His fist collapsed to the table with a thud. "I'm allowed to feel something."

I knew better than to keep pushing. "Did you know Klaus was a fire wielder?" I asked. "Everett's a third-year, right?"

"Yeah, Everett told me on the first day. And I had no clue that Mother rode a—"

"Daigthorn wyvern," I said before he could finish.

"Why would our parents lie to us? I mean, I wasn't called to Winter. How the hell am I supposed to win Serpent for a realm I haven't visited? Monty says my light quell will come when I bond. He's taking us to the mountains to find our dragons."

I breathed loudly. "I'm forced to spend eternity in the Winter trails freezing my ass off until I find mine. I swear it's colder here than it was in the North." But I knew that wasn't true—knew I'd never felt Winter's true brute force until a few days ago.

"Thanks again for kicking Bridger's ass the other day. It almost makes up for abandoning me," I said mostly as a joke.

"Anything for my little sister. I never knew the Thorne family was so passive," he seethed. "I can't protect you there, Sev. You know it kills me, but Monty says we risk expulsion if caught in other realms, something to do with our quells affecting the wards."

I dropped the faint shield. "I think Bridger killed Klaus, and every time I listen to him, it feels wrong. I thought it was Archer at first—thought he chose me to be under the Night realm because of guilt," I said. "Everything reminds me of him, Knox. I wonder if he sat in this very seat or if we've walked the same stones."

The shield Knox formed fell. "Klaus wasn't killed. Everett would have told me. You can read about every student in the library, and they clearly state murder by dagger or killed by a wyvern as the cause of death. Klaus drowned while riding his dragon."

Hearing Klaus drowned severed whatever invisible thread I'd sewn myself back up with—the pain of Klaus would never stop.

Malachi passed by our seats and said, "I'll go with you to the library, Sev. I've been needing a book on poisons."

And I swore her hearing was as strong as her swing.

Knox shrugged. "Go ahead, but you'll need at least a second-year to take you there. First-years don't have clearance."

"Monty can let us in." Malachi grinned. "We'll go after combat."

I nodded at Malachi. "You certainly are observant," I said.

* * *

Myla won the dagger Charles had given me in combat, and that seemed to be my last tether to the North as she sheathed it against her ribs in a leather strap. I wasn't sure why she was my opponent, but I was sure it was intended to break me down even more.

Monty waited by the library doors impatiently after class. A navy-blue leather vest covered his tanned skin, and underneath, a low-cut shirt revealed tufts of black hair curled on his chest. After his morning shower, he smelled like he'd drenched his entire body in cologne.

Daylight dripped from his fingers as he twisted his wrist, and the door to the library unlocked with a click. "You have ten minutes. I have a Serpent meeting at eight to discuss the trial today," he muttered.

Malachi blew a kiss toward him. "I owe you."

The library was over thirty feet tall, with rows of dusty books. Cully would be in heaven if he saw the dragon-shaped bookends. A chandelier of flame lit the room with a feverish heat. Most of the covers were rebound with the intricate snake crest I'd seen in Archer's hand.

I remembered when Cully snuck into my room with a new folktale, secretly reading it to me. Reading poetry and fiction was frowned upon, and I figured every book here was a historical passage. Perhaps that was why he never got the chance to write where he wanted.

I asked Malachi, "How do we navigate? Nothing is labeled... I don't see any signs of what is what." I scanned over the colossus of books, then started down one row. *'Antecedent Quells,' 'How to Turn Anything into a Weapon,' 'The Dangers of Mind Reading Vol 8.'* No rhyme or rhythm orchestrated the aisles as I brushed over the spines.

"Every book you touch has meaning to you. The library is warded, so you don't discover something you shouldn't have," Malachi yelled from the row over. "Trust me, I just picked one up on wind turbines and how my quell can be used in farming. Just have faith that the right book will find you."

I picked another one up titled, 'Winter Shields.'

"Earlier today, you seemed spooked. Are you alright?" I wanted to ask about her wyvern, but I didn't know how.

Malachi grunted as the sound of books fell. "Yeah, I'm used to everyone being out to get me. I suppose I didn't think the note would be so cruel. Someone wants me dead, like always."

I grabbed a silver-spined book titled, *'Snake Enigmas.'* The inside cover was a picture of a golden egg.

The book dropped from my grasp, opening to a page depicting a black snake devouring an entire town. It showed a man commanding his enigma basilisk to reap havoc on a realm. I flipped a few pages over, skimming the gruesome attacks over the centuries.

"Bernard Herring was the first to bond with a basilisk. He forced the creature to commit horrendous acts throughout Verdonia. All fourteen children bonded with snakes following the brutal attacks. B. Herring was murdered by ~~redacted~~*, and all fourteen children were sentenced to death, as were their enigmas. All six grandchildren are known as the Forgotten Children. Cleminore Herring consumed the throne as queen of Verdonia, banning the enigma bond with all snakes. The Serpent Academy was built as* ~~redacted~~ *became known, threatening the throne…"*

Malachi cleared her throat, and I slammed the book shut. "My family's history is a bit more confusing than yours. I think half of my ancestors were hung to death."

"Sorry, the book fell." I scrambled to put the book back on the shelf. "I promise I wasn't digging," I said.

"You wouldn't have found that book if you weren't curious. You can ask me anything. The king's family has always been an interesting topic amongst the followers." Her throat bobbled. "You have no idea what it's like to be accused of treason simply because my last name is *Herring*."

"I don't understand. Cleminore was Bernard's wife?"

"His sister. This was before the title was earned. My family has a history of bonding with snakes, large snakes that will listen to your command, and those eggs will bond with you. The power was too great, and it created monsters... deadly monsters that eradicated entire realms, leaving the land bare. Cleminore made each of her children prove they were worthy of the throne by killing the very beast that destroyed villages—a snake. She placed dark magic wards on all lindworms and made it a test to prove their loyalty to Verdonia, as they are the rarest and deadliest snake known. Kill the lindworm and consume the title. This academy exists to ensure power is passed down in good faith. Cleminore knew the throne was never hers, and at any moment, it could be ripped away, even by her own children. In some way, she was the least power-hungry of my entire family. I am the last of my bloodline to keep Verdonia in the Herring name."

"Five more minutes, Malachi, and not a second longer," Monty yelled from the library doors.

Malachi rolled her eyes and handed me a book. "These are all the students with last names starting with B who attended the academy. I skimmed through it, and unfortunately, Knox was right. It doesn't list Klaus's death, only that he drowned somewhere on the trial grounds."

She raised her brows and tapped her finger on a line. "Did you know your brother Charles was born at the academy? That means your parents conceived here. No wonder your mother didn't claim Serpent her year. It's strange, though—the parchment on his entry looks different, almost like it's been tampered with or corrupted." She snapped the book shut, stirring a cloud of dust into the air. "Your family might not have decades of betrayal, but I'm sure the more you dig, the more secrets you'll uncover."

I clenched my fists and said, "It seems everyday I uncover a new lie."

Her eyes lit with excitement, dimming before settling into a grin. "Welcome to the Serpent life. You're a legacy, and that comes with secrets."

I blinked slowly, nearly choking on the air. "Estella mentioned my mother was pregnant, but I wasn't coherent. It just… doesn't make sense. My father was already in power when Charles was born. Why would my mother stay another year here?"

"Yeah, his place of birth lists the academy's coordinates. That must be a first in Serpent history. I'm all for getting hot and heavy, but to risk getting expelled by not being careful. That's why they make mycris for us to smoke to avoid such… disasters. I couldn't imagine facing trial while pregnant."

"Do me a favor and never repeat that." I closed my eyes, cringing.

"Speaking of hot. Monty's a hothead, and before we get locked in here." She glanced at the door. "We should leave."

I followed Malachi outside the library, stuffing the book under my armpit.

Monty didn't look at me as we stepped out, and I doubted he knew my name. "Meet me in two hours by the sparring fields," he whispered to Malachi.

Malachi sucked on her bottom lip. "I'm staying the night with Monty. Strictly professional."

"Professional? As in warming his bed?"

She snickered, walking the opposite way. "Finally, someone who understands me."

Perhaps today only left me more curious about Malachi's family. I'd never heard of a snake enigma. It all seemed barbaric, and no wonder some years no student won Serpent if one had to kill a beast of that size and live.

The Serpent will mark you. Was it bravery that made a Serpent?

But I knew it was power—the taste of it, the luxuriance it brought. This castle was made of the finest gold. And I didn't doubt the scaled walls were real.

A dizzy spell came on. It was as if the wards of the library knew I didn't belong, and that twist in my stomach lingered. Sleep would claim me fast, and as the lantern-flecked halls swallowed me within those seas of stars, I wished the moon would hover for longer. I knew a broken nose only held someone back for a day or two before that power grumbled and groaned to breathe.

Chapter 8

"Are you ready?" Bridger asked, standing beside the entrance of the Winter trails with a bandage covering his swollen nose.

I tucked my freezing hands under my arms as we walked. Callum, another third-year Winter, joined Bridger. His pale eyes and golden locks reminded me of every Winter male I'd met— sharp, cold, and detached. But his rounder face and wider eyes, paired with his meaty frame, marked him as a Winborrow native.

"I was ready yesterday," I hissed under my breath. "But, I suppose a broken nose is a worthy excuse."

I tightened an extra bandage around my wrist to secure it, bracing for the pain that would surely return soon. Archer had reset the bone, sparing me worse agony, but the excruciating ache lingered.

Callum sneered. "You'll pay for your brother's mistakes today, don't worry." He kicked my shins, sending me sprawling face-first toward the scaled ice wall. The last bit of warmth in my lungs escaped in a sharp gasp.

I froze, staring down the wall. My head spun as I crawled back onto all fours, the height making my stomach churn. I bit my tongue, refusing to answer him, choosing silence over retaliation.

If I didn't return to the academy with a quell or at least an enigma, Archer might ship me off to Malvoria—or worse, Bridger would kill me here and now. All it would take was one kick, and I'd tumble fifty feet to my death. The Winter realm would claim my body, and Bridger would claim the Serpent title.

Bridger's lips curled in a cruel smirk as he planted his feet, watching me. "Your mentor told me you're to bond with the first creature that looks at you—even if it's a pigeon. Strict orders from Archer."

"A pigeon?" I mocked.

"The Serpent of Shadows isn't of sound mind. Allowing a Winter under his mentorship is… blasphemy. It's either your head or mine."

I stalled, dragging out the conversation. "Where are your wolves?" I said through gritted teeth.

Callum shot Bridger a glance. "Scale the damn wall so we can move on with our lives."

My gaze locked onto the icy wall below. Gripping the slick snow, I began to descend, balancing on the first ledge. Slowly, step by step, I focused on breathing through the sharp jolts of pain radiating from my wrist. Bridger and Callum's whispered conversation drifted to me as I edged further down, their white and golden hair stiff in the lashing wind.

Bridger had been right earlier—death would be kinder than this. I'd pissed him off before he'd even met me.

The sound of shuffling boots drew my attention. Bridger leaned over the edge, his lip curling with malice. "I can't allow you to claim the Serpent title, Severyn."

Before I could respond, he uncurled his fist, blasting snow down onto my spine. "You knew this was coming. You knew where this would end when we were alone next."

An icicle shot down, slicing through my fingers and pinning a thin piece of skin to the wall. I groaned, my foot wobbling on a precarious shard of ice. Snow whipped around me, twisting into sharp, violent daggers. Three more struck, driving into my exposed skin as I clung desperately to the wall.

"Do not let him see your weakness, Severyn." I shot forward, hearing the same voice leading me to the lake. *"You do not bow to him."*

My cheek pressed against the cold barrier. Breathing slowly with each pound in my chest, begging for this torture to stop. Callum and Bridger would kill me. They'd claim I fell. I knew Knox would send a letter home. I knew dying in Winter was worse than being called to another realm. I'd grown, breathed, and lived in Winter all my life.

Failure. I was a failure.

I ground my teeth to hold back another scream, gripping a stone with my sore wrist. I'd take that damn egg hidden under my bed and bring it to Archer. I would forge a bond with that griffin if it were the last thing I did.

Bridger allowed me a few more steps before he swung an icicle at my ribs—Callum joined, and it was ice on snow pelting at my body.

My blood froze to the wall, staining the blue ice a pale pink. I kept my head low, hoping Bridger wouldn't see the crystallized tears falling from my cheeks. I had painted a masterpiece that stirred fear as the next students who dared to claim the title would see my blood, my fury in those handprints. Would Malvoria still accept a broken body?

Would father still accept me, knowing I'd failed? Knowing I did not die in glory but as a weakened mess of fragile bones.

Bridger pulled his arm back, and I knew the next blow would be the one that took me out. "Please don't," I begged.

"I need to claim the title, Severyn. No hard feelings. I'll give your mother the decency to live, but I'll ensure your father knows I was the one who killed his last possible blood heir." He pushed his palm forward as a pointed icicle aimed straight for my broken wrist.

But the ice never came. Instead, a darkened ray speckled between my stiff hands, coated with a dazzling sand texture almost resembling crushed starlight.

Bridger hissed, "No fucking way." His stare locked towards the clouds.

A black-scaled dragon, nearly three times the size of a griffin with a pearlescent underbelly, broke through the tree line, blowing a flurry of darkened air before dipping towards me and flying off with a howl. Frost-licked branches snapped off, falling to the ground with a groan. Dust glimmered between my shaking fingers, illuminating a trail.

I took another shaking step down. Bridger's arms were crossed, and he was pissed off.

I nearly cried tears of joy as my feet touched the solid ground, and before I could catch my breath or warm my frozen fingers, Bridger stood beside me.

"Find your damn enigma," Bridger growled.

Bridger could portal. There was no way he climbed that fast. And to the left stood Callum.

My feet sank into the snow, boots dusted with that same brilliant sheen. "Do dragons normally enter the frozen realms?" I asked.

"That dragon hasn't been seen in nearly two years. I suppose the Serpent was keeping tabs on you, and now that he's seen what a pathetic, shivering ball you are, I don't think he'll bother us anymore," Callum hissed.

That was Archer's dragon. It had to be.

Damien mentioned it was missing. That creature was everything I suspected Archer's enigma was: jet-black scales resembling a swirled midnight sky, slivered violet eyes that matched the shirt buttons he'd worn at the Rite.

"Who are you?" I asked Callum as the frozen ground tracked my steps.

"You speak when I say," he spat. "And to answer your question, I'm the one you'll bow to if you make it out alive."

Teeth clenched to stop the chattering, I hissed, "Time's ticking. Don't the odds lessen once you're in the third year?"

"Shut the hell up and find your enigma," he barked.

There were no eggs nearby, no mature griffins waiting for me to spot them. I expected to find a single feather laid for me to stumble upon and for a bond to anchor itself into my bones.

I knew in my marrow that I didn't belong here. The cold could wash over me—consume me in its frosted cloak—but I would never call back and take it as mine. Perhaps I broke, knowing my father's legacy would die without a fight. But to hell with these assholes. I was never good at listening. My family could attest to that.

Defeat hung in my slouched shoulders as Bridger and Callum watched me like a lost dog. My breath caught on a gust of lashing wind. I would never be what I was expected to become. Never the perfect Serpent daughter who married power and surrendered her name. I couldn't even bond with a damn griffin.

"I don't think my enigma is here." I faced Bridger, and his hands slid into his pockets.

"I know. Your mentor doesn't seem to like that answer. Perhaps that's why his dragon swooped in to save you." Bridger's blue eyes flickered to mine, colder than the ice crusted to my brow. "Or perhaps… it was guilt that saved you. Your dead brother is the only reason you're not in Malvoria."

"What do you know about Klaus's death," I cried, breaking under the weight of his words. "I would rather be in Malvoria than spend another day under your leadership."

Liquid pain stained my cheeks. I felt broken-legged—a hand dragging me to the finish line.

I was supposed to be a legacy here.

"I'm not sure Malvoria would take you in your state. You're weak and without a quell. You should have stayed home, gotten married, and done your job as a wife. This isn't the world for you." Bridger opened his palm, releasing a flurry of snow. "You can stay here for the night… the wards will open for you at dawn."

"There are beasts. You can't be serious." I ran towards him. "Bridger, I am sorry you hate my father, but that is not my fault."

He shoved me back. "I need to impress your mentor, and it seems bonding with your enigma is the only way. His vote counts, and I doubt he'll bid on you. He'll understand." Bridger waved dismissively, already at the top of the cliff, staring down. I didn't know where Callum went.

I stumbled towards the ice wall, slamming my fist into it. "You can't leave me stranded here!"

No voice responded—not even the echo in my mind.

I wrapped my arms around myself for warmth and kept moving. This was cruel—beyond evil, leaving me to freeze out here. I made my way to the cabins visible in the distance, where warmth surely waited.

Twisting the handle of the closest one, I collapsed on the floor with my head between my legs.

"Destroy the old version of yourself. Shed your skin, Severyn. You must kill off whoever you were before." It was that voice again, softer.

"I don't know how!" I screamed.

Silence.

"Find him. You are the only one who can save him."
"Find who?"
"I cannot speak his name. He has been waiting for you to find his remains."

Familiar howls sounded from the outskirts of the trails. Bridger's wolves... he'd sent them to watch me. "The moment I enter those forests, I'll be hunted by the beasts."

"You are not like him. You are not courageous. He chose wrong." The voice ripped abruptly from my mind, leaving me with a splitting headache that took all but an hour to shake.

I curled into a ball under a pile of woven blankets, the scent of dust and moth balls drawing through my breaths. I'd never seen outside the Northern barriers and was told to strip whatever essence I had to survive. To detach myself from all I knew before I could exist. The academy wouldn't break me—it would tear me into flesh and bone like Bridger's pack of wolves would once they clawed the door down.

This world was harsh, but the title was earned, not given. I could choke on my breath a thousand times, but it would not mean my lungs were stronger. And a broken bone was only weaker, more brittle, once it healed.

I grabbed the handle of the door.

As I stepped towards the flurries of whipped ice shards, the dagger heated in my fist—that dull, sleek-handled blade Damien gave me.

If I kept walking, would I meet Spring? Would flowers bloom on my path instead of wilting to death and morphing into slush under the harsh cold? Would Spring melt into Summer and bring on that radiant heat I craved every Thaw? If I decided not to cowardly hide in the shadows of the cabin, where not even a lantern flickered with life, would I survive the night, the next one, and the one after that, until all I heard was the thrashing of the waters as the boat took me to Malvoria?

Every ache and bruise on my flesh screamed where Bridger had struck me. I hugged my body, the only tender touch of comfort I'd felt since entering the academy. I kept walking through the frost-licked path, searching for my quell to break through my skin. Slivered, beastly eyes stalked my way, waiting for the moment I stepped beyond the curve. The same creatures that Father's shield had kept at bay.

Ashen claws reached and reached.

I walked an hour into the flurries. Through the pelting winds, I dragged my boots across feet of growing snow, tracing over the ice plains and the peaked mountains, sheltered only by the crunch of each step. No signs of life, no flutter of wings called to me from the bushes. I couldn't see beyond the haze of pale. My eyes burned and stung as a shield of white blanketed my path. I was too far along in my trek to turn back, and my joints were stiff and too frozen to walk one more step. The thick snow softened my landing as my knees gave in, my fingers slate grey, dull as I believed my blood had frosted to my veins.

No screams sounded from my frost-bitten lungs as I stared above. Winter claimed me as I lay to die in a Frozen Valley.

It wasn't wings I heard, but boots. The soft crunch as someone approached me from behind.

A faded shadow drew closer. Using all my strength, I turned to see the ghastly grin on Callum's face as he unsheathed a dagger from his side and walked closer. "Did you miss me?"

He'd frozen my vocal cords with a raise of his hand. Frozen my tongue from screaming as he sliced my leg.

I couldn't move—couldn't scream. I'd gone limp. Flashes of white and red stripped my sight with each heave of his blade. My blood tasted like screams.

"Worthless," he muttered, slow and cruel. "Bridger, care to take a stab?"

A set of silver eyes watched, blonde ends curling toward his jaw. Bridger stepped closer, and I knew he'd take out his revenge on me. "Your brother told me I can't touch you, but he didn't mention Callum." He flared his nostrils. "And he pissed me off, so I don't give a damn what he orders."

Stop. Please stop. I screamed in my head. A glove shoved between my chapped, snotty lips.

Thirteen. He'd marked me thirteen times. The same day as my birthday. The same day, I heard of Klaus's death. Thirteen was only a number, but when the gurgled breaths dulled after ten, those last three had my pleas begging for him to end me.

Callum sunk to his knees, brushing a strand behind my ear. "Such a waste of a pretty face. I couldn't bring myself to ruin it. Here ends the legacy of the Blanches." He clicked his tongue. "Such a shame."

I clawed back. Heaving my spine into a mound of crimson snow. "Please," I stuttered in pain. "Leave me alone!"

Bridger scoffed. "Make her undesirable. Carve your name, mark her. I don't care. She'll be dead before the sun rises."

Callum dragged the blade against my exposed thigh. "Scream my name, Sev. Tell me to stop."

"Bridger," I forced a breath through my teeth. "I did nothing wrong."

"You did nothing. That is correct. Your villagers starved for years, and you sat in your estate reading, smiling down at us peasants." He wiped his nose. "I begged your father for medicine for my mother once. He had his guards restrain me. You are a coward, Severyn."

"Then kill me!" I screamed. "Don't… torture me. I didn't know, I swear!"

Bridger clenched his jaw. "I prefer misery." He lifted my iced hand, holding the sharp metal against my fingertips. "Say my name, Severyn. Cry out to your fortress before I cut each one off one by one. Hopefully, you were taught how to sew."

When I didn't respond, he pressed the blade harder. *"Stop! Please."*

Callum gripped my jaw, forcing me to face Bridger. "Say it, Severyn."

"Bri—Bridger!" I cried.

Callum snickered. "Let the hounds tear the rest of her clothes off. She'll freeze before dawn comes."

I couldn't cry. I couldn't scream. I lay there for what felt like hours, the cold biting into my skin, deeper than the frost ever had. A strange shape loomed through the mist, gliding between the trees like a shadow untethered from the earth.

The snow stopped falling, but only where that shadow passed. Then, it came into view—a dragon, wide-winged and immense, skimming the ground before landing a few feet away.

Terror rooted me to the spot. I couldn't move. I couldn't run. My voice trembled as I whispered, "Don't hurt me."

The dragon tilted its head, dark as midnight, its eyes gleaming like fractured amethysts. Slowly, it unfurled one massive wing, draping it over me like a shield.

Winter, my home, seemed to hold its breath as I gazed through the cracked veins of the dragon's wing. They stretched like rivers frozen mid-flow, yet within them, I swore I felt warmth—a heartbeat.

For a moment, I wondered if I had died.

Archer's dragon stayed with me the entire night. When the sun rose, it felt abrupt, as if the moon itself had turned away, unable to bear witness to my suffering.

I couldn't help but wonder: did Archer send his dragon?

Chapter 9

Muffled voices spoke, and it took me a moment to realize it was Bridger's. "I told you she is not a Winter. It nearly killed her for you to understand that," he whispered. "She can't bond with a single enigma and is literally repelled by snow. How do we know her true bloodline given her brother's calling?"

I blinked, staring up at the dim lanterns on the bedside table. Ringing and humming mingled with scattered voices.

Bridger stood at the foot of the bed with the headmaster beside him. "I chose Winter for her. It's what her father wanted. Of all Fallon's children, she's the only one who is weak."

"Her mother had one of the most powerful quells in the academy's history, and her brother bonded with the Gemini dragon. What did you expect? The Serpent has me by the neck," Bridger said, exasperated, flinging his arms in the air.

The headmaster was silent, his thumb strumming over his beard. "Speak to Jenessa and find out why a beast escaped through the wards and onto the trails. The girl was—was brutally attacked."

My tongue felt frozen, like my body had been a night's breadth ago. I didn't make a sound. The wards were fine. It was Callum who'd—who'd attacked me.

Bridger was there. He watched. I swore he got off on my pain.

"I refuse to be her mentor, not if that Serpent is making demands. I didn't want to leave her there alone. Perhaps the academy can make mistakes, such as heiring a mad leader." Bridger's combat boots clicked as he stormed out.

I melted into the mattress, sinking my neck into the curve of the wrinkled pillow as the headmaster followed. Flashes of last night lashed through my mind like a whip cutting through a shield. The sound of my clothes tearing under his dagger, the grin as he watched me shiver until I begged. My throat was hoarse, raw from screaming. My eyes darted wall to wall, searching for Estella, but the infirmary was empty.

I shoved the white linens off my legs and pulled at the loose dressings covering my wounds. Welts and bruises laced my aching skin. My fingers traced the tender, purplish areas where Bridger's ice daggers had punctured me. Callum had cut my clothes, jagged and deliberate, to make it look like a snow beast had attacked.

But I survived.

I fell asleep for what felt like an hour until the door creaked open. I blinked and saw a flushed Damien. He was the last person I wanted to see like this, and I didn't have it in me to be scorned or accused of wandering into the forests alone.

He clenched his jaw, taking in the sight of my bruised skin. "Malachi couldn't find you this morning. I thought you were—"

"Dead. I nearly froze to death," I said, pulling the cotton shirt down. "Still no quell, and I think my enigma is nonexistent."

His eyes flashed. "You look… terrible. What happened?"

"I'd rather not—not talk about it. I'm sure your brother has already called the boat to Malvoria."

"Lucky for you, he and the other Serpents are gone." He took a step closer, his hand brushing against the wooden bedframe.

"Gone?" I leaned forward.

"As in taking care of their Serpent duties. They are still leaders of realms. They have people to care for, politics to sort out."

I knew being an arrogant, attractive ass wasn't all a Serpent was. "Right," I said.

"You're covered in blood, Severyn. There's a bath on the second floor." He went to help me up, but I pushed back.

"Why are you helping me? I told you I'm being sent to Malvoria," I hissed. "You have no reason to be nice to me."

His jaw tightened. "Because we are friends."

Your friends should be your enemies, but I'd be dumb not to lean on Damien. Damien might be the only person who could take me back to the lake in the Summer forests. "I didn't think you'd want to be after I ran into the woods."

He grinned. "I don't blame you for running off."

I needed to heal. And a bath—a hot bath I'd kill for. "Friends," I said. "I guess that's fine."

Damien grabbed my elbow, steadying me through the halls. His eyes reminded me of a fire with fresh mulch laid to devour, the flecks of amber, green, and orange distant rims around his pupils. And something whirred beyond that clenched jaw as I leaned against him.

"You are freezing." He ran his palm over my bare arm, avoiding my wrist with every tender graze.

"I don't belong in Winter." The words escaped before I'd thought them through. "I don't know what to do. My father's legacy depends on me."

"You do not want to be the leader of a frozen valley, do you?"

"I do not wish for my father's name to die." The half-truth was perhaps worse than a lie.

"So, you would rather be miserable for your entire life?"

I was silent.

We were on the west side of the castle. A serpent-shaped lantern trailed along the ceiling with candles flickering from the large body of the porcelain snake. The creature's scales were carved into the walls, glinting like jewels under the light of flames, casting our conjoined shadow on the stone ground. I shuddered at Malachi's story about lindworms and wondered if those scales were of the slain beasts.

Damien stepped into the crystal-lined bathroom, forcing out two students who were towel-drying their hair. Damien was protective, something on the verge of sweet, as he gathered a spare set of clothes and a towel from the closet for me.

"I'll guard the door. Take your time," he said with a subtle grin.

"Thanks," I said. It was the sincerest effort I could manage with my aching bones and skin. The door closed with a groan.

A faucet glinted back, opening to an oversized quart tub. I twisted the knob, and the water steamed, instantly soothing the welts and bruises. Mirrors wrapped around the ceiling, forming an iridescent pattern. And I couldn't help but look up and see the hollow girl staring back——her body was nearly translucent under the shoddy light. I hardly recognized myself. I looked weaker, a shell of a woman after those excruciating hours on the frozen ground in Winter.

And perhaps I'd wilt before I could become reborn, before the old me simmered, willed to whatever voice was in my mind.

After an hour and pruned fingertips later, I dragged my numb body out of the steaming water. I dried off with a cotton towel, changing into fresh academy attire untouched by blood.

Damien pressed against the wall as I stepped out. "You look better. More like a human than whatever you were before."

"I guess that's a compliment," I whispered.

"Take it however you like. But I'd like you to take it as a compliment."

I'd have to face another brutal day tomorrow. "Bridger won't stop. He'll kill me." I don't know why I didn't mention Callum's attack.

He scratched the stubble on his sharp jawline. "Bridger was the one who found you. It's very rare for beasts to escape the wards." His hand was on my backside as we walked towards the grand hall. Night speckled a sea of stars through the wide oval windows as he continued, "I'd say the Winter trails will be off limits until a full investigation is done."

I'd be spared for a few days until they realized Callum had done it.

We sat on a stone bench near a wooden fireplace in the grand hall. An aide brought us mugs of hot chocolate. Damien appeared softer in this light, and I again noticed the scars on his chest.

I hardly knew him. I didn't even know his quell and here he was, escorting me to the bath.

"On the first night here, you mentioned never telling strangers your quell. Can I know now?" I widened my eyes, giving him the same doe-like pout I'd seen Malachi flash at Monty.

Damien chuckled low. "Why don't you guess it?"

I took a sip from the velvet-swirled hot chocolate. "You are a student mentor for Summer. So, I'd say heat control?"

Damien scoffed. "My Gods, are you stereotyping me? No, I have two quells. Dragons often live hundreds of years and choose to continue after their rider passes. Emerich gave me glass manipulation." He opened his palm as a crystal-clear dagger struck from the center. "It comes in handy when there are no weapons around. I can also portal through mirrors, but I'm a little rusty." He pulled down his shirt, showing me the scars I'd noticed.

Our scars matched. I imagined the power within that quell. Glass was everywhere. "Could we both travel through mirrors together?" Bridger and Callum could portal through the snow—the possibilities with glass were endless.

"I've never tried it, and I don't think I would ever take that risk. It nearly drains me if multiple mirrors are around." Damien raised his palm, and that glass dagger shattered into a million whirling crystals.

"It's beautiful," I whispered.

He kept his eyes on me, nodding. "Beautiful… or deadly."

"A quell can be beautiful."

"Listen, I'm going to teach you how to fight. I want you to be able to protect yourself in case something like that happens again."

"Who—told you?"

He blinked. "Combat. Bridger broke your wrist, and he won't hesitate to break your legs next time you're pinned against him."

"You don't have to do that."

"Is it stubbornness, or have you spent too much time alone with your thoughts to trust others?" He raised his voice, loud enough for three students to glance over. "I could make a grand gesture if that's what you want."

"Grand gesture?"

"Well, no one's beaten me in combat yet. I could fake a limp for a day and tell everyone it was your doing."

"That'd have the opposite effect. Fine. Teach me combat—but after the healer comes."

"Okay, but on one condition: I want to get to know you. I want the real Severyn. No pretending, alright?"

"I already told you. I'm an open book."

He shook his head. "What's your favorite color?"

"Is this necessary?"

"Yes."

I rolled my eyes and took another sip. "I like yellow. Like the sun. What about you?"

"Don't judge me, North, but I like green. And the only reason I was interested in getting to know you is because I get to see my favorite color whenever I talk to you."

"Should I limit my blinking?" I asked.

"No, that would be sort of terrifying."

I laughed. "Thanks, Damien. You managed to make a shitty day, not so shitty."

* * *

The healer arrived three days later.

He mended my wrist with his quell without touching the swollen joints, even smoothing over the cuts and welts. I had grown so used to the constant pain that walking without shudders felt strange.

The Winter trails were warded off, allowing me three days to rest. It seemed a fifth of the academy either broke or sprained something in their bodies during the first week. I didn't feel bad when I saw Bridger in line, waiting to fix his nose.

I hoped they'd have to snap it again to reset it. That his screams would wake the sleeping griffins across the mountains.

Spring was warmer than expected, and thawing hardly felt like an event here. I saw a boat along the coast, and my nerves ignited, thinking it was the Malvoria ship, but it was just a cargo boat hauling supplies. Griffins flew overhead, strapped with heavy gear, their vicious glares making me avert my gaze quickly.

I missed warding that morning. Without my quell, Cain deemed me useless at projecting a shield or ward. Myla sparred with me during combat, and not being placed against anyone seemed worse—it meant I wasn't worth a fight. I had nothing to give them. Myla, however, seemed stronger, her limbs filling out as the first week passed. A fluffy, flightless griffin cried from a pile of leaves, its black feathers and golden eyes gleaming with life.

"Her name is Haziel," Myla exclaimed, glancing at the lump of feathers every other second. "I'm a full-time griffin mother now."

Myla bore two daggers sheathed against her ribs, trophies from her triumphs in the last two battles. One, a copper-stained blade from Autumn, and now mine. I also kept Damien's dagger—not that it counted toward a win, but he'd earned enough last year to boast a small collection.

"She's adorable. Hopefully, she grows big," I said, flexing my fingers on my left hand. The healer mentioned I'd have full strength back within a day.

"I wonder when they'll open the Winter trails again. It's bullshit. We're missing prime field training," she said, jamming her knee into my chest and pinning my arms at my side. Her curls swayed as she hovered above my face.

That tightness returned—guilt. "I'm sure it'll open in a few days," I said as she dragged her body off me. Every muscle groaned as I sat up, resting my arms on my shaking knees. "On the plus side, you're getting stronger. Three more wins, and you'll earn a sword. I'm sure you'll be considered for lead to claim when they choose at the bid."

"Yeah, I've been getting private lessons. Bridger says my quell is stronger than most first-years."

I wiped my arched brow, sliding closer to her on the grass. "Did you want to eat dinner later? Perhaps I need your powerful snow to bring my quell out."

A wrinkle formed between her eyes. "I'm—I'm actually busy. Bridger's taking me griffin riding. I can't ride Haziel for at least two more seasons."

I smiled back, though I felt the distance growing between us. "Have fun," I said through clenched teeth.

Antonia jammed the dull end of her dagger against Alaric's throat. "We're not getting back together," she hissed.

Jace pulled her off him. "Toni, relax."

I narrowed my eyes at Myla. "The Night students scare me."

Myla leaned closer, kicking up a tuft of grass. "Rumor is Alaric and Antonia dated back at home. He broke up with her before they left for the academy. Seems like Alaric regrets his decision."

"Lovers turn rivals," I whispered. "It's hopeless here."

Her brows scrunched together. "Not as hopeless as rivals to lovers."

She meant Bridger. I gazed at the clouds and hoped they'd stay as rivals. "Bridger is not worth hopelessness."

Her face turned a deep shade of red. "He doesn't see me as anything other than a first-year."

"Bridger… wants to kill me," I said. "He—"

She cut me off. "It's not personal, Severyn. I mean, he told me about your father and I don't understand how you were so ignorant to what was happening in your country."

Rage simmered low in my gut, but Damien interrupted us, twirling a dagger before I could respond. "Mind if I steal Severyn for a bit?"

Myla shrugged once she saw my slight nod. "As long as you return her in one piece, or I'll have my griffin peck your eyes out."

He winked at Myla. "You'll have her in whatever shape I see fit once she knows how to fight."

Damien led me to the dragon fields and introduced me to Emerich, his spiked-horntail. Without Cully's stories, I'd know nothing about dragons or their breeds. Emerich's neck was long, nearly twice the length of Archer's dragon, and his scales shimmered like glass algae—sea greens and blues reflecting the light across his broad body. Over fifteen feet tall, his horned tail was jutted with spikes.

"He's quite the comedian," Damien said as we approached.

"What's he saying?" I asked.

"He says your enigma is dead. But that would mean you'd have to bond with one for that to be true. Emerich thinks he's a know-it-all because he survived three wars."

I shuddered, believing he was right. The borders to Winter were still down. Keeping silent put Myla and dozens of Winter students at risk. But what Callum had done to me burned inside my mind, and I wasn't ready to speak of it.

"What else is Emerich saying?"

Damien listened for a few silent beats as Emerich hummed a low vibration deep in his throat. "He says you were chosen correctly and that you should be patient. He also thinks I should hold your hand."

Emerich made a noise that sounded like a chortle—as if the dragon found humor in Damien's feeble attempt at flirting. "I thought we were going to spar."

Damien leaned closer, sweeping a finger along my palm. "And… I hardly know you."

I'd gotten my firsts over with when I turned eighteen. Most males feared Father, more so Charles. Sometimes, I regretted not waiting. If Myla could salvage lust in cruelty's eyes, what did I have to lose?

A Summer and Winter seemed as appalling as dating a rival.

His eyes scanned the field as he softly cleared his throat. "It's only chivalrous if I hold your hand before I have a dagger against your throat." And in a quick maneuver, Damien pressed a blade against my spine.

I breathed three shallow breaths of crisp spring air before twisting from his grasp—face to face with his hazel eyes.

"Don't let me win," I said, unsheathing the dagger he'd given me. Our blades clanged. He was quick on his feet, dodging my every swing and landing a few blows on my shoulders.

He leaned in closer. "Not a chance."

Winded, I asked, "Are you from a title?"

"My father's a Summer Serpent. He's a cruel man."

"Aren't all Serpents? What did Malachi mean when she mentioned boarding school?" He wrapped an arm around my backside, and I ducked.

"How about whatever idea you've made about my life stays that way? I'm not the kind of man who'll tell you his entire life within a day."

I grinned. "So, you're allowed to ask me personal questions and hold my hand, but I can't know more about you?" I desperately wanted to know more about Damien. Even now, after he claimed two Serpents ran in his bloodline.

He twirled the blade in the air, humor touching his eyes as he said, "Disarm me, and I'll tell you a secret."

I cocked a brow, reaching for the blade clutched in his grasp, but he yanked away with a false smile. "You didn't think it would be that easy?"

I huffed. "Don't go easy on me."

We fought until the sun set, streaking the clouds with color. He countered every stride and lunge with ease, until we both crashed into the grass. Cold metal pressed against my throat, and his hand tightened around my waist. I pushed against him, but he squared his hips over mine, trapping me. He brushed a fleck of dirt from my chin with his thumb, his touch unexpectedly gentle.

His cool breath hit my face, taunting his blade before me. "Unfortunately, you did not win."

I laughed to myself as I leaned up and bit his jaw. It was not hard, just a gentle bite, but it was enough for his shoulders to tense and the blade to slide against my collarbone and hit the ground.

"I believe I just did," I hummed.

He rolled off me, eyes on the dusted sky. "We both know that move doesn't count. I am a man, Severyn. Of course, I will crumble if a beautiful woman bites me." I watched his eyes whirl once before he sighed. "I was in a boarding school for six years because I told the truth. Now, the reason I shall let your mind sort that out."

"That's not *fair*."

"Hey, you never answered my question about wanting to be your father's heir."

"My brother Charles would have been better suited."

"It seems we're both living a world within our siblings. Mine happens to be the biggest asshole on the Continent. Now, you'll understand Archer was why I was sent away."

I scoffed. "All the more reasons to hate him."

He nodded, changing the topic. "I'll walk you home. Dragon riders don't like it when bird riders step onto their fields."

I laughed. "My brother warned me that I should avoid dragon riders."

He rolled his eyes. "Your brother seems like a smart man," he said.

I was unbonded, powerless, and without any weapons. Whoever wanted to attack me would have an easy kill. Honestly, I didn't care because for the first time in two years I laughed.

Chapter 10

Warding was brutal that next day, leaving me with a splitting migraine as I forced my shield to cover my trembling fingers.

I was the only one without a quell in the entire academy. Six students were forced onto a boat as per their Serpent's request while I was recovering in the infirmary, and I dreaded the next time I saw Archer, knowing I'd seen his dragon's midnight wings fly in earlier.

I overheard Antonia whisper to Jace from a row behind us, "Ciaran is back. I thought for sure she was dead."

Jace responded, "He's still weak. You can blame the Blanche freak for that one."

I whipped around. "What the hell do I have to do with Archer being weak?"

"Not you," Antonia sneered. "But it's nice to know you were eavesdropping."

Myla gripped my shoulder. "You're in no position to start a feud with people who know where you sleep."

I shrugged her off. "Antonia, it must be hard."

She grinned back. "What?"

"To be broken up with because a title is greater than love. But seeing as you called my dead brother a freak, I'd say Alaric dodged a bullet."

Barred teeth hissed at me. "Let's hope I don't have your key today. Drowning seems to run in your family."

My key?

A moment later, as we left warding, Myla asked, "Did your brother die here?"

I hesitated. "Yes. I think Archer placed me in Night because he had something to do with it." I didn't mention Bridger as my primary suspect. I knew she wouldn't believe me.

"It makes sense. When my father passed, I felt like I owed him something. I'm his only child. But I'm not from title. My mother could hardly afford to feed us—and here he was, living a life within golden ice. She knitted traditional gowns for the visiting Serpents of Ravensla, but it was never enough."

Wishing for her triumph was my downfall. There was something worse than loving your rival—it was the one person you trusted becoming one. As much as I wished Myla and I were the same, we were two different stems. She'd grown with a hungry belly, a starved mind for what existed within my life. And a bee would never sip from both our nectars.

A blaring siren had me nearly on my knees—

Pressing my palms to my ears, I cried, "What is that?"

Myla grabbed my elbow. "Bridger told me there's an unplanned trial happening today. They call it the Trial of Despair. Apparently, more students should have failed by now, and this is a way they kill off the weak. He—he told me not to tell you."

I followed behind Myla's grip, pooling beside the dozen students at the academy's entrance. "All I have is a dull dagger," I hissed. "Myla, what the hell is the Trial of Despair!"

Myla unsheathed the dagger she'd won off me from across her ribcage, leaving her with only one. "Take it. I can use my quell." She shoved the dagger into my chest. "I got you, Sev. You can trust me. Just… hold your breath like we did in the caves."

Myla's grip faded. My knees slammed into stone. I gripped the empty air, and the ground beneath me disappeared.

Slowly, I faded, sinking. "Myla," I whispered.

Water and waves sloshed through my treading fingers. Algae streaked across my line of sight as seaweed brushed against my ribs in a valley of green. I hadn't taken air in. My lungs began to burn and beg for oxygen seconds later. I tried to untangle my foot, but a tight chain around my ankle stopped me from floating upward.

I felt the weight of whatever held me to the ocean floor tugging me down as I flailed my arms through the current and swam closer to the chain around my ankle.

My ears popped as I lowered—the daylight breaching from the surface, melting into shadows.

Without releasing air, I couldn't swim any lower to see what I was tied to. I turned around, waving my hand as my fingers tried to pry off the chains while I slashed the blade repeatedly into the metal. I couldn't breathe. I couldn't calm myself down.

I had about forty-seconds before I would pass out.

Thirty-nine, thirty-eight. My lungs needed air. *Thirty-six.* My throat started to close, and a metallic taste burned on my tongue.

Knox swam towards me, his arms cutting through the water with precision. His hand slid down my body, fingers brushing my shoulder as he reached for the chain with a rusted key. Bubbles escaped his nose in a struggle as he tried to force open the lock, but it wouldn't budge. His lips moved, but I couldn't hear him.

I swore he was crying. His eyes were wide with panic, desperate, as his hands fumbled with the key. His gaze locked on something behind me, and for a fleeting moment, I saw the raw anguish in his face.

I twisted, my heart slamming in my chest, to see Everett—chained, like me. The sight of him, so close yet so unreachable, shattered me.

He mouthed, *"I'm sorry."*

Knox swam towards him, every stroke frantic. He reached for Everett's leg, fingers trembling.

The key slid into the lock. It fit. And with a snap that echoed in the deep, the chain shattered.

The sound of it breaking felt like the final straw. I wasn't the one he could save.

I was the trial. The test of burdens—how loss would destroy him, whether grief would ruin him, and how much his mind would stray. A leader could never crumble. I was Knox's test.

Ten... nine... eight. I lost count. I glanced toward the daylight as a cloud rolled over the sun, the saving grace I yearned for, but darkness had already become my home. The shadows and souls of the academy students now surrounded me. And soon, the Blanche family tree would have new ink bled onto its pages—my cause of death: drowning.

Bright flickers below caught my eye, shimmering within the inky debris. A familiar freckled face met my gaze. Klaus. He hadn't aged a day since he left us that snowy morning.

Had death already claimed me? Tears salted the sea as I reached for him.

He smiled, then pointed upward. "Breathe, Severyn. You need to breathe."

I cupped his cheek, knowing the air in my lungs had been squeezed dry. I hadn't seen those tawny golden eyes in over two years. Finally, I understood my father's search for something to match my mother's eyes—autumn's warmth had no wrath over that hue in Klaus. No griffin feather could ever resemble them.

I shook my head, rattling the chain in waves.

"Yes, you can," Klaus urged. "Come on! Breathe! Breathe for me. You need to survive to find me. I need you to breathe so you can find me."

"I miss you," I whispered those words, my last breath slipping away before I sank beneath the weight of the chains. Seaweed curled around my limbs, dragging me to the sea floor. My cheek pressed against algae and fish bones.

For the first time in a week, I felt peace as Klaus lay beside me. He looked too young to be here, too innocent to have lived through these trials. I knew he was my age, but in that moment, I felt like a child again. Starved—not just for air, but for time.

I deserved to live. Klaus deserved it more.

I wondered about the ghosts of the academy. Did they stay here, stranded in the depths? Did they believe they had won the Serpent title?

Klaus pointed again to the surface, tracing shapes in the algae and seaweed with his finger, showing me how the light shone through. I wished for his eyes, that ability to see beauty in chaos. That half-grin had me wondering if I had only joined the academy to see it again... even if it wasn't real.

"You aren't real," I said. "You died."

"I know, Sev. It's not your time. Trust me."

Maybe I'd lose my mind to stay here. Grow gills and fins, just to see him for a moment more. I'd climb mountains to chase that strayed mind—fighting for a second to count his freckles worthy of a galaxy.

"Find my name, Severyn. Find it within flesh and bone, where a heart beats beside it."

He squeezed my hand, but nothing but the current slipped through my fingers, a stark reminder that Klaus was gone and my mind was playing tricks on me.

Perhaps I was mad.

Another Blanche failure. I could hear the town gossip—the months of silence at the dinner table as Mother lit two candles before each meal, silently sobbing. Cully was destroyed, while Father stared at the serpent crown in his office, wondering where he went wrong. His body slowly giving up, wards broken, the cries of snow beasts breaching through. His golden ring lost in the shallows of the academy forever. Charles married, making Father proud, producing an heir for the Serpent title. No one would mention me again. No one would dare dwell on the failures.

Klaus turned to me once more. "It's time to breathe."

I parted my lips, feeling not water, but cool air and softness. It rushed through my lungs, expanding my ribs. I opened my eyes to see Archer staring at me, water beads dripping from his hair. He pressed his lips to mine again, and another wave of air filled my lungs.

I shoved him off. "Did you just kiss me?" I spat salted water, my eyes burning as more liquid poured from my mouth.

"No," he said, choking on the words. "I saved your damn life. You weren't breathing." He wiped his chin, his drenched tunic clinging to his chest, showing every rippled muscle.

In his hand, a similarly shaped key that Knox had held glinted, rusted from the past trials. And seven others lay scattered by his feet, each shaped differently.

The screams started all at once, drowning out everything else.

Realization sunk in. My life cost seven students' lives. Rage filled my blood. Tears fell from my eyes with every blink.

"How could you?" I hissed so loudly that I didn't care if others heard.

"How could I save you? You're welcome." I heard his words, but he didn't speak them out loud. My mind whirled as he repeated, "Your breaths are owed to me. I won't have your death on my hands."

Where was Myla? Damien was beside Malachi, who was coughing up seawater. Everett leaned against Knox, the life coming back into his flushed cheeks.

My heart began to pound. Crying out Myla's name, I staggered through the students. "What kind of trial is this? This is…" the words wouldn't form. I couldn't breathe until I saw Myla.

I held the frosted dagger to my chest, yelling back at Archer, "You should have let me die. Now Myla's key is probably in your pile. Why was my life worth more than theirs?" I stared at each key one by one as if I heard their names echo silently.

Archer walked away without a word. He doesn't care. His reputation means everything, and it is worth more than seven lives. I clutched my gut, leaned over, and threw up more seawater.

Bridger grunted from the shore. "…I found the fifth body. Her name is Myla," he said to a Valscribe journalist. "Cause of death: drowning." The journalist jotted in a notebook, continuing on as more students emerged from the water.

He carried a dark-skinned girl in his arms. She was lifeless. Her lips were blue-hued, parted as water dripped from her lungs. A severed chain dangled from her ankle, the lock untouched. Her chest hadn't moved. Why was her chest not moving?

Myla. Not Myla.

Bridger shoved me off I touched her cheek. "She's dead," he said causally. "Myla Reinhart is dead."

My knees buckled. "No… save her. She can't die!"

"Severyn, go back to your corridors. The trial has ended." He closed his eyes. "People die here. Get over it."

I crashed to the ground. Grief was raw, a blistered welt on my heart that never seemed to heal. And Klaus's wound had reopened. Myla. Not Myla.

Damien ran to my side. Only his ankles were wet. "Severyn, are you okay?"

Bridger shouted again, "Lynch, get Blanche out of here. She's a fucking mess."

A gasp sounded from behind me. Myla opened her eyes, sucking a deep breath in. And my entire body flared toward her. She met Bridger's eyes—seawater spilling from her mouth. He placed her on the dock gently as she caught her breath.

"Give me a minute." She rolled on her knees, hand flat against her chest as she coughed.

Bridger knelt beside her, patting her back. "We need to get this chain off you."

Grief consumed the docks. And I couldn't dare meet any of their eyes. I caused those cries, the wails, the shock… seven lives. I was worth seven lives.

I took off back to the estate. My slacks weighed me down, chafing my thighs. Malachi was safe, and Myla was alive. It was the only thought that got me through the halls.

* * *

I huddled under my blankets for the next hour before a soft knock sounded at my door, and Damien clutched two cups of tea as he stepped inside. "Figured this would settle that saltwater in your stomach," he said.

I thanked him and we sat in silence on my bed for a moment. "Archer had seven keys," I said. "Why would he save me?"

He shrugged. "Archer does what he wants without consequence. He placed you under his mentorship, and I doubt he's willing to let you die without proving whatever he told the headmaster at the Rite." Damien slid his hand inside his pocket and pulled out a necklace with a glass cylinder-shaped pendant looped around. "Listen, if you ever need me, simply hold it, and I'll be there before your first tear drips."

I inspected the necklace, tracing a thumb over the clear, roughly cut pendant. "Did you make this with your quell?"

Damien blushed, lowering his gaze. "Yes, after today—I realized how terrible I would feel if you were in trouble and I couldn't help you. It's just glass, Sev. Not a diamond or anything of value."

"I love it. That's very sweet of you. Thank you." I twisted my torso. "Could you put it on me?" I tried to keep it together but couldn't stop my shuddered breaths.

Damien carefully lifted my hair and placed it over my shoulder. His arms surrounded me as the glass pendant touched my chest, and his fingers clasped the chain, slightly stroking his thumb down my spine. I didn't want him to leave. Not tonight… not when I could still hear the shattered screams as six students lost someone.

Damien's fingers glided toward my jaw, angling me to face him, and those hazel eyes consumed me. "You'll be okay," he whispered. "I promise."

"Nearly dying takes a lot from you," I whispered as his touch slipped from my face.

"Find your light and hold onto that. Some days are worse, but it only means tomorrow will be brighter."

As Damien turned to leave, I asked, "Do you know who had my key?"

The silence whispered back, and I knew his next words when he clenched his jaw and faced me one last time. "I did. Malachi went into the water to save you and nearly drowned herself in the process. But Archer… he'd taken the key from her. Archer killed six people today to save you. Three were Night students. The rest were Winters. I won't tell you their names unless you wish to know."

Disgust rolled in my guts. "I don't know what to say."

"Then don't say anything, but you are here to live another day. This is normal, Severyn. People die trying to prove themselves. This trial wasn't about you today. It's another way the academy gets rid of the underperformers. I might be an asshole for saying this, but I'm glad he saved you when I couldn't."

I didn't have it in me to be upset at his bold assumption that my life was greater than seven. "I was collateral damage," I said. "I was my brother's test."

"Rest and be thankful you have a tomorrow." Damien stepped out, closing the door behind him.

As I tried to rest my eyes, a familiar voice whispered through the shadows, as if that leaking starlight had punctured holes in the windows.

"Find him," she called. *"Only you can awaken him."*

Chapter 11

Today, I breathed for Klaus. Having no right to feel my lungs expand and take my first breath of the day. But I was returning to that lake today, even if it might kill me. And Archer had callously saved my life—not knowing I'd risk it a day later.

I ate breakfast—cold oats and fruit as Malachi sat beside me, Myla across. She seemed shaken up from yesterday's trial, fiddling with her fork. Cormac and Margaret joined us. I fidgeted with the glass pendant as Malachi twirled wind within her finger, playing off Myla's snow.

The air was somber. A heaviness billowed in my chest as we all sat silently.

Bridger stopped as he passed us, resting his gaze on Myla, and I knew that stare, the longing in his eyes. Myla also noticed his stare, her snow falling onto her lap as her cheeks flushed. It was like a child seeing stars for the first time.

And I couldn't stop that lust between them as Myla softly waved.

Malachi nudged her. "So, are you and Bridger seeing each other?"

Myla's gaze lowered to the stone table, then onto me. "No," she said in a whisper.

Malachi strummed her fingers on the table. "Come on. Please give me something to gush over. I need details. Have you guys kissed? You both left together yesterday? His face when he thought you were dead was… heartbroken."

Margaret flashed a grin. "Mal, that is morbid. But is *it* cold?" She raised a quick brow. "Summers are too warm for me. I prefer Night males."

"*Who*?" Malachi asked. "Tell me it's Alaric. Antonia stole my dagger in combat, and I'd do anything to get back at her."

"Jace and I had a moment during combat," said Margaret. "But… he's in love with Antonia. I don't blame him. The cutthroat, hot persona is one way to have men swoon you."

I couldn't believe we were talking about this.

I curled my fingers around the edge of the table. "I heard the Winter trails are opening today. Hopefully, those beasts won't be escaping again."

Myla dropped her fork with a loud clang. "Hopefully not. But I think we both know what happened."

Malachi made a face. "I am so glad to be an Autumn. Severyn, you finally have a tan. You were nearly translucent for a few days."

I shoved the dagger Charles gave me toward Myla. "You can have it back. You won it."

Myla didn't reach for it. "It's yours. You need it more than me."

I grinned. "Thanks. Tell Bridger I'll be late for the Winter trails. I have something I need to do."

Myla stuttered. "We're not seeing each other, Sev. I—I know what happened to you. I know what Callum did. Bridger tried to stop him. He's not the bad guy here. He's… sort of sweet."

I wasn't willing to tell the truth. If Myla wanted to further her relationship with him, who was I to stop it?

Malachi raised a golden brow. "Now you two are keeping secrets?"

I shook my head. "I'll tell you tonight, Mal. Right now, I need all the daggers I can get."

Malachi didn't hesitate as she pulled a dagger sheathed to her ribcage and stabbed the end into the table. "Severyn's going for blood, and I support it!"

* * *

I met Callum's stare as he waited outside the Winter fence. Ice glazed the pit of my stomach.

He'd seen me and was probably waiting to tell Bridger I'd broken the rules and stepped into the Summer trails. I didn't care.

Past the bend, the zip line came into view. I gripped the cold metal handles, the weight of my body pulling against the line as I glided over the crashing waves below.

My boots hit the moist ground with a jolt, sinking slightly into the dew-speckled earth. The air was crisp, the scent of damp leaves mingling with a faint metallic tang. Ahead, the wicked forest loomed, its shadows stretching long and jagged in the morning light.

I was insane. I was mad, but I didn't give a damn because I was not willing to spend three years hearing a voice in my head with the off chance that Klaus might be alive.

A low growl rumbled from the bushes. My heart quickened, but I forced my legs to move, breaking into a run towards the lake. Vines lashed out from the underbrush, curling around my ankles and calves, their grip tightening with every step. Pain shot through me as they pulled taut, the coarse texture burning against my skin.

The forest was restless today, determined to either keep me away—or trap me within.

I slashed through the thicket, the blade of my dagger cutting cleanly into the tangled foliage. Gritting my teeth, I hauled myself forward towards where I thought the lake might be. Shadows closed in around me, disorienting and dense, until I spun in place, my breath coming in shallow gasps.

Then came the guttural growls. I turned to find three black, sinewy beasts stepping from the bushes, their yellowed eyes glowing like embers in the dim light. Their claws raked through the sand, carving jagged furrows as they crept towards me.

I couldn't take them all at once—hell, I wasn't sure I could handle even one.

Veined hearts pumped behind translucent, ashen flesh. Engorged canines dripped as they caught the scent of my sweat and fear.

I bolted towards the water. But three more creatures picked up on my presence, drawn by the sound of my hurried breath as I hacked through the dense undergrowth. A vine lunged at my leg, its barbs digging into my ankle.

Reacting swiftly, I sliced through the sinewy appendage, causing a corrosive yellowish slime to ooze out. It burned through my thick socks as I kicked away the coiled-like tentacles. Two more assailants closed in, their forms almost wrapping around my throat and threatening to drag me deeper before I managed to regain my footing.

Gods, I was not dying today because of a plant.

Flesh met rotted wood. The beast spread its bat-like wings, crawling on all fours, snapping its jaw at my face. I fell to my knees, my fingers dipping into the cool bath below as the rotted bridge groaned under my weight.

I was doing this for Klaus, to silence the voice in my mind. My only choice was to slide into the murky lake.

A set of jaws snapped in my face.

"Swim. Now"

I slammed into the lake spine-first.

Brown sludge lined the surface as I dove down, tucking the daggers into the hem of my waistband.

Yesterday, I begged for the sun to graze my cheeks and for fresh oxygen to fill my lungs, and today, I was sinking deeper, swimming further into the depth of shadows.

My left ear popped as I searched the still, algae-laced waters. My arms beat faster, but my lungs burned. I had gone mad. No other word could explain why I was frantically skimming my fingers along the rocky bottom.

My elbow brushed against a tangle of weeds, and I recoiled, heart pounding. I couldn't see beyond the heavy shadows, the water darkened by debris that blocked any sunlight. My foot grazed something leathery. I kicked back, tracing the shape with my hand—large, rounded, almost skeletal. I ran my fingers along what felt like ridged ribs.

It was a creature.

I swam over what seemed to be the form of a dragon, my fingers grazing its torso. But then, something else caught my eye—what looked like a human. Its skull was hollowed, the eyes eerily absent, gutted where a rider's gaze should have been. Algae clung to the bones like a funeral shroud.

And then, I saw it.

That ring, still golden and shining, looped around the right index finger of the slate-grey skeleton—identical to the Serpent ring my father had gifted Klaus before he left for the academy.

There he was. Only bone and gold were left, his clothes mere particles floating around me as the months turned into years. Perhaps this was how it should have gone, with me resting with him as our lungs gave out in the same depth of water.

His dragon was beautiful. Pearlescent scales dressed the creature's frame with a midnight ink underbelly, fading into the murky waters. I grazed my hand against its spine, feeling… warmth… which was odd.

Even light itself held no wrath over the glory of what this beast was. I could almost hear Klaus's laughter as he rode in the sky.

"*Come back to me.*" I mouthed—not daring to touch his fragile bones, afraid to disrupt whatever quiet world he'd entered. That was my last bout of air before I clawed my way back to the surface.

Klaus was only gold and bone.

My fingers were the first to slice through into the air. My lungs were next as a dozen fanged, winged creatures snapped at the water's edge. I found what I needed to see: that even the bravest could wear glass concealed as a diamond.

That voice in my mind was as silent as the moon on a sunny day. It did not laugh nor mock my feeble attempt at hope. It wanted this to happen. Lured me here for some reason—

"I did what you asked!" I screamed, feeling the rip of claws slash the water around me. I stared directly into their beady eyes as I waved a dagger violently, my chin dripping with sludgy lake water. "Stay back!" I hissed over and over.

I threw Damien's dagger, striking the beast's shoulder with a growl. The others hissed, stepping back on their hind legs as drool dripped from their snarled teeth. "Get back!" I yelled again, my voice hoarse, still struggling to breathe.

I gripped Malachi's dagger, feeling the wind within my throw as it struck another beast. Only one dagger remained, yet four creatures lurked within the bushes.

Suddenly, a silver-tipped arrow shot through the trees, striking a beast down. The bushes shuffled, and a shadowed figure stared me down. Archer Lynch. He looked like he might shoot an arrow right at me from how he aimed his bow along the woods.

A beast lunged for him as he dragged his arm back, shooting it in the chest. "Get the fuck out of the water," he said. "Now."

Rage and something else filled his blue eyes.

The water beneath me bubbled as Archer grabbed my wrist, dragging me over the lip of the lake. Rolling onto my back, he shot another creature from behind.

"You wouldn't understand why I came here," I said, taking another breath.

"I know damn well why you went here. Do I need to sleep in your hallway to ensure your safety?"

He pulled me to my feet with the bow tucked under his armpit. "What are you talking about? How—how did you find me?"

He threw a dagger over my shoulder. "It doesn't matter."

"Why haven't you sent me to Malvoria yet? And why was I worth more than seven lives?" We were both running, but my drenched slacks weighed me down.

He didn't respond, and perhaps he would drag me to the Malvoria boat if we did survive the woods. "I don't owe you an explanation," he hissed. "This was reckless, *Severyn*."

"Then don't owe me. Tell me why you saved me. Tell me one good reason so I can stop wondering."

Archer closed his eyes. "Curiosity will get you killed. Stop asking questions and be thankful."

"Archer! On your left!" We were nearly halfway out of the woods before a death dweller lunged and pinned Archer to the ground.

Its claws sliced into his chest. Archer grunted, forcing an arrow over his shoulder, missing the snapping, snarling creature—

My hands became hot. So hot that a sweltering heat boiled in my gut, rising towards my inflamed cheeks. I reached for the last dagger, aiming at the beast, and before I could breathe, a flame struck from the center of my trembling palms.

Flame.

I fell as the flame smothered the beast in a grasp of fire, crawling back and circling my fingers like withered ropes. Black smoke curdled from its hissing muzzle, collapsing into a pile of ash.

I killed it with flame.

I stared at my palms, then at Archer, who I swore was more shocked than me. "My quell…"

"Antecedent quell," Archer breathed, cursing as the trails neared our sight. "You stole Klaus's power."

"I didn't steal it!" I snapped, my voice breaking with desperation. "What the hell is going on?"

"A quell passed through a dragon is only strong through the bond of a living enigma. That dragon down there is a rotted corpse."

He knew all along where Klaus was—knew it was only bones that held him together. But I had felt scales on that dragon. I had felt… warmth. I had felt something.

"It called to me and has been since I got here. It led me here, Archer. I swear!"

We dove over the warded trail. Archer stumbled towards a cabin, his steps uneven. "A dead dragon cannot call to you," he muttered, clutching his bleeding chest.

"You're bleeding."

"I'm fine." He opened a cabin door and collapsed on a cot. "Do you know how to bandage? I won't be strong enough to make it back tonight. There's bandages and cloth in the closet." He pointed a finger towards the furthest wall.

I wriggled off my outer layer, slopping the wet garment onto the ground. The once-pristine white sheets were already soaked in blood. I had seen my fair share of wounds from Father and Charles's beast hunts, but nothing like this. The sight of so much blood unsettled me.

I grabbed the first-aid kit from the linen closet, my hands trembling slightly as I sat on the edge of the bed. I hesitated for a moment before carefully pulling the remnants of his shredded shirt away, revealing the extent of the damage.

I wiped his chest down with an alcohol pad, forcing myself to remain steady despite the chaos swirling in my chest. Three deep claw marks were carved below his breastbone, the torn skin weeping crimson. His toned muscles twitched with every move of my hand.

I had never seen a more beautiful man, writhing in pain. Gods, he was… I couldn't even finish that thought.

"Does this hurt?" I asked softly.

He grabbed my wrist as I swept below his beating heart. "Stop."

My breath hitched. The towelette slipped from my fingers when my eyes landed on something unexpected—something impossible. Five familiar letters scrawled across his ribs, their penmanship unmistakable.

Klaus.

My heart pounded, each beat louder than the last. My voice trembled as I spoke, questioning my own sanity. "Why do you have Klaus's name marked on your ribs?" My hand hovered over the name, shaking. I knew that cursive K—it was the way he signed his name on cards during Winter Solstice gifting.

Archer's gaze hardened, his jaw tightening. "Klaus and I were bonded riders. Our enigmas were Gemini twins. Ciaran and Naraic."

'Find my name beside a thumping heart and flesh.' Klaus's words echoed in my mind, but I pushed the thought aside. It had to be a coincidence—some cruel twist of fate.

"Damien said you were… weak," I said, my breath stifling in my lungs as I wrapped the bandage around his chest, tightening it with care. My eyes didn't leave his. "Is it… because of Klaus?"

"Ciaran is weak, but hopefully, she will live another decade," Archer replied, his voice quieter now, almost mournful. "She enjoys being here and knowing Naraic rests." He paused, his gaze darkening with the weight of memory. "Your brother was my best friend, Severyn. Protecting you was a promise I made to him."

"How did Klaus die?" I pinned my arms to my side, leaning back on my ankles as far away from him. Yet, my eyes stroked the dark hair trailing the deep curve near his abdominal muscle.

Fuck, I was alone in a cabin with a bleeding ruler who, thankfully, didn't notice my stare.

"There's more danger to this academy than those beasts in the forests." He rolled onto his side, his chest moving up and down, and suddenly, I was fixated on his every move. "I can't tell you."

"Why is everything restricted? Students should be aware of any attack at the academy." I returned the first-aid kit to the linen closet but stayed across the cabin. I was wrong about Archer. It took everything in me to take one more step back to him.

"As I said, curiosity will get you killed. Stop asking questions a first-year should not know," he said with a breath of annoyance.

I stared at my blistered palms, where fire had willed from my veins. *Fire*, the thought of begging for snow to frost over my limbs, only to draw flame within those pleas, caused my lids to brim with tears.

And so, the girl who willed to know what lived beyond those plains of ice saw too much too fast. What would I tell Knox? If he'd even believe me, and if Myla would still trust me as fire boiled within me.

"Do you think my quell will go away?" I asked.

Archer stared at the wooden planked ceiling. "It would be in your best interest."

I pulled the drenched top over my head, wriggling out of my sopping slacks, throwing my clothes into the corner, covered only by the wraps around my chest and under bottoms. He kept his eyes on the ceiling as my spine faced him.

And I knew what he thought of me. Knew I was that annoying friend's sister he felt indebted to protect as he clenched his jaw.

"You wanted me to find my quell, even telling Bridger that I bond with a pigeon if it's the last thing he does," I said.

Archer rubbed his index finger over his temple. "You have no idea what happened today, do you?" he asked.

Two cries sounded above, swooping low past the window to reveal pearl-white scales. I rushed to the door, feeling a blast of heat against my face as I yanked it open. Two dragons appeared. One soared higher, its wings spread wide, lavender eyes watching me with an intensity that rooted me in place. Its black underbelly glinted in perfect contrast to the other's shining white spine. Their horned tails sliced through the air in unison.

They were nearly identical, their size and form a mirror of one another, except for the inverted scales.

Archer limped behind me, towering over my shoulder. "You—" he began, his voice low and uncertain. "This is not good."

I couldn't tear my eyes away. "Is that—?"

Archer cut me off. "Naraic and Ciaran. And one of those dragons is supposed to be dead—was dead."

Naraic's wingspan stretched over thirty feet, his brilliant pearl scales shimmering as he landed. The impact shook the ground, his claws sinking deep into the soil. His neck curved gracefully, and those lavender eyes locked with mine.

"What do I do?" I hissed at Archer. There were protocols for approaching creatures. Griffins liked their back feathers stroked before a flight, but a dragon? I had no idea what might provoke or calm one. One wrong move could end with me in flames.

"Walk forward," Archer instructed. "And be still."

I forced myself to take a single step towards the pearled beast, gathering what composure I had left. Ash drifted from Naraic's flared, algae-stained nostrils. His wings were batlike and torn— exposing the veiny bones beneath. He looked like a creature caught between life and death.

I reached out, extending my hand towards his cheek. The back of my fingers grazed a scale, its surface cool and smooth. I exhaled slowly, my breath shuddering as time seemed to pause.

"I found you," I whispered. "You were Klaus's dragon?"

"You were the only one who could," Naraic's voice rasped in my mind. It was not the same voice that had called to me in the Winter forests.

I turned to Archer, my voice cracking. "He's been down there for two years… rotting," I said. "How is that possible?"

Naraic growled, and my attention snapped back. *"Will you accept our bond, a promise to protect Verdonia, to give your life to me and our connection, and I will give you my protection, my soul?"*

A bond?

Archer hissed at Ciaran, "She isn't ready. Not yet, but I will train her to be Klaus."

I would be a dragon rider. Had there ever been a dragon to live in the Frozen Valleys? I wouldn't hesitate—not when two sets of lavender eyes stared at me, capable of ending me with one breath.

"Yes," I breathed.

"Open your palm," demanded Archer. "He needs to mark you."

I needed time to think, but my blistered fingers uncurled without thought. "I accept your bond," I said.

Then Naraic blew a breath of fire at my fingers, marking my right palm with an intricate relic of flames that swooped between my knuckles. My hands tightened as a gag of ash shoved between my teeth, rising through my aching lungs. A tether synched, and something in my ribs snapped in place.

Ciaran watched me from afar, bowing low. "A bond to Naraic is a bond to Ciaran," Archer said low. "Two dragons, one soul."

I nodded at the same dragon who'd turned Bridger's icy daggers into shadowed dust. Those wings I'd felt along my bare spine as I lay there.

"You found him," the same voice whispered. *"I knew you were brave."*

It was her leading me here to find her brother—and mine. The thought nearly had my eyes filled with tears. She'd saved me that night. Kept me warm under her wings.

I turned to stare at Archer. "I heard her in my mind."

Archer reached for my arm, twisting my palm to stare at the swirl of flame. "We must bond too, but we'll do that when neither is covered in blood. Enigma bonding can be draining. Rider bonding can be deadly and… personal."

"Bridger mentioned rider bonds were forbidden," I said.

"There are three types of bonds, and I don't care to explain them. You can manage your own research."

My head whirled. I couldn't remember how to walk. I stared at Archer, knowing beyond those eyes was sheer annoyance, knowing I was the last person he wanted to bond with. "This is a lot to take in," I whispered. "That's why you saved me at the Rite? Because of Klaus."

Naraic and Ciaran huffed before taking off into the skies. Archer dropped my hand. "You should rest," he said firmly.

I didn't want to rest. I wanted to understand this. "How did I save Naraic? Was he trapped in some petrified state?"

His voice was low. "The same way you saved Myla. You possess a forbidden quell, meaning if anyone finds out your dragon is Naraic, they will wonder how a dead dragon rose from the grave."

A wave of sickness washed over me. "Myla was *dead*," I said, stepping back, nearly tripping over my damp boots. "They'll strip me of my quell like my mother."

And from his silence, I suspected he knew that part.

Archer gave a cruel, arrogant smirk. "Just stay out of my way. No one must know about Naraic. We say you bonded with a cousin of his if any of the third-years recognize his scales."

I tucked my head between my knees. "I'm going to be sick," I said.

Archer threw a cool shadow atop me, simmering that flame inside my rolling guts. "You are inheriting Klaus's flame at his advanced level. The hardest part will be controlling it and keeping yourself… cool. It takes most students months for their quell to slay a beast."

Through the gleam of darkness, I shook my head. "Am I still in the run for my father's title?" I'd willed flame—breathed ash. I was a beast in the eyes of the Winter wards.

"No, a fire quell cannot exist within Winter's lands. You are in the run for my father, Victor Lynch, as the heir to Ravensla. Damien Lynch will become your student mentor. Immediately." He pressed his lips together. "Since you two are well acquainted already, hopefully, he won't consider you a rival."

And if I hadn't shattered yet, I had now.

Damien was my rival.

Chapter 12

Cold sweats roused me sometime before dawn. The skin on my backside stuck to the cotton sheets, slick and clammy from the night. The memories of yesterday clung to me like a heavy fog as I stared at the bloodied sheets Archer had discarded in a pile.

I stepped into the early morning light. Archer had mounted Ciaran, her wings stretching wide across the sandy path. Behind her, Naraic lay sprawled, his wings slightly healed. The bone was no longer intertwined with flesh and visible veins, though the scars remained.

Scars. What happened to him?

"I'd suggest putting your slacks back on to avoid scale rash. But I have a few ointments that can help if you insist on flying back to campus like that." The humor was back in his eyes—healed as if a restful sleep was all he needed. He looked stronger, and I didn't know that was possible.

Was the Serpent of Shadows weakened for two years? Was I seeing the flesh of a new man dressed in unscathed leather?

Heat rose to my cheeks. Yesterday's clothes reeked. I'd deal with scale rash if it meant I wouldn't have to slide my legs through crusted slacks.

"How do I... get on the dragon?" I asked, staring at the creature.

"You'll need to swing your legs over his neck." Archer said, gracefully descending Ciaran and stepping towards me. His eyes assessed me—head to kneecaps. "And you... are shorter than Klaus."

Naraic pinned his neck down, snarling. "I think you're offending him."

Archer shimmied out of his leather riding jacket and placed it over my shoulders. "Take my jacket for now, and I will find you a spare that fits you when we're back at the academy."

I shoved my arms through the jacket's oversized sleeves, the heavy leather settling awkwardly against my bare thighs. The weight of it pressed down, and I bit back the urge to throw it back at him. His smug grin practically begged for retaliation. "Thanks," I muttered through gritted teeth.

"I expect that jacket back," he said, his tone clipped, barely audible. "I know first-years enjoy the thrill of speaking to a ruler, but I'd rather not be associated with you."

I glared at him, fingers brushing the half-moon relic pinned beneath the faded serpent emblem on the leather. "Don't worry. I wouldn't be caught dead wearing this around campus."

Lifting my leg to climb, I stumbled back. Archer caught me with one hand. "Watch yourself," he said. "Or is mounting something too complicated for you?"

"I can mount anything," I said.

"I doubt that."

"Boost me, and I'll get it next time," I said. Were we talking about the same type of mounting?

Then Archer curled his hands on either side of my waist, effortlessly shoving me onto Naraic's spine. I couldn't help but notice how his fingers lingered slightly on the jacket's sleeve.

Archer touched my calf, angling it inward. "Keep your knees locked and your legs tight against Naraic's ribs." His fingers brushed toward my thigh but stopped short. "Naraic will sense where you want to go, but if you need to veer a certain way, use your thighs to nudge him in whichever direction you wish. You do know which is left and which is right, correct?"

"You don't have to be arrogant," I said, then a wave of heat hit me. I wobbled forward, and a cool shiver ran along my spine. I blinked up, and it seemed all that sickness disappeared.

Shadows… he was using his shadows on me. A silken black sheet bathed my trembling arms. Silently, I watched him mount Ciaran, his calf muscles tight against her ribs.

Huffing, I said, "You should ask someone before inflicting your quell on them."

He gave a blank stare, and the shadows dragged back. "If you vomit on my jacket, feel free to keep it. It might earn you a few challenges during combat. You seem to need all the help and handouts you can get." He eyed the iced dagger Myla won off me.

Naraic took off first, his wings raised, beating within the air. I lurched forward, keeping my grip tight on his neck as the air ripped past me. "Sorry," I said, unsure if Naraic heard me. I knew Charles had a rider bond between him and Lorna and their griffins, but it seemed unnatural to speak in my mind. I knew nothing about bonds.

We glided above the castle, and I tried to keep the blazing heat from knotting around my stomach. The land spanned for miles and miles, sheltered by jagged peaks flecked with snow towards the northern side. Golden tints stained the grounds as Day rained dawn across the academy's vast landscape. I saw the crimson wall hidden within the Winter trails, nearly the joy from me. Spring was wild with untamed flowers like a rainbow had wept over the lands. The Night trails were a swallowing shadow of brittle trees and moonlight within a sea of stars.

I wouldn't fly any closer to that dark oasis.

Naraic went easy on me. I knew those scars on his scales, where a few were torn, meant he'd lived through the worst of the land's shows. I wasn't his first rider, and I didn't think Klaus was either.

The wind beat against my sweat-licked brow, curling through the folds of Archer's jacket.

I felt alive, and I had gone too long without that feeling.

Naraic landed, tucking his wings in. And I awkwardly slid off, nearly faceplanting into a pile of dragon shit as I stepped forward. Archer stifled his laugh as Ciaran's midnight wings crept low. He gracefully jumped down, walking towards me with a pool of midnight shadows following his every step.

He opened his palm, glancing at the jacket he'd given me. I shrugged it off as a wave of his spiced musk sucked through my senses.

"You're a natural, Blanche," he said. "I suppose you are Klaus's sister after all."

It was the first compliment he'd ever given me, though it came wrapped in a thinly veiled insult.

My knees wobbled as I handed him the jacket, gaining my balance. I asked, "What happens now?"

"Listen, Severyn," he began, "nothing changes between us. I am still a Serpent, and you are still a student. You will see me when I seek you out. Because when I tell you this will end badly if anyone suspects that dragon is Naraic—" His eyes darkened under the hood of his brow. "I'll be at the fields for dragon training. Try not to get in my way."

I nodded tightly. "In that case, may I be dismissed, Serpent?" I sneered low.

A grin crept to the side of his mouth. "Shower, you smell like a corpse." His nose wrinkled at the jacket in his hands.

* * *

Grey sludge drained from my hair. It took three washes for my skin not to reek of dirt and whatever else was lying dormant in that lake.

Damien waited by my room after my shower. "Alright, where have you been all night?" A slight annoyance, perhaps concern, tinged his voice as he leaned against my door. He glanced at my sopping hair I'd hastily braided in two, leaving the single strand of my birthmark loose.

How do I tell him? Would he care? Did this mean Damien would always be a part of my life, tied to Archer somehow? Deep down, I felt closer to Klaus than ever.

I uncurled my fist and showed him that swirled relic of flame on my palm. "I got my quell," I said.

His eyes lit up as he ran a hand through his tousled brown locks. "That is an antecedent relic, meaning you also *bonded*?"

I nodded. "You'll have to teach me some riding tricks."

Damien let out a loud sigh. "I don't know anything about griffins, Sev."

"Well, it's good that I bonded with a dragon then. I'm no longer in the run for my father's title." Speaking it out loud boiled venom in the back of my throat.

Failure. Grief. Loss. Our name would die. And that feeling was utter numbness.

The halls seemed tighter—suffocating as we walked to class. "I suppose I am your student mentor now, huh? Seeing as that quell is used to keep Summer wards strong. Luckily for you, there are two Summer heirs needed. We could both become Serpents."

I was happy Damien didn't see us as rivals, but why did Archer say I was in the run for his Father's title when there was another vacant heir?

"I guess on your next Summer outing, you can finish showing me around the trails there," I said.

He grinned back. "Does that mean you are finally taking me up on that offer to show you around the academy?"

"I guess so," I chuckled. "The dragon I bonded with is a cousin of Naraic, my brother's dragon… His name is… Skia."

Skia was the first thing that came to my mind. It was also the name of the mountain that surrounded our home in North Colindale. Hopefully, Damien didn't know his geography. I'd become good at lying—lying in the letter I wrote to my parents and lying to Damien now.

Damien had no reason not to trust me. But I couldn't risk him knowing… not when my mother was stripped for bearing a forbidden quell.

He asked softly, "I didn't know you had another brother?"

"I have four. Three are alive. Klaus… died here."

"That's common for riders to bond with an enigma related to them," he said. "Most griffin eggs here are descendants from the first year the school was built. Dragons also tend to find familiar bloodlines if their rider dies. It's called Dragon Roots. I'd bet the flame quell has passed through centuries of your bloodline. Every hundred years, hatchlings branch out and find new bloodlines." He shrugged. "It's a strange way of discovering your distant relatives when their dragon roots with yours."

"Here, I thought I had only iced blood. Hopefully, Bridger will stop trying to kill me." But I knew deep down Bridger becoming my father's heir was worse than anything I could have imagined.

"You've just entered another ballgame, North. Dragon riders are ruthless. You've missed a lot of combat classes. Most first-years should have earned a sword by now. If anyone duels you, you're dead within seconds."

I looped my arm with his. "Well, it's a good thing I have an awesome friend who will bring me up to speed on everything I've missed." I cocked my head, giving him the widest doe eyes I could muster, and it seemed to work. "And you promised to train me."

"You're lucky you fascinate me," he said with a grin. His finger twirled my neval streak. "Not many beautiful riders these days."

We stopped before the warding classroom. His eyes shifted to my lips—or was it mine on his?

Damien was unlike Archer. His eyes held a darker intensity, which I hadn't thought possible. Archer was the Serpent of Shadows, yet somehow, his brother seemed to inherit all his perfect leftovers.

He huffed as Myla cleared her throat, brushing past us. "She's sitting with me today, dragon rider."

Damien smirked. "She's all yours."

I grinned, shaking my head before following behind her.

Damien sat across the room with the second-years. I slipped into a seat beside Myla and Malachi. Oddly, Antonia and Alaric were in our row, with Jace strategically placed between them for reasons that were painfully obvious.

Malachi smacked the warding book closed in front of me. "I thought you died last night. A warning is appreciated when you decide to stay out all night after telling me you needed daggers," she seethed. "I nearly sent every guard to search for you."

I uncurled my palm to show her the flame relic. "Bad news, I lost your dagger, but the good news is I got my quell."

Malachi smacked my shoulder, studying the swirled mark I'd shown her. "A fire quell?"

I held my grin back. "A lot happened last night."

Myla widened her eyes. "Between you and Damien? I saw you two in the halls."

Antonia straightened her posture, obviously listening to us. "No, not that. Stop talking. I have missed too many classes. I will explain everything later."

Professor Cain stepped into the classroom and instantly perked up. "I sense a new quell in the room," he said.

Malachi twirled her finger, and a gust of wind raised my hand unwillingly. "That would be Severyn!"

I stirred for a second, clearing my throat. "Um, yes, sir. I found my quell yesterday."

Cain motioned for me to step forward. Damien held his grin on me as I walked towards the center of the class. "Open your palm, dear." Cain motioned at my hands, his gaze tight on the swirled relic. "A fire quell can become destructive easily in warding, making the shield deadly. But this relic is antecedent, meaning this is not your natural power, yet a given one from a fallen rider." Cain stepped back, knocking into the table and shattering a glass vial. "Oh, dear—"

I felt everyone's eyes burning into me as I stared at Professor Cain. "What is it?" I asked.

"Blanche, you may sit down. Herring can take over."

His reaction startled me.

Myla squeezed my elbow as I retook my seat. "We are quite the opposite, I suppose. You're fire, and I am ice."

"I guess we are." My voice was low, barely a whisper. "It doesn't matter to me."

Malachi rose, stepping towards the center of the class. She opened her palm, and a flurry of wind brewed from within, whirling around until nearly every paper in the class flew and fluttered like a storm was silenced to four walls.

"Someone test my shield," she yelled over the prowling winds, nearly throwing students to the sides.

I opened my palm, igniting a small flame, but Damien beat me to it. Tiny glass shards rose from his hands. He flicked his wrist at her shield, and the fragments ricocheted off, falling to the ground in a thousand pieces.

"Excellent, Lynch. You've been practicing. Now, a glass shield is not something I would want to step inside." His core chuckled loudly. "No one wants to be pulling out shards from their face for a month."

Antonia raised her hand. "I thought antecedent quells were rare."

Professor Cain straightened his crooked glasses back on his nose. "There are three types of quells one can gain: your natural quell, which you are born with, and a vested quell, which is the power your enigma gives you. Normally, after years of bond. An antecedent quell is passed on after a previous rider passes, and the enigma consumes that power. That power may be decades old. Most only obtain their natural quell. But an antecedent quell can be passed on through hundreds of bonds."

Antonia crinkled her nose. "Is it normal for a Winter to gain a fire quell?" She flattened her hand. "Who's to say that I won't strike daylight from my palm in a year from now," she hissed.

Cain pressed his lips together. "I believe the enigma chooses where you will reign or live. Now, that is only speculation."

I nodded at Malachi as we practiced our shields. "Should I be worried about dragon training?"

"Monty and Archer are great teachers. But you are behind." Her eyes narrowed slightly, puckered lips smacking. "I'm sure everyone will play nice today."

"Play nice?"

Noon struck, and the clock's chime sent the class scattering. I lingered behind, my steps faltering as Malachi glanced over her shoulder, sensing my hesitation. She paused, but I waved her off.

Professor Cain bent to sweep up the shattered glass, his movements stiff and distracted. I crouched to help, tossing a jagged shard into the bin. "Professor," I began, my voice low. "Earlier, you felt… something in me. Can I ask what it was?"

Cain froze mid-motion, his hand gripping the broom tightly. "Severyn, I'm not sure what you mean," he said, though his eyes betrayed unease.

A sting ran through my hand as a shard nicked my finger. I winced, blood welling at the cut. Meeting his gaze, I pressed, "I know what I saw, sir. You can sense quells, can't you?"

He glanced over his shoulder, his face paling. "Death," he murmured, the word heavy and sharp. "I felt death inside you."

The air seemed to thin. My steps faltered as I backed away, nearly knocking another vial from the table. "I'll… see you tomorrow," I managed, my words tumbling over each other as I slipped from the room.

He called after me, but I was nearly halfway down the hallway.

Death. I choked my next few breaths of air down, using the stone columns to keep me upright. I needed to focus on combat next. I couldn't afford to be dizzy. Not when nearly my entire class had earned a sword. Cain sensed quells. Had he felt that bond between me and Naraic and that forbidden cure that rose him from his grave?

My spine groaned against the pillar, eyes glazed on the narrow hall leading to the foyer. I'd willed death, life. I wasn't sure. It took everything in me to push open those iron doors and head towards combat.

There was Malachi, leaning against the railing outside. She shoved a quill inside her riding leathers when she saw me. "What were you writing?" I asked.

She pursed her lips. "Don't be mad, but I sent a letter to your mother. Knox gave me your address. I wanted her to know Astoria was in good hands." There was another letter behind the one she wrote—the same golden parchment we received during the first trial.

I lifted a brow. "I'm not upset. She would be happy." I glanced at the golden letter. "Is that the trial letter we received?"

She half-hugged my waist as we walked to combat together. "Oh, yeah," she said, awkwardly. "Tell me what your mother is like?"

And I struggled with what to say. Who was Fallon? But I knew the woman who raised me, and I told Malachi all about her. I told her how my mother lost her sight, knitted all our clothes by hand, and made the best potato and beet soup. That was all I knew. I never knew the version she did—the one who rode a wyvern and was stripped of the death quell.

But the more I found out, the more I felt like I knew her— hidden in disguise with a faux frosted coat. The lies she'd spewed for years. Was it lies? Was not knowing of her forbidden power considered a lie?

The wind dragged through us. "You're lucky to have a family," she said softly. "I would love to meet your mother one day."

"We could fly back during Winter Solstice when we have our holiday. It's the most beautiful time to visit," I said.

Malachi grinned. "I'd love to."

I should have asked about her siblings. I should have wanted to know more about Malachi and her family. I sensed that soft part in her, but I couldn't for some reason.

We reached the combat grounds, and my heart dropped when I saw Bridger and Damien pinned against each other.

Summer and Winter.

Bridger struck two icicles into each palm, raising them above his head before thrusting them at Damien's shoulder. With a swift motion, Damien caught them mid-air, his muscles flexing with power. He let out a primal grunt as he threw the ice down to the ground, shattering it. The shards scattered, and with a flash of movement, glass whirled around him, forming a dozen sharp spheres that shot straight for Bridger's chest.

Bridger cursed. "Not so small of pieces, man. I don't want to spend the next day picking shards out of my arm."

Damien countered each Bridger's throws, always one step ahead. "Come on, Bridger. You can break a helpless first-year's wrist and torment her for days, but you can't fight someone your size?"

Shit. They were talking about me. But… I never told Damien about most of the torment.

Malachi nudged me. "You should know Damien wins every round."

I rolled my eyes. "He can't win every round."

"We both know what you are doing," Bridger hissed. Three icicles grew within the frost. "This is hardly fair." He glared at the combat professor, then aimed those three daggers at Damien's heart.

Damien dodged the ice with a quick shift. "And what is it that I am doing exactly?" He cocked his head to the side, grinning.

"You're a filthy mind reader. Turn off your quell, and let us see how well you fight," Bridger spat.

Mind reader. Had I heard that right?

Damien mentioned he had two quells. Flame churned in my guts, and I thought I'd hurl ash if I moved. I glanced at Malachi, whispering, "Did you know?"

"We're allowed secrets, Sev," she said. "Now you understand why Damien always wins. I'm guessing he pretended to get to know you?"

For a heartbeat, I wondered what Damien knew about me. But he shrugged at Bridger, not tuned into the tornado of my mind.

"And why would I do that? Your mind is interesting. Fuck, you love replaying that memory of her for me." Damien hissed and pinned him to the ground with his boot over his throat. "Shall I break your neck? I'm sure the healer is up for a challenge today."

Bridger spat blood as he sat up. "I'm done. You win this fight."

A growl released from Damien's parted grin. "I should drag you to Summer and let you shrivel in the sun."

Bridger snarled, lashing his hands around Damien's ankle. "At least I've made her scream my name. I should have carved my name into that bitch like your brother did. But you should know I never hurt her."

Damien took his boot off Bridger's neck. "But you watched. You allowed someone to torture a student under your mentorship. You enjoyed it." A tremor ravaged his spine. "Don't make me regret not killing you today."

Professor Knight snapped his fingers and Damien backed away. Then he gestured to me. "Your Serpent informed me you've inherited a Summer quell. Today is Night versus Summer for first-years."

I had no time to question as Antonia stepped in front of me. Three silver daggers sheathed her thighs, including one I recognized on Malachi before. Her hair was braided back. Shadows followed her quick steps—followed my trail of ash like a phantom ghost stalking my every move, including my courteous bow. She reminded me of a cat with her slicked hair and feline composure.

Monty yelled, "No quells, first-years."

She shot a vicious smirk at me, curling her fingers. I felt for my dagger and swung at her side. Ropes of flame twisted inside me, and I swore if she cut me, I'd bleed ash.

I met Archer's gaze—knuckle under his chin. Eyes watching my every breath.

My hands touched her arm, and she jolted back, curling her bottom lip. "She's going to burn the fields." Her finger pointed toward a burnt patch of grass with a charred impression of my boot. Myla flicked her palm barely above her hip, and a hiss of steam sounded from my skin.

Monty called the match. "Severyn, forfeit your dagger to Antonia. The use of quells in your first year is prohibited during combat."

I didn't bother asking why. I knew Monty would make up some bullshit reason that our quells were unstable. And perhaps he was right. Maybe I couldn't control this quell.

I threw her the dagger Charles gave me, and she dragged her finger down the tinted-blue handle. "This shall look lovely with my collection," she said, placing it into a leather holder as she joined Alaric.

I supposed they were back together.

Combat was over, and I was back on day one—daggerless.

Damien left without me. I ran after him, yanking his elbow. "What the hell was that?" I asked.

"I believe Monty was scolding you for using your quell," he said sarcastically. I followed him past the infirmary doors and towards the dragon fields.

As spring yielded to summer's heat, the air grew heavier, pressing against my skin. I tugged off my cardigan, knotting it around my waist.

I turned to Damien, narrowing my eyes. "You can read minds."

He stiffened, his usual smirk faltering. "I don't know what you're accusing me of," he said smoothly.

"You know exactly what I mean." I stepped closer, heat rising to my cheeks. "You can read minds, since when?"

"For about six years," he said. "It's common in Summer to gain your quell during Harvest Festival."

I curled my hands into fists, fighting off the ravenous burn in my fingers. "How does it work? Can you read my mind now?"

"Normally, it's a blur of voices all screaming. Once I know the sounds, I can learn to shift through them. I've gotten quite attuned to your sound." He closed his eyes. "Yes, I can hear your mind right now, Severyn."

"And are you reading my mind now?" I muttered.

"Not intentionally, but see, we're conversing, and I hear two of your voices. I never lied. I told you on the first night we met I prefer to keep my quell private. The thing is, Sev, you lied to me today. Quite frankly, you lie a lot."

My face fell. "I have no idea what I'm doing, Damien."

He stopped walking and grabbed my wrist. "Do you trust me? I know it's only been a week, but… I want you to trust me."

He looked ashamed, and as my silence screamed back, I couldn't control the voice in my mind. "If you know everything, you'll understand how alone I feel right now."

"Answer my question. Do you trust me?" His hand glided the shaft of my forearm until his fingers curved my neck, my jaw.

I leaned into his touch. "Yes," I breathed. The first truth to spill beyond my tongue and ink-stained fingers.

I trusted Damien.

"I won't let anyone hurt you." He brushed my streak behind my ear. I curled my hands around his jaw, leaning in to kiss him, but he shifted back. "You don't want to kiss me, Sev. Not now."

I leaned back on my heel. "I thought you liked me. Do you… not…" I cut my breath off, biting my tongue.

"I'm two things, Severyn. One, I don't overshare. Two, I don't believe in fables. This is not the moment for our first kiss. Not when you've been in the forests for a night, lying about the most important bond in your life."

"I'm… sorry." Flinching, I kept my gaze low. "I should have told you the truth."

He changed the topic. "Cain's shield snapped when he felt your power. The man is a hound for sensing quells and saw something dark in you today. I saw his mind." A gust of wind hit my face.

"Archer thinks Myla died that day at the trial," I whispered. "I… saved her. Revived her—I'm still trying to grasp it."

His hands smothered my lips. "I'm not the only one whose quell can listen to silent conversations. We'll discuss this later."

I nodded.

Chapter 13

Rows of dragons lined the sprawling fields.

Emerich's sea of green was the first one to approach us. Ciaran's midnight scales gleamed under the sun. Archer was nearby.

A few dragons circled the grounds for prey. Most lounged, waiting for their riders.

A senior student I'd never seen before made his way across the field, eyeing me down. He looked to be from an Autumn realm, bearing the same amber-colored eyes as Malachi. He wore a Serpent pin, and I assumed he was in the lead to claim the next heir.

"The pigeon fields are on the other side of the campus, Winter," he said with a cocky grin. "Saw you here the other day. I figured someone would have told you."

A shadow flew above, and Naraic landed behind me with a growl, curling his snarled lip. He placed one claw protectively in front of my boot. "This is Skia," I said. "My dragon."

The redhead jerked back, and his eyes darted between Naraic and me. From that beat of silence, I feared he knew who Naraic was. I didn't imagine there were many white-scaled dragons in Verdonia, but he certainly was the only one at the Serpent Academy.

He scoffed, muttering as he walked toward Tydon, the Serpent of Autumn, "That thing looks like a walking corpse."

Archer appeared in a shadow beside Ciaran, leading her to the middle with a leather riding suit shrugged across his shoulder. Malachi stood beside a lean, grey wyvern, and my heart sank seeing Astoria for the first time. Horns trailed the beast's slender neck. Her right eye was scarred, and the dragon looked like she'd survived a war and back, with patches of discolored and torn scales.

Archer threw some leathers at me. "Change," he hissed low. "Your clothes will be shredded the moment you're airborne."

I glanced around, conscious of the dozens surrounding me. "In the middle of a field?"

Archer threw his arm up, and darkness swallowed me whole. I quickly shrugged off my uniform and slipped into the form-fitting leather suit and matching black jacket. Stepping out from the shadow.

Archer dropped the shield and addressed the crowd. "Normally, we don't have riders joining us this late, but Severyn Blanche has bonded with Ciaran's cousin, so I've made an exception. I hope you are all kind to her during her first session."

Monty grinned, his eyes lingering on the leather suit that clung to my form. "Damn, Winter," he muttered under his breath.

But my attention was elsewhere—on Damien. His gaze was like a weight on my back, heavy and unwavering.

Knox mounted his silver wyvern, a creature that could have easily been a distant relative of Astoria. Nearby, Everett climbed onto his burnt-orange scorpius-blade, its piercing golden eyes gleaming fierceness.

I couldn't help but watch Everett and Knox. They were too close—too familiar. It was strange to see Knox so carefree, laughing beside his rival, and for a brief moment, I felt a pang of jealousy. I'd never seen him like this.

Antonia arrived a moment later. "Alright, let's see if she's as fast as her legacy mother," she said.

Archer gestured to the crowd. "Everyone mount your dragons. Today, we'll go over the basics and obstacle obstruction."

A few groans rippled through the group. I knew Archer did this for me, but the intensity of the other riders' glares still hit me hard. As I approached, Naraic bowed low. I grazed my heel over a rib as I mounted. "Sorry," I whispered, struggling to lift my leg.

Damien noticed my struggle. "Do you need a lift?" he asked.

Testing his abilities, I stared.

He raised a crooked brow, his lips marred by a slow smile. He placed his arms around my waist and lifted me. My leathers held Naraic's scales more tightly than on our first flight. I balanced, wrapping my arms around his broad neck.

"Stay close to me," Damien yelled as he approached Emerich.

Archer took the lead, and Ciaran's black wings spread wide, staining the clouds with a smudge of darkness. Naraic clawed at the grass before beating his wings and taking off.

Further down the field, metal poles struck through the ground with large circular obstacles. Emerich skimmed through three of them with a twist of his wings. Naraic followed suit, ripping us through two.

"He's fast. You should try out for the Skyfall race in a few weeks," Damien's voice echoed through the mulched sky.

The wind smacked my face. "What exactly is the Skyfall race?" I asked, wing-to-wing. "Apparently my mother won two years in a row. Also, I don't feel very welcome here."

"It's a dragon race through every trail and realm. You get your portrait on the wall of legacies, not to mention points at the Serpent Bid. And about the red-head. Forget him. He's only pissed Malachi will claim his leader spot at the bid."

"I have more questions. Do I dare ask what happens at the Serpent Bid?"

"Yeah, the Serpents bid on who they want to earn the title," Damien explained, his voice casual. "It also determines the leader of each sector. Some say the more bids you get, the more likely you are to become a Serpent. It's a bartering system across the land—think of it like a lottery. Whoever gets placed first gets a shiny pin and the chance to duel the Serpent during the year-end trial."

We went through another hoop. "That sounds barbaric—" Naraic took a sharp right turn, narrowly swinging me off. I caught my breath, finishing my sentence, "So, the Serpents choose the heir?"

"Not exactly," Damien corrected with a smirk. "The Serpents bid on the top six for the final trial. It's also a system for bartering and deals. Say, your father voted for me and I won—then he'd get his share of the spoils. Serpents make all the official bargains there. I take it you don't know much about it?" He grinned, then pointed toward the horizon. "Enough politics, follow me."

"Bargains?"

Naraic grunted, and I tightened my thighs in assurance as we followed Damien over the sprawling mossed peaks. Naraic flattened his wings as we dove over the mountain and flew above the sea. The grey water seemed to stretch forever, and I felt small on this island, knowing Winter brewed in Frozen Valleys and Summer's belch was a hot wince compared to me.

Naraic clawed the water with a single nail, misting my boots. "It's breathtaking," I said. The whooshed flame in my guts simmered, still tingling in my clenched fingers.

"Wait until we're no longer in the academy, and you have your entire life to fly anywhere in Verdonia. When I looked at you, I knew you weren't a griffin rider."

"And dragon riders have a certain look to them?" I asked.

"You are a natural rider. Most first-years wouldn't dare fly this far from the fields. Your mind is… chaotically the most peaceful thoughts I've ever heard."

"How can something be chaotic and peaceful?"

"You never gave up when most would. I mean… you were completely isolated for your whole life."

I stared off distantly, unsure how to respond to that.

Naraic was in my head. *"Do I have permission to show off? I can do a backflip."*

Speaking through our bond felt strange. *"I don't think I can hold on."*

"We have lots of time to practice before the Skyfall race."

"Did you… want to do the race?" Naraic veered left, back to the field.

"I never got the chance before."

My heart strummed a half-beat in my chest. *"Okay, we can do it. But let's avoid flips until I can get on you without help."*

"Fine."

Naraic looped through three obstacles, up and down. My stomach whirled before he descended, carefully coming to a gallop before Ciaran. "I said no flips," I seethed at Naraic.

"It was only a test. Now the Lynch won't think you're weak."

Archer nodded, shielding a flat hand over his eyes from the sun. "Good job, Blanche." His voice hinted with humor. "But it's not very formal to be lifted onto your dragon. Perhaps Damien Lynch should keep his hands to himself."

I ignored the last part, wiping my brow. "How do I sign up for the Skyfall race?"

Archer pursed his lips together, and that humor dimmed. "No," he said.

"I wasn't asking for permission," I scoffed.

"Your dragon is far too weak for the Skyfall competition."

Ciaran huffed. "I think Ciaran would disagree."

He eyed Ciaran down. "I told you she was not ready."

"But I am ready. I just need some training, and *Skia* wants to," I hissed. "You said I'm a natural rider."

"As your Serpent, I forbid you." He crossed his arms over his broad chest, and we began a staring game. Eyes of silver held me hostage—until shouting started across the field.

Archer brushed past me, his words causing my throat to tighten. "Someone has fallen."

A split second of fear came when I turned around to see the auburn hair of the male, stilled, as his legs jutted in an unnatural direction.

Everett.

Knox approached the bloodied figure. Then, a distant wail sounded. I couldn't stop the all-consuming grief. I ran towards Knox, ripping his thrashing hands away from Everett's broken body. Death, as slow and quick as it could be, knew no bounds,

Damien ran, skidding to his knees and pressed his finger against Everett's pulse. "He lost his balance and fell."

Monty shook his head. "Always a shame when an experienced rider falls. One less to claim the title." He swayed his eyes over the surrounding Day students, including Knox. "Who will be the next lead, any takers?"

His scorpius-blade cried a mournful hum, her head slumping over Everett's body. I dragged Knox away from Everett. "It's okay, Knox. Everything will be okay," I shushed, wrapping my arms around his neck.

Knox paled, his chin trembling as he faced me. "You don't understand, Sev. I—I cared about him… I wanted more time! I deserved more time."

My throat tightened, tears streaming down my cheeks. I had no words of comfort. "I'm sorry, Knox."

He shoved my reaching hand away. "I want to be alone."

Archer threw a shield of shadow around Everett's body, his eyes slightly glazed as he commanded, "Class is over. Get back to your dorms. Now."

The crowd of riders began to disappear back to the castle, whispering amongst themselves. Even Monty didn't stay for his own student.

Antonia's fingers twitched as she stood pale-faced towards Archer. "Sir… he—"

A shadow shoved her across the field. "Antonia, leave."

Damien motioned with two fingers as he called my name.

I crept through the shield of shadows as Damien spoke to Archer. "Should we send a letter home to his parents?" I asked, trying my best not to throw up as I stared at the blood-soaked fields. Everett's neck was broken, and his arms were pinned unnaturally back.

He was dead. I knew he was.

Damien glanced at Archer, hesitating. "I don't think that will be necessary."

"He deserves a proper burial," I cried. "He deserves to be mourned!"

Damien crouched, his voice lowering. "Myla was dead on the beach. You brought a dead dragon back from the grave after two years. You can save him."

Archer clenched his jaw. "You can't be serious. It's… unnatural."

I shook my head. "I can't… I'm not doing that."

Damien huffed. "Your mother played God during her time here. Perhaps this is nature correcting itself by giving the daughter of death herself the ability to heal. There's only one way to find out." His eyes traced the caked blood crusted on Everett's ear.

"I can't."

He gripped my wrist, dragging me down. "Sev. Let's try. Knox won't recover from this. I read his mind."

I nodded as I sank to my heels. "What if it doesn't work?" I whispered.

"Then he's dead," said Damien. "But your brother needs Everett."

I pressed my hands against the grit of Everett's cheeks like I'd done with Myla. Knox lost his brother. I wanted Knox to be happy.

We all waited, hovering around Everett as if we'd see that first thump of his chest. I fell back, staring at Damien. "My mother's quell may have been dark and willed death, but I am not the light."

Everett heaved forward, his palm flat across his chest. "Holy shit." The color drained back into his cheeks as he ran a hand through his blood- and dirt-caked hair. "What happened?"

"You fell off Iridis," said Archer, placing his palm on Everett's chest. "You broke a few bones—it's best not to make sudden movements until the healer can look at you."

Archer met my gaze. Fear—or something—stared back, but I couldn't miss the hint of disgust in his curled lips as he helped Everett up.

Wind slashed through the shield of shadow, and in stepped Malachi. "Don't worry, I'll take him to the infirmary," she said. "Sev, make sure you're home tonight. We have a lot to discuss."

Damien helped me off the ground, brushing a flake of blood off my thumb. "You are the light, Severyn."

I nodded through a wave of sickness. Ropes of flame withered around my guts. I saw Archer's slight curl of his outstretched fingers as shadows simmered my burn. He seemed to be the only one aware of the nausea roiling inside me.

Archer whispered, "Not a word of this to anyone, not even Knox. Malachi can listen through the wind, so there's no point in keeping it from her."

I leaned against Damien. "They're going to strip me of my quell," I said. "Professor Cain suspects something dark in me already."

Archer rolled his shoulders. "Just lay low for now. Training for Skyfall will only draw unwanted attention to you. If the professor suspected your forbidden quell, he would have told the headmaster by now. The healers are a bandage compared to you."

My head began to whirl. "I need sleep."

Damien exhaled. "I'll walk you home."

Chapter 14

I sat on my bed beside Damien, fisting the cotton blanket. "Do you think they will force me out of the academy?" I asked.

"Saving a life is hardly a negative thing. You gave Everett a chance today." Damien leaned closer to me, our shoulders brushing against each other. "You were meant to find Naraic, albeit you lied to me about him, but he was yours to bond with."

"You always seem to know what to say." Heat rose to my cheeks. *Of course*, he did. He was reading my mind.

Damien sighed loudly. "I don't do it often, and I shut myself out whenever I hear my name in your head. Shielding works, but it gives me massive headaches after hours of holding it. I don't want to invade your privacy."

I laughed nervously. "I guess there's no hiding anything."

Damien groaned, jerking his face towards the door. "Malachi's thoughts are loud. She'll be here in three, two, one."

Malachi stepped inside. "Was I interrupting?"

I flashed a quick wink at him. "No, Damien was leaving."

"Good, I'm exhausted. I spent an hour beside Everett. He nearly tore my hand off as his bones reset. Knox knows he's alive. He nearly fainted when he walked into the wing." She swayed her hand, gesturing to the slim distance between Damien and me. "We have much to discuss, including your quell, Naraic, and why Damien Lynch is sitting on your bed close enough to kiss you."

Damien raised his hands defensively. "I'll see you tomorrow, Sev." He closed the door, and Malachi turned on her heel and faced me.

"Archer wasn't joking when he said you can hear through the wind," I said.

Malachi fell into her bed, sprawling out. "Okay, go ahead and ask."

"Ask what?"

"About Damien. What do you want to know?"

I laughed nervously. "Nothing is going on between us. He's kind to me."

Malachi waved her hand. "Their mother died when the three boys were teenagers. Their father, Victor, is the Serpent of Ravensla. They have another brother named Kian, who's a year younger than us. Their mother, Reina, was a Shadow, born in Demetria, the Night City, and she was a bargain to marry Victor."

"Their mother was a bargain?"

"Most Serpents do not believe in love. They feel marriage is only a contract to bind realms. In Victor's case, he bartered the sunlight to a few realms in exchange for marriage. He's a power-hungry man."

I stopped her before she could go on. "Malachi, I'd rather him tell me. If he's comfortable." I crawled under the covers, extinguishing the lantern on my side. "Besides, we are just friends. I'm not sure he wants to be anything more than that."

"Not from the way he stood up for you in combat. Damien would be the last of my worries. When Klaus passed, Archer shut his borders down for months. Everyone was surprised to see him as a mentor this year. It nearly killed him losing Klaus. They were friends."

That pain was back in my throat, a mix of guilt and something else. "You knew?"

"Gemini dragons are extremely rare," Malachi said. "They're two bonds forged into one, like that three-headed dragon my grandfather has. Ciaran is yours, just as much as Naraic is. I think the entire Continent has kept an eye on those two. Most years, no one claims the title, and lindworms are nearly as rare as Gemini dragons. It's a battle to the death, but the real kill shot is the one who takes the power of the Serpent."

She yawned and stretched. "I don't believe in coincidences. You were meant to have this power, and you were meant to find Naraic." She rolled her eyes. "And you can't keep secrets from me. The wind hears all."

"What is the wind saying now?"

She laughed. "That we found our first thing in common. We are both evading death."

I traced the moon's glow on the ceiling. "Thank you for being my friend. I didn't have many growing up," I whispered. "And taking care of Everett. I don't know how you handle all this grief."

"Of course we are friends," she said. "I find comfort in faults, and when you're the last sibling alive holding onto a dying title, you tend to fade into the grief and sadness."

* * *

A week passed since Everett fell. Knox didn't question it, and I was thankful.

I avoided Professor Cain in class, quietly warding my flame in the back of the oval windowed room. And I thought Cain feared me a little, feared the wispy black flame I'd drawn all week.

I'd won a single dagger off Margaret all week, and with whatever the Serpent Bid was, I doubted my lone dagger screamed leadership material.

Damien led the Summer students into the trails. He wasn't a hands-on mentor. Saani waited by the entrance for him after we'd strolled aimlessly for hours. Even the beasts of Summer seemed subdued.

Dragon riding had been postponed for three days due to a Serpent outing. I'd watched Archer and Monty fly westbound outside my window, Ciaran's midnight wings cutting through the clouds. Night and Day were breathtaking: the moon and stars tangled in Monty's golden rays. It was almost impossible to believe we had enemies when our opposites lived as neighbors.

A pull tightened in my chest as the days dragged on, and by the third, that tether snapped, coiling around my ribs and squeezing my heart. I didn't understand the longing for something I barely knew, the suffocating ache that gripped my lungs every time I glanced at the stars.

Knox was my opponent today. We'd fought as kids until we bled or screamed for Charles to intervene. Knox never went easy on me. I'd managed to land a few hits, even pressing the blunt edge of a dagger to his throat, but he always turned the tables, kicking it from my hand to reclaim the only dagger I'd won all week.

Damien met me at the fields later that evening. He looked freshly showered, his hair slicked back. I caught a trace of his cologne from several feet away. "I want to take you somewhere tonight," he said, his voice smooth. "A quiet place I found during my first year."

"He smells nice," Naraic rumbled down our bond, lounging in a patch of fresh dew.

I smirked. "He does."

"I thought he put cologne on for me."

Damien stepped closer. "Need help mounting?" he asked, reaching for my waist before I could answer.

I might've let him, just to feel his arms around me, but I turned as his fingers brushed my ribs, my breath catching. "No, I need to do this myself. But thank you for the offer."

"Klaus was never this awkward on his dates. Don't ask about them; he'd scorch me from the grave," Naraic teased.

I glared at him, forgetting to use our bond. "Remember when I saved your life?"

Damien arched a brow. "I can't hear what goes on between you two, you know," he said, running a hand through his hair. "Though, sometimes, I wish I could. Naraic makes you laugh."

"He thinks you wore cologne for him. He's disappointed."

"What was that? You embarrassed him. Now get on me so we can leave this misery," Naraic grumbled.

Climbing onto Naraic was far from graceful, but I managed.

"Thank him for noticing," Damien said, winking as he mounted Emerich.

I ran a finger along one of Naraic's scarred scales. "If you're good, he might give you a chicken head. He has a few dried ones tucked away."

Naraic hummed and we took off into the veiled sky, following the current of Emerich's wings. We circled the castle, its stones swallowed by the black void below the clouds. Emerich banked left, leading us towards the Spring forests. The shield warding those vine-wrapped borders tingled against my skin as we entered. The air was thick with lavender and dew, each breath refreshing and sharp.

Damien pointed to a clearing below. Naraic followed, though less gracefully, his bat-like wings snagging on brambles. He hissed when a thorn clipped his scales during the landing.

The clearing glowed softly, lanterns hanging from trees, casting warm light over the daisies, and pale peonies carpeting the ground. Petals drifted across a broken cobblestone path in the gentle breeze. Damien dismounted Emerich and approached with an outstretched hand. "I know you don't need help, but please, take my hand."

I nodded, letting him pull me down. Our chests brushed, our breathing syncing as he steadied me. "Don't we risk expulsion being here?" I whispered. "This is Spring territory."

Damien smirked, his eyes glinting. "The girl harboring a forbidden quell is worried about expulsion?"

His hand brushed against mine, lingering just long enough for the warmth to reach me. "So, why are we in the Spring trails at night?" I asked, my voice carrying the weight of a thousand unspoken questions.

"Spring has special wards," he explained, his gaze sweeping across the clearing. "This place is shielded, suppressing quells. It's the only place where I can find peace." He raised his hands, as if to demonstrate the silence that hung in the air. "Here, I can't read your mind."

I held my palm out, eyes trained on it, waiting for a flicker, a spark, anything. But nothing came. The bond with Naraic, usually a steady hum, was eerily quiet. "Do you not enjoy hearing my thoughts?" I asked, the question slipping from my lips before I could stop it, my voice quieter than I intended.

The silence between us deepened, thick and heavy.

Damien exhaled. "I don't. But I know I'm in for a lifetime of brutal honesty, even if no words are spoken." He took my hand again, leading me towards a faint blue glow emanating from the bushes. A soft trickle of water dampened my face as a hot spring appeared through the trees.

"You mentioned you gained your quell at Harvest?" I asked.

"Harvest is a huge festival. It's the only time Summer's wards are down. I started hearing thoughts when I was fifteen."

"Malachi mentioned your mother… I'm sorry about your loss." I cringed, hating how I sounded. It was the same awkwardness I despised when people brought up Klaus.

Damien's voice wavered. "My mother went missing when I was fifteen. No one knew where she was, but I knew the truth. My father… he killed her. Archer didn't believe me until he became a Serpent. I was sent to boarding school at sixteen. Hearing that Archer claimed a title and I was accepted into the academy felt surreal. I haven't seen my father since."

I brushed my thumb over his knuckles. "You can't blame yourself for that."

"In a few weeks, my father will place his bid, and it won't be my name. Archer will make his bid, too, and it won't be yours. He may even drag you back to the Night realm after this year. He tries to shield his thoughts from me, but I know he's already plotting how to exist as a Serpent while bonded to your dragon."

I shook my head. "He can't do that. I deserve to be here just as much as he does."

"The moment I met you, I heard your thoughts and thought I was listening to my own. I thought, for once, I could have something that was only mine." Damien's fingers laced with mine. "You know I'll protect you. I don't know why, but I can't stay away."

"I feel the same way," I whispered.

"I've heard of worlds without dragons or quells. Where love isn't a contract but a promise. A man at boarding school spoke of such lands. I've often wondered if these wards are meant to keep us in."

"You remind me of my brother Cully. He always made me wonder what else is out there."

Damien sighed, gesturing to the spring. "Care for a dip?"

"Is it safe?" I asked, eyeing the bubbling water nervously.

"If I say yes, will you go in?" Damien grinned, already pulling off his shirt.

I looked away, my cheeks heating as I saw his toned figure. "Fine. Turn around."

Damien chuckled. "Severyn, I don't know how to tell you this, but seeing your bare shoulders is hardly scandalous."

"Then don't turn around," I muttered, slipping my outer shirt and slacks off.

Damien followed, his presence warm and steady as he wrapped his arms around me. His thumb gently brushed my cheek, sending a shiver down my spine, before he leaned in, his voice low. "I'm ready for you to kiss me."

Before I could form a response, his lips were on mine, soft and insistent. Everything else melted away—every worry, every doubt—until all that remained was the heat of his touch, the intensity of his kiss.

I pulled back slightly, my breath shaky. "It took you long enough," I teased, my smile barely containing the warmth spreading through me.

"I wanted to kiss you that first night. And yes, Severyn, you were sort of flirting with me, but you're terrible at it," he laughed. "This was easier than I thought."

His forehead pressed into mine, and we stayed like that for what felt like hours.

Kissing a Summer student was borderline callous. But frost never coated my fingers. I wasn't his poison. It would have made the perfect fable—ice and warmth, forced to sever. But two titles were up for grabs. And perhaps lust was my poison, but fuck, did making out with him feel like a damn cure.

He said, "I don't know anything, Severyn. But I know I care about you."

I rested against his chest, thumbing over the droplets. "I care about you."

"It's easier this way," he said softly.

"What's easier?"

"Nothing. We should head back. It's past midnight," he whispered once the air touched our sweltered faces. "Forget I said anything."

I shook my head. "Okay. *Yeah*, we have class in a few hours."

I was thankful he couldn't hear my racing mind while we waded through the water silently to shore.

Naraic and Emerich waited for us outside of the hot spring opening and flew us back to campus. We neared the shadowed dorms, and I thought he would kiss me again. I knew *he knew* I wanted him to from the screams in my mind.

But all he did was smile as a whisper escaped his clenched jaw, "Good night, Severyn. I enjoyed kissing you, but I don't want us to rush into anything."

I stifled the hoarse voice in my throat. Even my flames were simmered. "Good night, Damien."

I caught my breath as I leaned against the stone wall, my heart still racing from the kiss. Damien had kissed me. His presence lingered, warm and electrifying. I hugged my clothes to my chest, trying to steady myself before I made my way to the bath to wash off the remnants of the hot spring water.

The heavy stone door creaked open as I entered, the sound echoing through the room. I filled the large quart tub, the steam rising as the water swirled into the basin. With a sigh, I dropped my remaining clothes in a soft mound on the tile before sinking into the water. The warmth enveloped me, a welcome contrast to the confusion and heat still lingering in my chest.

I glanced at my reflection in the glass mirrors. I knew I would regret staying up this late once dawn hit in five hours. I knew, regardless, I would be tossing and turning in bed thinking about Damien—

The bathroom door creaked open.

I screamed, pressing myself into the corner of the tub. Archer stood frozen in the doorway, clutching his ribs. His eyes widened before he nearly slipped on the tile, spinning away. "Shit, why are you up? You could've locked the damn door."

No, no. Not now.

"The lock's broken," I stammered, my heart racing. "Damien guards the door for me." My eyes flickered to his bloodied skin, the lacerations that marred his arms and shoulders. He reeked of liquor.

Archer tensed, glancing at the mirror without looking at me. He didn't dare. "Get to bed. It's past curfew," he snapped, waving toward the door.

A cold knot twisted in my stomach. Four days. He'd been gone for four days. I reached for the towel, my voice barely a whisper. "You didn't answer my question. Why are you bleeding?"

"I'd rather not have a conversation while you are indecent. Please, Severyn, walk away." He raised his palm, and the lanterns flickered before going out one by one, leaving us in the dark.

"Well, now I can't see." Striding toward the door, I used the wall to balance myself.

He opened his palm, releasing one shard of pure starlight that hung to a lantern. "Is that better?"

"No. Tell me where you were." If Klaus's death wounded him, what would his loss do to me? I was weak. My bond with Naraic was weak.

He sighed, his voice heavy. "There were a few attacks in Verdonia. We lost nearly a hundred guards today. An Autumn realm has been destroyed." His shoulders slumped forward, and for once, I believed the mask he wore had slipped.

"Is Charles…" I couldn't bear to finish the question.

"Your brother is fine. The wards at Malvoria should hold for a few months."

The tap dripped behind us, the sound echoing through the starlit room. Darkness had never appeared so radiant, prisms of light scattering across the stone walls. He hadn't turned around yet, but I saw it—the breaking—within the slight tremble of his spine.

When power slipped, it was loud—the shakes, the quivers. Archer couldn't hide misery from me. I'd grown up around it.

"And what about you?" I stepped towards him, daring to reach for the cut on his shoulder. "Are you okay?"

He raised a hand. "I am fine, Blanche."

I gave him a flat stare.

"Let me see your cut." My fingertips skimmed the slice on his neck, and his eyes, like chips of ice, met mine.

He didn't pull away. "Your hands are warm," he muttered. "I'm not… used to it. Warmth."

Built like a fortress, I couldn't help letting my gaze wander as I took him in. If he were a statue, it would've been made from the finest clay, every muscle and bone perfectly chiseled.

"It's the flame," I said softly.

Lowering my hand, his fingers closed around my wrist, sending a shock of panic through me. A silent yelp escaped as he twisted my body, slamming me against the wall. His shadow relic flared beside mine, rimmed with ash, cold and unyielding.

"I don't want you to care about me," he growled, his voice low and dangerous. "I don't want you around me."

I stared at his hands gripping my wrist, my heart pounding in my chest. "I didn't steal Klaus's power, if that's why you hate me."

"I could easily kill you," he growled, leaning in so close that I could taste the shadows—coal and mist swirling between us. "I want to kill you, but I won't. Naraic's bond is weak. Your life is in my hands. Don't think for a second that Naraic chose you, because he didn't."

A cry broke through my tightened throat, and ash-like flakes swirled in the space between us. What was happening? He saw it—his eyes tracking the darkened specks on my skin. Our skin. His gaze ignited, a storm of fury and fire.

"How am I supposed to treat you?" I asked, my voice cracking. "You disappear for days… I… want to know you."

His thumb skimmed my jaw, brushing away a single drop of water. "You knew I was safe. You can start by pretending all you know is my name."

I swore he stole the breath from me. Maybe I had known he was safe. There was darkness looming in his irises, the same dusted shade of ash coating our bodies.

"Let me go," I hissed.

"And then what? You run to my brother?" His gaze flicked to the pendant around my neck.

I raised a brow, refusing to rise to the bait. "No, I'm going to bed."

He stepped away, his figure nearly swallowed by the shimmering starlight. "Don't use this bath anymore. It's not safe."

I couldn't force myself out of that room quickly enough. Clutching the towel to my chest, I darted to my dorm.

What was that?

Chapter 15

Damien arrived at dawn every day for the next week. We'd spent most afternoons on the fields with Naraic and Emerich racing through obstacles for the Skyfall tournament. We never spoke about that kiss, and I feared Damien regretted it—and I tried my best to forget it.

Or perhaps he'd seen Archer and my encounter. My mind had coaxed that memory up more than once since it happened.

Myla gained her first sword two days before, a silver-handled blade from the Day realm. And Archer made it clear he didn't want me to race. His kindness faltered when we returned to advanced dragon riding. Not that Naraic needed it. I'd learned that Naraic was seventy-one. But he was forbidden from speaking of past riders—another ward. Professor Cain hadn't pressed on my quell either, but I couldn't help but notice his lecture on forbidden quells during our history lesson that morning.

Cain tapped his quill on his wooden desk. "Back in the settler days, quells knew no bounds. There were even quells that absorbed the powers of others. Forbidden quells disobey nature, such as those involving life and death. Twenty-seven years ago, a Serpent Academy student could kill with a single touch. Her wielding knew no limits; anyone who stepped towards her shield met a fatal end. Does anyone know what happens when someone is found to possess a forbidden quell?"

Malachi raised her hand. "Their quell is stripped from them."

Professor Cain shouted, "Excellent, Herring! I suspect you are familiar with forbidden quells."

Antonia raised her hand. "How many forbidden quells have been found at the academy?"

Cain pushed his square glasses back. "About ten. The most recent was two years ago. It's never a good thing when one is found."

I asked without raising a hand, "How are they found?"

"Well, Severyn, the Malvoria guards are trained to seek out those harboring forbidden quells. Usually, I can suspect it as well."

Antonia smirked. "Say her name. Fallon Blanche harbored the forbidden death quell, and her daughter sits among us. How do we know Severyn isn't one of them?"

Cain clenched his jaw. "I suspect many things of Severyn Blanche but not a forbidden quell."

Antonia rolled her eyes. "The daughter of the death quell should be watched. I don't feel safe knowing she sleeps doors away from me."

Professor Cain nodded. "Antonia, if you are scared, might I suggest strengthening the shield in your room." He flicked his wrist, shattering her shadow shield into a crumble of darkened spheres. "Class will be dismissed tomorrow as I have a meeting with the guards," he muttered. "Now, let's see those shields."

We shielded for the rest of the class. My flame whirred and hummed, growing from my relic into a fiery ball. The flame warmed me, and Myla, who sat across, cursed as her ice melted into a puddle.

I quickly shot an apprehensive grin at her, whispering, "I'm sorry."

Myla pursed her lips. "It's fine," she hissed, slamming her warding book closed and moving three chairs over.

Cain called the class, and I waited for the rest of the students to leave. Damien must have read my mind and knew I wanted to stay back and speak to the professor because he gave me a nod as he left the room.

I strummed my fingers on the table as Cain organized his desk. "Professor Cain, did you know my mother?" I asked.

His eyes hardened on the stone ground. The door slammed shut as he raised his palm, and every vial and liquid shuddered. He spoke quietly, "We attended the academy together."

"What happened to her?" I prepared to be shocked. It seemed nothing about my mother was expected.

"I've always sensed quells, and when Fallon's quell arrived, I was sick for a week. Your mother confided in me. I tried to help her, but I knew then what power she held."

My chest tightened. "Did you tell anyone?"

"I had no choice. Your mother was something the academy hadn't seen before, something forbidden and unnatural. I tried to warn her, but the king took one look at her and stripped her of her quell. I can't speak about what she went through here." His eyes closed as if a memory haunted him. "Your mother was born in Ravensla. The flame makes sense," Cain muttered. "Fallon lived a tough life before coming to the academy."

"What?" I gasped. "My mother was born in Ravensla?"

Cain pressed his lips together. "You are the burning heir of Summer, Severyn. Victor Lynch and your mother fought for the same title. Those two were… chaos together. I am glad to see you and the glass-wielder as friends."

Damien and I were rivals… and I was simply another Bridger stealing his rightful heirship. "What did you mean before when you sensed something in me?"

"A life saved demands remission. A life saved is a life lost, and you are not strong enough to hold that. It is called a Soul Weaver or as the forbidden passages say… a necromancer. You possess the extraordinary ability to heal beyond blood and wounds—you can heal the soul."

"Are you going to tell the headmaster?" I whispered, fisting my riding leather jacket.

Cain closed his eyes. "Does it make me any better? Those who survive having their quell stripped are an anomaly. I—I'm tired of holding that darkness. You cannot save lives, Severyn. Seven souls linger to you… I can hear them screaming. And that is the darkness I sense in you."

Seven souls. Archer had seven keys. Meaning a life would have to be lost for me to save one.

It all sank in. Guilt and shame reefed my insides. "I have to go."

I ran from that room, from the walls that seemed to suck me in further, from his eyes that held onto me with such might I could not bear another second.

I was simply a vessel between life and death. I ran to Naraic, dropping to my knees. My hands pressed into the dirt as I met his violet eyes. He already knew my whirling thoughts but still nuzzled his sharp snout into my chin.

"Who am I to say should live?" I'd gotten better at speaking only through the bond.

"Perhaps those lives should not have been taken in the first place. Your quell broke through when Archer saved you."

"Do you think I would have bonded with another dragon if Klaus were alive?"

Naraic was silent for a moment. *"I do not."*

"Why?"

"We knew you would come. There is no reality where Klaus survives. I know the names of each rider who will choose me, living and unalive. I knew you were next. I just didn't know how exactly."

"You knew? Klaus knew?"

"When a dragon is born, we have roots. Every hundred years, a new root grows... every hundred hatchlings have a choice. Our bloodlines are tied, yet Ciaran and I were the hundredth egg and when our first riders chose us, it split us between flame and shadow. I did not know how you would find me. I just knew you would."

"I don't understand."

"You will someday. When you are ready to understand."

* * *

Damien waited by the fields for our private combat lesson, dressed in traditional Serpent Academy black and green. The breeze picked up, yet I sensed summer would be in full rein within the following days.

Picking through my mind, Damien gave me a tight-lipped expression. "Do you want to talk about your conversation with Cain?" he asked, placing a clipped sphere in my hands.

"No. I'd rather spar until I can only think about my sore body."

Damien cocked his head. "And you choose sparring to be that activity? I can think of other ways of getting hot and heavy that don't involve a knife to your throat." He twirled the dagger in his fingers. "Unless you're into that."

"I'm not in the mood to pretend flirt. Not when the Serpent Bid is in a month, and I have yet to keep a single dagger in my possession during combat." I pressed the dagger's soft side into his chest, forcing him to step back.

"Pretend flirting?" Our daggers clanged as he lunged forward.

I grunted. "Yes. We kissed, and you now pretend like it never happened."

Within a second, the dagger was against my neck, his hazel eyes burning into my gaze. I held my breath as his other hand gripped my wrist. My back slammed into a tree as he skimmed the blade along my neck, not hard enough to draw blood.

"Do you want me to kiss you?" he mused.

Damien never scared me, but the look in his eyes was more primal. "Not like this."

"Your mind begs to differ. I'm a man of class, Sev, but my thoughts of you are more crude than the fable you've made about us in your mind. I'm not willing to risk a rider bond forming between us." He leaned in, and our breath formed as one. "You are always lost in thought." It was a complete topic change, but I was too annoyed to be embarrassed.

I watched his knee bend, bracing to pin me down. My spine scraped against the bark, jerking as his dagger tore through the air. I quickly swung at his leg, and a curse broke our feud of huffing.

"I don't care about a rider bond. I want you, and I don't know what you want."

My heart pounded.

If my mind were my setback, I'd engulf every thought in violent flames. I would breathe in smoke through every word spoken to me.

"You clearly know nothing about rider bonds and how they are formed."

I slammed my palm into his chest and hissed, "I do not disagree with you. Perhaps I've been rather distracted, and no, I don't know how those bonds are formed." Damien was the worst sparring partner I could have chosen. I needed someone who would not go easy on me and could not predict my every move. Preferably someone I hadn't kissed.

I dove right, but he was already there, his hands around my waist, pulling me closer. Our hips pressed together, and the dagger slid from his grasp, sticking into the grass. He shifted closer, and those hazel eyes softened under the moonlight.

"Stop," he whispered, his grip tightening, drawing me closer. "I wish I could shield around you, but it's difficult, and I'm afraid if I let you in, you won't understand my mind."

I swallowed the burning down.

"I understand," I said.

But I wasn't sure if I did, because it was happening again. Those tight grips of his fingers around my body made me believe he wanted me in another way. I knew I was clueless in every sense of romance, but this was not me being naïve. This was everything I'd read in the fables.

But Damien had told me he didn't believe in fairytales.

"Damien, I am in the run for only your father's title," I whispered in one defeated breath. "My mother was a Ravensla native. I didn't know." But clearly Archer did.

His forehead leaned into mine. "I know. I didn't want to tell you."

"This complicates things."

He shook his head. "My whole life has been a blur of jumbled thoughts and fragmented conversations. Constant noise. But with you, Severyn, I find peace. So forgive me for saying this, but I don't care about the rivalry. I never cared about earning a title. Your mother was born in Ravensla, and if you claim the Summer title, you'll become my father's heir."

"You may not want it now."

"You'll know when I change my mind because I could kill you without you ever seeing it coming. I hear every thought, every nerve that dares to move inside your body! And I'm afraid I'll hurt you someday." He hovered over my heart, dragging the dull end against the button loops on my shirt. "I'm fucked up, Severyn."

I reached my arm up, and he grabbed my wrist, pinning it against his chest.

He got close. One hand on either side of me, a breath separating us. I didn't push him away, but perhaps I should've been terrorized. Reckless, dangerous madness. Or, as Cain described, chaos.

"Damien," I breathed. "You don't scare me."

It was a lie, and he knew it.

"It doesn't hurt yet. Let's enjoy it while it lasts," he said.

He meant us. Someday, we would hurt the other.

* * *

Malachi's shadow flickered under the doorway of our room after Damien and I parted ways in the grand hall. I lingered outside, waiting for a moment of peace before facing her inevitable chatter about her latest date with Monty.

I desperately needed sleep.

But when the door creaked open, it wasn't Malachi. It wasn't even human.

A black-scaled creature lunged at me, its gaping maw lined with needle-sharp teeth. I screamed, stumbling backward over the shattered remnants of a golden eggshell. The creature slithered across the stone floor, its hiss slicing through the air as it coiled and struck again.

Panic coursed through me. I reached for my flame, but fear clogged my veins, and all I could muster was a wave of sweat. It lunged again, sinking its jagged teeth into my ankle. Pain seared through my leg as I kicked desperately, my breath hitching in terror.

I screamed again, kicking harder, but the creature's grip tightened. The pain was unbearable as I clawed at its eye, jabbing my fingers into the soft, wet iris. It reared back with a shrill hiss, but it didn't let go.

My vision blurred. The skin around my ankle turned pale, the bone nearly exposed. It lunged again, and in my scramble, I slammed my head against the tile floor. Stars exploded behind my eyes, the world tipping sideways.

Death had courted me many times. Born in the chrysalis of darkness, the womb of a woman who killed with her eyes and touch, perhaps I was destined to die this way—poisoned, broken.

Forbidden.

Maybe I saved those keys for myself.

In and out of consciousness, shadows engulfed me. I awoke on a velvet bed, a cold draft brushing against my cheekbone.

I groaned, stretching my arms as the memory of last night surfaced. The tight bandage around my ankle was a cruel reminder. Where the hell was I? The windows were shattered, letting in the icy wind. I limped toward the jagged frames and realized I was at the top of the castle, overlooking the griffin fields.

My clothes hung loosely, draping off my elbows. I gripped the wooden bedpost, steadying myself as my gaze landed on twelve silver-tipped arrows mounted on the wall.

And then, I saw it. That violet-eyed buttoned dress shirt hanging from the closet.

I snapped my fingers, summoning a small flame.

My knees buckled. "Holy shit!"

Archer stepped out of the shadows, his face carved in fury. "Someone tried to kill you by putting a snake in your room. When I find out who did that…"

"I did," I interrupted, my voice dry. "I found it on the first day. I thought it was a griffin egg… honestly, I forgot about it."

His thumb pressed against his temple, his jaw clenching. "You what?"

"I found the egg," I repeated, my tone defensive. "I kept it."

He studied me, his silver gaze piercing. "You poisoned yourself. I give it a year before the venom spreads to your heart." His hands curled into fists. "How could you be so reckless?"

"There's a cure, right?" I nearly fell back onto the bed.

"There is, but do you deserve it?" His voice was ice. "Do I deserve to be tied to you for the rest of my life, knowing how careless you are? Every time one of Naraic's riders dies, it weakens Ciaran. Fortunately, our bond is still weak. I have nothing to lose if I let you die."

I stifled a sob. "You wouldn't let me die."

"And why wouldn't I?" His voice dropped, venomous. "You're nothing but an inconvenience to me."

My throat tightened as I glanced at where the mark of my brother's name was etched into his skin. "Because Klaus meant something to you. If you let me die, you dishonor him."

His teeth bared in a silent snarl. "Don't bring Klaus into this."

"Why not? Because he was your friend? Because I'm just his annoying little sister? If you don't cure me, I'll find the cure myself."

"There is no cure for snake venom on this island, and the academy does not tolerate students who bring deadly serpent eggs into the castle."

The weight in my ankle finally registered as I collapsed. Cold hands caught my elbow, yanking me upright. Archer leaned in, his lips curling in spite. "Your entire foot is already numb. Perhaps by winter, you'll be gone."

"What do you want from me?" I whispered, holding his glacier-like gaze. "I thought we were… friends."

Archer's jaw tightened, his tall frame casting me in shadow. "I'll give you the cure on one condition."

"You're going to make me wait?" I hissed.

His icy stare bore into mine, unyielding. "My condition is this: I want you to take my father's title. You have a season to prove to the Serpents that you're worthy. In return for the cure, your life will no longer be your own. You'll be my personal weapon. I'm done playing games, Severyn."

"I can't do that to Damien."

"Dying for a boy you've known for weeks is desperate, Severyn. I'd rethink those words as you begin counting your breaths."

"Fine," I spat. "I'll try."

"I've warded our conversations so Damien cannot hear," he added coldly. "Whatever happens between us, he will never know."

"What about my leg? I can't feel my foot. How am I supposed to ride Naraic? Archer, you can't be serious."

"You'll regain feeling once you have the cure."

I clenched my fists, forcing back tears. "Why are you doing this?"

"I'm going to barter something at the bid, something your father needs to survive," he mused. "And I believe a few Serpents will quite enjoy that offer."

Anger flared within me, heat rising through my chest. Archer shifted his fingers, snuffing the flame in my hand with a shadow.

"Where are my clothes?" I snapped. "I can't leave your bedroom in your shirt."

"You don't have to worry about that. Half the academy already thinks you're fucking my little brother."

"Is that a problem?" I asked, cocking my head.

Archer scoffed. "You can do whatever you want, Severyn. But Damien will only hurt you in the end. My father wants Ravensla to stay in our family's line, but Damien will ruin it. The land will become barren before his first term ends if he claims the title. He's unstable and reckless. And you're just as foolish for trusting him."

"Is that so? He told me he doesn't even want the title."

My heart froze as his silver eyes darkened. I shoved my trembling hands behind me, refusing to let him see my fear.

"And you believed him?" He clicked his tongue. "You're a foolish girl. Do you simply fall for the first man who is kind to you?"

I ignored his last words. "How does *this* benefit you in any way?"

"A Serpent never reveals his barter before the bid." He stepped back into the shadows, and I found myself tracing the outline of his shoulders, following the sharp line of his jaw. He was wickedly beautiful. And I hated that I called him beautiful.

I fisted the oversized shirt, smelling only his rich whisky scent. Heat boiled within me. I could play his game. He wanted a pawn, but I would be the queen, and I knew my power. I was his gambit, and to hell would I allow him to break me.

'We knew you would come.' Had Archer planned this? Was it a lust for power, to bid something my father needed if I won Serpent? I remembered that letter, the swirled quill marks stating a failed bargain for my freedom would leave the Winter shield to shatter.

My freedom. Had father bid my freedom, and now whoever claimed it was taking it back?

* * *

I sat beside Naraic in the field the next day. With warding postponed, my thoughts simmered under the heat of the morning sun, my legs stretched out in its warmth. I'd already rewrapped the bandage on my ankle twice.

How could I keep this from Damien?

"Is Archer always an arrogant bastard?" I asked through the bond to Naraic.

"No."

"What was he like before?" I imagined becoming a Serpent did something to you. It rotted your mind from the core and made you feel invincible.

"Kind. When Klaus died, that kindness left. It is only a matter of time before you will care for him. Whether you like it or not, a bond will form between you. I trust Archer with my life, regardless."

"Why? He doesn't deserve our trust... not when he's forcing me to lie to Damien. Why would he ever want me to become his father's heir anyway?"

"Perhaps something far worse will become if Damien claims." Naraic stretched his wings in the single shred of sunlight, holding firm through the clouds. *"We are all bonded. Ciaran hears everything... Archer as well."*

"Through this bond?" Heat rose to my cheeks.

"I've cut her off, but Archer is strong enough to break through sometimes. His bond with you is different than most."

"Sometimes?"

"Ciaran called to you to find me. Archer could hear her. He knew what you were to him. Knew it from the day he heard your name. Trust him, Severyn."

"Why didn't you tell me?"

Silence.

"I did not know what you would be like."

Naraic didn't trust me at first because I was not Klaus. "I have combat in ten minutes. I'll find you at the fields in two hours."

Naraic grunted, tremoring his spiked tail.

I smiled at Myla as I reached the fields. After I melted her ice in class, it felt like a week had passed since we last spoke. Two swords were sheathed on either side of her narrow waist—one silver-tipped and the other with an opal handle from the Day realm. She had more weapons than any other first-year, even surpassing some seniors.

Professor Knight made Monty the instructor today. Monty acknowledged me with a swift nod as I stood across from Knox, whose eyes flared at me and my empty hands. I had no daggers.

Monty stretched his arms with a groan. He moved like the afternoon sun, casting rays of light across the grass.

"Those who have swords will spar against each other. Daggers, you will team up," Monty announced. His eyes narrowed at the two of us who were daggerless. "Those who do not have daggers will be granted the use of quells. Robi, you are against me. Severyn, you will duel Archer."

Heat prickled my palms. A shadow coiled at my feet, and in a heartbeat, Archer was standing inches away. Darkness spilled from his hands, fluid and graceful, stealing my breath. I bit back the curses threatening to slip free.

Draped in a black sleeveless top, his muscles rippled, veins pulsing with life. The serpent tattoo on his neck seemed alive, slithering and tightening with each of his movements. He leaned in, his closeness that of a predator savoring its prey—I was the prey he'd been hunting for hours.

A phantom wind teased my hair. "Be respectful and bow, Severyn Blanche," Archer said smoothly, dipping his head just enough to feign respect.

"Like hell," I hissed.

Monty craned his neck, flashing me a crooked grin. "She's a feisty one."

Archer lowered his head, hands laced behind his back. He motioned with his eyes for me to go first. *"Shall I heat you, Severyn?"* His voice was a static stroke in my mind.

Archer could speak to me telepathically, and it was worse than having my thoughts devoured by a mind reader. I didn't want his voice colliding with the walls of my mind, let alone to hear Naraic's and my private conversations.

Heat surged through my veins, pooling in my palms. Facing Archer made it easy to unleash the anger buried deep in my bones. I poured every bitter thought, every unsaid curse, into the black spark coiling in my hand. It slithered into a silent flame, snapping at his leather shoes just as he stepped back.

Too many channels converged—one Damien controlled, one only Naraic could hear—all fusing into a chaotic, unrelenting current.

I screamed in my mind, *"I wouldn't if I were you."*

A faint response echoed back, *"Are you threatening a Serpent?"* His brow arched in spite.

"Threatening you would be lighting your face on fire." I scoffed, shaking. Every vein within me felt like it might burst and spew molten blood.

"Is that all you have, Severyn?" Archer raised his palm, and a thundering shadow rippled from his body. His eyes glowed black as darkness consumed half the combat grounds. *"Now fight me or give up like you always do."*

A shaded rope seized my waist, dragging me closer. Archer grabbed my wrists, pinning them to his chest. I struck my flame, scorching his fingers and whatever fabric lay between my wrath.

"No," I hissed. *"I can't control it."*

"Keep your palms open. Klaus could light fires with his eyes. Do not wield the flame. Become it." He lifted his chin. *"Consume me."*

He was training me to use my quell. To control it. And as much as I hated him, I needed to learn.

A pale light shone from Monty's eyes, shredding through the darkness and turning the field into a haze of grey smog. Archer didn't release my wrists as I tried to pull back. Even his heart didn't quicken.

I braced, my body shaking. "I can't!" I yelled.

"Burn, Blanche," he said louder, his voice cutting down our faint bond. *"Burn me."*

His chest must be blistered by now—my fingertips branded into his skin, marking him with my own relic of hopelessness.

He kept my hands pinned above his heart. Three, four, five beats. That rhythmic hum picked up.

"You are the weakest one here. Not a single dagger, and you expect to fill Klaus' shoes. Show me what you have, Blanche."

I lifted my eyes to his shadowed face and swore his breathing became uneven. I gripped his shirt, fingers curling into the fabric.

He shoved my wrist towards the sky as ash rained from the clouds. The willow tree behind us burst into flames, and the grass beneath my feet formed a ring of fire. Every nail on my hand flickered with flame. Smoke, ash, and screams consumed the combat grounds.

And he didn't snuff out my fire with shadows. Instead, he allowed me to burn.

"She's going to burn the grounds to nothing," Everett hissed.

"Let her," Archer growled. Something dark flickered in his eyes as he held me against his chest.

Three more trees burst into flames as my eyes darted around. I fell to my knees, curling into a ball, burning my own flesh as I tried to stifle the ravenous flames. Hands gripped my shoulders—not Archer's, but Damien's.

"Look what you did," Damien yelled at Archer. "She's a mess!"

"I'd hardly call that a mess," Archer replied, throwing two daggers next to my knees—one with a handle dipped in ash, the other silver. "Severyn has earned quell rights during combat."

"Only second and third-years can use quells during combat. You saw her… she is… unstable with her power, brother." Damien's lip curled slightly. "You'll kill her if she can't control it!"

A gust of wind blew the ash away as Malachi lowered her arms, surveying me and my trembling body.

Archer squared his shoulders, staring at Damien. "Fire quells require release, brother. Severyn's skills are above the average flame wielder for a first-year. Would you not agree?"

"I agree there's a reason first-years are barred from quell use in combat," Damien replied. "You're making a mistake."

I had earned two daggers, but at what cost? Damien didn't believe I could handle it. Even Knox hesitated to step closer. The only comfort was his familiar golden eyes, staring at me from across the field, reading me up and down with his invasive quell.

I knew it was terror rippling from every pore in my body as Knox broke his hardened stance and cleared the distance between us. "Are you alright?" Knox asked.

"I'm fine," I said with another lie. Perhaps he sensed my fear. Maybe I would never be able to lie to Knox again.

It wasn't until I felt his arms lift me that I truly shattered. But the tears never came. They stayed locked behind dry eyes, replaced by a sudden, unnatural grin tugging at my lips. Knox was forcing me to be happy, shielding me from the humiliation of crying in front of my peers.

"Let's eat dinner together," Knox rasped. "They're serving cabbage soup tonight—do you remember how Mother used to make it after our first harvest?"

I nodded, following him across the courtyard.

The first harvest back in Northern Colindale was always a celebration. The sun blazed, brighter and warmer than it would be for the rest of the year. Fields sprawled with lush vegetation and ripe produce. I'd carry a basket through the orchard, plucking hellebore petals along the way. Mother would begin her canning rituals, and the entire valley worked tirelessly, sowing the next season's seeds before frost claimed the soil.

The train tracks always signaled the frost's arrival—the steel groaning as cracks splintered along its surface, screws glistening with a thin veil of ice. Life had felt simpler then, I thought, staring at my raw, blistered hands.

My ears rang as Knox gripped my shoulders. He deserved to know the truth. I could trust him. "You never liked Mother's soup," I teased, still giddy from whatever quell he'd inflicted on me.

"Better than whatever roadkill Father and Charles would bring home. I will never forget when we fried squirrel tails that one frost." Knox shuddered at the thought.

"Nothing quite like Colindale food," I said as we entered the large dining hall across from the library. Six rows of fifty-foot wooden tables were centered with green velvet benches. Savory spices wafted through the air. A serpent sculpture hung from the ceiling—lights flickered from the scaled body. Dozens of students sat, eating soup and sourdough bread. Knox went to the large pot and carried two bowls in his hands.

"What will we tell Father when he comes for the Serpent Bid? None of us are in the ranks to take over for him," I began. "It will ruin him."

"Then let it. The academy placed us, knowing our history. The Blanches have reigned over the frozen valley in Colindale for a hundred years. Father must have known about Klaus."

I knew Mother was born in Ravensla, but this unknown Day blood—what made it so powerful that Knox was chosen for the run for the next heir? I had never considered my father crumbling before, but if I counted Charles, this would be the third failure in his lineage.

Words, truth, sat on the edge of my tongue. I had to tell him about Everett. How that dragon had not only been Klaus', but he'd given me Klaus' quell.

I slowly stirred the soup, and chunks of ripe beets sank. "Knox, there's something I need to tell you."

"If it's about Damien, I already know. He asked me about you when I first bonded with Relic. I let him have my words, told him he'd be my second kill if he hurt you."

"It's not about Damien. It's about Klaus." Shuddering, I raised a hand. "You killed someone?"

Knox leaned back on the velvet bench with a raised brow. "Day's initiation. Anyway, what about Klaus?"

"My dragon's real name is Naraic. He was Klaus's dragon."

Knox pulled his brows together. "That can't be. Everett told me Naraic died along with Klaus."

"I brought him back to life, Knox. I saved him. Naraic gave me Klaus' fire antecedent quell." I swallowed hard, hoping I could do the same with my words. "I saved Everett that day. He was dead, Knox."

Those golden eyes showed a whirl of emotions as an unfamiliar gaze held me. "Everett told me you were the first thing he saw when he woke up. He made it seem like you saved him. I couldn't understand…"

"I couldn't let his death destroy you, not after Klaus. I should have told you, but this quell I have is forbidden. If anyone finds out, it will be stripped away, or I will die."

"The power of resurrection," he scoffed. "I won't tell anyone, Severyn. You know you can trust me. I know Klaus was always your favorite, but I'm still here for you."

I had to believe that our blood was enough. That Knox would keep that loose promise and guard it with his heart.

I wouldn't know what I would do without my brothers.

* * *

I'd been exhausted for the better half of the day, nearly collapsing into my bed as a soft knock sounded at the door, and I could tell it was Damien by the smooth rhythm.

"Come in," I called, and the door unlocked with a *click*.

Damien stepped inside wearing a black tie and a traditional academy dress shirt. We'd all lived in dirty combat clothes for the first few weeks. I'd forgotten we had other outfits besides bloodied, torn fabric and leather. His hair was damp, and a clean shave marked his sharp jaw. In his hand, he carried a leather-bound book.

"I brought this for you. It's all about fire quells. I figured you were more of a reader than a hands-on learner."

"Thanks." I grinned. A natural smile, not the forced one Knox compelled on me for two hours as we sat in the dining hall.

Edged on the bed, Damien placed the book on his thigh. "What Archer did today was wrong. I know he is a Serpent, but he had no right to push you like that."

"I'm fine."

Damien ran his fingers through his hair, staring at the empty bed across the room. "Is she ever here?"

"She stays with Monty most nights now. Something is bothering her. I think it concerns the letters we received on the first trial."

Damien peered towards the window as if capable of seeing another world within that glass. "It's a scare tactic. Some of us need to know our demons. For some, it's a quest we need to figure out before we claim our tile. They say the sanity trial is an all-knowing power that senses secrets. I assume Malachi is trying to uncover something she needs too."

"The king's granddaughter is trying to uncover something? Can't she just… snap her fingers and have anyone at her will?"

"Well, Monty's eldest siblings are his personal guards at the capital. Malachi is not the type of person who throws herself at power. She wants something from him, something that requires trust."

"That sounds exhausting. I feel bad for Malachi."

Damien shifted to lay beside me, resting his chin on my shoulder. "Perhaps, but people do desperate things when in need."

The pale moonlight poured through the windows, casting soft shadows across the room. I yawned, burying my blistered fingers under the woven blanket. "I wonder what her letter said. Are you able to read her mind?"

"It's shielded under the academy wards. I'm sure it involves her title, or she wouldn't be spending time with Monty."

"Mine was vague—said I was part of a barter."

"Did you ever figure out what it was?" he asked.

I shook my head. "It has to do with my father's shields."

"Serpent barters are serious, Sev. Archer tried to barter with any realm to break his bond with Ciaran after Klaus died. No one in the entire Continent was powerful enough to do it."

Sadness dragged through me. Perhaps there was one other who carried the loss of Klaus the way I did.

"He tried to break his bond? Is that possible?"

"Ciaran had not been seen since Klaus died. It nearly killed him, and now that you are bonded with Naraic, Archer can't afford to lose you… Gemini dragons normally only bond with one rider. Something must have happened for their dragon root to splice between shadow and flame."

He sure made me feel replaceable the other day. I'd never been needed or used to someone's advantage, and now, one of the most powerful Serpents needed me. Archer was a manipulator, and I'd bet anything he'd give me the cure only if it came to my death—his weakness.

"Promise me we won't let anything get between us, Damien. I don't want to lose you… I'm sure you've read my thoughts by now."

I leaned closer to him. Damien was the air I needed to survive. My mind held all those clipped thoughts, and I didn't care if he knew.

His voice had no disdain or hidden sense of betrayal, but his words cut like a knife. "Severyn, this isn't a game. This is our dynasty. It will break us someday, but let us be one piece for now."

My lips tightened, knowing there was truth in his words. "It doesn't have to break us."

Damien shot a half-grin at me. "For now, North. For now."

Chapter 16

Summer was in full swing. Parched leaves dotted the overgrown paths, and sweat clung to my skin, a second layer. I felt like a flower, desperate for sunlight, as a tan darkened my complexion. The more I realized how suffocated I'd been all my life, the more I despised myself. It was a cruel thing, to blame my home, my heart—one that no longer beat for the chill of winter.

I earned another dagger from Alaric. I was two away from gaining a sword, thanks to Archer.

Antonia glared at me as I sheathed the speckled grey-handled blade along my ribs. Twirling her black-glazed sword, she hissed from across the field, "Don't get used to it, Blanche. Fire needs fuel, and you're nearly starved for air. Archer only pitied you because of your brother, and you know it."

She left with Alaric before I could respond.

Myla ran after me, Haziel squeaking as her barbed black feathers broke through. "Sev," she called. "Callum asked to be against you in combat this week since you gained quell rights. I wanted to warn you." Bridger stayed a few steps back, arms crossed over his chest.

"Thanks for warning me. But I can handle him."

"He's pissed. Thinks you're getting special treatment since Archer gave you two daggers."

I licked my chapped lips. "Do you believe him?"

She sucked in a breath. "Maybe. It's not exactly fair you've advanced to quells in your first year."

"Why doesn't Bridger vouch for you? Since he's so close to Jenessa."

A wax of frost billowed from Bridger's fingertips. "Leave her, Myla. People like Severyn will only know luxuries and handouts. She'll never be like us, and thank the Gods above, her father's title is out of her hands."

"You will never be my father's heir," I hissed at Bridger. "I'll make sure of it."

I didn't owe Myla my life anymore—not since I saved hers. But the pain of what we were hurt. I lost Myla on the Winter Trails to the heart of someone who'd rip mine out if he got another chance.

I walked away before I said something I would regret even more.

Another three days had passed.

The ripple of shadows hit me before I saw the black wings slicing through the horizon. Archer had been gone with Ciaran for three entire days, not that I was counting. I'd grown used to his absence for my own well-being, though Naraic remained restless, his gaze drifting towards the clouds each night.

There he was on day four as I was heading to combat. Archer stood beneath the charred willow, leaning casually while Monty sparred beside him. The other Serpents watched with sharp, calculating eyes. A nervous flutter stirred in my stomach, but the cold weight of truth quickly smothered it.

I was his weapon.

Professor Knight read out the names of opponents: "Knox, Myla. Severyn, Callum. Malachi and Damien."

Callum gave a low chuckle. "You're up, Blanche," he said, stretching his muscled arms as if he already felt victorious.

I waited four days to hear his name and mine together since Myla had warned me. He'd finish me off here. He'd end me weeks before the Serpent bid, where my father would be forced to face the potential new heir of his land.

And I lied to Myla when I said I could handle him. I… did not want to feel ice crawling through my lungs again.

I owed it to the cold showers I forced myself to endure every day since that explosive fire that happened with Archer. My fingers were nearly healed, with only slight scarring on the nailbeds.

Callum bowed before me. "Ladies first," he said.

Myla kept her eyes on me. We'd both felt that shift when I became a Summer. Perhaps it was envy in her eyes as she watched the spark ignite in my palm.

I glanced at Callum's boots. The same ones he'd worn that night. Thankfully, the impression didn't scar. But a mind tended to scar differently than a body. Aches and bruises mended—but Callum had ensured his scars were deep.

Golden eyes narrowed, sizing me up.

Damien spoke in my mind, *"He plans to strike you on your left and steal the dagger sheathed at your ribs."* I quickly glanced at Damien, but he was mid-bow to Malachi, grinning opposite me. *"Do not make it obvious I am helping you. Keep your eyes on him,"* he hissed back, ripping out of my weak shield.

I did not bow as I said, "I'll take the red sword if I win."

Callum surveyed me, eyeing the daggers along my thigh and ribs. "You have nothing that I want. All those daggers are basic and easily found throughout Verdonia. Although, I've heard the Serpents are more keen to speak and bet if they recognize their home dagger. This sword was my first one. Said to have been wielded by the Forgotten children a hundred years before."

I drew the flame back. "I must have something you desire, Callum."

Frost licked his lashes, eyes turning pale as snow. "Put in a good word for your father at the Serpent bid. Not that his opinion matters, but to have his daughter brag about me… Gods, that will be something."

"Fine." Flame boiled in my guts from that barter. I needed a sword, and I wouldn't win them all—not when it would take another few weeks for me to earn another dagger. Weeks I didn't have.

Frost coated his fingers, traveling towards his elbow. An icicle struck from his palm, pointed and deadly, like the ones he'd used on that helpless shell I was weeks before. He held it high, aiming straight for my heart. A chill sucked down my lungs. Callum veered left as Damien had warned me, and I dove opposite, dodging that first blow that split a tree behind me.

My flame grew twice in size, reaching above my head in a whirl of ash. I snapped it at his chest, branding a mark along his t-shirt. The ice melted in his hands with a simmering hiss.

"Does Damien know you're screwing his Serpent brother? Saw you leaving his room the other night," he seethed. "But I'm not surprised. A girl like you gets everything she wants with a smile. I don't think spreading your legs for a ruler was necessary."

I heard his words—heard them but could not process them beyond the rage that filled me to the brim with fire.

Fuck Callum.

Snow fell onto my forehead, melting with a hiss. "My father could create avalanches with his quell. A snowflake is hardly enough to stop a dozen beasts from attacking your realm. Might I suggest practicing more? How about it? Ward against ward."

His voice was hoarse as he raised his hand again. "Did you believe that was all I had?" The temperature dropped—only for me. It seemed every bone in my body was set on ice. My blood slowly froze. Legs numbed and stiffened as they wobbled to a defensive stance.

My fire dulled, frozen in a blaze. Then, all at once, not a single spark ignited.

"When you give up, scream my name this time. Fuck, that was good," he growled.

I was losing, but at this point, I might have been dying, and it was that same bitter cold I'd felt as I collapsed on the Winter trails. My fingers greyed, fearing they'd snap with one twist of my knuckles.

A distant breath sounded in my mind. *"Is that all you have? Oh, Severyn, I thought you were dangerous."*

It was Archer and he wasn't even looking at me.

That bastard was speaking to me through our bond. *"Klaus would have burnt his toes off by now. What does it take to bring that flame out? Is it anger? Because I will piss you off if that is it."*

"Try it," I screamed in my head. I didn't care if Damien heard. This was life or death.

My fingers wouldn't budge. My throat seized, frozen from the spit in my lungs. A crystalized gleam of ice splintered toward my elbow, like a lake growing that first layer of hardened frost.

"It's not working," I cried in my mind. *"My flame is gone."*

"I didn't want it to be you."

My chest tightened as a single, jarring, heated pulse echoed through me.

"Because I am weak?" I asked.

"Because you are his sister, and I try to hate you more every day because you will never be him, but I am reminded that his blood runs through your veins. You are his last shred of warmth capable of making me feel something other than despair. Wield the damn flame, Severyn. Wield it now, or I will force it out of you through any means."

"How?" I cried. *"Do... I wield it?"*

"I could turn you on. Even the sound of my voice ignites you."

Another blow of ice hit my lungs. *"You don't. That won't work."*

"I don't believe you. You could leave my bedroom in my shirt again. But we'd actually fuck, unlike the rumor Callum just spread about us." He dared to breathe down our bond again. *"Does that heat you, Severyn? The thought of you and me alone."*

"Not in any realm would I—"

My clothing was soaked in thawed slush. That flame sputtered out, growing claws as it circled me. "Get out!" I choked aloud, ash coating the backs of my teeth. "Get the fuck out!"

Then, a black flame slammed into the stone steps, slithering. Callum yelped as his shirt caught fire.

I became the flame. I traveled up his sleeve, consuming every fiber in my wrath of heat. Callum rolled on the ground, arms flailing. I let him suffer for a moment, let his clothes burn to ash as he'd left me bare and stripped on the iced grounds.

I walked three steps towards him, pressing a firm boot on his chest before I grabbed the hot metal handle of the sword, bowing as the flame sucked back into my palm.

I leaned down in a whisper, "My father will know precisely who you are and how his daughter took your first sword."

Smoke and smog veiled us, but through the grey haze, Monty crossed his arms as he said, "Severyn Blanche has earned her first sword. And damn... she's got some angst in her."

The words I never thought I'd hear. And Callum was silent on the ground, rolling around in blistered, naked pain. Myla helped him up. "You didn't have to burn his entire clothes and leave him naked, Sev." She scoffed and took him toward the infirmary.

"I'm not sorry," I hissed.

My body felt thawed, as though I'd been frozen in a glacier for a hundred years. My teeth chattered uncontrollably. Damien wrapped his arms around me, pulling me close against his chest. "Let's get you warm," he murmured. "Your skin is freezing."

I nodded, refusing to glance back at Archer's shadow. He wouldn't know he'd been the one to save me. I wouldn't give him that.

There would be no Skyfall training today. Not when my fingers couldn't form a fist, and hiding felt far safer than facing Archer again after those crude comments he spoke through our bond.

Damien didn't head toward the Night Hall. Instead, he kept walking, guiding me towards the golden spiral stairs that led to the Summer dorms.

"Where are we going?" I asked.

"My room, just for a moment. The halls are warmer than your dungeon of a corridor."

Stepping beneath the sun emblem, the Summer halls were bathed in light. Paintings of suns adorned the stone walls, and the air felt warmer here, tinged with the scent of citrus that lingered in the dusty corridors. Shadowless stone floors echoed under my quiet steps, while the wards hummed as we neared his room, buzzing like electrified gnats around the wooden frame. Damien waved a hand, and the door clicked open.

His room was twice the size of mine and Malachi's, with a queen bed in the center, its black duvet stark against the pale stone. A large armoire stood against one wall, and shelves filled with books stretched from floor to ceiling. Shards of glass—blue, sea green, and others—were scattered across his desk, catching the light in fragments.

"Glass?" I asked.

Damien picked up a dark shard and twirled it between his fingers. "I've been practicing projection with sea glass from the South. This one's from my bedroom back home, and this one," he nodded toward another, "was from my dorm at boarding school."

I watched him as if studying a puzzle I might one day solve. "You can see through glass, like a portal?"

He clicked his tongue in amusement. "As Malachi can hear through the wind, I can use glass as a one-way mirror." He rummaged through the armoire and pulled out a three-inch shard of broken glass. It looked like it had once been part of a compact mirror. "I stole this from Bridger's room. I thought you might like it. I assume it's from North Colindale, and I know you miss home."

To me, it looked like any other handheld mirror. "What am I supposed to see?"

"Come closer and look into it. I'll try to project what I see into your mind."

I held the shattered mirror gently, careful not to cut myself or further fragment the glass. Wild emerald eyes stared back at me, mimicking my own, but they seemed sharper—more cunning. The streak of white in my bangs and lashes appeared brighter, more striking. Then frost spread across the mirror's surface, and the reflection changed. No longer were those my eyes staring back, but slivered hazel ones. A house on a hill, with a frozen lake stretching before it. Then, it was North Colindale. My home.

The bitter cold was only… bitter, tainted with Bridger and Callum's greedy, cold hands. I stepped back, and Damien had seen it all, reliving that moment.

Then I was Bridger's eyes, which only lasted a second, but a bloodied, pale me lay half naked on the frozen trails. A wolf carried shreds of my fabric in its snarling mouth.

"I should have killed him that day during combat."

That sword felt heavier on my spine. "I have healed."

"I haven't, not when he still walks. I see his mind." Damien shuddered. "I see it from his eyes and live through it. He does it on purpose… to torture me."

"Bridger needed revenge and got Callum to do his dirty work. He needed to feel strong, and I will never allow him to hurt me again." I swallowed my whisper. "And maybe I needed to feel it not to be so weak."

He cupped my jaw. And then, I felt him in my mind, resting along the childhood memories as if each chapter of my life was immersing him further and distracting himself from his restless one—as if I were another book on his shelf.

No breath escaped me as his forehead rested against mine. "Just say the word, and I'll keep my distance. Tell me to stay away, and I will, Severyn. I know what Callum said wasn't true."

I couldn't fix what was broken, but I could mend. I could piece him back together, one fragment at a time, from whatever darkness haunted his past. I could be the silent wave that carried him to shore.

"Stay," I whispered, releasing the breath I hadn't realized I was holding, the taste of ash still lingering on my tongue from the battle. His fingers curled gently around my ribs, and I leaned into him, grateful for his steady presence. His face was a mask of blankness, but his eyes softened—unaware that my world was crumbling in silent flames.

I could feel myself falling for Damien.

His lips brushed the curve of my neck, nuzzling the delicate glass pendant he had given me. "I'll catch you," he murmured to the thought, his lips warm against my skin.

* * *

The next few days blurred as Naraic and Emerich pushed their limits, training for the Skyfall race. A dozen second-years joined us, but none moved like Malachi and Astoria. They weaved through the obstacles with flawless precision, rings of light cutting through the night sky. Thunder rumbled, lightning crackled, and wind lashed through the trees. Each rider used their quell to throw off the others, but Malachi and Astoria were untouchable, as if the storm itself obeyed them.

I hoisted myself onto Naraic, and he shot into the air, Malachi retreating with the wind. "Astoria won Skyfall with your mother two years in a row," she said, a smile tugging at her lips, her wyvern just a wing's length ahead. "Dragons are forbidden to speak of their past riders, but your mother wrote back. Isn't that incredible?"

A wave of warmth flooded through me. My own mother hadn't written back to me. But I had lied in my letters, speaking of the black-horned griffin I had bonded with, unknowingly describing Myla's hatchling instead. I knew my lie would shatter in three weeks, but I clung to the story of the girl thriving in the Winter sector.

"What else did she say?" I asked, forcing a grin.

"I told her we're friends, and we are both competing in the Skyfall race."

I gaped. "You told her I was competing in the race?"

"Yes, should I not have?"

Naraic lunged toward a hoop, circling as Malachi followed suit. "I told her I bonded with a griffin. She'll think I'm mad!"

Astoria cut in front of me, and Malachi reached into her leather pocket and pulled out an envelope. The same ones we had at home. "Read it."

I grabbed the letter, unfolding it and nearly falling off Naraic as I stuffed it inside my dagger's sheath. "I will later."

"I want it back."

"Fine." I guided Naraic down, lowering to the fields. I pulled the letter out, and each swirl of black ink made my stomach sink. Her writing was slanted, with blotches of ink stains in parts where she hovered her quill over longer.

But it was my mother's writing.

Dear Malachi Herring,

Astoria was a wonderful wyvern. I bonded with her by the volcano near the end of the Summer border. I remember that day like it was yesterday. She was just an egg, but I knew she was mine. I got a few burns and nearly lost all feeling in my fingers for three years from the volcanic ash. I hope she didn't give you a hard time during your bond. She can be feisty.

I always thought Severyn would claim her—I am glad you two became friends. Riders are for life… hold onto that.

Astoria is powerful and drawn to those who wield such strength. I am honored she chose you. We won Skyfall during our first year… something to keep in mind.

All the best, Fallon Blanche

I folded the letter in half and handed it back to her. "Did she give you a hard time during bonding?"

"Yes. She made it clear that I was not her first choice. I will never be you, Severyn. Your mother's blood was stronger, and you will follow her path."

"I haven't told them I gained a fire quell," I admitted.

"Please write back to her and tell her the truth. Everyone here fears what their parents will think, but they do not control their destiny. Astoria chose me because you were already chosen."

We knew you were coming.

I never thought Malachi could be jealous. I blinked and silence fell between us.

Once a mask of unnerved coldness, her face brightened as I wrapped my arms around her. "Astoria chose right."

Riders are for life. Was that always the truth? When Mother was at home in a world that did not answer to her. When the world deemed her forbidden?

Malachi pulled away. "A few of us are meeting at the docks for drinks tonight. Bring Damien along."

"Who's all coming?"

Her eyes glittered. "A few Serpents and those participating in Skyfall."

"Serpents?"

She flicked a wave of blonde hair over her shoulder, the ends damp from the sputtering rain. "You'll have to find out."

I approached Damien and Emerich near the tree line. Something on his face told me he'd listened to every word between Malachi and me. "So, are we going to the meet?" I asked.

He widened his eyes. "I have no idea what you are talking about," he said, holding back a grin. "I really do try to give you privacy. Tomorrow, I will teach you more about mind shields. You'll need the protection during the Bid."

I leaned back on my heels. "Do I dare ask why?"

"You're still learning to crawl. You can do more damage concealing a lie than with a sword."

I shuddered. "Well, at least I have a sword now."

"And you earned it."

* * *

I showered and changed into a more traditional uniform—a black skirt that fell just above my thighs, paired with tights perfect for the rainy weather that had lingered all afternoon. Damien, however, wore the same button-down shirt from yesterday. As we neared the group of students, a strange impulse made me want to pull away.

Their eyes weren't filled with fear, but something else, something more unsettling, as we approached. Archer and Monty each held a gauntlet, swirling a dark liquor inside. Two other Serpents stood nearby, taking long drags from tightly bound rolls, releasing reddish smoke that curled through the air. The scent was floral, perhaps wild Muddvein—known to calm muscles when inhaled. Malachi, ever the bold one, sipped straight from a bottle of red wine, her eyes lighting up with excitement as they met mine.

I squeezed Damien's hand, knowing how many voices were in his mind. Malachi wrapped her arms around my neck, shoving the bottle toward my lips, then dragging me out of Damien's grasp and into the crowd.

I took a sip—mainly because I knew I'd choke if I didn't swallow. She matched me in every way, right down to the boots. In fact, I might have been wearing hers.

She reached for a drag of the roll, and a plume of copper smoke blew from her nose. "It's mycris," she said, "One puff every three months prevents unwanted pregnancies." She snickered. "Hopefully, you two are being safe." Her eyes dragged between Damien and me.

"Oh, we haven't—" I said. But I grabbed the mycris from her fingers and inhaled anyway, leaving a gritty, medicinal texture on my tongue. Better to be safe with how much time Damien and I were spending together.

Damien got between us. "Severyn, we should just hang out at your dorm." He reached for me, but scattered light danced low, distracting me. "I don't really like crowds," he added with a mutter.

Monty stepped into my line of sight. "Well, if it isn't the newest flame student." He gestured to his drink. "It's good. Try it. It's a mix of phoenix tears and rum." The liquid sloshed as he pressed the rim to my chest, eyes dancing up and down my body.

"*You're* offering me a drink?" I asked.

"*Do not.*" It was Archer in my mind, louder down that bond. "*...take a drink from Monty Garcia.*"

"*I'm feeling parched,*" I hissed in my mind, catching a clip of his shadows further down.

I grinned at Monty. "Thanks," I said, sipping the potent liquor. I turned to offer Damien some, but he was gone. I figured the drunk ramblings were too much for him.

"I've been watching you during combat. You're a little firecracker, aren't you?" Monty chuckled. "First, you're a Winter, and then you come out of nowhere with a fire quell. I might know who I'm placing my Bid on." He flicked the edge of my neval streak with a smirk.

A warmth bloomed in my stomach, and it wasn't my quell. My limbs loosened, and I found myself leaning closer into Monty without thinking. "I didn't know you knew my name."

A rope of silken daylight bound around my waist, pulling me nearer. "Of course, I know who you are, silly. It's only courteous to finish the drink." His voice dropped low as he leaned in. "Tell me why I should choose you at the Serpent Bid."

His lips hovered near mine, and I was wrapped in that tether of light, warmth spilling from his breath and tickling my nostrils. "Better yet, show me," he purred.

I opened my palm, sparking a single flame. "What did you want to see?" I grabbed the bottle and took a heavy swallow. I knew this was reckless, knew Monty was not a Serpent I cared to impress, but I needed all the bids I could get.

Monty pinned my arms down with his lips close to my ear. "That's not impressive. I want to see you use only your eyes."

I felt everyone's attention on us. Even Archer stared. But that stare was desperate. Primal.

Shit… no, his stare was dangerous.

"Fine," I said. I was up for a challenge. I focused on a tree behind me, forcing my arms at my sides. I swayed back and forth before Monty steadied me, his hands tightened on my hips.

"Careful," he said, leaning in. "You know nevals are hunted in some areas of Verdonia," he whispered.

My lips parted with a flick of his wrist, tilting the remainder of the gauntlet down my throat. His intoxicating voice hummed to the cage in my chest, and whatever liquid he poured down my throat forced every muscle in my body to numbness. "I don't think you'll last very long in the real world."

I swallowed hard. "What do you mean—hunted?"

Then Malachi snapped at him, "Monty, you're going to scare her!"

"If she wants to be a Serpent, she has to handle it," he barked back, and his hands slid along my thighs—Oh gods. I couldn't shove him off; whatever he'd given me was too strong. His lips pressed to my neck, inhaling as a gritty tongue licked toward my ear. "You're mine for the night. Would you like that, Severyn?"

Someone grabbed me from behind. My cheek slammed against a thumping chest, and I looked up to meet Archer's pissed-off gaze—just as his fist collided with Monty's jaw. No shadows. Just a brutal punch. "Get your fucking hands off her," he growled.

Monty spat blood, a grin curling his mouth. "Come on, Archer, I only wanted to know what all those stories were about. Why, every year, the scorpion riders come searching for those freaks."

"What is he talking about?" I slurred. "It's a bloody birthmark." Shit. I gripped the fence lining the drop to the ocean, teetering back on my heels.

Archer's spliced-knuckled hands gripped me from behind. "Ignore Monty and get to your dorm before you make an even bigger fool of yourself." His wild blue eyes, like stormy waves crashing against my chest, burned past me. "I'm about to break every finger of Monty's that touched you. Maybe I'll hang his tongue while I'm at it."

I wrenched myself free. "I'm not leaving."

His jaw clenched. Without warning, he scooped me into his arms, draping my legs over his shoulder. My arms thrashed, head hanging like dead weight against his chest. "You're infuriating, Blanche. What the hell were you thinking, taking a drink from Monty?" We were already halfway across the courtyard. "Do you intentionally drive me mad?"

Heat flared in my thighs from where his hand gripped me. "Our deal is off," I hissed.

"Our barter ends when I say it ends. You drank liquor mixed with phoenix tears. Aphrodisiac. Makes you either infatuated or spills your deepest secrets. You can't handle either, clearly."

I dug my fingers into his solid arm, the eyes on his neck locking onto me like they could see straight through to my soul. "You're infuriating and controlling, Mr. Serpent of the Night." I mimicked his voice, daring him.

We passed through a shadow, and suddenly, we were in the Night halls.

"How did you—?"

Archer raised my hand to the door. "Unlock it. Now."

I twisted my wrist like a key, and Archer dropped me onto the bed. "Sit," he demanded.

I wiped my brow, ripping my shirt off to cool the boiling heat coursing through my body.

"I'm hot," I said, fanning my palm over my face, trying to keep my head steady as the world tilted.

Archer rolled his eyes, tossing a blanket of shadow over me. "Then take your clothes off. No sense in overheating."

I sat up, ignoring his crude suggestion. "I know you're not going to let me die. We're already bonded. Why else can I hear you in my mind? If I die, you'll be left as weak as you were when Klaus died."

The words hit harder than I intended, but damn him for thinking he could control me.

I swallowed a breath of shadow that clawed at my airways. "There are many ways riders can bond. Your brother and I had a simple ward between us." His chuckle rumbled deep in his chest. "Some fuck as a way of initiating the bond. Physical closeness. Sharing quells. A kiss is sometimes enough to forge the bond. But a rider bond only ensures protection when the other isn't around."

I could feel his gaze on me as my legs spread slightly, his eyes following the movement. "And what would you do?" I asked, my voice a whisper that held far more than it let on. "Not that I care how you would bond with me."

A shadow pooled around me, thick and heavy. Archer slid forward, faster than it would've taken him to cross the room. His mouth hovered near my ear, one hand grazing the hollow of my neck, sending chills through my spine. "You're very interested in my answer for someone who refuses to listen to me. You've been practicing for Skyfall after I forbade you." His jaw tightened, his breath hot against my skin. "And why the hell am I constantly on your mind when I told you to forget about me?"

"You're a conceited asshole," I said.

His other hand rested on my thigh, nails scraping across the fabric, tearing it effortlessly. "Overheating? That's a sure way to die before the poison does its job."

I felt my pulse race as I slammed back into the pillow, frustration bubbling inside me. "You are the poison, Archer."

Those blue eyes devoured me before narrowing to where his stroking thumb knotted in my see-through tights. "Do you want me to stop?" he said slowly, arching his veined neck. "Or can you feel the bond rattling between us, Blanche? We could keep going, and all your reckless little thoughts will be wound within mine."

I shook my head, trying to find a voice to escape my dried lips. Softly, I responded, "Don't stop."

That heat narrowed between my thighs.

Madness. I was mad to want more. For my body to sing from his touch.

He shifted closer, eyes on my lips. I'd regret this, but the burning desire to be touched by him was nothing more than the poison Monty gave me.

I wanted him to touch me.

Or maybe it was a wicked curation of my wildest thoughts.

Perhaps he was the poison, leaching into my veins until even my blood was dyed with shadows.

His fingers went higher up, nearing the hem of my skirt. "Is this where Monty touched you?" Thunder rumbled in the distance, shuttering the stained-glass windows.

A faint breath released through my nod. "You didn't… have to punch him," I said, tracing the shade crawling the walls, the same dark beauty enveloping his sharp cheekbone.

Ignoring my words, he ripped another line through the fraying fabric, and I swore my skin sizzled. "For someone who refuses to listen to me, your body sure enjoys the sound of my voice," he groaned, lips brushing against my neck. "You drive me mad. I'll drive you insane. Deal?" His finger scraped higher, grazing the edge of my panties before squeezing my thighs.

"Why do you care so badly about controlling me?"

"It's not control, Severyn." His other hand slipped over my chest, undoing three buttons. "I simply don't want you to overheat from you thinking about my hands sliding up the inside of your wet thighs. Your crush on me is adorable."

I ground my teeth. "I don't like you. You're the one who carried me home."

"If it weren't me, you'd be bound with daylight tethers now. Monty seems to have his eyes on you. Do you enjoy the attention of a powerful ruler?"

"You believe I am that weak? That I'd allow Monty to take me home?"

"That drink brings out desires, and you've yet to kick me out."

"Desires are foolish."

My body betrayed my mind. I craved him more than I cared to admit. What the hell was wrong with me?

He traced a shape over my underwear, daring to slip it over and touch my skin. I breathed through the ash, biting my lip to silence my pleasure. "Oh, Severyn. If I was cruel, I might have caved to you, but pleasuring you after you've been poisoned by a drink is not on my mind." He slipped his hand out, his thumb skimming a scar on my thigh, then another, pausing as he traced each jagged line. When he reached the fifth, his breath hitched. "Who did this?"

"It doesn't matter," I hissed.

"It was Callum, wasn't it? Did he… where else did he hurt you?" Anger rippled in his voice, yet it softened into something unfamiliar, something almost tender. "Tell me what he did to you."

"He made it known that he had marked me. To ensure I was undesirable."

Archer's hand hovered, and shadows melted over the scars, dark tendrils brushing my skin like whispers. "You will never see torture in these scars again. If anyone dares to harm you, I'll mark you myself until shadows are your desire."

I fisted the covers over my thighs. "I don't need your protection. And you can leave now."

A flicker of something unreadable passed through his gaze. It seemed to take every ounce of restraint for him to stand. "Keep telling yourself you hate me. Maybe one of us will start to believe it." The shadows retracted into his palm. "Get some sleep. You have a big race coming up."

Before I could respond, Archer disappeared. I traced the faint, glowing marks left on my thighs as if he had painted my body with starlight.

Shadow and stars couldn't erase Callum's scars entirely, but it was five fewer lines to bear.

Moments later, Malachi stumbled inside, red wine dripping from her soaked blouse. "Shit, did you hear that thunder?" Her eyes darted around the room, and she shook the ends of her damp hair.

I swallowed hard. "Yeah, I did."

Malachi collapsed onto my bed, her weight bouncing the mattress. "Sorry about Monty. He can be… aggressive when he gets an idea in his head."

Desperate for a distraction, I blurted, "What do you know about neval hair?"

Her lips tightened into a grim line. "There's been someone hunting anyone with that mark. They have been for nearly four decades. How did you not know?"

"Someone's hunting me? And what are scorpion riders?"

Malachi yawned, stretching her arms like she hadn't just dropped a bombshell. "I figured you knew. Ask me tomorrow.

It'll take at least an hour to explain, and I don't have the energy right now."

She reached for her lantern, but before she could extinguish it, I flicked my gaze to the candle and stole the flame, snuffing it out myself.

"That's… an interesting trick," she murmured, her voice laced with surprise.

And in the enveloping darkness, I allowed myself a small, proud smile.

* * *

Pounding sounded at the door. Hastily, I glanced out the window where the sun broke through. I'd slept in, and Malachi was gone, and from the looks of my whirled covers, she tried to wake me as well.

I outstretched my hand toward the door, falling out of bed as it unlocked. Gods… my head pounded.

"Severyn," Damien gasped, surveying yesterday's clothes on my body and the rips in my stockings. "Did you trip walking home last night? Your tights are shredded."

I waited for the spiraling questions once my thoughts of last night leaked out. I changed quickly, asking, "Where did *you* go last night?" He held the door open as I ran my fingers through my tangled locks. "I was worried about you."

Walking to combat, Damien kept his eyes low. "Monty's thoughts are loud. He wanted some personal time with you, and I wasn't interested in seeing you swoon over him. I understand the desire for power, especially for someone like you."

I stared at him. "You thought I was interested in Monty?"

"Well, there was someone on your mind last night," Damien sneered. "And your thoughts are muddled after I left, so I don't know what happened."

I didn't know what happened last night. I couldn't tell him about Archer taking me home and how close we were. "Nothing happened."

He'd only marked me with his shadows.

Damien grinned. "I trust you, Severyn." He pushed open the iron doors as we left the grand hall. His boot kicked a stone, chipping along the onyx path.

"Good," I whispered. Liquid lies coursed through my heated veins.

"That was some storm we had last night," he chuckled low. "Did you know that when certain quells are shared, they can create a new power? Fire and wind can create a tornado, but fire and shadows make thunder and lightning. How interesting is that?"

My body iced. "That is interesting."

Damien glanced at the glass pendant around my neck. "Your necklace is twisted, Sev."

My cheeks heated. I gripped the chain, centering the pendant. "Nothing happened between us. He walked me home," I hissed.

"Oh, I *know*."

I let out a choked breath of ash. "Good."

"I think your barter with him is quite cute, though. I never saw it coming," he muttered, "now you understand when I say that whatever friendship we have will shatter in a few months."

I did a complete spin to face him, grabbing his elbow. "Then you must have heard why I made that deal, Damien. I'll die if I don't get the cure. You know it killed me keeping this a secret from you."

Somehow, he knew. The shield Archer placed between us, warding our words, had failed.

A mask of cold slicked his features. The Damien who walked me to class was gone within a night's breadth. Power. Damien chose power over me, over my life.

"That's a bit dramatic, Severyn. It didn't *kill* you. I thought it was rather easy for you, how every day you'd smile at me, and I'd pretend I didn't know. Perhaps I do want that title. It is mine to claim, and you said it yourself—you're just another Bridger trying to claim heirship."

I wanted to cry for how cruel he was being. "I suppose your decision has been made then."

Damien tightened his lips. "What is it they call us? *Rivals*?" He shrugged. "We have a few more months until we truly shatter."

Chapter 17

The days leading up to the Skyfall race all seemed to blend. The trails were warded off in preparation for the race. Flying overhead was forbidden, and those who attempted to do so would be scorched.

Dozens of visitors from across Verdonia flew in to witness the race. Various quells rippled through the air as cloaked figures strutted through the courtyards. We were told not to converse with them. A few Serpents showed, and I waited for frost to brim the windows as Father's loud boots entered, but he never came.

Knox spent the last day trying to convince me to back out, telling me how dangerous the race was. Naraic nearly cindered his pants when he wouldn't take no for an answer.

The Serpents left two nights before, likely to ensure their borders were secure with the influx of riders making their way to the academy. Archer knew today was important. Even if he'd warned me this race would draw unwanted attention to Naraic.

But I thought he might have shown at least.

No one wanted me to race. But as I stood on the fields with two dozen riders, listening to the headmaster explain the rules, the nervous jitters in my gut only grew stronger. He wore a grey cloak sewn with gems down the side and black slacks. His yellow eyes, matching the dimming sunlight, darted toward the guards stationed near the castle doors.

"The map goes through every realm. Silver ribbons are worth one point, and gold ribbons are worth two. If a rider falls, do not save them; that will only slow you down. If your feet touch the ground, you are disqualified. If your dragon dies, you are disqualified. You can kill and dismount other riders, and using quells is encouraged." The headmaster stared at the clouds as he continued, "I must warn you that the wards are down, meaning creatures and beasts of all sorts will lurk through the skies."

I glanced at the edge of the field, where a hundred or so students crowded with binoculars, their white-knuckled hands gripping tightly. Most of the bird riders stared at the dragons in the field's core. Myla's lingering smile caught my eye, keeping me focused.

I would not die.

A few Valscribe journalists jotted down notes, their pens flying across parchment as they documented the arena and our names. The fear of my name appearing in the Serpent Press frightened me. But it also... intrigued me. I assumed Cully hadn't written an article worthy of earning his access here yet.

Oh, how I missed Cully.

The headmaster cleared his throat, raising a single hand high. "Does everyone understand?"

We all nodded. Malachi, standing to my left, ran a hand down Astoria's sleek grey scales that matched her leather jacket. The dragon snarled low, its neck rolling with a tremor.

Malachi nudged me in the ribs and whispered, "The king has arrived."

I glanced back, spotting Knox first, then the king a few rows ahead, surrounded by armored guards stationed at each corner of the castle. They were fully encased in silver swords and steel. The king's long ashen hair, streaked with blonde highlights, glinted in the sunlight. He leaned on a black snake-shaped cane, his golden-scaled suit shimmering with jewels and rings adorning every finger. He reminded me of a snake.

I swallowed the bile rising in my throat. "How many riders normally die every year?" I asked Malachi.

"Depends on how brutal the race is—usually three."

"Those odds are terrible."

"Did you think we flew through a few hoops and called it a day? This is called Skyfall for a reason," she hissed back.

A chilled breath of shadows filled my lungs when Ciaran's wings breached the academy wards. The other five Serpents followed close behind. I forced myself not to stare, not to care that this was the first full breath I'd taken in two days. But his appearance wasn't to reassure me—it was to impress the golden-scaled man whose eyes lingered on Malachi.

Was it selfish to put Ciaran through this? Knowing my odds of death, knowing it coursed through my mother's blood? But I couldn't back down. Not with a hundred eyes fixed on me and my trembling hands. I gripped the chain around my neck, and Damien caught my gaze, giving me a tight nod. I knew he was upset—knew we were already shattered. Not into brilliant glass shards he could shape into art, but into pieces that never fit in the first place.

Light clipped the sun, and the king appeared beside the headmaster with a snap of his fingers—daylight.

The king wielded the quell of light.

"Welcome to the hundred-and-first Skyfall race," he began in a rasped voice. "As another year comes before us, I'd like to reflect on the greatness our Continent has strived for—for the students who became warriors and leaders, for the memories forged during their time here. The Skyfall race is a deadly obstacle course, and we are reminded every year when a rider does not return." The king raised his cane, and the crowd held their breath. "Remember, leaders are made, not born. The title is never deserved."

A distant horn blew.

We all mounted. I ran my hand down Naraic's scales. *"We got this."*

"Don't fall," he said through our bond.

All the dragons took off into the sky. Naraic pounded his talons along the dirt, rising high towards the hoops. I yelled at Malachi, "Good luck."

"See you at the finish line." Her voice drowned within the sheet of rain pelting from the darkened clouds, drenching me— causing me to slip. I clung to Naraic's ribs as the wind pounded into us.

"Most of the obstacles are in the forests. We'll need to get low," Naraic barked down the bond.

"It's against the rules to know the maps before. Why would you risk that?" I hissed, latching my grip tightly.

"I've done this before. Never made it to the finish line."

I went numb. "Naraic—what are you saying?" I cried as we dove through a hoop, wings tucked tight, and I reached, missing that first golden ribbon by a hair.

"I am saying exactly what you are thinking."

Two other riders chased through the same obstacle. Astoria ripped through a hoop further ahead as Malachi tied a golden ribbon around her arm.

I caught one last glance at Knox below; his face said it all. The wide, fear-licked eyes that watched every clench and swerve of Naraic in the sky—watched the wind pound into me as I leaned.

I thought Klaus died in glory. I thought the heavens cried out for him as his body smashed into that lake and the earth devoured him, accepting his noble sacrifice, but his death was for nothing. He died on this exact day for a race. I gripped Naraic harder as his wings stretched out. A flame struck from my palm, and I lit the last hoop on fire, along with those six remaining ribbons—a third year halted as his dragon hissed, nose-diving down.

We narrowly missed the last obstacle, circling back as Naraic swooped under, twisting through the willow trees. My ribs smashed into his spine as he flew through, and I tore that golden ribbon off the metal pole, waiting until I caught my breath to tie it around my wrist.

The rain slashed my face, cutting into me like severed glass. We dipped low, and Naraic's barbed tail scored along the grass as he went through two more hoops.

The crowd cheered as I blew a flurry of blackened smoke toward them. A few students whispered amongst the others. The headmaster had a monocle on—eyes on me as he stood beside the king, bracing for the wave of heat. As I tore past them, I heard his words to the king, "…Fallon's daughter."

I was Fallon's daughter. I knew that statement was a curse. I was the daughter of death, riding on her snow-white resurrected beast.

I met the king's slivered gaze, which wavered between Naraic and me, devoid of any discernible thought. A hiss of breath whispered through the wind. "Nobody enjoys a show-off," he said, voice clipped.

Naraic huffed as he dove toward the Day realm. No lunge of the wards repelled us. No electrified field protected the trails as speckled light broke through the clouds, suffocating the rain with that bright beacon above. Knox had never struck me as pure radiant with the worms he'd dug with his bare hands and the roadkill he'd made necklaces with from vermin bones. But this was his realm—his *calling*.

We glided above a large lake, lunging through two more hoops, stealing those golden ribbons each time.

Naraic groaned in pain, snarling his snapping jaw. "What is it?" I screamed.

Then I noticed a shard of metal pierced into his scale by his ribs. A flash of spiked tails slammed into my side. A third-year Night snickered as her silver-tipped fingers threw metal shards toward us. The same woman I'd seen Archer speaking to on the first day during the Rite.

The lead to become his heir.

"Care for a little fun, Sev?" she snickered.

Gasping, I reached toward the fragments lodged near a scale on his ribs. "I'll tell Archer you attacked us. He'll never trust you."

She raised her silver-slicked hand again. "He can't believe you if you're dead."

We dove down, skimming over the water before lurching into the sky. I wielded a leash of flame, hanging onto Naraic's neck with one hand, snapping the cindering whip toward her with a *hiss*.

"And you can't claim his heir if you're a cindered corpse."

She choked, eyes narrowing to slits before flicking her wrist, and a shard of metal clipped my ear. "You little, *bitch*."

"Naraic!" I cried. "We need to fly."

Pain, horrible pain, pierced me. A pool of warm crimson trickled down my cheek as she grew two more jagged daggers, sharper than the last, mirroring the trees with the sleekness of the metal. She thrusted, and one tore through across my shoulder, shoving me backward.

I needed to lose her off my trail, but the thought of ending her willed in my thoughts, dangling as the only option to save Naraic.

"He'll be glad he doesn't have to protect you anymore," she hissed, shoving her blonde hair over her shoulder. "Your brother is dead. He shouldn't carry that burden of ensuring your safety simply because they were friends."

I curled that leash back. I had never thought so callously about another person's death, but seeing Naraic in pain did something to me. It ignited not only a flame but rage.

I ripped out the shard from my shoulder with a hiss.

Anger surged—funneled through my boiling veins. I willed that flame to reach her, to wrap around her neck and drag her down.

"Fly!" I screamed, and Naraic took off, ripping Delair off her dragon.

She was bloodied and shaking on the ground, and her flesh peeled over with cindered burns. I had done that—for Naraic. I reached over to his ribs, tugged the serrated metal out with a grunt, and threw it toward the ground.

"I killed her," I breathed.

"Her shield was weak."

Riders flew above and away from me, unwilling to risk their lives for the lower hoops I'd set ablaze. We passed through the forests, and two more golden ribbons decorated my wrist. Daylight became the cool breeze of autumn leaves.

Then Naraic cried a howl I had never heard come from him before. It wasn't a pained noise, but the sound twisted my stomach.

I saw Emerich's sea-green scales through the clouds. "Damien," I called.

Moss-flecked peaks lined the horizon. Mist veiled us in midday showers, and I was thankful it wasn't that beating rain from before. But when Damien didn't answer back, Naraic chased after Emerich, whose spine was riderless.

Fear gripped my bones as Emerich let out that same howl. A cry of *mourning*.

"Damien," I yelled, leaning over the whirl of clouds with each lower of Naraic's wings.

We followed Emerich through a trail, and I saw a leather jacket caught on a branch. We flew lower, nearly gliding above the lush grass.

A figure was on the grass, lying too still and calm for my liking. Tears clustered under my lids when I saw Damien's bloody face and how his back was contorted unnaturally. Naraic flew closer.

"Breathe, Blanche," Naraic barked.

Damien's chest rose, and I took my first breath.

We got as close as we could without dismounting.

"Damien, look at me!" I screamed. "You're not dying today."

His eyes whirled before focusing on mine. "Sev. Leave me. Win." There was no blood; he must have fallen on his back.

"What happened?"

"Hail. It pelted me, and I slipped."

"How dare he…"

He strained to shake his head. "Everett… he can wield ice. I've never seen a dragon rider wield it before."

Everett? "Why would he attack you? He's our friend. We— we saved him."

"You saved his life, Sev. I…" he groaned, trying to get to his feet. "It doesn't matter. You need to go. I need to rest for a moment, maybe a day. This was your race, Sev."

"You're disqualified. I'm not leaving you here to get attacked by beasts."

He leaned up on his arms, groaning in pain. "I only did this for you—to get close to you. And I'll never speak to you again if you step one foot on this ground." He meant it, although I figured Damien had already chosen that silence between us.

I could feel Naraic's beats getting quicker. We needed to fly. "Can you stand? Try and get back on Emerich." I looked through the trails, but only thick bushes and winding vines surrounded us. He would never make it out alive. "Please," I whimpered.

He stood up with a grunt. Emerich dipped as low as he could, and Damien grabbed his neck, shrieking, but managed to mount Emerich. "Ride, Severyn. Now," he said.

"I'll meet you at the fields," I said through tears.

Damien nodded, loosely sprawled atop Emerich. He would survive—and that was enough for me.

We soared out of the forest and into the heart of the canyon. Towering crystalline formations appeared as colossal daggers thrusted from the sky to the ground, forming a natural stone labyrinth. Those jagged spires refracted the sunlight of Autumn's muted sun, splintering dazzling colors that danced across the canyon walls. The narrowed gorge was a twisted path barely wide enough for a single dragon to navigate through.

Each sphere seemed honed to razor-sharp perfection. Naraic's wings beat in place as he felt my hesitation. "It's not worth it, Naraic. It's not worth your life," I said.

"There is no other route. I can do it."

And I believed him because perhaps he had done it before.

Naraic tucked his wings in as tight as he could, weaving through the spheres one by one, striking each hoop and tearing that golden ribbon loosely tied along the metal. Seven. I had seven ribbons laced around my wrist, fluttering through the ripping wind.

Raw amethyst lined the bottom of the canyon. My heart beat with each of Naraic's wings, and our breaths were in sync. I was his eyes, and I'd die with him if we went down. And I felt that invisible tether between us, as if our veins were connected through our bond—heart and lungs pounding as one.

I clung tight to his scales, feeling every twitch of his muscles as we glided through the maze, veering right, left, down… Pain ripped through my lungs as Naraic's wing tore into one of the spheres.

He growled twice, tremoring a roll down his spiked spine. *"Do you anger people when I am not around, North?"* Naraic hissed. *"Not even ten minutes have passed, and another rider is trying to end your life."*

A dagger swept past my cheek.

I turned to face two dragons. Alaric's teeth barred as he stared at a third-year Autumn student, the same one who'd mocked me for standing in the dragon fields weeks before.

"Brantlyn," Alaric hissed low, dodging another dagger. "This is a race, remember."

"I know those scales," he hissed at me. "You're a freak, *pigeon.* What kind of black magic did you do on that beast you ride? Tell me, or I'll consult the Malvoria guards, and I know the royal guards aren't afraid to rip forbidden quells from the students here."

I didn't know his name until now, yet he wanted to kill me. I should have listened to Archer. Fuck, I couldn't think of him right now.

Brantlyn aimed that next dagger at my heart, and Naraic's wings were already pressed against the stone with nowhere to fly.

"He's not a freak," I said as Naraic smashed against the rocks and the dagger flew past us, nearly grazing his entire left wing to the bone. "He is mine."

"Leave her and race," demanded Alaric. "Severyn has done no harm to you."

"I think I'd rather kill her before she burns the academy down," he said, thrusting another dagger at us. "I watched that dragon die two years ago."

"No!" yelled Alaric as he lunged through the air, taking the strike in the stomach.

He met my swollen gaze as he crashed into the sharp abyss below. Seconds seemed like minutes as he gripped the bloody handle. He stared up at seemingly nothing and then shifted his silver gaze at me.

"Toni's going to kill me… if I survive." He tried to lean up, but a sphere was punctured through his shoulder.

"Alaric, I'll save you!" I cried. "Don't move."

"Tell Toni… I love her. That I'd choose her if I could go back," he said. "Please, Severyn. I need you to tell her that."

Then, a sound that mimicked death itself sounded through the crisp air.

Brantlyn's dragon was caught between the barbed crystals, screeching as its talons tore into stone and spheres.

"Naraic, we need to help Alaric!"

"Your humanity is not greater than your life. You do not carry his burdens. Nor his sacrifice."

Alaric screamed at his silver wyvern. "Let me die! Release the bond so you can survive. I won't be your last rider."

I always thought an enigma bond was for life, but I wondered if Klaus had demanded Naraic release the bond before he drowned. If those were his last words.

Naraic roared a breath of deadly ash, cindering Brantlyn until only charred bones clung to the dragon's spine. *"That redhead was rather annoying, don't you think?"*

And Malachi had warned me three deaths were normal during Skyfall. And I had witnessed each one.

Alaric's wyvern tore through the spheres, shredding its scales along the path before taking off into the sky. I felt the punch in my throat, the stillness as we glided out of the labyrinth.

"Does that happen often?" I cried. "He released his bond!"

"You will never see that again in your lifetime."

"Klaus never—"

"I had no choice."

"It nearly killed Ciaran," I said out loud.

"I did it to save Ciaran. This is more than a promise to protect. Ciaran is my other half. She is my sister, hatched in the same egg. We are one. Our bond is unbreakable. I ensured Ciaran and that rider of hers would live. I released the bond to find you. Dragons can only bond to the blood of our fallen riders. You were chosen the moment Klaus took his last breath. Klaus knew you were coming. Most dragons prefer to break the bond once a rider naturally passes. Our blood has been synced since before you were born, North."

A shadow swallowed us whole. Above, a crack of moonlight fractured the darkness, its pale glow the only source of light. Naraic's scales shimmered faintly, a constellation of silver beneath the scattered stars. Below, a restless grey sea battered jagged rocks, the crash and hiss echoing like a mournful hymn.

Shrieks rose from the forest ahead—sharp, hollow, like whispers torn from a nightmare. The overgrown path twisted into the black.

My stomach churned, a queasy knot tightening with every wing beat.

Naraic moved with quiet purpose, his snout brushing something I hadn't noticed before—a golden ribbon, swaying gently in the cold breeze.

Flying through the Night realm forced my thoughts to whirl on *him* as I soared through his mimicked land. *"Why didn't Archer tell me on the first day?"* I asked.

"He was waiting for you. Patiently. Your brother was cunning. He knew I would find you. He just didn't know how."

"Archer is willing to let me die unless I prove myself," I said, "willing to let me betray Damien for his own sick barter over his father's title."

"He knows your potential."

"So, you are on his side. He forced me to lie to Damien."

"You agreed."

"I can't see anything in this darkness."

Naraic sent a rumble down the bond, a laugh if I could call it that. *"Your eyes will adjust someday."*

We plunged deep over the belly of the mountains, and I clung to Naraic's scales to stop the motion sickness—to hold my breakfast down. Every breath was devoured by darkness, consumed by that sickening shadow. Even my quell had cooled to a soft vibration. We broke through the clouds and into Winter.

I grabbed the ribbon from Naraic's snout, tying it with the others.

White engulfed my vision as Winter's icy breath slammed into me. We narrowly dodged three hoops as hail lashed our bodies—sharp, relentless.

Hail.

I saw Everett. His veins bulged, dark and gorged, as he pulled Winter's air into himself, grunting with every heave. Iridis's wings flailed wildly, her movements erratic, like a bat tangled in a net.

"Everett!" I shouted, my voice swallowed by the storm as we drew closer.

His flushed face whipped toward me. "Severyn—I didn't mean to attack Damien! Iridis—she lost control. I don't know what's happening to me!" His golden eyes were wild, pleading, as though I could help him.

"I think Iridis gave you a quell. A snow quell," I said. "You need to leave this realm before it kills you."

Ice rained down on us. I didn't flinch but flared my quell to salvage the last remnants of warmth. A burst of blood vessels streaked his eye crimson as snow thickened, nearly knocking Naraic from the air.

Iridis suddenly surged forward faster than I'd ever seen a dragon fly.

"How is that possible?" I muttered to Naraic as we seized the last silver ribbon left from the wind, barely managing to peel it from the freezing metal.

"A snow dragon existed a hundred years ago," Naraic said, his voice echoing in my mind. *"The Forgotten killed them all. Everett must have Winter blood."*

Ahead, the ice wall loomed. My eyes traced the half-submerged caves where Myla and I had nearly drowned trying to recover those eggs. Gritting my teeth, I urged Naraic to veer right, bypassing the Spring realm entirely. There wasn't time for all the ribbons.

And I had no idea if I was in first or last place.

Heat slammed into us. The muggy breeze carried the tang of salt and debris, a curling sea stretching into the horizon.

Naraic hissed sharply as two griffins appeared alongside us. Unbonded. Wild. The headmaster had warned about the rogue creatures.

One struck first, slamming into us with feral force. I lit my flame, smoldering a feather to the barb.

But I didn't see the second griffin until its talons tore into me, ripping me from Naraic's back by the claws. I flailed, reaching for Naraic.

And as those claws released me, Naraic's thoughts filled my mind—not of me, but of Klaus. His screams reverberated, golden hair streaming in the wind as he hurtled toward a glinting lake below.

"Release the bond, Naraic," Klaus cried. "Release it now! Severyn will find you—I've seen it."

Naraic obeyed, the bond snapping like brittle glass. Water rushed up to meet me, cold and suffocating.

Yet I was still falling, and a lake didn't await me.

Klaus's final words echoed through the fading bond, a whisper swallowed by the deep lake water: "Find Severyn. Protect her with your life, Naraic. Thank you—thank you for everything."

And as water consumed my dying brother's lungs, that last call through their bond was the least expected words I would ever hear. *"Tell Archer to protect Severyn when she finds you, and I forgive him for falling in love with my sister."*

Those were Klaus' last words before that bond was silenced.

"We will, Klaus Blanche. We will protect Severyn."

I waited for the impact... for my body to crack against the earth, not deserving of the soft blow of lake water. I reached for Naraic, but I fell faster than he could dive.

Wings encased me. And it was not Naraic who caught me, but Ciaran's black-scaled neck. She shoved me toward her spine, and I held my breath, wrapping around her.

"Ciaran?" I asked.

She didn't answer—our bond was too weak, or she knew allowing another rider on her was against some unspoken rule.

Seven riders ripped past and through the valley of wild griffins, snarling and tearing through the air. I hugged Ciaran as we took off. Naraic was a few beats behind.

But through the haze, I hadn't seen that silver-backed wyvern headed for us with two dangled limbs tucked low with aged scales.

Naraic attacked first, shredding the wyvern's right wing down the middle with a strike. The wyvern hissed, snarling and biting into Naraic's neck.

No.

I felt his pain as mine, nearly blacking out right there.

"Retreat, Naraic!" I hissed.

Naraic took a swipe, and I felt each pound, each claw tear into his scales.

The academy dimmed in the mist, and I buried my face into Ciaran's scales because I couldn't watch him die.

As wing beats halted, I swore I would see pearl wings falling below me, but only torn grey ones lay in that valley of green.

"Ride," Naraic growled, *"and be fast."*

Ciaran forced herself to the fields with each beat of her muscles. Wind slashed my face, and I turned to see Malachi's fingers waving beside us.

"No hard feelings," she yelled, realizing whose dragon I rode a heartbeat later. "Is that *Ciaran*?"

Ciaran slashed through the violent wind thrown at us. "She saved me," I said. Then, Ciaran snarled, unleashing a shadowed breath at Malachi.

Naraic slammed into Astoria, forcing them to veer a hard right and allowing Ciaran and me to take the lead. *"Don't look back. Keep your eyes on the field,"* barked Naraic.

I saw that soft glow of the finish line where no dragons waited victoriously. Then the wind ripped us back ten feet, and Malachi jerked in the lead. *Damnit.*

I struck a flame, tilting off Ciaran's neck as I wrapped the fiery whip around Astoria's tail. I pulled back quickly, and Malachi veered down. We were wing-to-wing now as we neared the finish line. I struck Astoria again on the underside of her belly. Her wings arched, slowing with a hiss.

Naraic followed, and we hit the ground hard. I gripped Ciaran's neck with all my strength, spinning as Malachi crashed beside us in a roll. I rested on Ciaran's body, feeling the weight of every eye in the crowd fixed on me and Archer's dragon. Her pale violet eyes steadied me as I tumbled off, landing hard on my knees. Naraic followed, curling his tail around Ciaran's in an unspoken bond.

Malachi swarmed me with a sweaty embrace. "You won, Sev." She wiped a streak of blood off my cheek. "You won Skyfall."

"I dismounted Naraic. I fell. I'm disqualified." I could hardly feel my left leg at this point. I leaned against Naraic, whose snout nudged me toward the headmaster and the king.

"Your feet never touched the ground, North," growled Naraic.

A few seconds later, the headmaster adjusted his wind-blown cloak as he lifted my arm. "Severyn Blanche wins Skyfall with eleven ribbons."

Those words did not taste victorious. Not with Naraic bleeding from his torn scales. Alaric was dead. And I killed Delair. What had I *done*? Everyone stared, including Archer, whose eyes locked on Ciaran's protective stance behind me.

A second breath sounded in my mind. *His.*

The king dug his snake cane into the grass hard, balancing upright. His voice was louder than the faded scoffs of Archer down our bond. "Severyn is disqualified. That is not her bonded dragon," the king said.

The crowd went silent. I couldn't tell the truth, not when Naraic was supposed to be dead. The headmaster gasped, realizing a moment too late that the pearl one holding me from falling was. Victory lasted moments before the remaining sixteen riders flew in. Before, I would be stripped of my quell in front of the entire school body.

Like mother like daughter.

Malachi boldly confronted the king with a voice only a blood relative could use. "That dragon chose her. Severyn won."

"Dragons do not choose between riders," the headmaster spat. "Doing so would nearly break the bond between dragon and rider. And that creature she rode is *already* claimed."

Pride wasn't worth dying for. I'd take being disqualified rather than answering why Naraic was alive.

The king surveyed me. Naraic and Ciaran rested together, and I hoped I was the only one who could see their matching scales, that the underbelly of Ciaran was of the same pearl texture as Naraic's spine.

"They do if their dragons are bonded. Severyn won the race, and I will not strip her of that victory." Malachi held her chin upright.

Strip. She would not strip me of my *victory*. She'd get my life stripped from me if she didn't *shut up*.

The king stared at me with a familiar gaze of green, deep-set eyes, yet I could have sworn they were amber before.

"Very well," he growled. The king gripped my wrist, raising my hand in the air. "Severyn Blanche has won the one-hundredth-and-one Skyfall race." His voice muffled through the ringing in my skull.

This victory would cost my life. I was sure of it.

* * *

The infirmary beds were full of riders. Damien groaned in one, leaning against the wooden headboard as he saw me. "I heard you won, congratulations." A wrap was around his waist with ice packs melted into the sheets. And I lost count of the bruises on his ribs.

He was broken.

"Hardly," was all I said, having no energy to explain the events leading after and how pissed I was at Malachi. "How are you doing?"

"The aide says I'm lucky to be walking. I dislocated seven disks in my back and my neck. It will take a week for me to get back on my feet and probably a lifetime of pain," he said with a groan.

"I saw Everett. He didn't mean to hurt you."

"He came out of nowhere and froze Emerich's scales, and I had nothing to grip onto as I fell. Maybe when Everett died, and you saved him, it did something to their bond. We know nothing about your quell."

I furrowed my brows. "I wasn't going to let him die. You were the one who convinced me to save him."

"I know. You did what you had to do. There is a reason why your quell is forbidden. I hoped I could train you to shield before the Serpent bid, and that offer still stands."

Something distant and unsettling stirred, and I could feel the change between us—it felt like I'd grown new skin over the weeks, shredded that faux frosted coat. "I'll be waiting for you to heal."

He half-grinned. "You can't get rid of me that easily, Sev."

Chapter 18

I scrubbed my skin raw, scrubbing all that blood off until my palms were flushed red. Surprisingly, the leather vest remained intact even after griffin claws had ripped through the backside. Bruises and wind burns covered my face and aching body. I was sure my blunt land on Ciaran had broken a rib.

I stared into the shattered mirror and finally realized I had won Skyfall, just as my mother had. I always believed we were not similar, and I could never endure what had happened in her past. But the longer I was away from her, the more the resemblance became uncanny.

The air was tight and cold in the hallway as I returned to my room. The lights flickered, stretching into endless darkness. I collapsed in my bed, not knowing I had closed my eyes before sleep had taken claim of my mind, dragging me into a depthless coma. It was Naraic. Our bond had finally snapped in place, enough for me to feel everything he felt. Enough that it took Malachi shaking me to wake up.

Her blonde ends brushed against my face, whispering, "The king has called for you. He wants to have dinner."

I shrugged Malachi off as a dream. "Go away."

"Get up." The wind ripped through the duvet, snatching it off my body. "I won't ask again."

I shook my head. "The king has called for *me*?"

She grinned. "Yes, you won Skyfall. It's tradition to have dinner with him. Now, I suggest changing and combing your hair first."

I got out of bed and began yanking a brush through the ends of my hair. "This is your fault. I was okay with losing, and now Naraic's life is in danger because you had to be noble."

"All I said was Ciaran was bonded with your dragon. He doesn't know you rose him from the dead. For all we know, Naraic was in hiding for two years. I thought you'd be happy you won. It's an honor to be invited to dinner with the king. Smile and accept anything he offers."

I cursed under my breath, rifling through my closet for the nicest academy clothes I could find. Malachi tossed me a white, long-sleeved button-down and a black skirt from her closet. "Wear this," she said.

"Thank you," I muttered, pleating my bangs back. I stopped mid-braid and stared at her, raising a brow. "Can you come? Please."

She dusted a fleck off my shoulder. "No, I can't come. I wasn't invited."

"Fine."

A knock sounded at our door.

Three guards stood motionless outside, their silver armor faintly glinting in the dim light, swords strapped in rigid precision across their backs. Without a word, they flanked me, their heavy boots echoing through the stone halls as they led me upward—through winding staircases and towards the highest door in the castle.

A serpent statue loomed atop the academy's tallest peak.

Dawn brushed against the melted shadows of Night, their meeting drenched in Autumn's weeping haze. Summer's warmth lingered on the edges of Spring's tender lush, clinging to the barriers of Day's golden light. People had died to see this view. Killed… like me.

The air felt stale and heavy, each gasp dragging through my tightening chest. Behind me, the door clicked shut.

A golden cloak draped along the stone tiles, glinting pure light within the stained-glass window—not a sea of stars, but the sun. Half-drunk, a goblet of wine perched in the king's slender hands, stained with red film. He wore no crown—but the sight of him had me bowing amidst the ache in my shoulders.

I was seven again. My father, years younger, fewer wrinkles, with his hand pressed firmly on my back. "If you are ever to grace the king with your presence, first you must bow and smile." And so, I did. "If the king offers you something, you take it."

"Your majesty," I began, my voice trembling. "It is a pleasure to meet you."

I took my first step towards the large mahogany dining table carved with intricate designs. A crystal chandelier hung over the table, scattering embers across the room. Another empty chair, arched claw-footed legs curled into a spiral with a deep-purple velvet cushion, faced the twenty-foot slab of wood, covered with every delicacy I could imagine. Fresh ham with cranberry sauce, stuffed turkey, and every vegetable—even ones that would never grow in the bitter cold of the north.

The king turned to face me, curiosity beaming in his wide green eyes. I sat without hesitation.

He strummed his empty fingers along the table. "Severyn Blanche, where have you been hiding all these years?"

"Sir, I was born in the Frozen Valley of Northern Colindale. It isn't exactly a place one leisurely visits." My breath was shallow. I didn't linger on his aged face for too long.

He hummed a low tune I couldn't quite place. "You willed flame. It always fascinates me when students are called to a realm they have never stepped foot in. This academy was designed to have great leaders flourish in the lands. Some of the strongest blood has been poured to create the trials, the wards that keep Winter chilled and Summer hot. My, the academy's founders imported every flower and vine from across the lands."

A chill ran down my spine. "My mother was born in Ravensla, your honor. If chosen to be a Serpent, I will do my best." I kept my hands laced in my lap and didn't dare take a sip of the red wine the aide poured before he did.

He swirled his goblet thrice, legs of red crawling the glass rim. "Fallon Blanche could have taken the entire Continent at its reins. I see you in her. She sat in that same seat twenty-six years ago." He gulped a heavy sip, a grin curling his thin lips as he jangled a lavender pendant on his wrist. "You have her eyes, my dear."

I sipped the wine, tasting berries and oak. "Her eyes are gone."

"She bartered them for her life. Your mother, as powerful as she is, was also reckless."

I dared to ask how.

"She chose to give up her quell to live in the North. She chose babies and a family over her life. Anger claimed her. A quell is what makes us, Severyn." He leaned in closer. "Do you understand?"

There was something uncanny about his eyes and how they lagged from the rest of his head.

"And is that life so wrong? Perhaps she didn't want that." I stabbed a pork loin, cutting into the meat as the king took another gulp of wine, spilling it down his speckled grey beard.

"Your mother could have been a Serpent. She gave up her life to raise Charles. And when he joined the academy, I closely watched him. To ensure he would not turn into the weapon that was your mother. Then, when he bonded with a griffin, I let my guard down. He was weak, weaker than Fallon. But when Klaus came along and took after his mother's dragon rider days, he started showing signs of a forbidden quell. I knew I was a fool to believe her blood would not taint her children."

His shoulders rolled back, placing a leg over his knee. "I knew Naraic and Ciaran from when I was a young boy, and I was devastated to hear about Naraic's passing, but it seems those emotions were for nothing because a dead dragon has risen." His stained lips quivered. "Dare to explain, my dear?"

"I found him alive, sir. He bonded with me." Liquid lies coursed through my veins. I was committing an act of treason.

"Do not lie to me, Blanche. How did you revive the dragon? Tell me, or I will kill it again and force you to necromancy the creature." He straightened his head, fists slamming onto the wooden table. Those green eyes whirred, and I swore he'd stolen them from my mother and shoved them into his eye sockets.

I had to calm my breathing.

"I want to ensure you will not kill Naraic or Ciaran if I tell you the truth." I swallowed hard as I mentioned his name. "That includes Archer."

A wicked smile curved his lips. "You have my word."

"Ciaran led me to Naraic. He was wounded for two years. He—he wasn't dead," I stuttered. "That is the honest truth, your Highness." I forced a smile, trying to control my breathing amidst my lies.

"I don't think I quite believe you." His eyes narrowed, then a cold mask slicked over his features like the dead of winter.

Someone screamed torturously behind the wooden door before it groaned open, and Knox fell to his knees, gagged with a cloth. "Severyn!" he cried. "Turn around."

It all happened so fast. The sound of his neck snapping—his body lying lifeless as he took his last breath. My scream set every curtain on fire. The table was ablaze, cindering whatever food touched my wrath. I went rigid, forgetting how to walk, even how to crawl, as I moved toward Knox's body on my hands and knees.

A leash of light bound me in place. "How—how could you?" I screamed at the king with such hatred that it took everything in me not to set him on fire and cinder that golden cloak to ash. I wanted this to all be a nightmare.

Pain and guilt were all I felt. All I would ever feel again.

"One less Blanche to fight for the title. Will you allow your brother to die, or will you save him?" The king's voice was so venomous I thought I would need a second cure.

Knox was dead, and only I could save him.

Chapter 19

I pressed my palm against Knox's pale cheek, knowing that action would cost me my life.

Live, damn it. I willed every ounce of strength and hope in my veins for Knox to breathe again. Myla didn't take this long to wake up, and neither did Everett. Something was wrong. My hands trembled as I pressed them against Knox's chest.

Live. Please. The thought surged through me like a desperate prayer, my breath catching as I conjured up death's waxing, boiling presence through my lungs. I would never forgive the king if Knox didn't survive. How would I write to Mother and Father, telling them that two of their sons had died on the same day, two years apart?

The king chuckled, a sound more akin to a desperate scoff. "And to think I believed you were something extraordinary."

Seconds felt like hours as I held Knox's cheek. My tears blurred his face, and I barely registered the soft claps from the king as he leaned back in his chair, whispering my mother's name. "Fallon Blanche's daughter can wake the dead, considering she wields death."

Knox shot forward, his eyes blazing with confusion. Relief crashed over me, and I sobbed uncontrollably. The king, amused, sipped from his goblet, his green eyes glowing. "You are just like your brother, Knox. You saw a forbidden quell and did the right thing by bringing it to the headmaster's attention. Honesty has its rewards at the academy."

Betrayal crashed over me like a tidal wave. My heart sank as the truth hit me, boiling in my gut like venom, curdling every ounce of trust I had in Knox.

He wouldn't meet my gaze, his lips pressed tight, chin lowered. The troublemaking brother who never cared for curfew, who seemed carefree and loyal, had betrayed me.

"What are you going to do with me?" I hissed at the king, the fire in my voice barely masking my fear.

"Nothing, for now," he replied. "I'll let the Serpents deal with you at the Bid. No one likes knowing their neighbor is more powerful." He waved dismissively, and three guards stepped forward, flanking him as he turned towards the door. Before he left, he glanced back, his green eyes sharp. "Oh, and you should know—every rider of Naraic's has died. He will always choose Ciaran."

I shuddered, rage and exhaustion clashing within me. The king's words gnawed at my composure, and I leaned against the table, my fiery gaze locked on Knox.

"Have you nothing to say to me?" I demanded. "I trusted you."

Knox's voice broke, his words shaky. "Nothing that would make sense. I noticed a change in Everett. He seemed withdrawn, and I assumed it was because he was homesick. Then you told me how you saved him, and I felt sick. It seemed unnatural, Sev. I didn't know what to do. The headmaster promised he wouldn't expel you until he discovered the truth. I didn't know it would lead to this."

"Well, it has led to this, Knox. I watched them snap your neck in front of me. How could you not come to me first?"

"The academy is here to help us strive to be our best. You would have stopped me, and I feared if the king found out at the Bid, he would kill you immediately. This was me helping you. They stripped Mother of her quell. Klaus is dead. I couldn't lose you, too."

I clenched my fists, my voice sharp. "I expected this from Charles, but not from you."

I left him standing there, the weight of his betrayal pressing heavily on my shoulders. My steps echoed down the spiral stairs as I descended, my energy spent. The lanterns flickered and extinguished one by one as I passed, as if the academy itself knew I had nothing left to give.

The Night halls loomed before me, cold and uninviting. The door wouldn't open on command, forcing me to summon my last bit of strength to twist the brass handle. Malachi's lips moved as she spoke, but I couldn't hear her words over the ringing in my ears—the ringing of Knox's scream, the haunting sound of Alaric's bond breaking. I felt her at my feet, untying my boots, and then, as the covers tucked around me, she kissed my forehead with a small, comforting smile.

I slept through warding and avoided combat for three days. My walks to class were silent, Damien absent from my side. Naraic couldn't fly until his wings healed, and even then, I feared reopening his wound. Students whispered as I passed, their eyes following me. Winning Skyfall had made me infamous. Even Monty, who I thought was still angry about Archer's punch, smiled at me in the halls.

That evening, I had my portrait painted for the grand hall. I sat still for three hours, the rows of framed faces staring back at me, each one poised and etched. Twenty-six frames down, I found my mother. Her old name, Fallon Berret, was inscribed beneath her image. Her portrait captured her before she lost her eyes—a younger version of me, down to the white birthmark on our bangs. Her green eyes gleamed with happiness, her full lips curled into a radiant smile. She was everything I had imagined and more.

I leaned against the wall, my chin high. I wouldn't become my mother. I wouldn't let the king steal my quell, my eyes.

My life.

"You could have at least smiled in your portrait. In fifty years, the new students will believe we tortured you," Archer said, his voice dripping with sarcasm as he appeared from the shadows. He wore a grey suit, his polished leather shoes gleaming in the dim light.

"Half true," I shot back, forcing my mind away from that one night.

"Someone needs rest. Is Damien keeping you up at night?" he drawled, his smirk infuriatingly casual.

"Yes, in fact, I was needing some well-deserved rest." I turned to leave, but his hand gripped my wrist, pulling me back. The rush of that night overwhelmed me, the memory all-consuming.

"I heard the king invited you to dinner," he said in a low voice.

"I ensured Ciaran and Naraic's protection if that's what you're asking. Please let me go unless you need me for something else, Serpent." My voice wavered as I held back tears.

Archer recoiled slightly. "He knows about the Gemini dragons?"

"He knows about my quell. He forced me to watch Knox die and then save him." My voice cracked as I stifled a sob, the mental image of Knox's neck snapping fresh and vivid. "If you've come to annoy me further, I'm not in the mood."

"I had no idea. Ciaran told me she saved you at the race. I assumed any third-year would have pieced together what you were to me once they saw you on my dragon's back."

What I was to him.

"I need the cure, Archer. I'm weak. My left leg could hardly hold me for two days after the race."

He grabbed my wrist again, a hint of humor touching his grin. "That's normal when riding dragons. You're gaining muscle."

I yanked my hand free, my patience gone. "I'm not in the mood. I understand you dislike me, but we both know Naraic chose me the day Klaus passed."

Tears burned down my cheeks, and I didn't bother to wipe them away. Then, unexpectedly, his arms wrapped around me— strong, unyielding, pulling me into the solid warmth of his chest. My cheek pressed against him, and for a moment, the weight of the world eased. His hand lifted, brushing a tear from my face with surprising gentleness.

"I never wanted this for you," he hissed, his voice low and raw.

"What do you mean?"

"For us to care for each other. Knowing only the other's name was simpler. Now, fear and death bind us, and I'm not sure how long I can pretend your tears don't hurt me."

I melted into him, something stronger than gravity anchoring me against his chest. For a fleeting second, it felt like I could breathe again. Then, as quickly as it began, he dropped his arms. His face paled, and without another word, he turned on his heel and disappeared into the shadows, leaving me alone with the aching void of what remained.

***

Damien was walking on the seventh day with only a limp. Knox hadn't said a word to me either, even as we silently were pinned against each other during combat, and I knew he let me win that day. I knew him throwing me a dagger my way was his version of apologizing.

I spent that afternoon with Damien, learning shielding. We sat by the docks as the darkened sea crashed into the sand. We didn't talk about Skyfall, we didn't talk about anything other than preparing my mind for the Bid.

Damien clasped his hands together. "Lesson one of shielding, Serpents possess advanced powers, meaning they can crack you open with their quell and see into you. Pretend your mind is made of solid metal, Severyn. Block me out," he said.

I gripped the wooden dock, strumming my fingers over the splinters, forcing an invisible wall up. Metal curled around my mind like bent iron. There were still gaps where Damien managed to break in and throw my thoughts back at me—where I relived, over and over, Knox's death.

Damien knew how to break me. I tried to push away every memory he ripped out, but his brute force always found the cracks. In a few rare moments, I had managed to kick him out entirely, but he always returned, and any shield I built up melted the moment he crept back inside.

"Use your quell, Sev," Damien said, his voice low but commanding. "If your shield isn't metal, make it cindering flames. Burn me out."

Flame sparked in my palms, but I contained it. I siphoned it inward, as I'd done with the lanterns in the hall. I whirled that flame around my mind, and when Damien crept inside, I scorched him out with a whip of snapping fire.

Damien hissed, flinching back. "Shit, that one hurt."

"How was that?" I asked, my voice tight.

He leaned on the dock, nodding slowly. "This whole time, I was going about it the wrong way. My shield is glass—thick glass, might I add. You needed something familiar to build yours."

I crept closer, building up that fortress of smoldered ash until my mind pulsed. The pressure was so intense I thought I might burst a blood vessel and spew liquid flames from my parted lips if I moved too quickly.

"Again," I hissed, repeating it three times over.

He nodded. "Let's try something different."

It became a warzone within my skull—sharp glass penetrating the perimeter, finding my weaknesses. He burrowed a hole within, dust and debris contaminating my thoughts, planting an image in my mind.

And… suddenly I was trapped.

I was bare, bowing to him as he wore a crown. It was a world where I lived under his reign. My lips were on his in the next frame, his hands on my body. Frozen inside his mind existed a reality where he was a Serpent, and I was beneath him.

Bowing to him. Married to him. Trapped.

"Damien, stop!" I shouted, my voice cracking.

I reached for the dagger hidden beneath my skirt, but the trance he'd trapped me in withered away as he pinned me down. My blade clanged against the wood below.

"Once you're stripped, you'll have nothing," Damien said. "But you can stay with me, Sev. We could be happy together."

He thought I'd enjoy that fantasy—even thank him for the possibility of his savior complex. "No," I said firmly, my voice cold.

Damien stifled a laugh. "You think the king will let you live because you're bonded to a Serpent?"

I exhaled sharply. "No."

He grabbed the dagger from the dock and slid it back into the sheath along my thigh. His hands gripped my waist, his body pressing firmly against my cracking ribs. "Did you think I'd hurt you?"

His pounding chest weighed against me. My fingers skimmed along his ribs, where I felt the hidden sheath of his blades. "I will never live under your reign." I tried to grab it, to yank it out, and place it between us.

"Your enemies should be your friends, Sev. You learned this on day one."

I swallowed bile, choking on the weight of my own words. "And what do they say about lovers?"

His thumb traced a fallen tear along my cheek. "That two should not feast with only one fork. You are not my lover. That kiss between us was a mistake."

I stared up, willing the tears to stop. If that fantasy came true, I'd become my mother—a woman who had lived beneath the power she once held. Beneath the reign she could have claimed and the followers she could have led with her unstoppable wrath.

And for once, I saw us clearly.

Rivals.

* * *

Naraic's wings were scabbing over, and I'd finally taken my first full breath in over a week. With Ciaran resting beside him, I sat with them after my *eventful* shield training with Damien.

Gods, I needed to clear my mind.

It was two weeks until the Serpent Bid, and every day seemed to blur into the next. I had a sword, nearly onto my second. I'd won the Skyfall race, but was that kind of power feared? Would they see through the metal and ash and decide I wasn't worth the risk? Would Father allow them to kill me right then and there? We had four days off for the annual Harvest Festival, and most students with flying enigmas had already left for home.

I spent the last hour with a quill and paper, trying to phrase a letter to Mother that only she would understand.

How did Thaw go? Have Father's shakes gotten worse? I tried to be everything I wasn't. I spent a week in the Winter realm, only to be called to Summer and bonded to a dragon. I won Skyfall and had dinner with the king. I've bonded with a Gemini dragon whose other rider is a Serpent. Academy life is nothing like I expected. I could use your guidance.
Love,
Severyn Blanche.

I'd written this out a dozen times—crumpled paper strewn at my feet. I'd probably never send it. The chaos that would ensue when Father saw my flame and knew his title was doomed kept the words in my hand instead of the mail.

Ciaran rumbled behind me, raising her wings as Archer approached. He tossed dried chicken heads toward Naraic and Ciaran. Naraic roared, snapping one mid-air.

Archer nodded as he mounted Ciaran, his speckled blue eyes meeting mine as he adjusted a bag strap. "Where are you going?" I asked.

"Somewhere I'm not surrounded by children," he replied, raising a brow. "If you insist on specifics, I'm going to see my brother Kian in Ravensla."

I scoffed. "We are all adults here, in case you forgot. You're only two years older." Dark clouds gathered above, cloaking the field in shadow.

I realized then that I always felt him when he left—the pull of the tether snapping along the borders of each country. I didn't have it in me for him to go again, for those nights to suck me into their silence, for anxious thoughts to rattle my bones as I waited for him to return—injured or worse.

"I must have forgotten." He grinned, his tone playful. "You seem to disobey every one of my commands like a child."

"Can I come with you?" The words escaped before I could stop them, and I wished I could immediately pull them back. "Naraic doesn't like being away from Ciaran for too long. I should also visit the country I'm supposedly up to rule…"

"Naraic is seventy-one years old. He can manage three days without his sister. And besides, who will keep Damien occupied?"

"Damien is twenty-two years old. He can keep himself occupied," I shot back. "Besides, I need air. And before you point out that I'm standing in a field, I mean I need to get off this damn island for a few days."

His lips pressed into a thin line, and I braced for the refusal. What I was asking bordered on inappropriate. "Fine," he said finally, his tone clipped. "But I won't stop for you. It's a six-hour flight to Ravensla. I hope you understand that."

I forced myself to suppress the grin threatening to rise. "I understand." My fingers laced behind my back as I tilted my head, feigning innocence. "I mean, I did win Skyfall. Perhaps it's you I'll be stopping for."

"You won with my dragon."

I rolled my eyes and left with nothing but the clothes on my back.

Chapter 20

Naraic had a rough start, tilting left as we glided over the grey ocean of silken waves. Starlight guided us north along the coast, and I saw how far the academy stretched, how those ice peaks never melted, and how daylight shattered only in one quadrant.

Riding with Ciaran and Naraic was something of a dream—their wings were in sync, each breath timed, nose to nose. Our veins became one as each pound of his chest matched mine, along with that much softer beat I thought might have been Archer.

Evening twilight held high, consuming that last bit of orange-hued sunset until we rode through the pitch-black night. I kept my eyes on the sea above, masking the oiled waters below, even as sleep groaned in my dry eyes, the salt stinging with every blink. I dragged my arm along Naraic's neck as hours passed. It was unbelievable that Archer made this trek every other week to attend to his Serpent duties.

If I won Serpent, what would become of us? If we were worlds apart? The Night districts were on the other end of Verdonia, near the capital… near Malvoria.

If I won the Serpent title… those callous dreams never reached beyond my whirred thoughts, never touched the light, even more so now as my life was strung with withered cords as the bid approached.

Heat blew against my face as we entered Ravensla. I wasn't tired anymore, but my legs throbbed from tightly gripping Naraic as the wind picked up and the claw-like waves ripped through the greyed sea. The dragons' wings tucked low as the city bloomed before us. Rows and rows of villas traced along the shoreline. Castles jutted through the sand dunes. Summer's air was hot and heavy, sucking through my clenched throat as we landed.

Ravensla. My mother's hometown.

A dozen other dragons lounged lazily along the sandy shore. Archer casually tossed the last bits of dried chicken at Ciaran and Naraic, the dragons' tails coiled around his waist. With voracious delight, they devoured the treat.

"Stay close, right by my side," Archer commanded abruptly, seizing my hand and yanking me beside him. "The city is dangerous this time of year."

All those hours of fighting sleep faded. "My mother was raised here," I said in awe, gazing at sculptures of sand carved into humans and dragons—almost frozen in time as snarled snouts gaped along the cobblestone path. Each wrinkle on those feared faces was captured art that only years of sculpting could create. Each scale was different, detailed to precision.

"I know," he said. "Klaus told me your mother was born here. Seems like your family hid a lot from you."

I couldn't keep my eyes off the sculptures. "Are they—" I couldn't say the word. That art had to be real at one point, breathing and living years before.

"Ravensla has a dark history. They are mummified travelers from the settler days. The stories speak of a woman who could turn anything breathing into sand."

"Was it a forbidden quell?"

"Yes, there are good people with dangerous quells and evil who seek to find them. Take Seekers. Most of Verdonia's scriptures of the future were written during the Forgotten days when quells knew no bounds. But those Seekers were worked until bone jutted from their fingers, and they practically bled ink." He continued, "It wasn't until one wrote the story of the king's bloodline that the Herrings killed off every Seeker in Verdonia."

"They weren't stripped?" I gasped. "Do you know what the scripture wrote?"

A city appeared before us, dazzled in lanterns, shabby brick buildings, and tapestries strewn within the narrowed streets.

"It did not speak of secrets or death but that of a forbidden love story. It spoke of an overthrown crown by a mixed blood. Seekers are perhaps the most dangerous quell to exist. To know the death of you and everyone you love and care about, to know a world exists beyond your time."

"Malachi will take the throne. She deserves it," I said.

"No. Monty has plotted Malachi's death since day one of the academy. It is scribed that the blood of a Herring will stain the lands. She's aware. Why do you think she has spent every waking moment with him? Malachi stands in the way of anyone taking the throne. Her mother was killed, and it drove her father mad. She had five siblings who all died at the academy. Malachi is the only living Herring who can take the king's throne, but it is down to one of us if she dies. The rise of a new line of royalty."

Archer looked off into the distance, past the lurching sea beside us. "I've heard stories that some wrote of a Lynch taking the throne. I tried my best to bury that. Then, I realized how deadly that quell was, how mad it made people." Archer shook his head.

"Did you go mad?"

"Nearly. Klaus's death didn't help. We bonded fast, unlike you and me. I believe we are night and day when it comes to our differences. I knew you had to grow, that I would have to let you fall before you could fly."

"You mean to die? You are withholding a cure from me."

Archer scoffed. "There was no cure. Those snakes are deadly but not poisonous. I wanted you to see what you could be, and I don't trust Damien. I know you like him, and he's your friend, but Damien knows your mind—knows what you want to hear, Severyn."

I steeled before the rage heated my veins. "He doesn't trust you, and I don't blame him."

Archer cocked his head. "And why is that?"

It wasn't ash I choked on, but the truth. "Your mother. Damien knew about her death, and you never believed him."

"Not believing him was the worst thing I'd ever done. But you must understand—we were raised to be Serpents. Your brothers were, too. My parents never had a marriage of love and laughter. We spent our entire childhood fighting with swords and brawling until we bled. I was raised to be great." His voice grew along the path, echoing back. "I didn't believe Damien because that meant my life was damaged."

"How do you know I wasn't raised to be a Serpent? Damien was sent away to boarding school. He needed someone while you were partying at Serpent gatherings."

Archer looked down. "I assumed you never wanted the title. Klaus was trained and already had his quell, but you were different. You seemed lost. I spent many hours with Klaus. You seemed to be a proud topic of his… I can see why."

I brushed a loose strand of hair back. "Klaus had his quell before he joined?"

"You never knew?"

I wondered if all secrets craved air, if they could never truly exist without light, without voice. "Do we ever… truly find ourselves?" I asked, my voice barely more than a whisper. "Is being a Serpent… worth it?"

We walked the dimmed pathway towards the city. "I still ask that. I'm not as cruel as you perceive me to be." He let out a breath of air. "You did kill my lead heir. Perhaps it is you I should be worried about?" He raised a brow, the humor replaced with something I couldn't understand.

"She was after Naraic. I had no choice," I said.

"First blood is always the most impressionable."

How many lives had he taken? "Do I dare ask who your first blood was?"

Disdain crossed his features. "Perhaps another day. Right now, we need to find an inn that has a vacancy. The Ravensla Harvest is quite grand this time of year. Most of the wine for the Continent is produced here. It harbors some of the finest fruits of our land." His fingers grazed mine. "Scavengers are everywhere, and someone like you they would love to get their hands on."

"You mean my neval streak?" I swallowed hard as I glanced back at Naraic and Ciaran, curled up together and resting. It reminded me of the house cats we had back home and how their fur would blend as one as they slept by the windowsill.

"I meant your beauty, but your neval streak is quite a stir around these coasts."

My stomach heated. "In other words, I am tradeable?"

Eyes ahead on the bright city, he said, "Take the damn compliment, Severyn."

"Is that an order, Serpent?" But as soon as I said it, his face fell.

The city welcomed us with dancers dressed in flowing silk garments and bedazzled eye masks as they performed along the streets. Lanterns hung from the brick and sand buildings, and colorful fabrics were strewn across the wooden canopies, leading through winding paths made entirely of cemented sand and seashells. Vendors beckoned us toward their wooden carts of trinkets, masks concealing everything besides their eyes. The streets smelled of cooked meat and citrus, and then we were in the cluster of the city.

A crowd circled around a man whose face was half teal scales. An arched mustache curled the slender frame of his face. Gold coins danced by his feet as the spectators watched his show. His hand raised, and out came a translucent dragon, no more than the size of a rabbit. It flew around the alley, doing flips and swirls in the air before dragging back into his hand like tethered smoke.

I stopped dead in my tracks. "What is that?" I asked Archer. "It's mesmerizing."

"An illusionist. You don't want to get trapped by one. They can alter your mind and force you to see things. It's an older quell, not very useful unless you wish to spend your life as a street performer."

"Do you believe that all quells should be a weapon? I mean, it's sort of beautiful how he can create art with his mind," I said.

"I enjoy beautiful women and sunsets—a quell is not beautiful. A quell is your worth in a world where power is everything."

I didn't hear his response. A soft buzz sounded, almost like static crawling along my eardrums. "Can we stay for a moment?" It was as if my mind was roped with chains to the performer, and even taking one more step, I felt I'd miss something great.

Archer grabbed my hand, pulling me along. "See, this is how they get you. All he wants is gold." He tugged me harder, but I would not go. "Severyn, please—"

My boots felt heavier. My eyes laced on the man in sheer delight as he tipped his black hat and smiled at me, raising a glowing palm. "A taste of what you need the most," he said. "After that, it's five coins per minute."

I asked as heat sucked through my lungs, "What do I need the most?"

And nothing could have prepared me to see Klaus standing before me. *Klaus.* He looked the same as two years ago but he wore a Serpent uniform. His arms were crossed, staring at me as if he had no idea he was dead, as if the shock in my eyes concerned him.

"Are you alright, Severyn?" he asked, wavering between Archer and me. "Just ignore Archer. He's a grump."

I counted his freckles as if I'd forgotten how many his cheeks bore. I stared into that golden-flecked iris, a once broken promise of his northern bloodline that boiled into steam.

Oh, Klaus.

"Never better," I said. With every gulp, my throat dried like shards of glass were poured into my airways. I wrapped my arms around him, but the empty air ripped through my broken heart. "You're not real," I whispered, stepping back, but something dragged me out of the alley with a tightened, chilled grasp around my wrist.

Klaus waved at us. "But the show was just getting good, Sev. You can't leave now! I told Mother I'd keep my eye on you," he yelled, his voice drowning out as the crowd swept him away in a flurry of smoke and ash.

It took going down three alleyways for me to come to my senses. Archer cupped my cheek, kneeling beside me—beneath me. He was shielding my mind with shadows. Darkness swirled my vision, stirring his face. My chest thundered loud enough for him to check my pulse. His blue eyes held me upright. His lips moved, whispering my name until my hearing was back.

"What was that?" I seethed, catching my stolen breath.

"I warned you. Illusionists can contort your mind in cruel ways. There is no sense in getting wrapped in one. I wouldn't be surprised if those same people were standing there tomorrow until the soles of their feet were blistered and bloody." He hesitated before curling his fingers around my jaw, and I leaned into the coolness of his shadows, knowing if I heated anymore, I'd faint.

"Sometimes we see something we want so desperately it is hard to escape," he whispered, his voice dropping to a near caress.

"I saw Klaus," I said through my barred teeth, a lump forming in my throat. "How is that not a forbidden quell?" The air ripped from my lungs fast.

"There is no harm. He did not bring Klaus back to life. You simply imagined him. Some people enjoy being in a dream state." Archer's gaze lingered on my face longer than necessary, his thumb brushing just faintly over my cheek before dropping away. "We should go."

"I feel sick," I said, clenching my fists. "How many people surrender their life savings to imagine something?"

We stayed in the dark alley for a moment before Archer grabbed my arm and pulled me up. "More than you think. It might take a few hours for your mind to settle. It's best to sleep it off."

I nodded as we moved deeper into the city. Townhouses and shops framed the cobblestone streets. Archer turned sharply, leading us towards a narrow building. Above its door, the word INN was etched into a wooden beam, its once-bold letters now faded and cracked with age.

The air inside smelled of dust and wood. A red velvet couch dominated the waiting area, paired with a coffee table at its center. Books, paintings, and tapestries adorned the walls, their colors muted.

Behind the desk, a man with a black patch over one eye glanced up, his single eye darting to Archer. He scrambled out of his chair, adjusting his rounded glasses with trembling fingers as he bowed deeply.

"Mr. Lynch," he said. "It is an honor to have you here. How may I serve you?" He fumbled for a quill and paper, his hands shaking as he awaited Archer's reply.

Archer shook his head. "We are here visiting Kian. I should have sent a letter ahead of time. But are two rooms available tonight?"

"Kian—yes. Your family home is quite a way out of town in Grimswire." He looked down, afraid to meet Archer's eyes. "We only have one room left in our hostel section. It is not Serpent grade, sir. You understand with the festival how rooms fill up in Ravensla."

"Lynwood, it is fine. I don't expect to be treated differently now that I am a Serpent. We will graciously take whatever you have."

"Very well, sir, and?" He glanced towards me with such genuine delight I swore light rippled from his iris.

"Severyn Blanche. My Father is the Northern Serpent in Colindale."

That light seemed to fade. "Fallon Berret, is that your mother?"

Archer raised his hand. "Lynwood, we have traveled far today, and Severyn was caught in the illusionists' wield. We can all get to know each other tomorrow."

Lynwood nodded as he went behind his desk and fumbled in the drawers before grabbing a rusted key and handing it to Archer. "Very well, room sixty-one. It is down the hall and to the left. Make sure you drink water. Those traps can be exhausting.

Your mother must have warned you of them. I always found her lost among their wield."

"She never mentioned them," I said, wanting desperately to stay five minutes longer and speak with Lynwood. But another patron entered seconds after Archer opened the door to the hall.

We went through the tight halls, where a rusted sixty-one plaque hung above one of the various painted doors. Archer turned the key, and we both stepped into a narrow room, small enough to fit only one bed with a bright patterned duvet and a yellow-painted armoire that looked a hundred years old. Inside, no extravagant tapestries covered the cracked walls. While the city noises were faint, there was no sign of settling even as midnight struck.

Wait—

"There's only one bed," I whispered.

Archer unsheathed his daggers and bow, placing them atop the armoire. Then he went to unlace his boots, nodding toward my stare. "It's one night, Severyn. I promise I don't bite."

My throat tightened. "Oh, I don't mind." I shared a bed with Myla for two nights on the trails. Sharing with Archer couldn't be any different. At least, that's what I told myself.

Archer studied me, squaring those broad shoulders as he pulled off another layer of protective leather garments that fell to the wooden boards with a clunk. "We can be friends, Severyn. You know that, right? I told Klaus I'd protect you, but you do not seek comfort in others. You… do not trust willingly, and I know I haven't put myself in the place of that position."

I shrugged off my leathers, eyeing him down as more of his clothes seemed to strip from him. How many layers was he wearing?

"You want to be my friend? Now, after you lied to me for weeks, claiming I was poisoned." I nearly scoffed at the idea of a Serpent being my friend. I didn't see him as Klaus's friend, and if I did, would it make me admire him more? He prided himself on being something great, and there was no concealing what people would do for power.

The more clothes fell to the floor, the more bare muscles I saw. I didn't know skin could be beautiful and that a wicked man could wear it proudly. *Why is he so attractive?*

"We don't have a choice. Either you hate me, or we make this work. I apologize, Severyn, if I've overstepped."

I waved a hand. "You're a Serpent. I would have to oblige if you demanded that we be friends."

His eyes went up and down. "You're quite flushed. Are you overheating?"

"I'm fine, but clearly, there is a power dynamic here."

His cold mask slipped briefly as something distraught narrowed in his blue gaze. "I see you as my equal. And if our places were switched, I would expect the same." He sprawled onto his back, leaving space for me beside him. He even dared to pat the bed as if I was a begging dog seeking his approval, his affection.

I hesitated, shrugging off the final layers of my leathers before slipping beneath the woven blanket. Curling up, I rested my head against the pillow, letting the tension ease from my body.

"Equal," I hissed under my breath. "You only want to control me."

"What I want, Severyn… is not to control you. I feel very protective of you." I felt his bare back against mine, the shudders of his breath as he faced the wall. And I swore I heard our faint bond rippling between us.

"Goodnight, Archer," I mumbled, unsure if the sound reached him.

That night, I dreamt of growing up in Ravensla and living in a towering building made of sand. I saw winded streets fluttering with tapestries as I stepped through the narrow alleyways. I dreamt of the heat on my body as a silvered mask concealed my face. It wasn't my life, but it was enough to feel as though this should have been, that I'd been trapped in a frozen castle, not knowing what the sun felt like. I had seen the clouds, not knowing the sun existed.

The moon seemed to hover longer as if the strained sun wore itself out from the festivities.

Chapter 21

A pale white gown was placed on the bed that morning. Gold lace traced the slim fitted bodice, elegantly flowing past my knees with a pearl-lined hood hung from the backside.

Archer was gone. His bow, his daggers—everything packed. For a moment, I thought he'd left me stranded as punishment for kicking him in my sleep.

Descending the stairs, I made my way to the reception area. There he was, seated with Lynwood, a steaming cup of tea in hand. Another cup waited on the table across from him.

He looked different today. A flowing white tunic, neatly tucked into black slacks, hung perfectly on his frame. His bow rested across his shoulder, and his damp hair was combed back, gleaming faintly in the morning light. He appeared impossibly normal, yet effortlessly striking.

Lynwood turned to face me, his one eye gleaming with that bright light I had seen last night. "Good morning, Severyn. I hope you slept well after the illusionist got to you."

I nodded, forcing my gaze away from Archer. "I'll be sure to avoid them from now on."

Lynwood's eye danced between Archer and me with a curious expression. "Is this your first time visiting the city?"

"Yes, actually, my mother was born here. You mentioned you knew Fallon?"

"Fallon was unforgettable. She came from no title, and her parents were scavengers. My parents always fed her. She wasn't like the others. She never stole. But when the king visited and invited her to the academy, your mother made her mark during her days there. Top of her class, everyone thought she'd win Serpent that year. Ravensla had gone years without a Serpent. The city was nearly barren before Victor claimed heir."

"My mother was a scavenger?" I nearly choked on the tea. I thought of those ratted, cloaked figures I'd seen overlooking the grounds as we flew.

"Yes. Most scavengers don't possess quells, and for hers to be forbidden was rare—Fallon was rare. And that birthmark certainly held its name." His eye flickered to my bangs.

I nodded at Archer, sipping my tea. "Was your grandfather not a Serpent? How did the city go years without a leader?"

Lynwood strummed his fingers along the wooden coffee table. "Veravine Almera ruled over Ravensla as Verdonia's sixth Summer Serpent for two decades. Rumors say she fell in love with the king when they were at the academy. The queen had her killed, knowing she couldn't compare to Veravine. There was no heir for Ravensla, and as many lands turned ashen with the attacks from the Forgotten, we all waited until a Summer student would claim heir. Scavengers nearly took the land over for those years. I'm sure Victor is keeping close tabs on your brother to hopefully bear him an heir. Victor poured his blood and tears into reviving the land. He did what many could never do."

"And the king allowed his wife to destroy a land over a rumor?" I asked, glancing at Archer. "Wasn't the king scripted to have a forbidden love?"

"Well," Lynwood began. "A rumor like that could destroy a marriage and a Continent—one life is not worth that fallout. Veravine was our leader. Her flame warmed our hearts. The country truly loved her. Not to take away from Victor's accomplishments."

Archer crossed his arms, his expression unreadable. "That story could have been about Veravine. Most of the literature from their time at the academy was burned."

"I try not to feed into all that nonsense," said Lynwood, fixing his crooked eyepatch. "Seekers were known to spread rumors as payback."

I could only imagine being forced to write until bone protruded from your fingers would make anyone mad. "Do you know anything else about my mother? Forgive me, I feel like I never knew the real Fallon."

"I knew the real Fallon," he said, clutching his teacup tighter. "This was nearly three decades ago, and my memory isn't the best regarding the minor details. Fallon never returned home after that. Even her parents never... came back for her. We weren't sure where they came from. Scavengers come and go; they barter whatever odds and ends they can get their hands on. Fallon was the black sheep of the street dwellers. I remember my mother brushing the tangles from her hair once a week and washing her torn clothes. She never stole, never once."

He glanced inside his teacup. "I wondered how she was. I heard she married a Winter Serpent, and I think Fallon just wanted a home." Lynwood placed his mug down. "Please tell her I said hello next time you see her."

Archer studied me as if my entire life had just been laid out for him to analyze. "Klaus never mentioned your mother was a scavenger. I don't think he knew. But it makes sense why Winter did not call to you now. My father's roots have been in the Summer for centuries. But Father was the first Serpent on his side. I would be curious to know where Kian is called next year when he gets his letter."

Archer stood up. "Speaking of Kian, we should be heading out soon. It is an hour's travel out of the city by horseback."

"We can't ride Naraic and Ciaran?" I asked.

"The city has a no-flying ban during festival season," Lynwood said. "Some creatures are volatile. Best not to have bloodshed in the skies."

We said our goodbyes and headed towards the city's core, where the architecture was even more breathtaking in light. Horses trotted along the paths, hauling wagons of fruit. Dust blew within the wind's flurry as crowds drew by. Colorful cloths of rich reds and yellows were strewn across the buildings as makeshift tarps. I saw a few scavengers with their hoods drawn as their inky eyes stalked the crowds with curled fingers beckoning. One darted across the street, snatching a woman's gold bracelet from around her wrist. I shuddered. That was my mother's life of never knowing where her next meal would come from and bartering whatever she could to survive.

We stood in the alley for a moment, and then Archer faced me, hitching my cloak over my head. "Don't leave my side," he said, offering me his hand.

I hesitated for a moment before taking it, my pulse quickening at the subtle warmth of his touch. Tightening my grip, I followed as we sprinted through the crowded streets of Ravensla.

A black stallion awaited us near the stables. Archer helped me up, his hands lingering briefly on my waist. I steadied myself on the horse's broad spine, adjusting to the size difference of Naraic. "He's a bit different than Naraic," I chuckled nervously.

"Serpent—" a man hissed, running towards us with his hood pulled over his head. A dozen eyes shifted as Archer's name hissed under their breaths. He waved casually as he mounted the horse behind me, his movements fluid and practiced.

"You get used to everyone knowing your name. I hoped the clothes would allow us to blend in, but I suppose not," he murmured, his voice low and edged with amusement.

Jerking forward, I instinctively wrapped my arms around his ribs as he softly nudged the horse. "Never leave my sight here. There are good people in these streets, but if they see a woman with me, some may try to take you and sell you back at a price I am unwilling to find out."

I tightened my grip, my cheeks burning at the closeness. "How much am I worth?" I scoffed, trying to mask my flustered nerves.

"Priceless," he murmured, his tone so soft it barely reached me over the clatter of hooves.

Heat rose to my cheeks again, and this time, I couldn't hide it. I didn't know how to respond, so I left the galloping stallion to take us through the never-ending paths.

The sun held high, soaking onto our backs as we rode eastbound. We passed by a few smaller towns near the outskirts of Ravensla, each just as vibrant as the last. A few scavengers walked through the desert lands, heavy woven bags high on their shoulders, chains and trinkets dangling from their baggy clothes. A row of sand warriors jutted in the distance. And I imagined the ferocity of that woman who stood before them, the fear staining their widened eyes as that woman struck them and made them into the sand.

Sand turned into grass, striking a lush garden of ivy and bramble. And it was as though we had entered another realm. The sun was hidden behind a cloud bank, giving a few moments of shadow. We entered another township, crossing over a wobbling bridge where ocean water drew through the coastal village, winding along the paths. Grimswire. I read the silver sign as we passed under it. A few large ships swayed in the current, docked to stone. This village was richer than the others as guards patrolled the streets, ensuring each passing had met their eyes. The golden-haired guard nodded at Archer as we carried on. Colorful fish swam in pools beneath us. We passed a clock tower, and a few pointed buildings made from silvered stone and other fine materials.

And it was as if every metal was welded to create this town. The grounds dazzled with a brilliant glow of diamond-crusted paths as we approached a gate that opened at our arrival, where willow trees and shadow surrounded a large estate. The home was a shrunken-down castle with ivy trailing up to one point. Archer jumped off the horse, helping me down as we walked to the front doors.

"You grew up here?" I choked.

"Yes. Grimswire was where I was born." The door opened, and a male stood near the opening. *Damien?* He had dark hair with a tanned complexion. That same sharp jawline and dimpled left cheek as Damien.

No, it was Kian, the third Lynch brother. This entire family was beyond attractive.

"Archer—" Kian wrapped his arms around his brother's neck, then his hazel eyes flickered at me. They were darker around the iris, flecked with brown swirls within. "And who is this lovely creature?"

Archer's hand hovered the small of my back, his touch light. "Severyn Blanche. Remember her face because she will be your mentor next year," Archer said with a grin.

"So, she is the girl from your letters?" Kian responded with a soft chuckle that struck the hair on my spine to rise. "You are right—she is beautiful. If I were you, Sev, I'd run away now."

What was happening? Archer wrote letters about me. I swallowed hard, failing to keep my voice steady as Kian embraced me with one slender arm. "Damien and I are great friends, too."

He snapped his finger. "That's right, it was Damien who wrote about you. I suppose your little romance ended when you got pushed in line to take the Southern throne. Not all is fair in love and title." Kian took a step back, allowing us to enter. "Make yourself at home, Sevy. There's a fresh pot of tea on. Your room is on the second floor across from Archer's. And if you get scared at night, my bed is always open."

Sevy. That's a new one.

Archer jabbed Kian's ribs. "Be respectful."

Kian smirked. "I'm only looking out for Severyn. Surely she hasn't had enough Lynch in her life." He nudged me as I walked past him. "You know I'm joking, right?"

Warmth hit my face. It was a sense of welcoming. I prodded Kian back and laughed. "Right now, you seem to be my favorite."

The walls were dark gray, their shadows deepened by the flickering light of a log fireplace. At the center of the room lay a fur rug, unmistakably from some Summer beast, its hide stretched and worn with age.

A painting hung on the wall depicted a family of five. The mother, fair-skinned with piercing silver eyes and auburn hair, rested a graceful hand on the eldest son's shoulder—a boy of about twelve. Beside him, two younger boys grinned wide, their toothy, mischievous smiles brimming. My gaze caught on one face.

Damien.

And then, standing tall at the edge of the frame, a man with a dark complexion and hazel eyes froze me in place. A serpent tattoo coiled around his neck, nearly identical to Archer's.

I lingered on his stare longer than I intended, a chill prickling my skin. There was darkness behind those smiles, a shadow I couldn't ignore. Any warmth I'd felt in the room evaporated in an instant.

Damien had to live knowing what his father had done, and no one believed him. I felt for Kian being left alone in this grand home as his two brothers ventured off. I saw myself in him, but at least I had Knox. My family might have had secrets, but none like this. Nothing that made my skin crawl.

I quickly looked down, and Archer studied me. "My father is not here if that is what you are wondering."

I turned on my heel, glancing between the two brothers. "I wasn't," I said, crossing my arms over my chest. "Well, are we going to enjoy this festival or not? Or was this dress for nothing?" I twirled once, showing off the slim-fitting gown. I had to admit Archer had good taste.

Kian snorted, softly punching his brother in the arm. "Archer does not partake in festivals. Good luck getting that hard ass even to smile."

There were a few beats of silence. "Would you like to go?" Archer asked.

I shot a coy glance at Kian, who pressed his lips thin. "Yes," I said. "I thought you'd never ask."

Archer seemed annoyed, but I didn't care. I wanted to soak in all that Ravensla had to offer. "Very well, but you'll need more daggers on you." Archer motioned with his eyes to the spiral staircase beside the living room.

"I think my flame is quite useful," I said, following him through the home and into a room with armor, swords, and daggers hung on the walls. The air smelled of wood and musk, but mostly Archer, and maybe it was strange I could pick his scent apart.

"Did our fathers make barters? These are from North Colindale." I recognized the iced base of two.

"Serpents are always making bids and barters. Having a few daggers doesn't mean much," Archer said. "Besides, your father doesn't barter much these days."

I couldn't quite tell where the others were from—besides the red-handled sword, which matched the one I had earned off Callum during our match. He had referred to them as being crafted for the Forgotten Children a century before.

I asked, "What exactly do you plan to barter with him, or was that another lie?"

Archer reached for two matching black-tipped daggers. The silver handles were etched with crescent moons. "Your father's land is full of diamonds. He could have any Serpent at the reins if he wished. Northern Colindale is one of the richest lands in Verdonia, and I hoped to make a deal with him." He grabbed two leather holders, kneeling as he cupped the back of my leg and raised it. He changed the topic swiftly, eyes on me. "Some say receiving a dagger from a Serpent is an honor."

His bare hands skimmed my thighs, and I leaned into the touch. "What do they say about a Serpent kneeling before someone?" I asked.

Archer tightened his clasp of the leather sheaths, his pupils flaring beneath his dark lashes. "Naïve."

"Do you think you are naïve?" I asked, and he rose two heads above me.

He considered my question. His one hand was still cupping my leg. "I think I lost all sense the moment Naraic bonded with you. I mean that in the nicest way possible. You do not wield to me. Being headstrong is a blessing. You will make a great Serpent."

"Damien says you will force me to step down and follow you."

Archer glanced at the pendant on my neck. "Coming from the man who gave you a necklace to watch your every move."

I looped the chain around my index finger. "Damien gave it to me in case I need help."

Archer scoffed. "Help?"

I bit the inside of my cheek. "Damien means well. He cares about me."

"If you insist on allowing a male to see and hear every breath that escapes you, then perhaps I was wrong about you."

"Your protectiveness is not needed, especially not with my heart."

"Your heart… does not beat for him." A distraught gleam hinted in his eyes. "I do not wish to shatter your heart again with my words."

He meant Klaus.

"Then who—who does it beat for? If not a man whose only words have been kind and certainly no lies have uttered from his lips."

The sheer closeness of him caused my flame to spark. "Damien was the one who caused Everett to fall. He wanted to test your quell. I am simply ensuring you understand what my brother is capable of." His eyes froze on the glass pendant. "He watches you through the glass. Think about it, Severyn. He can portal through mirrors. When I found you in the bath… he was watching you." His jaw clenched, rage whirling in his eyes.

A shiver ran down my spine. He wouldn't. "How do you know?"

"Antonia saw him. He used his quell to shield Everett's mind, forcing him to fall. When I learned about Delair attacking you during Skyfall, I knew Damien had tainted her thoughts. She would never go against me and willingly attack you. You don't understand the power of a mind reader."

"He… watches me?" I ripped the pendant off my neck that suddenly seemed suffocating, throwing it across the room. It was glass… he could see through glass. He could see me.

"He watched me *bathe*?"

"He brought you to the one bathroom that is full of mirrors. It's disturbing if you ask me."

"No," I whispered. "That's just—"

"How do you think he knew about our barter?"

"I figured he'd broken through your ward," I said.

He got close, so close his breath touched my lips. "I should be insulted, but I'll allow you to believe I am still your enemy because shattering your heart seems to dampen mine."

Choking on shadows, I stayed silent for a beat. "Are you insinuating your heart beats for mine?"

"When I feel you in my veins miles away, I begin to believe so."

I shook my head. "What happened to only knowing the other's name?"

"I knew more than your name before you had ever heard of mine." He sheathed another dagger into a holder, lifting the hem of my dress. "And I would have stayed suffering because I promised Klaus I would protect you."

And I knew right then how much my brother meant to him. Did Archer know his last words?

Chapter 22

Nothing could tame that wildfire of anger that brewed in my veins as we went toward the festival.

Kian wore a black leather jacket and a sword over his shoulder. It was a short walk toward the bustling core of Grimswire. The sounds of the gathering grew louder as we approached. A violin played a higher note, along with the strum of a guitar. The melody was the same as what my mother hummed while cooking and sewing. The city whispered its history along the aged stones and the chipped buildings. And I was immersed in a world of shattering light, quells, and the rich scent of cinnamon and citrus. Town folks danced under the fading sun. My gown blew within the flurry of dust.

"The finest wine in all of Verdonia," Archer said as he passed me a goblet shaped like a flower, the stem narrowed and slender. Bubbles rose from the bottom up, and I tilted my head back as Archer waited patiently for my approval.

"It's good. Better than anything I've ever had," I said, taking another sip to drown the thoughts of Damien away. At least a buzz could tame that pounding in my mind.

Kian held his hand out before me. "Well, if you aren't going to ask Sevy to dance, don't mind if I do."

Archer kept that hard-ass stance, resting against the bars overlooking the canal. "I do not control Severyn. If she wishes to dance, don't let me stop her."

Kian grabbed my hand, bowing slightly. "May I?"

I rolled my eyes. "You may." And he spun me thrice as we danced with the other villagers in the town's core. I dipped back, laughing, spilling the wine.

"Have my brothers driven you mad yet?" he asked. We did something like a waltz, feet swaying with the music as my hand rested on his shoulder.

"I have three of my own," I yelled over the music. "Four, I mean."

Kian widened his eyes, wiping his brow dramatically. "No younger sisters?"

"I am afraid not."

Kian stretched his arm out, swinging me towards the crowd as he laughed. "Don't be pissed at what I'm about to do."

His head nodded slightly before two firm hands gripped my hips. I turned to meet Archer, nearly slamming into his chest. My feet stilled as he awkwardly adjusted his hands higher up on my waist.

"I never knew you could dance," he said. "Don't let this get to your head."

"My father taught me," I whispered. "I always assumed I would be married off someday."

A slight grin curved at the ends of his lips. I knew this meant nothing, but I couldn't stop my blood from heating as he held me close to him.

"And if that were the case, you would never know who killed that man you were forced to marry," he whispered. "It might have started a war."

I traced the ripple of shadows that followed our every sway. I was naïve to believe any part of him enjoyed this. Our breaths were in sync. Our hearts beat as one—I felt him in my veins, and I think I had for a while. I glanced at those beautiful lips. Those eyes of wonder and grace worthy of an ocean named after them as I traced every part of his face.

"You wouldn't dare," I said. Was Archer jealous of the hypothetical possibility of me marrying a man?

"I would have been the nightmare that haunted you forever if we hadn't met. A name you hated, a fate you'd accepted. Klaus wanted me to protect you, and that meant stopping you from being forced into a marriage with someone else."

It was true. My body wanted him—there was no denying it. As for my mind, I'd admit it had strayed too far.

The shutters of our bond rippled, forcing a seal—

But I was nothing more than a setback on his journey to greatness.

"So, all I am is your best friend's little sister?"

"No." He shook his head. "What are you doing to me, Blanche?" he whispered close to my ear. "First, I kneel before you, and now I am dancing with you. Have I proven myself to be friendly yet?"

"Have I tamed the Serpent?" I asked. If I washed away with the shadows once those lanterns struck through the ground turned on, I'd accept my fate.

"You have done more than tame me." There was a pause after, and I couldn't meet his eyes even on my tippy toes.

My flame relic glowed, illuminated by a shadow, as did his— but it was speckled in ash. I leaned into him. And every part of me wanted to seal that bond between us, even the unwilling gnaw in my gut. I believed he also felt it when he leaned in, the slight arch in his shoulders that swallowed me against his body.

"How's your heart?" he asked slowly.

"Bruised, I suppose. I'm mostly angry at myself for not seeing it."

Archer stopped dancing, and I slammed hard on that final twirl into his chest. He reached within the slit of my gown and stole a sheathed dagger. Steadying me, but his face went cold—so had that burn within his palm. He hitched my hood over my head as he pushed me behind him.

"Keep your head down," he hissed.

I followed Archer's gaze as three six-foot-long scorpions scuttled along the path, their steel pincers snapping. First came the scavengers, but it was the four figures that followed them that chilled my blood.

Their expressions were wicked, eyes cold and unreadable. Pointed, rusted spheres scraped against the stone. They wore scuffed fur vests, the fabric stretched tight over their muscles and scars.

The glass slid from my grasp, shattering onto the ground.

"Scorpion riders?" I hissed.

"Yes, they are called Bribers around here. Much like Scavengers, but their enigmas are scorpions," whispered Archer.

The one male leading grinned, liquid black eyes hidden beneath his brow bone's shadow. A giant scorpion hissed, claws ready to attack. The entire crowd went still.

"I heard a Serpent was here," he yelled. Scars covered his skin—marked with foreign relics. He pulled his cloak down, and a mound of black curls shaped his narrowed face.

It took everything in me not to grab Archer and force him to stay back. I knew his shadow quell could strangle them if the Briber attacked. But those silent pleas never escaped as Archer stepped forward, and our weak bond rippled.

"What do I owe the pleasure, Detria?" Archer asked.

Detria raised his chin as if tasting the air. "Are we not allowed to enjoy a festival? All are welcome during Harvest in the South."

He opened his arms wide, stealing a goblet from a woman's hands and slamming the wine back. "And the wine is simply to die for me."

"You know your kind is not welcome in the South, let alone Verdonia. I would not want a fight to ruin such a beautiful festival." Archer's voice was calm and assertive. "Now, what is it you seek? Because I know it is not oranges." Archer glanced at the second female Briber, who was peeling an orange with a knife.

She grinned a wicked white smile, glancing at me with violet eyes. Her blonde, nearly white hair curled above her slender jaw.

Detria made a silvered-toothed grin. "We hear you are harboring a neval girl. Her blood sells for a hefty amount of gold. Give her to us, and we will be on our way."

I kept my eyes low. He wanted me. Monty was telling the truth. Ash choked up my lungs. Kian flickered his gaze towards Archer, not daring to glance back and give me away.

Was I truly priceless, or were those just empty words?

"You are on my land, Briber. Leave now." I had seen moments of Archer's quell within the flickers of darkness, but never like this.

The sky muted to grey, and whatever shield Archer had used to conceal his shadows was now at full rein. Ripples grew from his open palm, and I realized I was in one as sounds bounced off the shield Archer had put off, echoing with a dissonance that could only be shouting. Flames shot from my palms—and even that shadow could not hold back my cindering ash.

Detria curled his fingers at me with a slight beckoning that made my skin crawl. "This is your father's land. You have no say here. We will leave peacefully, but we need the neval."

Were the Bribers our enemies?

"Why do you want my blood?" I asked with slim confidence.

Detria's scorpion hissed, lunging at me with two sharp pointers. "Some say your blood holds power. I don't ask questions."

I aimed my flame at the scorpion's face. Archer drew a bow, and I lit the tip seconds before it struck the Briber in the leg.

Detria groaned, yanking the arrow from his skin and snapping the metal in half over his knee. He stared between Archer and me as if he could see the shield extending between us and my pathetic attempt to hold my own up.

"Sabitha, grab her," Detria hissed at the blonde girl, raising a hand. An invisible force slammed into me. Two scorpions jumped, one pinning the hem of my gown with its claw. "Not only are you a neval, but you are also bonded to the Serpent through your enigmas and a barter. How peculiar. It seems the price of her blood just doubled. Tell me who you are, or my scorpion will force it from you."

Sabitha raised a golden ringed finger, willing the scorpion to snap its pincers.

"Tell him," Archer said, that calmness still in his voice. "Scorpions draw from the soul. He's already taken from us."

"Severyn Blanche," I said. "Daughter of Fallon Berret and the Northern Colindale Serpent."

The scavengers hissed, scurrying in place like rabid wolves. Detria raised a brow. "Reveal your face. Let me see." He approached me, ripping the cloak off my head with three bony fingers.

His thumb brushed my trembling jaw before a shadowed claw roped his wrist, bounding him back. "Do not touch her," Archer growled.

The scavenger with the scar on her cheek grinned, her excitement as vile as her rasping voice. "Fallon was worth every piece of gold when she was bought. I only wish I'd been the one to find her."

I froze. "My mother… was bought?"

"The price of being a neval," Detria said coldly. "Severyn is already marked in the eyes of our buyer. She's worthless to us now."

"Who's buying nevals?" My voice shook, and I struggled to choke down the tears threatening to spill. "It's just a birthmark—it means nothing!"

But the truth clawed at my chest. My mother was bartered like a trinket.

Detria's voice dropped, edged with disdain. "The neval mark comes from a single bloodline, much like our scorpion enigmas. If someone wants all the nevals, it's not our concern what they do after we catch one." His gaze slid to Archer. "I couldn't care less whether Severyn lives or dies, but I'd watch yourself, Serpent. Being bonded to something like that could stain your reputation. Anything worth hunting is only good for food… or gold."

Another scavenger, his dirt-caked fingers curling like talons, sneered. "We'll gladly take her off your hands, sir. We know plenty of places to bury her bones."

The Bribers vanished, their spheres cracking against the ground, and the scavengers spread out, muttering strange chants under their breath. Panic rose in my throat as my knees gave out, the weight of my silk gown folding beneath me.

Kian reached me first, his hand steady on my shoulder. "Bastards," he spat. "They've got no dignity. Don't let them get to you. My father's probably already tracking them. They won't get far. For the record, I think your neval mark is badass."

I could barely hear him over the pounding in my ears. "Did you know?" I asked Archer. "Did you know my bloodline was hunted?"

Archer's expression remained unreadable. "All marks mean something," he said carefully. "We don't know much about nevals. Klaus had the mark, but we never left the academy. Your mother has it too—" He broke off, flicking his wrist.

In a blink, we stood in the shadow of his estate near the gardens.

"A scavenger either found your mother or stole her," he said at last, his voice low. "It's hard to believe Lynwood's claim that she was born among scavengers. It's unheard of for them to have quells. Whoever her parents were, they didn't want to be found."

I clutched my arms to still their trembling. "Or they were killed. They said their buyer already has me." My voice cracked, my vision swimming with the blur of Archer's blue eyes as he leaned closer.

I needed answers, but I couldn't risk the academy's expulsion by leaving to find my mother. My mother had hidden me, locked me away in North Colindale. She knew. She must have known.

Had she married my father, hoping his blood would suppress hers? Had she hoped the griffin riders' weaker bloodline would shield me from whatever curse I carried?

Archer's voice pulled me from my spiraling thoughts. "I'm with you, Severyn. I will… protect you with my life. I swear it."

His words carried an unfamiliar softness that sent a shiver down my spine, though I wasn't sure if it was fear or something else. Before I could respond, Kian's voice broke through the tension, his steps hurried as he jogged towards us.

"You could've portaled me too, ass. I *am* your brother."

Archer turned, his irritation flickering as he pointed a hand at Kian, showering him in faint starlight. "Not now, Kian."

I pressed a hand to my stomach, nausea twisting with the weight of everything. As I doubled over, Archer's cool shadow grazed my forehead, soothing the worst of it.

"Who uses Bribers?" I asked, my voice strained.

Archer's composure held firm. "The Bribers cause trouble across the realms. Serpents sometimes pay them to settle debts or failed bids." He hesitated, as though choosing his next words carefully.

"Are you warded from speaking about it?" I pressed. "I deserve to know. I'm not weak, Archer." His hand, steady and deliberate, moved to the small of my back.

His darkness was still—so still it felt as though even the air dared not stir around him. "We've been fighting a century-long war for Verdonia's lands," he said finally. "The Forgotten Children want to reclaim what they believe is theirs. Centuries ago, when settlers arrived in Verdonia, they gained quells from the lands they were born into. But not everyone fit neatly into a realm. Some bonded with creatures—scorpions, snakes, spiders. They were outcasted, shoved into any realm that would take them."

His voice grew quieter, darker. "The outcasts' power frightened the king. When Cleminore took the throne, she turned on her own children, deeming them too dangerous. Most fled before they could be killed. The Forgotten have returned for revenge. But before that, they cursed the lands, severing them between seasons, light, and darkness. The original six God's blood created the borders of the realms."

"And my birthmark?" I asked.

Archer's gaze bore into mine, unyielding. "Most nevals carry forbidden power. That's why they're after you."

I bit my lip, tasting blood. "So, the Bribers are working with the Forgotten?"

He shook his head. "I think the king is behind this. He found your mother and stripped her of her power. And now, he's singled you out. Damien might be involved—"

"No," I said sharply. "He wouldn't betray me."

Archer sighed, pressing his fingers to his temples. "I need you to keep being his friend. He can't know we suspect him."

I clenched my fists. "You've warded our conversations, but I can't stop him from reading my thoughts."

"You're safe with me," he said softly.

The unspoken tension between us lingered. I dared to wonder—what were we? Allies? Enemies? Something in between?

Kian crossed his arms. "If you're done conspiring, can we eat? I'm starving."

Archer rolled his eyes but nodded. "Then we shall eat."

* * *

Dinner was roasted chicken, steamed broccoli, and some southern delicacy of spiced peaches. I'd helped myself to seconds, even reaching for thirds of the peaches. The food at the academy was nothing compared to this, and the North never had any spices imported, at least not a large enough variety to be considered a delicacy.

I wondered how the second harvest went back home—if Sivil had planted a lush garden, if her daughters' eyes lit up when they saw the basket of cabbage, knowing their bellies would be full that night. Today was a celebration for every land, and the Summer borders didn't seem starved for food.

The aide joined us for dinner as if she were part of the Lynch family, and that told me everything I needed to know about them. Kian was polite, even offering to take care of the dishes so the aide could have the rest of the night off. I'd learned her name was Della, and she was a refuge from a barren Spring realm. She'd lost her quell when the Forgotten raided her village.

After dinner, I sat in the bath for an hour, soothing my sore legs. The bruises and welts from Skyfall had dulled to a light brown. Slowly, I was healing, inside and out.

Archer had left a shirt of his for me to wear to bed. After my bath, I noticed the flicker of light under his doorway. The floorboards creaked as I went to the spare room and crawled into the unfamiliar bed, believing I had never touched such soft sheets as I sank into them.

I tried not to think of Damien and how wrong and naïve I was to believe he wanted to help me.

Power. He had chosen power. He was too kind for a cruel world, and I was too accepting of a friend—for anything he wanted to be. I would have taken those silent walks to class and believed I had found worth. I knew I deserved more, and maybe I found myself along the way.

I tugged those white sheets over my chest and glanced out the darkened windows. *Glass*. He was everywhere. Everywhere, I did not want him to exist. He was my cup at dinner that held my water, the reflection in the mirror. Could he see me now? Could my anger reach him from this far away, across the ocean?

"I'm pissed at you," I huffed under my breath.

Pissed didn't do my rage justice. I was done, but I still had to be his friend. I had to keep it up until I knew why, and this wasn't because Archer had told me. It was because nothing would soothe my restless mind besides an answer I was satisfied with.

Sleep pulled me under its heavy wing, but nightmares held me there, clawing at my mind. I dreamt of a scorpion, its claws sinking into Klaus's chest, its venom stealing the life from him. I woke screaming, my heart racing as shadows danced along the room's edges.

The door slammed open, and Archer strode in, shirtless, a dagger clenched tightly in his hand—the same one he'd confiscated from under my dress earlier. His chest rose and fell with sharp breaths, his gaze sweeping every corner of the room.

"Why are you screaming?" he demanded, his voice edged with panic. His eyes darted from shadow to shadow, seeking danger.

With a hand over my heart, I managed, "Nightmare."

His shoulders relaxed, and he lowered the blade, though his knuckles remained white around the hilt. "You scared me. I thought someone had broken in."

I sat up, running trembling fingers through my hair. "I dreamt… a scorpion killed Klaus. It felt real, like it was my enigma that did it." The words tumbled from my lips, disjointed and raw.

Archer moved closer, the tension in his frame slowly unwinding. "You're safe," he murmured. "I've warded the entire estate." He gestured to the bed, where faint shadows curled protectively along the edges, almost alive.

I watched him, his silhouette stark against the dim light. "Tell me your nightmares," I said softly, the vulnerability in my voice surprising even me. "Tell me something that makes me believe you feel anything at all."

His throat bobbed as he swallowed, and for a moment, I thought he wouldn't answer. "I don't like bats," he admitted, his voice quieter now. "They swarm my entire realm. Sometimes, I dream they're destroying my village while I'm away. And…" His voice faltered before he continued. "Losing Klaus nearly killed me. For months, I couldn't find a reason to smile. But yesterday…" His eyes softened, meeting mine. "Yesterday was the first time I smiled, truly smiled, since his death. And it was because of you. That's selfish to admit, I know, because his death led me to you. But it's the truth."

The words left me stunned, a knot tightening in my chest. "I'll never be happy Klaus died," I whispered, my voice breaking. "Knowing me… it wasn't worth his life."

Archer leaned against the doorframe as though it was the only thing keeping him upright. "You asked for real, Severyn."

"I know." My voice wavered. "Did Klaus… want us to be friends?"

His hesitation was brief, but telling. "Yes," he said, stepping into the room, as though the very act required courage. "He did."

I exhaled slowly, the shadows above me seeming to shift and settle. "And if we became… more than friends?"

His gaze didn't waver, the weight of it pinning me to the bed. "He'd suspect the possibility."

"Klaus was a Seeker, wasn't he?" I asked, the question tentative. Naraic's cryptic words echoed in my mind, and I wondered if Archer carried the burden of knowing my brother had been touched by a forbidden power.

Archer's expression darkened. "They burned everything he wrote," he said, his voice tight.

My eyes drifted to his ribs, where Klaus's name was etched in delicate script beneath his heart. "Not everything."

For a moment, neither of us spoke. The silence was heavy, the weight of unspoken fears pressing against my chest. I thought of my own life—a tangle of secrets and shadows, of broken dreams that never seemed to hold their shape. Would they burn my belongings too, when I was gone?

Archer stood beside my bed, the shadows clinging to his form like ink painted onto muscle. It was as though the darkness itself had sculpted him, every line and contour sharpened by its embrace.

"You should go back to sleep," he said, his voice low, almost a plea. "Before I lose the will to leave you alone."

I hesitated for only a heartbeat. "Then don't leave."

The words hung in the air between us, daring, vulnerable.

Archer sank to his knees beside the bed, as though the weight of everything tethering him to this moment was too much to bear. His voice was barely above a whisper when he said, "You are my only warmth, Severyn Blanche. The only warmth I desire." His breath shuddered as he closed his eyes, his hand brushing the edge of the mattress. "And I am desperately lost."

For the rest of the night, his shield of darkness lingered over me, a silent protector. He slept on the floor, his presence steady, unyielding. And for the first time, I wondered if he was the only shadow I would ever welcome.

The last piece of Klaus was written on his body, etched into his skin, a memory he carried for both of us.

And as I searched for pieces of Klaus in the silverware, I did not expect to find him in the shadows.

Chapter 23

The following day, another gown was laid on my bed. This one was made of red silk that snugged my waist. The skirt pooled into a bath of crimson crystals as the neckline swooped against my sternum. It was delicate, yet revealing.

I thought I would ask Archer what receiving a dress from a Serpent meant, but humor seemed grim after last night.

Kian and Archer were outside sparring. Their backyard sprawled with rolling grass, fenced in by tall posts and crowned with a wraparound porch. A swinging woven chair creaked faintly in the breeze, adding a soft rhythm to the crack of fists meeting skin. Welts bloomed across their bare chests, sweat streaking their muscles like war paint. At least Kian had landed a few solid hits on Archer.

I stepped outside, the sun warming my shoulders. Kian spotted me and waved, his grin boyish despite the fresh bruise darkening his cheekbone. "Last day in Ravensla," he said. "You're in luck because tonight there's a quell show."

"What's a quell show?" I asked, stepping closer.

"Anyone with a quell projects it. It's a ritual for the Harvest Festival," Kian explained, brushing his damp hair back. "I might even gain mine today."

Archer snorted, nudging Kian's ribs. "He's a late bloomer."

I turned to Archer, who had wiped the gleam of sweat from his forehead. He gestured to the dress I wore, its red fabric catching the sunlight like flame. "You should show off your flame tonight. Red suits you."

I fisted the lace bones along the ribs, the corset hugging each shaky inhale. "I can't exactly run if someone tries to steal me again. What's with the dress?"

Archer's expression softened, a rare flicker of sincerity breaking through. "It's vintage," he said simply. "And, forget yesterday, they will not bother us again."

Heat crept up my neck, unwelcome and betraying. Before I could respond, Archer stepped forward and touched my shoulder, steering me towards the house. "Come inside," he said.

"Did you gain your shadow at the Harvest?" I asked, glancing up at him.

He nodded. "Yes. I was seventeen. The look on my father's face when his eldest son inherited his mother's Night blood—I'll never forget it. He never forgave me for it." Archer's voice carried a bitterness that deepened the shadows clinging to him. "I hope Kian's quell is warmer. For his sake. Though, surprisingly, you can't beat a quell out of someone."

"Your father... hurt you?"

Archer's jaw tightened. "My mother died a year before. I was a painful reminder of her, a failure in his eyes—the son who should've claimed his throne but instead inherited the wrong blood."

Rage flared in my chest. "You didn't deserve that."

A shadow of a smile played on his lips. "Now, don't go soft on me, Severyn. Remember, you're not supposed to care about me."

I changed the subject, though my anger lingered. "I wonder why Winters don't gain their quells until the academy."

Archer leaned against the dining table, his fingers digging into the wood as if bracing himself. "Klaus never wrote when he lived with you? That man spent nearly every waking minute with a notebook in his hands."

Thinking back to our family home two years ago felt like recalling another lifetime. "He read. Cully was more of the writer in our family."

Archer's knuckles whitened as he gripped the edge of the table. "I knew you were coming to the academy. Klaus knew he would die. And I knew you'd be placed in some bullshit realm, forced to bond with a creature that didn't call to you because Naraic was dead."

"Klaus told you about me," I said, more statement than question. The realization settled over me like a heavy cloak. During Skyfall, Klaus had demanded that Naraic break their bond. Now, the pieces clicked into place.

Archer's voice dipped lower. "Damien heard my thoughts, and he got to you first. I knew you'd go into that forest, so I followed you. But every time I saw you, I felt guilty. Guilty because I thought I'd stolen your chance to bond, to breathe. So, I stayed away."

His hand rose, daring to graze my cheek. The touch was fleeting but enough to make my breath hitch. "But fuck, you made it difficult. Twice, I had to drag you away. And it took everything in me not to tell you what I knew." He exhaled sharply. "Ciaran kept telling you to find him, and I forbade her from nearing you because all you would find was a corpse."

I pulled back, shaking my head. "Why are you telling me this now?"

His gaze burned into mine. "I never knew how they figured Klaus had a forbidden quell. Not until yesterday. Then, it all made sense. When I heard you scream last night—" He stepped closer, the space between us disappearing. "They tortured you in the Winter realm, and I did nothing to stop it."

My throat tightened. "There was nothing you could have done."

"I couldn't hold Ciaran back, but I had no right to intervene. She'd broken my command and saved you herself, as she did during Skyfall. I know he hurt you, Severyn. I know being rejected from your home is the worst feeling."

"Bridger wanted to prove I wasn't Winter-bound." The words tasted bitter. "I know it wasn't your doing, but it still hurts to know Ciaran was ordered not to help me." I hesitated, tracing the gem stitched into my gown's lace trim. "Did you know I'd be drawn to Summer?"

He shook his head. "No. I had no idea you'd be called to Summer or end up in the running for my father's title. But I knew you wouldn't make it far."

I shuddered, my fingers trembling against the lace. "The Serpent's life is cruel."

Archer's grin was crooked, darkly amused. "Not as cruel as the woman you're bonded to killing the closest thing to an heir you'll have."

"There's always Antonia," I shot back. "She seems to have her eye on you, Serpent."

Archer's laugh was sharp, cutting. "Antonia is not Serpent quality. To claim a realm, you must be conniving and willing to lay down your life. My father rebuilt Ravensla through barters and bribes, not sentiment."

I swallowed hard, leaning against the wall for support. "And would you lay your life down for your realm?"

Archer studied me for a long moment, his eyes unreadable. "I would," he said at last. "But it would be foolish without an heir. I'm not eager to drag my future children into this cycle. Better someone else take it than repeat this madness."

I managed a weak laugh. "Who would want to live in constant darkness? No offense."

"Only those who see beauty in shadows will understand," Archer replied, his voice low. "Light is a mask."

Before I could respond, he turned and left, his footsteps fading as he disappeared to shower. I stared after him, the words he'd left behind lingering in the air like smoke from a fire long extinguished.

* * *

We spent that afternoon at the estate. Kian gave me a full tour of the Lynch family home, besides one room I assumed to be Damien's. Was it untouched for the isolated years he spent in boarding school?

Seven bedrooms were fully decorated with beautiful paintings of Ravensla. A hand-woven mat carried my feet along the long halls, string and cloth made from the same rich golds and reds that decorated the city. A wine cellar, made to withstand war, held a hundred bottles, some aged from when Veravine reigned.

"Was that Veravine?" I asked, passing by a portrait of a woman. The face was smudged, unrecognizable over the years.

Kian nodded. "This was her home. Most of her belongings were gone when my father claimed the title, but Father kept this one, although her face was only a reminder of the destruction her death caused."

"Veravine… it is a beautiful name," I said.

Kian shrugged. "I heard she was hot, but she's dead, so that might be disrespectful."

I swatted his arm. "Do you even have a filter?"

He leaned against the stone wall. "Life is too fast, Sevy. I speak my mind."

I stared at that smudged portrait once more. It was a love that could crumble city walls. And it wasn't the Forgotten who stripped this land. It was the stain her blood made on the king's heart.

After my tour, we ventured into the Grimswire Night Market. Overhead, floating paper lanterns waltzed through the ashen sky, painting delicate veins across the clouds. Along the canal's gentle waves, candles swayed in harmony. Masquerade masks concealed the faces of the townsfolk, featuring beaks, snouts, and feathers in hues of silver and gold, all swirling through the bustling streets.

Above us, a clan of baby dragons performed an intricate dance in the sky, playfully chasing one another. It was impossible to choose where to look.

Archer rolled his shoulders once, eyes scanning the slowing, beating sun. "What do you say, Blanche? Are you ready to show the people of Ravensla how much you burn?"

"Are you calling me *hot*?"

"Maybe a bit of a hothead," he teased, glancing at my hands. "May I?"

"Yes," I said, a bit too fast.

A swift nod before a cool hand led me to a cluster of people around the bridge. "Do you enjoy it here?" he asked. "The heat must feel different."

"I think I'd have to see it without the glamor." I glanced at Kian, gazing at his palms, anticipating that surge of power to manifest. "I wonder what kind of quell Kian will have."

Archer draped his arms over the bridge, eyes nearly matching the crystal-clear blue water below. "My father will not be happy if it's shadows. The past Serpent of Night used my mother as a pawn and stole power from Summer so the Night realm could have heat and sun in certain parts. That is why Grimswire looks different than the rest of Ravensla. There is always a silver lining to all barters, bribes, and even deaths. My mother died for Night to have light and sun."

And she wasn't even a Serpent, but she'd laid her life to protect her home. "How does one steal the sun?" I asked.

"Daylight quells can trap light. There are a lot of alliances between Serpents. Good and bad. I try to keep mutual with all the realms."

"Are you and my father on good terms?"

His face stilled like he was about to get into a political ramble with me. "Your father is sitting on one of the wealthiest plots of land in the entire Continent. Whoever becomes his heir must make wise barters."

Not with the Winter storms growing worse. Not with his wards breaking. I feared if no one claimed title… North Colindale would become another barren land.

"I wonder if Bridger hated me so much because he knew the people did not have to suffer. It felt as though there was never enough food to go around. My father chose to starve his people," I hissed. I didn't blame Bridger—it wasn't forgiveness I felt but understanding. I understood his hatred for my father.

"You love your father. The man you know is his truth."

"I suppose he could have married me to a Serpent in exchange for seeds."

"As I said yesterday, you are priceless, Severyn. It would take much more than a rich man of title for your father to use you as a bribe."

"Why are you not married?" I blurted out. Archer likely had a hundred women throwing themselves at him. I could only imagine those marriage offers he received from across the lands. Beautiful females who'd offer their bodies to him and birth him an heir.

"I spent the last two years understanding what a Serpent is, and most of that time, I was weak from Klaus's death. I believe in love, Severyn. My parents got married out of a barter. I couldn't accept that, knowing my mother had given her life over one. Sometimes, I believe that there is more to this world than power. You must fight for what is right, and sometimes that is your breath and your heart."

Our fingers touched.

I went to tuck them behind me, but Archer wound his within mine, eyes laced above. "Sometimes what we want will never make sense. Nor will we deserve it."

I sucked a clipped breath in.

He had no idea how fast my heart was beating.

The quell show began. A dozen palms reached towards the milky sunset, and I'd never seen anything so beautiful, so unison. Cheers sounded from all around as quells rippled into the sky. It was a shatter of daylight breaking through, twisting, and curling with an illusionist's dragons. It was the blazing heat of a dozen Summer quells as the wind rushed around us.

I raised my palm, and a soft flame sparked from my fingertips, twirling in a snake-like slither through the golden sky. Archer cupped my cheek. We both stared up, and each one of those stars was cindered in flames.

I gasped slowly. Even the shadows below us were outlined with sparks. No ash littered my tongue, but a faint coal and mist taste sucked between my parted lips.

My right palm tingled.

"Archer—" A swirl of shadows broke through my skin, curling like smoke in the moonlight. It wasn't flame, but something cooler, darker. A crescent-shaped mark etched itself into my palm. The sensation wasn't searing like flame but a taut, almost chilling pressure.

"What is this?" I whispered, staring at the mark.

"Darkness," Archer murmured. His voice was low, like a secret the world wasn't meant to hear. "There are three types of quells. Ciaran chose you that day during Skyfall. I told her you weren't ready for it, but the more I try to keep you from the shadows, the more they seem to claim you."

My palms found his cheeks, the cool tendrils of shadow on one hand and the flicker of flame on the other, creating a strange and beautiful balance between us.

"Ciaran gave me a shadow quell?" I asked, my voice trembling.

"Have you ever quell shared?" he asked, his body close, his knee pressing just in front of my thighs. His gaze was heavy, searching. "I could teach you."

"No, I've never… tried it," I admitted, my voice unsteady.

"The easiest way to quell share is through touch," he said, his breath brushing my skin. His pinky wound itself around a loose strand of my hair.

"I feel you," I said, and only then did I realize how tightly I had been clutching his fingers. Red marks lingered on his skin where my grip had been. "I'm sorry."

He pulled me closer, just enough for our chests to graze. His hand tilted my chin upward, and the heat in his gaze made my pulse stumble. "Stay still."

A silver sheen wove through the air, tracing our breaths like a whisper. My words stuttered as I struggled to find my composure. "I—I care about you. I know you said I shouldn't, but—"

"Kissing you would be the easiest and most reckless way to quell share," he murmured, his voice dropping to a husky whisper. "But I've lost all the will to deny that desire."

"You don't want to kiss me, Archer," I managed, though the tremor in my voice betrayed me.

His lips quirked into a sly grin, and he leaned closer, his breath brushing against mine. "And why wouldn't I? Because I'm a Serpent? Or do you finally see me as your brother's friend?" His voice dropped, rich and intoxicating, as he whispered against my lips, "Kissing you is the most tameable thing I desire to do with you."

My breath caught as my gaze flicked to his lips. "You're a Serpent. What if someone sees?"

But even as I spoke, a voice echoed within the bond between us, soft yet commanding: *"Fucking kiss me. Now."*

Before I could close the space between us, his lips claimed mine. They were cool, soft as silk, and careful—too careful. The kiss was simple, but I felt the restraint in every movement, like a storm held at bay. And still, it set fire to every nerve, the shadows around us shuddering as if they, too, felt the pull of this moment.

"Like this?" I answered back.

"More."

"You want more of me?"

"Yes."

I nodded, and at that moment, I was a wick floating down the river, caught in the pull of the current, as I kissed him back harder. Chaos and shadows swirled around us. I kissed him like it was my last breath.

Maybe it always had been his to claim. Maybe he was right when he said my breaths were owed to him.

His hands tightened around my waist, pulling me closer, anchoring me to him even as I became acutely aware of the hundreds of eyes surrounding us, including the apparent journalist staring wide-eyed.

Thunder cracked above—a jagged sound that echoed in my chest as lightning streaked across the sky. The world seemed to hold its breath.

I tasted the wine lingering on his tongue, dark and rich. His shadows seeped into me, coiling in my lungs and stealing the air until a silent moan slipped between our parted lips. He claimed every curve of my mouth, every inch of me, as though he were imprinting himself onto my soul. His hands tangled in my hair, the grip firm and possessive, deepening that forbidden touch.

Every essence of Archer felt forbidden—and I craved it.

I needed him.

He pulled away just enough to lift my chin, his thumb brushing against my jawline as his eyes burned into mine. "I didn't think a flame could cast a shadow."

My lips trembled as I answered, my voice barely audible. "I didn't either."

We both turned to watch Kian as he raised his palm into the sky, and shattering starlight broke through. He fisted the air, smothering whatever dark quell had broken through. Archer grinned silently. He grinned as if his heir stood feet away.

"Kian—" I breathed.

Archer shook his head, tightening his fingers under my jaw. "Knowing you've let down your entire country is not a great feeling."

There was a moment of silence as the quells began to simmer, and our smoking shadows blew away in the wind. Archer dropped his hand, clearing his throat. "My father is here."

The skin on my back crawled. "Is everything okay?"

A tall, darker-skinned male appeared out of thin air in the center of the dancing. A teal suit framed his slender figure as white gloves covered his outstretched hands. I pulled away as if the pounding realization struck that Archer had kissed me, and I'd gotten a shadow quell.

Siphoning the seawater in a spiral, the Serpent of Summer raised his hands. Cheers sounded as every lantern sputtered once the water fell, simmering even me. A few civilians gawked and bowed while others curtsied. Archer's father was even more intimidating than in his portrait as pounding drums welcomed his grand entrance.

His eyes tightened on Kian with a quick nod. Archer gripped my elbow—portaling us back to the house through the shadows.

As dusk broke, he slung his bow over his shoulder, dragging me down to the entrance. "I'm not in the mood to converse with my father tonight. We'll make our way to Ravensla. I'm sure Lynwood has room unless you are up to fly throughout the night?"

"Is it because I am here?" I asked nervously.

He shut his mouth, no doubt contemplating his words. "As I said, some Serpents have good alliances. I don't have the best political relationship with my father."

I gripped his arm, forcing him to face me. "You are his son? Is that not enough of a bind to forgive the past Serpent of Night?"

"Not when that man was my grandfather," said Archer in a rush. He pulled me towards the black stallion as a single drop of water fell onto my forehead.

"Your grandfather was the past Shadow Serpent?"

My breath caught as Kian and Victor stood before us, and it was silent as if all the noise was stripped from the world, even my voice as Archer's father opened his arms for an embrace.

"Archer, my son. You've come home for the Harvest Festival. How… lovely." His eyes flickered to mine, wavering along my streak of neval. He clicked his tongue. "And you've brought North Colindale's daughter with you. How strange."

I lowered my chin. "Yes, sir. Your realm is beautiful, and your home is breathtaking," I stuttered.

He stared at Archer's hand on me. "Flattery will get you nowhere, darling. Archer, you seem to be leaving. Surely, you can stay one more night for your dear old father."

My veins chilled under the weight of the Serpent's voice. He had no idea I was up for taking his title.

I squeezed Archer's elbow, and he grinned, choking his words in a rush. "Of course, Father."

To crumble before someone was not weakness; it was suffering, and I wished for a night's breadth to see fear cling to his eyes. Instead, I saw raw vulnerability when the sun dimmed next.

And so, the bat of his father crept past us, welcoming Archer and me into his cave.

The next hour was filled with the sound of silverware on plates as we ate fire-roasted zucchini and sea-salted pork. Their aide kept her head low tonight, hidden in shadows in the corner of the dining room, not daring to speak a word or join us as she had the night before.

A wave of anxiety thrummed through me whenever Victor's eyes swayed over me. All it would take was one question: "What is your quell?" And he'd know I was a Summer and in line to become *his* heir. He must suspect.

"I hear your brother is the Malvoria Institute of Guards commander. Charles, right? I was there for three days. Does he ever have those initiations in line?" Victor said between bites of zucchini. "It's a shame he never went on to accept the title. He could have been a Serpent, a powerful one at that."

My fork slipped, clanging on the wooden table. "Charles enjoys his career. I'm sure he could have been a great Serpent." My voice was quiet, and I thought Victor might yell at me to speak louder.

"Well, now that Kian is a Shadow, I must ensure Damien succeeds. I would not want some stranger coming onto my land. I know your father was hopeful at least one of his children would become his heir. You can thank your Scavenger mut of a mother for that. For lack of a better word, her entire bloodline is mud."

I gripped the knife, contemplating stabbing his throat with it. "Excuse me. How dare—"

Kian's eyes widened to saucers. "Father, tell me about your latest travels. Malvoria is a long way from here."

My fingers curled around the dining room table. "If my mother was a scavenger, why did she have a quell?"

"As I said, your mother's blood was mud. Fallon knew I'd win Serpent our years together. She knew her best bet was to marry whatever man would look at her. Andri was roped into her lies."

Boiled tears brimmed my heavy lids. I clipped my tongue between my front teeth, biting down to stop the curses I was about to shout.

Then Archer's shadows bound my wrist to the chair, darkness rippling through my hoarse breath. "Well, my mother seems to live in people's minds. I suppose she made her mark."

"Your mother murdered innocents. It is not something to be proud of."

"That's—she's… my mother wouldn't hurt a fly."

"If I remember correctly, it was twelve lives she took during our Serpent Academy years… including her scavenger parents."

"No," I said. "I don't believe you."

Victor grinned, leaning back in the golden dining room chair as he crossed an ankle over his knee. "Not to worry, Severyn. I don't think any Serpent will have you on their mind during the bid. Your father owes me something. It's only a matter of time before that bargain catches up to him. You should be gracious that I never sent the Bribers to retrieve what was owed to me."

I seethed through my barred teeth. "What barter did you make?"

Victor snapped his fingers, and the aide rushed to clear the plates. "Perhaps you should ask him yourself," he hissed, and ocean water flurried as he raised his hand, vanishing before my flame could cinder through Archer's rope of shadows.

"That didn't go very well," I whispered.

"He knows I was shielding you," said Archer. "But that is all. If we leave tonight, he'll suspect we're hiding something."

I closed my eyes. "Then I suppose we'll leave at dawn."

If there were two people I never wanted to have dinner with again, it would be Victor and the king.

After dinner, I sat in the armchair in Archer's room. Shadows and dark wards swirled across the walls like sentinels.

I didn't regret coming here—not when I'd seen the beauty of Ravensla and met Kian. I'd protect him next year—if I was still alive.

I curled into the soft fabric of the chair as Archer stepped inside the room after his shower. I forced myself not to stare at the ripple of shadow dripping from his hair. He was something forged in my dreams, and the Serpent of the Shadows held his title well.

And I'd kissed him. Passionately kissed the Serpent of Shadows.

"What barter was your father speaking about?" I asked.

"My father made a lot of barters with Serpents, I don't keep track of them," he said.

I shook the thought away because I didn't want to ruin today.

I was still in that slim-fitted red dress when I got up and asked, "Could you undo the zipper for me?" My chin angled towards him as I watched him step closer from the corner of my eye.

A hand lowered on my neck, fingers dragging down my spine slowly as he undid the zipper as the dress fell against my body.

"Where would you like your serpent mark to be if you had a choice? Perhaps, your shoulder." His nails dragged against my collarbone and kept sweeping lower.

"Right there," I said as his fingers paused in the center of my spine. "I'd want it to be on my spine, wrapping along my ribcage."

He brushed his fingers underneath my gown, dragging the tips of his nails against my ribs, skimming my breastbone. "Right here?" he said, his voice thick and sultry. Then, as his thumb grazed my bare, hardened nipple, he didn't shift away.

I held my shuttered breath inside—fearing shadows would form within my next exhale. He tugged the dress down my shoulder blade, sweeping his thumb over my bare sternum.

"You never answered my question about bonding," I whispered into his touch.

Archer chuckled low. "You're still going on about our rider bond?"

I faced him, the bodice of my gown barely covering my breasts. "Do you trust me?" I whispered.

He nodded. "Trusting you is easier than staying away."

"Then bond with me," I said, pressing my palm on his chest.

He leaned into my touch, chuckling. "Not here. Not while my father is under the same roof," he said. "And I'd rather take it slow to hear every breath owed to me."

"What happens tomorrow? When we are back at the academy?" I traced the serpent on his neck. "Surely whatever this is can't exist in light. Damien will see my shadow relic."

"I don't give a damn what Damien thinks—not after what he's put you through. For that matter, I don't care what anyone thinks. But weeks before the bid, I don't want anyone believing you made it this far because of me."

"But I did. Without you, I'd be in Malvoria." I remembered the moment he said my name at the Rite. The anger I felt not knowing the truth. "You should have sent me to Malvoria during the first week."

He stifled his choke. "Perhaps it is you who owns my breaths."

"I want to see Night," I said. "Promise you'll take me there someday."

"First, you see Ravensla, now you want a taste of the entire Continent?" he mused. "It is a full day of flying. We'd have to stay in the capital. A Serpent can stay in a few regions without causing… political issues. It is more socially acceptable during festivals, and this was my yearly appearance for the Summer civilians."

"So high and mighty, planning out your ventures. I'm beginning to think life as a scavenger isn't so bad. Are they not free to roam wherever?"

Archer shoved a shirt into my chest. "The moment I became a Serpent and had to clean up a hundred years of political mess, I thought the same."

Shifting out of the dress, I pulled the cotton shirt over my body. "Thank you for letting me come with you. Ravensla is beautiful."

"I have seen miles and miles of beauty in my lifetime. I walked nearly every stone in Verdonia, but nothing compares to this. They say your home calls to you. They say once you find it, you know."

I hoped his words were true.

I rested on the end of his bed. "What *is* beauty to you, Archer?"

He angled his body in front, hands pinned before my knees. "Sunsets. It reminds me I have another day to live, to breathe. It Reminds me of my mum."

"Your mother would be proud of you. Being torn between your home and your blood must be hard. I feel like I've been relearning how to breathe since I got my letter."

He eyed my wrist where the scorpion had struck and slowly brought my hand to his lips. "I've given you my breath to breathe before. And I told you if anyone touches you, I will mark you myself."

And not a single flame willed within me.

"Can you… tell me about Klaus. The version you knew."

His brows furrowed. "Klaus was brave. He was the first to raise his hand in Cain's class, even if he was wrong most of the time. He could speak about anything, and… we were friends. The purest form of it. The day he wrote his death, he…" Archer choked. "He wrote your name. Wrote it with a smile and said I'd find that piece I lost in him… within you."

"You knew I would come?"

"I knew you'd seize more than a title. Perhaps my breath… perhaps I wished you would hate me. I wanted to be cruel, but I couldn't."

And as I searched for the same fork Klaus had used. The same sun rays he had felt… I never knew I'd find my piece of Klaus in the least expected place—hidden in shadows.

Chapter 24

After a long six-hour flight, we were back in Galthyn.

My legs throbbed as I dropped down from Naraic. The afternoon sun hung below the clouds. Ciaran and Naraic flew away mere seconds after we had touched the docks. I tugged at the leathers clinging to my clammy spine. There were a few awkward seconds between Archer and me as we walked down the docks silently and toward the academy doors.

"You have a trial in two days, Severyn. I hope I do not have to drag your body from the bottom of an ocean again," he said.

I spun to face him. "Does that mean you'll kiss me again?" My fingers slacked at my sides. We were nearing the Night hallway, and those halls seemed narrower, or Archer was closer to me than Damien had ever been.

Archer scoffed, and a shadow pinned me to the academy's wall. He got close. "Severyn Blanche, I am your Serpent mentor. If you were anyone else, you'd be dead." Shadow dusted to ash as my palm raised. "You're against me for combat tomorrow. Try not to moan in your sleep too much."

The door clicked open with a flick of my wrist. "I intend to do just that," I said, whisking into my room and closing the door. I still heard his soft breaths through the iron. I waited—hoping he'd come inside.

It was only empty thoughts with no substance. But then, the crush of reality weighed on my shoulders. Damien had lied to me. It was more than despair… it was suffocation. And starving those feelings would take a while to shrivel. Archer and I couldn't exist within these walls. He was a Serpent, and I stayed a naïve first-year.

But it was that soft knock behind me that made my bones melt. I knew that knock too well, and it still sent every nerve in my body on overdrive.

I opened the door, meeting Damien's grin. He shifted his hands to the pocket of his slacks, and of course, he wore that shirt I liked on him. Of course, he'd come here minutes after I had arrived back.

And I swallowed hard as I let him in foolishly.

I mustered up my best shield. Tightening that flame around my mind as he stepped closer to me. "Hello, Damien," I said.

"Where did you go for three days?" he asked. "Are you hiding from me?"

I could feel his satisfaction with the truth. "I was in Ravensla with Archer. I met Kian and your father."

This seemed to shock him. I got the feeling he wasn't used to being kicked out of my mind, but slowly, that brute force halted.

"You flew to Ravensla with Archer? That is a big trip, and Naraic is still injured from Skyfall." He smiled. "But I'm happy you're home."

I know what you did to Everett. My jaw clenched, withholding the passion, the fury in my blood to yell at him. His eyes glanced at my bare neck, and that smile halted.

"Your pendant is gone," he said.

I acted surprised, widening my eyes. "Shit, it must have fallen into the ocean."

Hurt, pain, and anger flickered across his face. Had Archer gotten it wrong? There was no way he could be this cruel and lie this convincingly.

It took everything in me not to embrace him because, as much as I dreaded this moment, my heart yearned for it. But my fingers began to tremble, just as my father's had when warding became too much. I knew, at any moment, the fire encasing my mind would simmer. I steadied my breathing because one heavy exhale would blow out that ash.

Damien brushed a strand of hair behind my ear, and slowly, that ash crumbled into shattered glass. "Is that all?" he asked.

And then he shoved himself into my thoughts, and gradually, I felt all those moments I had lived in the past three days slip out of the wall of fire I'd built. Some parts were missing, the spoken words blurred, but everything was there: his father's attacks on my mother, Kian gaining his shadow, the illusionist masking as Klaus. A scorpion hissed at the final moment, even causing Damien to step back. His wild eyes burned, not with rage but with desperate curiosity.

"I'm impressed, Severyn. You held that shield longer than before." He released that strand of hair with a grin. "I'll be here at dawn to walk you to class, as always. We'll need to do extra training for the trial in two days. Most first-years use those days to train their quells, but I suppose you aren't like most first-years."

He turned on his heel, pausing at the doorway. His grin widened. "Shadow quells cause nightmares. You may want to burn a lantern while you sleep."

My lungs begged for air as I collapsed onto my bed.

Fucking mind readers.

The following day, Damien did as he said. At dawn, he stood by my door, waiting as twilight streaked the sky. I dressed in warmer leathers, strapping knives to various limbs, including the two daggers Archer had gifted me. I grinned at Damien in silence as we left for warding class.

Professor Cain stood at the front of the classroom, drawing a large circle of chalk on the blackboard. His movements were deliberate, each line precise. Then, he turned to face us, his gaze sharp.

"I need volunteers to protect the circle," he announced. "Severyn, would you care to defend it? Myla will use her ice quell to break through. It's always fascinating when opposite quells clash."

I nodded, stepping to the center of the room. Myla joined me after a few beats, the tap of her leather loafers echoing on the stone floor. Closing my eyes, I pictured the circle in my mind, every line burning with intent. I raised my fingers toward the blackboard, drawing a flame tight around the chalk, each curve outlined in fiery precision.

My tether wavered as Myla flicked her wrist, shards of ice pounding against my fiery fortress. Ice collided with flame, steam rising in spirals as our quells waged war. But I held my ground, flames flaring brighter with every strike.

For a moment, I thought of Archer and the way his shadows had shielded me, protecting not just me but everything within his reach. I poured everything into the fire encircling the board, daring Myla to break through.

I flinched as her coldness reached my throat. It was… an eerily familiar suffocation, frost creeping up my spine.

I would not shatter.

I would not. Shatter—

The sharp, biting cold on my skin brought me back to that moment. My chest tightened as the ice crawled up my spine, and I couldn't escape it. I was there again.

Hands roped around me, pinning me to the frozen earth. Their laughter echoed along the peaks. A wolf snarled, shredding what was left of my clothes. Tears crystallized on my cheek, freezing before they could fall. A dagger scraped along my thigh.

My blood didn't boil—not yet. My scream was muffled by his glove pressed against my mouth. Winter, my home of ice, held me down.

"…the hounds can tear the rest of her clothes off," said Callum.

The circle was a ring of fire. My fingers began to shake as an icicle dragged along the edge of my barrier. I felt that dry scream clinging around my throat as every part of me was frozen, including the tears that clung to my cheek.

I would burn.

Boiling tears clung to my lower lid as I melted that ice. I burned the entire blackboard beside the circular cutout that fell to the ground, and even as Cain held my shoulders, I kept burning. I seared that memory of Bridger and Callum. I burnt their gaze that took in my frozen body, their greedy hands as they cut me, and laughed at Serpent's daughter and all her failed glory.

And Myla had trusted him even after knowing what *he'd* done.

"Severyn, that is enough," Cain choked. "You did what I asked. You protected the circle."

Knox clapped three times, elbow rested on his knee. Myla was in shock, but she was proud. I couldn't read Malachi's face, but it was something along the lines of fear, possibly because she had to sleep next to someone who could incinerate anything with their mind. Damien always looked impressed with anything I did, and I hated that more than ever because I still looked at him for sickening approval.

I fisted the shadow relic on my hand, and a cool wave soothed over my burn.

Cain cleared his throat. "There is a level to warding, though. Could you live in a world where everything around you was dead and burnt? The entire world cannot exist in flames while yours thrives."

I almost asked why not, but instead, I said, "I'll work on my control."

A nervous look stayed on his face as he watched me take my seat next to Malachi.

Damien raised his hand, and the Professor gestured for him to speak. "Could we practice quell sharing? With the upcoming trial, we might need it."

Professor Cain tapped his bony fingers on his desk. "Quell sharing is more advanced. Normally, that is a third-year course."

Damien crossed his arms over his chest, glancing sidelong at me, and I knew he was throwing my quell share with Archer at me. Knew he'd seen that kiss. That was no coincidence.

"I think we know each other well enough. And anyone willing to try should," Damien added.

Cain drew out a long breath. "Very well. But we will go outside." He glanced at the burnt blackboard, unwilling to risk his entire classroom turning into ruins.

The entire class emptied through the double-wide back doors and into the courtyard. A few students whispered, asking what quell sharing was.

Damien stood before us all. "Quell sharing is when your power combines with another student and creates something entirely else. Think of paint; when you mix magenta and yellow, you get red. That can be said for quells as well. Snow and rain create storms. It can also be beautiful and one of the most personal things you can share with another, so keep that in mind."

I was thankful he didn't use shadow and flame as an example. Most students were hesitant to group up. But no one dared to step closer to me, not after almost melting the entire classroom minutes before. Even Damien stood his ground, but I wondered what glass and fire could create and if we'd melt as one.

Malachi stayed quiet, but I knew damn well Monty had taught her how to quell share during the first week here. I never wanted to feel the ice in my lungs again, so Myla—we would never breach that.

"Severyn, would you be willing to try?" Malachi asked.

Wind and fire. I could only imagine the chaos we'd cause near all these trees. But Malachi knew how to control her quell better than I could, and perhaps we'd create something beautiful as Damien had described.

I nodded as Malachi grabbed both my hands between hers. I wondered if certain areas felt the power differently. Had Archer held my hand like this instead of kissing me, would thunder still have cracked?

The world around us spun into chaos, a furious flurry of wind tearing through the air. Trees groaned and smoked, their leaves snapping like brittle paper. I drew the flame from within, letting it surge through every vein until my chest burned and the air was stolen from my lungs. I doubled over, gasping, but the wind caught me, holding me firm as ash swirled into a spiraling inferno.

The vortex roared around us, flames licking at its edges as though alive. Our breaths fell into sync, and in that moment, I felt her power merging with mine, pulsing beneath my skin. The wind taunted, pushing harder, daring me to falter.

Then it happened. A flame ignited in Malachi's pupils, burning with a brilliance that stole the breath I'd just reclaimed. This wasn't like the quell Archer and I had shared before—this was something else. Something deeper.

Our quells collided, and suddenly, it all made sense. Wind and fire weren't meant to oppose one another. They were meant to unite, to create something unstoppable. Something deadly.

Shadows simmered below, not enough to draw attention from the watching crowd, but enough to dance around us. It was not a raging fire consuming everything within that sweltering wind, but I knew it could be. We could burn this academy into dust if we both tried.

Then Malachi let go, and ash rained down on anyone within a one-foot radius. The air sucked back into my lungs, and Professor Cain stood with his jaw nearly hanging on the grass.

"Now, that is a perfect example of quell sharing. That amount of control takes years to achieve, and most students can only quell share for a few seconds."

Something distant grew in her eyes as though she knew exactly what kind of force we could become together. She shrugged her slim shoulders. "See you at combat," she whispered.

Knox ran towards me. "Hey, I missed you during training," he said awkwardly. "I miss you, Sev."

Still catching my breath, I leaned against my brother. "We'll talk about it later," I said as we walked to the combat fields together.

Malachi traveled through the wind, already waiting and talking to Monty in a hushed conversation.

Without turning, Monty yelled, "Severyn, you're back on swords today. No quells allowed for this class."

I stiffened. Had I done something wrong? I stayed silent as Monty grouped us in twos. Archer still wasn't there, and I couldn't care. Those three days in Ravensla meant nothing.

Monty didn't take his usual space at the front. Instead, he angled in front of me, and it wasn't until everyone had already begun sparring that I realized Monty was my opponent. Unsheathing his sword, he did all those respectful gestures one did before tearing into the other.

"Why am I fighting you?" I asked, edging toward my blade.

"It is time someone taught you a proper lesson on hierarchy. You may have been given quell privilege, but you are useless in a hands-on battle," he said, not waiting for me to pull my sword out as he swung at my chest. "And I don't appreciate being disrespected by a first-year."

My cheek took a blunt swipe as I turned. Pain swelled in my jaw as blood dripped onto my collarbone. I dragged the red-handled sword over my shoulder and stepped back, the weight tilting me unevenly.

"I don't need to fight well when I can burn you into ashes with one touch," I hissed.

Monty laughed. He laughed in my face as he held the blade over his head, and our swords clashed together. The blood boiled in my veins, but I shoved it back as far as possible. He was stronger than me and had faster reflexes.

I dodged the double swipe but didn't expect him to be where I had veered. The tip of the sword stabbed into my right leg. My screams hallowed, drifting along the fields.

Again, again, again, our swords smashed into each other. I fought to get a wisp of air past my barred teeth. But he was always one step ahead. I frayed on the heavy line of passing out, dragging my limbs to rise. A sheen of white speckled my vision, my spine hunched with the weight of the blade. Not a single cut marred his olive skin.

I dropped my sword, relinquishing my triumph. "I'm done!" I yelled. "You—win." Hand on my shaking knee, I palmed my fingers to shield myself from the breaking light of his iris.

But that wasn't enough. Monty drew that sword out, and I met his ravenous, pale eyes as he stared at my thundering heart, knowing it was seconds away from dimming.

Darkness consumed the entire combat field. I flung out of the way as he stabbed his sword where my chest was seconds ago. Shadows consumed every bit of light, and even Monty had nothing to draw from once the sun was stripped from the sky.

Ashen rays soaked me, then two firm hands gripped my shoulders, and I was pulled through the darkness, through the rippling pain in my entire body.

Within one blink, I was in the infirmary.

Estella yelped, hand on her heart as she ran toward me. "Goodness, Severyn, you scared me."

I held my bleeding cheek. "I think I need stitches." I swung my gaze, searching for Archer.

She shook her head, inspecting my cheek. "I'll do my best not to leave you with a scar. It seems everybody wants to kill you but never finishes. You're lucky."

Luck. This wasn't luck. It was Archer saving me from Monty piercing my heart. I gripped the wall as Estella poured a stinging orange liquid over the wound.

"Combat got a bit heated today," I hissed through my teeth.

Estella raised a brow. "I'll say. They missed your nerve by a hair. You could have spent the rest of your life frowning, and how awful would that be."

There were a few beats of silence as she stitched my cheek. "It must be hard seeing all these wounds," I whispered.

She thought for a moment. "I usually don't see anyone more than once. Being in this room means you are weak or have a target on your back. So, who did you piss off, Severyn?"

"Monty, apparently," I whispered, "I don't think there's anything worse than pissing off a Serpent." Power had a level, and I had reached my peak to where others saw me as a threat. Monty—Monty wanted me dead. But why?

Estella shifted, dropping the thread and needle on the metal table pan. "Do you remember that story I told you about your mother's eyes?"

Distantly, I searched for the memory of my first combat class. "I remember. You said my father could never find that color of green again."

Estella held her chin high, those brown eyes narrowing as if the walls could hear. "That story wasn't about your father. It was about another man who searched all of Verdonia to find them. A man who'd be willing to steal the eyes of a stranger simply because he'd gone years without seeing that shade of green."

Something in my gut told me who it was, but I still could not dare say his title. "Monty wants me dead because—"

"Precisely," she hissed, lips thinner than the needle she used to stitch me. "Your mother suspected who her father was, but that kind of accusation could crumble the dynasty. I knew as soon as I laid eyes on you and when they shoved you into Winter that you were not born to follow, Severyn."

She held onto my shoulder, heaving forward as if all the air in her words were stolen. "The king is your grandfather, Severyn."

Estella's eyes shot toward the ceiling as she gripped her chest, dragging a hoarse breath through her lungs.

"Estella? Are you okay?" I whispered.

"I have guarded this for nearly thirty years, but it is time for a queen to reign. Do not—not let my last words be in vain. They will lie to you. They will hunt you. Don't—let them."

She was warded, just like Charles was.

She collapsed, and I dropped to my knees, holding her head in my lap. "Estella!" Her heart still beat, but her eyes were blank and dimmed. "Please wake up."

A tear fell from her eyes as she stared at me. "Your mother was my best friend, Severyn. Forgive her, please."

"What do you mean?" I cried.

Her eyes whirred, breathing falling. "You look just like *him*."

I could not save her. Not when whatever ward she'd been placed under was strong enough to silence her but cruel enough to keep her petrified.

I could not save Estella, but I tried. I held her there for hours, but no flicker of light shone from those still eyes. I had seen Charles and how it nearly killed him when we were flying to the academy. But that—that was nothing compared to the silent shudders Estella released. It was nothing as I cried any of my forbidden quell into her, hoping whatever God could hear my sobs would listen and release her, even kill her so I could save her.

Who else was warded? Who else *knew*? And that Daylight quell I'd seen in the king made sense now that Knox was called there. Malachi and I's quell share was powerful because we shared the same blood. Malachi was my—family. And this wasn't a rivalry between us. This was death, a forbidden secret breaking through the debris of shadows.

My cheek pulsed where her stitches were. I'd favor this scar for the rest of my life as Archer kept Klaus's last piece. It wasn't her name boldly scribed on my body but her mark and that gentle stitch of her mending fingers.

"I will find a way to save you," I said through tears. "I promise."

Chapter 25

I left Estella there. I had no choice.

I passed through the shadowed corridors and ran up those hundred steps toward the Serpent towers. I didn't know who I could trust, which scared me more than living a lie my entire life.

I imagined a younger Estella with my mother, her grey, wispy hair replaced by dark braids, their leather boots pounding against stone halls as they uncovered secrets at the academy. Had they stripped Estella of more than her voice? In another life, did she wield power beyond stitching wounds, now reduced to tending students' injuries as penance?

I pounded on Archer's door, urgency burning in my chest. When the door swung open, I stumbled in. My gaze caught the violet buttons and silver bows neatly arranged along the walls. Archer stood by the circular window, dressed entirely in black. He looked like he'd just returned from a Serpent meeting.

"How is your cheek?" he asked, voice measured.

"Estella is… gone. Petrified," I said, the image of her grey, lifeless eyes haunting me.

His sharp, questioning look told me he didn't understand. "And how did that happen?"

"If someone is warded from speaking about something, could they become petrified?" My voice cracked under the weight of the question.

"Death would be a kinder punishment," he said. "If a ward is forced open, it can lead to petrification or death, depending on its strength."

"Say it had to do with the king. Say it was a secret that could ruin lives." My limbs felt heavy, as if I, too, were on the verge of petrification. "If that truth got out, what would happen?"

"Yes," he admitted, his features hardening. "You shouldn't be here, Severyn."

"Do you… do you know who my grandfather is?" I asked,

"I was never certain." He closed his eyes briefly, as if the truth itself pained him. He knew what it meant: death, ruin, the fragile connection between us unraveling.

"Are you warded?" My heart nearly stopped as I watched him still.

"Not that I know of. But if Monty knows your bloodline, he will tell everyone. Tomorrow at your trial, I suspect it will become a hunt. I cannot protect you every moment. Taking you to Ravensla was a mistake. Kissing you was wrong. I am your superior." He pressed his thumb against his temple. "I'm sorry, Severyn."

"Is it because you want to kill me yourself and take the king's title? Am I standing in your way?" My hand drifted toward my daggers.

Darkness swirled in his eyes, feverish and untamed. "No."

"Then what is it?" I demanded. "You regret taking me there. I mean nothing to you beyond a bond forcing you to tolerate me."

"Because I cannot protect you every second. Because running is better than failing you. Because it would shatter Ciaran if you died… and destroy me." His words landed like stones, each one heavier than the last.

Archer squared his shoulders, hands in his pockets. "You've known me for two months. I've known you for two years. I waited for you, Severyn. Weak, but alive, because you kept me that way. For months, I wanted to see you. I even took a ship to your family's estate, hoping to glimpse you. Hoping you'd release me. And when you answered that door, I knew you would hate me forever."

Release him. The words felt like a chain tightening around my throat. He made me feel like a beast, holding him captive.

"Do you believe in me?" I asked, my voice barely above a whisper.

"Yes," he answered without hesitation.

"Then I won't die tomorrow."

"That first trial nearly killed you. They will only get harder," he said, stepping closer. His hand brushed my cheek, thunder rumbling in my veins. "All the Serpents will be watching. My father. Your father."

"I only care about one Serpent watching me," I admitted, the words slipping free.

His fingers curled around my jaw, lifting my chin. "You were slow to draw today. Sharpen your blades."

"Fine," I muttered, shadows pulsing beneath my skin. "It must be difficult, having your life tied to mine."

He chuckled, low and dark. "Infuriating. But I imagine having your life tied to a Serpent is no better. I leave for days, return torn and bloody."

I clicked my tongue. "I always know when you're safe."

"I spent two years with that feeling," he murmured.

"Why didn't I know?" My voice softened, thoughts swirling with thunder and flame. "Being near you feels like I have a hundred quells in my veins."

"You didn't know what you were looking for." Thunder cracked outside, shaking the trees. Archer leaned closer, his hand resting on my cheek. "Do you feel me now?"

Heat surged through my veins. "I feel you," I whispered, the space between us filling with shadow.

Archer was not the calm after the storm. He was the storm itself. And if I was to live in a world of shadows, I would strike my flame and light the path.

"Stay the night," he whispered. "Your room is not warded like mine."

I nodded, touching his cheek, feeling that cool darkness quench my burn. Lightning streaked the sky, flames trailing through the clouds. We were chaos together, and I wondered what would happen if we got even closer.

His eyes drifted to my lips, our breaths ragged. His hand settled on the small of my back.

I pressed my cheek to his chest, letting the silence wrap around us as our quells danced.

Chaos. Beautiful chaos.

"What is this?" I asked desperately. "What is this between us?"

"Our bond, and the past ones within it," he said softly. "This bond isn't ours. It's built on friendships and trust from before. The more time we spend together, the stronger it gets. And I… I don't have the strength to stay away from you."

"Then don't," I breathed. "We are friends."

He chuckled, low and warm. "Friends. Well, a good friend wouldn't keep you up before a trial."

He stepped back into the shadows, and my hand fell to my side.

"Fine. Then be my mentor tonight. I'm simply seeking guidance before the trial."

"As your mentor, I'm telling you to sleep. As someone bonded to your heartbeat, I'm begging you to rest." There was a faint curve to his lips.

"Is that a demand, Serpent?" I asked, tilting my head.

Amusement crossed his features. "Sure, Severyn. My first demand as a Serpent is asking you to sleep in my bed. I must be a cruel leader."

"The cruelest." I pulled my riding leathers over my head, dropping them below my feet with a thud. "And that isn't true. You demanded that I drop out of Skyfall."

"Ah, and did you listen?"

My daggers dropped one by one as I unlatched the buckles. I swore it took everything in Archer not to drag his eyes from my body for the third time.

"No." I shook my head. "But you were an ass about it."

The shadow he stood in emptied. Soft rustles sounded from the bed, and Archer perched on the silk duvet behind me.

"I meant what I said, Severyn. We shouldn't take this any further. I shouldn't be—staring at you. I shouldn't be contemplating shielding myself from you. I made a promise to protect you."

"You're allowed to demand things of me—allow me one."

A ravenous desire burned in his gaze. "What is it, *Severyn*?"

"Tell me next time when you decide to leave for days."

"Maybe I enjoy pissing you off, heating you," he growled.

His fingers knotted in the loose buttons atop the sheets. He went to open my fist, circling my shadow relic. I arched into his soft touch.

"I can't handle not knowing where you are on the Continent," I said, my gaze lingering on his lips, which seemed to edge closer with every heartbeat.

He weighed my words with a dark, hungry look. "Once we bond, you can speak to me through it wherever I am." His voice dipped, shadows curling around his shuttered breaths. His hands found mine, firm and deliberate. "Rider bonds allow no barriers. Once we bond, no shield you build will keep me out. Do you understand?"

"I understand." My voice wavered, but my resolve held.

He pressed his palm to mine, and I gasped as smoke coiled around us. Heat blossomed, not just on my skin but deep in my chest.

"Oh—"

His hand gripped the back of my knee as I reached for his jaw, my fingers skimming his stubble. The pull between us was unbearable, magnetic. I needed him—his lips, his touch.

The invisible tether between us tugged, synching the frayed edges of distance and silence that had lingered for too long.

"If it gets too intense, say something," he murmured, his breath warm against my chin. "Our bodies will react to the bonding process."

"I can handle it. Can you?" I teased, though my breath hitched as his proximity sent heat racing through my veins.

His lips quirked. "You consume my thoughts, Severyn Blanche. I nearly crumble every time I see or touch you." His fingers grazed my thigh, igniting sparks of need that coiled low in my belly.

"Take your clothes off," he said, his voice low, almost commanding. "You're overheating."

"I'm fine," I protested, though the heat beneath my skin betrayed me.

He hooked a thumb in my belt loop, a wicked grin playing on his lips. "I could always take them off for you."

I slipped out of my bottoms, kicking them to the floor. Sitting there, stripped down to my undergarments, I felt vulnerable yet alive under his gaze. His eyes lingered, tracing the lines of my body.

"Claiming my health is at risk to get me undressed? Convenient," I said, arching a brow.

"You're not undressed enough," he countered, his hands sliding over my bare legs. "I want to see all of you."

His shadows traced along my thighs, pulling a soft moan from my lips. "Bond with me," I whispered, my voice trembling with anticipation.

"Feel for it," he said. "And spread your thighs ever so slightly."

My thighs opened and he shifted his fingers up. "Like this?"

"Fuck," he hissed, sliding his hands even higher as felt my slicked inner thigh.

The bond snapped into place, a slow, electric tether wrapping us together. His thoughts brushed against mine, darkness swirling like ink in water. It wasn't invasive; it was a gentle, steady hand guiding me.

"Bond with me," I repeated, my plea more desperate.

His fingers slipped beneath my underwear as he rubbed his thumb over my heated core. Pleasure knotted deep as he moved deliberately, coaxing my body to respond. My thighs tightened, a shuddered breath slipping free as he nipped at the buttons of my shirt.

"If we're going to bond, I want your first thoughts of me filled with pleasure," he murmured, his voice like a growl against my skin. "You despised me days ago."

A black flame flickered to life on my palm. I was burning him, but he didn't flinch, didn't pull away.

"How am I supposed to feel about you now?" I whispered, my hand brushing his sleeve, the fabric singeing under my touch.

"Pleasure. Desire. Hate if you must," he said, his lips teasing the curve of my neck. "But for the next hour, I want every breath you take to be my name."

A finger teased my opening.

"Archer…" I gasped, pulling back to see the burn marks on his shirt. His skin, untouched, bore no sign of my fire.

"I can handle your burn," he said, his eyes alight with amusement.

I grabbed his jaw, kissing him deeply, fiercely. "Is that so?"

He pulled back just enough to breathe in the ash I exhaled, his shadows binding my wrists to the bed as I reached for him. "Slow, Severyn. I want to take things slow with you."

"This isn't fair," I bit out, struggling against the restraints.

He brought my wrist to his lips, kissing the flame relic there. "I thought you only had one demand?" His voice was a dark tease. "And you have a big trial tomorrow."

His lips traveled along my collarbone, down to my chest. One button at a time, he exposed more of my skin until my bare breasts faced him. "Please, touch me," I said.

His tongue licked over my hardened peaks, slowly, before he sucked them one by one. "It's not safe," he said, before he released the shadow tethers, leaving me breathless and aching.

"I'll be fine," I said, meeting his wicked gaze.

"I don't want to tire you out—for both our sakes," he said, his voice softer. "Rider bonds can drain energy. I could steal your entire quell for a day and leave you bare for the trial. As it is, I already taste ash in my lungs."

"I understand." I crawled farther onto the bed, and Archer rolled onto his side, resting his head on his hand as he watched me. The night breeze from the open window sliced through the heat between us.

"Sleep, Severyn. Please," he said, his voice gentler now. "Our bond is strong enough to hold us, even if we take nothing further tonight. This bond… ours… it's what we make it."

I turned onto my back, staring at the ceiling. "Tell me about Night. Distract me. I can't rest knowing half the school plans to hunt me down once they find out whose blood I have."

He brushed a strand of hair behind my ear, his other hand lightly tracing the edge of my flame relic. "I didn't think you were serious about a bedtime story," he mused.

"Please. Tell me about your home."

He saw the anxiety in my furrowed brow and sighed before speaking. He described the plains of shadows, the crystal mountains lining grey grass, and rivers of violet threading through the city. His voice softened as he spoke of owls hooting in wispy trees and the youngest heir to rule after his grandfather surrendered it to him.

And as I listened, the tension in my body eased, though the fire Archer sparked within me remained, smoldering just beneath the surface.

Chapter 26

Frost coated my lungs as I ran through the Winter trails.

The entire estate would be used for the Trial of Malice, but we could not use our enigma to fly, and not that I wanted Naraic in this bloody mess, but even my flame would not spark in this dry cold.

"Severyn," Knox yelled from the woods, and I hid lower behind the frosted bushes as he thrusted his sword—fresh blood coating the tip. "I know you're here. You can't hide from me."

I gripped my bloodied arm where he'd swiped me an hour before. Thankfully, the falling snow concealed my trail of blood.

A hand clutched my mouth. I turned to face Antonia as her dagger was tight against my throat. "Scream, and you're dead," she whispered.

I nodded silently, eyes attuned to the caked blood on her chin.

I saw Alaric in her eyes; his last words clung to my breaths, yet I knew this wasn't the time.

She got to her feet, kicking frozen dirt at me as she yelled after Knox, "She went over there." Her finger pointed further down the trail.

Antonia saved me when I did not deserve any kindness from her.

I gripped two daggers in my fists as they ran through the forest. The headmaster had referred to this as the Trial of Malice. But my brothers called it prey and predator, a childhood game I'd played growing up. The students were split in half, each marked as prey or predator. Each predator was to hunt and kill a student from another realm. But prey, we were told the longer we survived without wounds, the greater our chances of being bid on was.

I never believed Father prepared me for this—but he'd planted the seeds of succession even when our vocabulary was limited. We'd played games as children, not knowing our sticks and stones would turn into daggers and swords.

Knox wanted to kill me. Perhaps I read power so differently in everyone that nothing surprised me. Even Knox needed to prove himself, and his stunt with the headmaster nearly cost me my life… but I'd seen his eyes and knew no light shone through them, and whatever held him was darker than Archer's shadow.

This wasn't a trial but a game—Knox had no idea whose blood ran through his veins.

They hoped we'd kill each other before the Serpent Bid, and every secret that was starved down was too weak to fend, to crawl up from whatever silent cave it was buried under.

Knox was a pawn in someone else's game, and I wondered what was promised to him if he'd asked Monty to take the light of his soul to endure the pain of killing me. Priceless seemed feeble right now—priceless was whatever Knox was fed to believe killing me was worth it.

I'd gotten flashbacks of us playing as children in the woods. But instead, victory was doing the other's chores for the week.

Knox always won.

The cold wind wholly swept through and into my bones. I took off through the woods as my joints began to numb. Left would take me to Spring, but right would lead me toward darkness and into the Night realm. My quell would be useless if I got near that hot spring. I was running, not into the light of Spring shining through the trees, but into the darkness and to where I believed sanctuary was many weeks before as I went through this same trail.

The night crawled with me, consuming the trail with every heave of my breath. Soon, I became shrouded in that familiar blanket of cool shadow.

I caught my breath as I leaned against a cave, knowing the darkness was deceptive. My head jerked forward. Knox wasn't the only predator, as howls and hisses sounded from the forest. I gripped my daggers as yellow eyes stalked me from the trails.

I had to keep going. I struck my flame as I went through the slicked trails. Those beastly eyes walked with me, waiting for me to take one step over and kill me.

I took it back. I didn't care to see the Night realm, not when my heart was in my throat, and I could barely see my next step.

A figure approached, and I could barely make out Damien's features.

"Severyn," he called. A slick of sweat dripped from his brow as he caught his breath. "Are you prey or predator?"

"Prey." I took a step back as he drew closer.

"I won't hurt you."

"Are you prey?" I gripped the dagger harder.

"I am. I heard your mind, and I followed you here. I waited by your room this morning, but Malachi said you never came home."

I shuddered. "Well, I'm sure you have an idea as to why. I don't quite have a large circle I can trust right now."

I didn't have the energy to throw a shield up. Damien was in my mind, clawing over my visit with Estella... and probably where I had slept the night before.

He looked up at the night sky. "Listen, I'm not your enemy. You can trust me, Severyn. We need to survive this trial and claim what is rightfully yours."

I shook my head. Then, one of those beasts' paws slashed across the barrier. Damien grabbed my wrist and pulled me deeper into the Night realm as a seven-foot-long black creature with jutted grey horns stepped over the border, leathery wings extended from its hunched spine.

"We aren't safe here. Run!" yelled Damien. "The trail wards have vanished."

Damien unsheathed his sword, and we ran as fast as our legs would take us. The creature was gaining speed. Jaws snapping. Two more came from the other side, pinning Damien and I back-to-back. Those yellow eyes stalked around us in a circle, drool dripping from their engorged canines.

"Damien—" I swung the dagger as one of the creatures lunged for my chest, and I sliced it across the jugular. "We can't kill them all!"

We were trapped.

Damien slashed his sword. "Hell no, will I allow a beast to kill me." He held his palm towards the sky, and a thousand glass shards formed like floating crystals in the air. He twirled his fist and sent them flying at the beasts, striking them each in the chest.

They roared—but gained us enough time to take off.

I reached for the red-handled sword I'd won from Callum. I swung hard, clipping the broad shoulder of one.

"We're going to die here, Damien!" I yelled over thrashing claws. Liquid night drowned me in a pool of midnight sky, searching for any safe place to run.

I flung my simmered palm out, barely scorching the second beast to my left.

Damien pressed his spine into mine, and we walked a slow circle. "Do you trust me, Severyn?"

I panted, "Not exactly." There was no point in lying to him, not when my mind was screaming the truth. "I *want* to trust you."

He scoffed and grabbed my shoulders to face him. A million shards of glass whirled around us until we were portaled through the fury. A few cut me, slicing my knuckles and cheeks in a prismatic kaleidoscope of fragments.

Speckled light surrounded us, shattering off the mirrors of glass in every direction until we were both standing on the sands of Summer. It took me a moment to adjust to the sunset above. I skimmed my palms down my entire body, expecting glass to be lodged into my skin.

He touched my bleeding cheek, and a ripple of pain shot through his flared eyes. "Are you okay, Sev?"

"I thought you said portaling someone else was dangerous with your quell?" I snarked. "We just traveled through glass!"

Damien looked almost as surprised that I was in one piece. "I said I've never tried it with anyone else. It was either that or us getting mauled to death."

I gaped. "Next time, we travel through fire—let's see if you survive it," I hissed.

"My apologies, your majesty." He shot me a smug look and even dared to bow. I smacked him across the shoulder. "How low should I bow for you? My back's still sore from my fall."

"I've got a hundred reasons to be pissed at you, don't make me add 'asshole' to the list."

We began to make our way down the trails. Blades at the ready.

"I don't believe I've done anything wrong, Severyn."

I scoffed. "I know what you did to Everett during training. I know you only sought me out because of my neval hair. And that pendant you gave me was only to spy on me, Damien."

"Point taken—the Everett thing was wrong. And your neval hair only piqued my interest because they were *hunted* down when I lived in Basilyne during boarding school. You were this mystery to me. No offense, but a fragile female from the north didn't strike me as terrorizing. I gave you that pendant to ensure no one *tried* to hunt you down. I took it too far, Severyn."

"Well—" I cut my words short as Malachi stared across the trail. Blood dripped from her chin, her sword. She slumped her shoulders back, nearly collapsing into a pile of leather.

Predator. Predator. Predator.

She dropped the sword with a loud clang at her feet, face paled with one look at me. "He came after me. I had no choice, Sev." Tears clung to her, and I saw that gash down her arm. She'd been attacked. "*I killed him.*"

"Who came after you?" I asked, already feeling the sting in my eyes. I knew. I knew whose name she'd cry next.

"Knox—he isn't right. Knox is dead. He's dead, Severyn."

Knox was dead.

My body numbed. "Where is he?" I screamed, blinded by instant hot tears. I grabbed her arm. "Where is Knox?"

"Spring."

I turned so quickly to face Damien that the wind slashed my cheeks. "Portal me there, Damien. Now."

"Severyn, it's too dangerous. Our quells are weakened there. I hardly know how to portal myself without slicing my own skin up."

"I don't care. Portal me. Now." I swore I saw the shadow Knox lay in calling to me.

Damien nodded, gripping my shoulder as that same glass whirlpool spiraled around us. Shards sliced my skin like thorns this time. It was a ravenous pull, dragging me in, and for a moment, I saw myself in the shattered mirrors—the bloody, bruised girl in the bath, her wrist broken. An eagle-eye view of despair.

My sobs echoed through the fragments, a haunting chorus trapped in the void. *"You knew I was safe,"* Archer called, his hands pinning my body to the wall.

Clipped glass mirrored a wall of daggers, seizing moments from time—moments I didn't recognize, captured through another's eyes.

"Is this where Monty touched you?" Archer's voice was distant, pitched within the void of stolen time.

Damien had seen every moment of my life when he gave me that pendant.

Damien shielded my face against his chest. I flung back, crimson streaking my vision, metallic and heavy. Blood was everywhere, dripping down my cheeks, my arms. I screamed, prying a slivered shard from my hand, swinging left and right. My leathers were unscathed, but Damien… he'd taken most of the damage. A large gouge ran from his brow towards his eye.

I didn't have time to ask if he was okay. I spun in a full circle. "Knox?" I screamed among the roots and vines.

Damien held his bloody eye, pointing to the bushes. A body lay curled there, a hand limp on his chest. Knox's face was pale, lifeless. I ran, my steps frantic.

"Knox, I'm here!"

There are sounds capable of waking sleeping griffins. When the feathered cries tore through the wards, it felt like a piece of me died with each shriek.

"Severyn, everyone is watching you. Do not save him." Archer's voice rang in my mind.

"I don't have a choice."

Our bond went cold the moment my foot sank into Spring's mulch. Delicate florals waved in the breeze, scattered sunlight spilling through wispy leaves above. It was a trap—I knew it. The king wanted me to save him, to let the Serpents watch the live-action unveiling of my forbidden quell. I was the finale, the spectacle.

I'd wake more than griffins. I'd wake death itself.

"You're too close to the hot spring, Severyn. Your quell won't work here," Damien yelled, stumbling after me.

My life or Knox's. Either way, the Serpents would learn the truth. I gripped Knox's face between my palms, whispering, "A Herring's blood will not be spilled today."

Damien hoisted Knox over his shoulder, carrying him far enough for the fire to return to my veins. The molten heat surged, forbidden and uncontrollable. I swallowed the shadows on my tongue, the metallic taste clinging as I yelled, "Drop him. Drop him now."

Damien obeyed, lowering Knox to the ground. "Sev, you've already saved him once. We don't know what will happen a second time. Everett gained a Winter quell. It could be bad."

I looked to the sky, knowing Father was watching his son die before his eyes. "I can't let him die, Damien," I said, my voice cracking.

Blisters burned my cheeks as I wiped the tears away, placing both hands on Knox's face. Darkness swarmed the Spring realm, the sun and moon seemingly colliding in the sky. Knox gasped, his first breath shattering the silence.

I reached for Archer's bond, but all I felt was static, a cold hum rattling between us. He'd cut the unwoven cord the moment he saw me touch my brother. He'd done it to save Ciaran and himself.

For a moment, I considered pounding on Naraic's bond, daring to demand, *"Release me."* But I knew the cost—my death, days or moments away. Naraic deserved better than to be tethered to a death sentence.

I forced myself to stay grounded. Perhaps it wasn't my life on the line, but Archer's—he'd interfered with a Serpent trial.

The darkness faded to grey, melting into clouds before the light broke through again. Knox stirred, his face contorting as he sat up, shaking his head.

"What… what happened?" he asked, his voice weak.

Damien held his bleeding eye. "Your sister sacrificed her life for you after you nearly killed her and Malachi," he said, his words sharp and pointed. "The trial is almost over. It's nearing dusk."

Knox's face twisted in confusion and pain. "I don't remember anything. I would never hurt Severyn. Malachi is my friend."

Damien plucked a glass shard from his knuckles, glaring. "Then shield better next time. Someone compelled you today."

I didn't know a compulsion quell existed.

I pressed against the torn leather on Knox's chest, putting pressure on the wound Malachi's blade had left. "You need to act as if you're writhing in pain. I don't care if they keep you in the infirmary until the Serpent Bid."

I shoved him hard into the dirt, slicing a shallow cut against his skin with my dagger. "Do you understand?"

Knox nodded, clutching his gut with a loud, exaggerated groan. There was enough blood for his wounds to look convincing.

Chapter 27

After the trial, I sat on my bed for the last hour, waiting for the headmaster to barge in and demand how Knox was still breathing. But it was only Malachi.

There were a few beats of silence between us as she sat at the end of my bed, crossing her legs. "I guess we should talk," she began.

"How long have you known?"

She didn't hesitate. "Since we got those letters at the first trial."

"You've known for that long?"

"It told me two students were up for my title, and it was easy to narrow it down to Knox and you. After we quell-shared, I was sure of it. Monty pieced it together first. He plans to kill you. He hoped Knox would do it."

"All my life, I had no idea," I whispered. "Why didn't you tell me?"

"And perhaps that's how it should have been." Malachi shook her head. "My life is sad. But we are blood, Severyn. You are my family, and perhaps I enjoyed knowing I had one. Your mother's letters were so sweet, and I couldn't disappoint her."

"Right, bonding with her dragon should have been a dead giveaway." I pressed a finger to my temple. "What happens next? The people of Verdonia will not take lightly finding out there is a whole other bloodline set for the throne."

"Do you want the throne?" she asked.

I never had time to process the weight of her question. I hardly saw myself as ever being a Serpent, let alone ruling over the Continent. I slowly shook my head. "I don't see myself as ever being someone great."

"I spent my entire life being told what to do, what to wear, who I shall marry. I envy you. I truly do. For you to walk in and decide you do not want a title as callously as discussing the weather makes me angry for some reason. All five of my siblings never returned home from the academy. I've lost everyone I know. I swore that wouldn't be me. I made a promise to survive."

"I know. And that's why you deserve the title," I said quietly. "This isn't my life, Malachi."

"It isn't that simple, Severyn. Nothing ever is. Knox was compelled to kill us both, which means someone else knows. Monty can't compel. Someone knows, and they will do everything to pin us against each other. I don't want to die. If something happens to me, I want you to claim what is rightfully yours."

My head began to whirl. "Who could be strong enough to compel a student?"

"A professor, maybe. It doesn't matter who. It means that someone strong enough wants the Herring bloodline out of power."

"Malachi, we need to trust each other. I can't sleep here, not knowing if you will double-cross me the second I close my eyes."

Tears welled in her amber eyes. "I don't have much family left, Severyn. Once my grandfather goes, I will have nothing besides my father. I don't have it in me to lose you… and Knox. Blood is stronger than power, Sev. Nothing is chance."

I wrapped my arms around her neck, and perhaps I was naïve for believing Malachi Herring could be an alliance, but I'd rather die knowing I thought there was some good in this cruel world. All I saw before me was a shattered girl.

"Then I shall trust you with my life, Malachi," I whispered. "I'm going to need every ounce of hope at the Bid."

She sobbed into my shoulder. "We will survive, Sev. Us against the crown of thieving heirs."

* * *

Archer and Ciaran flew away the following day for a Serpent gathering. The lanterns in the room were already lit, and Malachi had left for the day.

She might have left in the night.

"Six students were killed yesterday. I'll be gone for a few days. Sharpen your daggers and train more," was all Archer had said through our faint rider's bond.

"Where are you?"

He took nearly two hours to respond, *"Capital."*

The bond went cold with the echo of my response: "Stay safe." I knew it didn't reach him.

Damien waited by my door, giving me a shallow nod as he heard my screaming thoughts. The walk to warding class was nothing but deafening silence between us. I couldn't hide my anxiety today, not with the Serpent Bid only days away.

Damien pressed a thumb against his temple. "Sev, you're very loud today. I'm worried you'll burst a blood vessel."

I scoffed. "It's my mind, and I have a lot on it right now."

"I can tell," he muttered.

"I'm still mad at you. Lucky for you, Knox seems to be more of an asshole."

"You can't blame me for being curious. I already paid for that mistake by breaking my back."

Damien didn't understand the full effects of his actions—how saving Everett had led to Knox confessing to the king about my forbidden quell. And no matter how many times I screamed my reasoning in my mind, all I got was a shrug of annoyance along my shield.

We entered the grand hall, and I nearly slammed into Damien, grabbing his shoulders to shield myself from the man standing in a royal guard suit.

"Shit, why is my brother here?" I gasped.

"It's never a good sign when Malvoria visits," Damien muttered. "It means they're hauling students who haven't performed well enough before the Bid—mostly first-years, but they take the odd second and third-year too."

Charles stood with his arms crossed, dusting a speck off his navy-blue suit. In his hand was a scroll, presumably filled with the names of students bound for the Malvoria.

Damien caught my wrist as I stepped forward. "His mind is clouded. I can't see it clearly."

"I'll meet you at warding," I whispered.

Charles's golden eyes caught mine. No smile curved his lips. Instead, he motioned at me with a curl of his fingers.

"I'll stay with you," Damien said, though I wasn't sure if he'd spoken aloud or in my mind because I was too distracted by Charles.

His haircut was sharper than the last time I'd seen him. I smiled tentatively, fingers crossed behind my back. "Hello, Charles."

"Good morning, Severyn," he said with a curt nod. His gaze flicked to Damien. "This must be Damien Lynch. Your father speaks very highly of you," he said. "He stopped by Malvoria for a visit."

Damien shook Charles's hand, smiling like he'd just been handed a medal. "I've heard great things about you, sir."

Of course, Damien knew about Charles. He'd seen every moment, every unwarded thought that crossed my mind.

Charles glanced at the scroll. "I heard you won Skyfall, Severyn. You will do great at the Bid." His breath hitched slightly, his hesitation barely noticeable. "I'm proud of you. I've put in a good word with the warden if Damien takes the vacant Summer title in Ravensla."

I wondered how long he'd known I'd moved to Summer—if he kept an eye on the roster every odd day to ensure I hadn't been killed.

"Do you need help finding the students?" I asked, letting the venom lace my voice. I wanted him to see my clenched fists, to know how barbaric this all was. I forced my flame down, cooling it with a mist of shadow.

Charles rolled his shoulders back. "You know I don't have a choice. The academy has no place for lesser performers. Malvoria will teach them what they're missing and turn them into great guards. Not everyone is born to lead," he said, his tone mechanical, rehearsed. "It's three years. It goes by fast, and the students are well-fed and housed. We aren't torturing them. All we ask is that they guard their Continent."

If they don't die first. I knew Verdonia needed protectors, but conscription was unjust, especially for students who refused to kill their peers in a trial.

"Is there anything else you need from me?" I asked, my voice strained.

Charles glanced at Damien. "May I have a few moments alone with Severyn?"

Damien's gaze hardened before he reluctantly walked away.

Charles skimmed his scroll. "There is one student. She was in Winter with you. Myla Reinhart. She's been pulled from the academy."

My heart dropped. "How is that possible? Myla has two swords and excels in warding."

A scowl crossed his face. "Not that it's your concern, but the academy doesn't feel she's suited for Winter. Better to pull her now than let her fail—or die. Her father was a lesser-known Serpent from a minor Winter realm. She has no true connection to her calling. At least after her term at Malvoria, she can return to Ravensla."

I seethed, my feet feeling molten against the stone floor. "Let me guess—Bridger Thorne said that. He's the third-year mentor for Winter. He knows Myla is performing well, and he's forcing her out."

"That isn't up to me. Your mentor and Serpent have full authority over your continuation here." He glanced towards where Damien had gone. "By the way, who is your Serpent? I didn't see your name on Saani's list."

"Archer Lynch," I said softly.

His golden eyes widened in surprise. "Both Lynches? That's a tough one. I don't understand why the Night Serpent chose you." He dragged his fingers over the scroll. "Sev, you need to stay on the edge. Don't draw attention. Win as many swords as you can. The lynches don't have a great history with our family." His voice lowered. "Father owes Victor a barter."

Charles was clueless. I wasn't just making waves at the academy. I was a tsunami, pulling the tide into my grasp before hellfire rained down. He only needed to glance at the dozen charred trees along the combat field.

"What do you mean?" I asked.

"Our parents attended the academy together. Some things don't heal with time. Mother and Victor were against each other for the same title. The barter Father made isn't something I can share, all you must know is you cannot let Damien win his tile."

I stared at my eldest brother. "I'm not a child, Charles."

"You're right. You're not a child. But I'm still your brother, and like the wards I'm under, they're meant to protect you."

I crossed my arms. "I understand."

He nodded. "Anyway, have you seen Myla Reinhart? Bridger said you two were close. I thought you'd want to say goodbye."

"Bridger is lying," I snapped. "He's trying to take Father's title. He's not a leader. He should be expelled for this—"

A whip of ice slashed the ground, silencing me. I jumped back as Charles's expression hardened.

"You're not in Winter anymore, Severyn. You shouldn't care."

I began to shake. "Please trust me, Charles. Myla deserves to stay. Bridger isn't—he's dangerous."

Charles chuckled darkly. "Being a Serpent means making tough decisions. Not all of them are good ones. You're young. Someday, when you're in power, you'll understand and thank me."

"Charles, you're making a mistake." I reached for him, but my hands curled around empty air. Ice crawled up my sleeve, numbing my fingers.

His jaw tightened. "Bridger Thorne will be the next Serpent of the Frozen Valley. The academy makes no mistakes. Get to class before my scroll grows longer."

My blood boiled as I stalked towards warding, cursing with every breath.

I hoped to catch Myla and warn her.

"Naraic, you need to take Myla away." Her griffin was still too young to carry her.

"The skies are too full."

But her empty seat screamed back like a thorn in my hand, a bloody thorn I'd spent a day trying to pry out. Damien met my gaze, and as I passed him, I heard him whisper, "She's already gone. Some woman escorted her out."

My mouth dried. "What did she look like?"

Damien shoved a mental image of Lorna riding Julian into my mind, the intrusive thought sharp and clear. Then, in the distance, Setrephia soared across the sky, her golden eyes scanning the academy grounds.

A scream pierced the air, distant but filled with unmistakable terror. It was already too late. Perhaps Charles knew I was a tsunami, and this was his way of attempting to control it.

Above was Haziel. Myla's hatchling griffin squeaked and cried, its tiny wings flapping furiously. The little creature wasn't strong enough to keep pace with Setrephia. Haziel tried—tried with everything she had—her sleek, fluffy feathers beating the air in desperate pursuit. But the distance only grew.

Charles had taken Myla.

* * *

Another two days passed without the Serpents. I believed this was a test of how long I could go without breaking. I did as Charles told me and was as quiet as possible. Even today, when I was pinned against Bridger for combat, I allowed him to walk away without his entire face melting off, and I'd say I deserved a medal of patience for that act of kindness.

I should have killed him. I should have held his heart in my grasp and demanded an answer. But Damien pulled me off him as I hovered my flame below his chin.

"Severyn, he pisses me off too, but Bridger is a student mentor. He was in the lead. It's not fair, but it happened," Damien hissed as we sat on the dragon fields next to Emerich and Naraic. "Malvoria needs guards, and Myla has a powerful quell. She'll survive the three years."

I closed my eyes, Haziel's cries of pain still echoing in my mind after two days. "Give me the rundown of the Serpent Bid. I don't want any surprises."

Damien leaned back on the grass. "We travel by boat to the Serpent estate. As the name suggests, Serpents bid on who they want to gain the title and be in the final trial. I am the current lead, but that could change. Most bid on their own children, but this year is full of hybrids. Our parents didn't grow up in the same realms, so it's hard to say what will happen. This year, it's based on skill—as it should be. Archer had nearly every Serpent vote for him his year. This bid is why I'm a mentor and first in line for the final trial."

He continued, "Then there's this thing called claims. If a Serpent is drawn to you, they can claim you, which means no one else can bid on you. The whole thing is all bullshit."

"A Serpent can claim you?" I asked.

"Any attention from a Serpent is good, but a claim is a bid that ensures you'll earn a title that year, like putting all your bets on someone. It guarantees no one will deem you unworthy or send you to Malvoria. But being claimed isn't ideal—you're essentially their puppet for the night. Honestly, the bid is all a sham. The lindworm chooses who will reign. This academy just prepares us for when it does."

"And if you object to being claimed?"

Damien chuckled darkly. "It's like warding—you can't break a ward unless you want to be petrified. You're bound by quell to that Serpent until we return to the academy. So, don't go winking at random Serpents that night." He nudged my ribs lightly. "Although, in your case, it might work in your favor."

"That's barbaric."

"If you gain a title, it's an automatic alliance with that realm. There are positives. For example, if Monty claimed Bridger, he could bargain his light."

"Archer told me your mother was a marriage bid. Do you remember how you found out she died… if you don't mind me asking?"

Damien's expression darkened. "My father's mind was never clear about it. Rage can shield memories. All I saw was her pale face as he stood over her still body. He said she was missing, and days turned into months. I told Archer, and he brushed me off." He paused, his voice tightening. "Boarding school was… something else. It was like being thrown in with all the misfits of Verdonia. I learned a lot about people. I learned how to be alone. Sometimes, I wonder if I even know how to be normal."

Despite what he'd done to Everett, I found forgiveness for Damien because I saw the cracks in him, the broken pieces no one else noticed. "That must have been hard."

"In some ways, I'm ahead of everyone here. I nearly ran out of books to read. So, when I encounter something mysterious, my mind has to figure it out."

His gaze danced along the clouds. "I know we were doomed to be anything more than friends, but… a part of me wishes I'd kissed you that first night. Part of me wishes you were still Winter-bound."

I sucked in a sharp breath. "Damien, I can't be anything besides your friend. Not when I don't know if I'll make it through the year." My voice wavered, but I held steady, hoping he didn't see through my lie.

He sighed, his voice tinged with resignation. "You're a terrible liar, Severyn Blanche. I see how you look at my brother. The worst part is… I can read your mind, but he seems to understand you more than I ever will. I thought it would be easier this way."

Flexing my fingers, I shifted the topic, unwilling to lead Damien on anymore. There was nothing salvageable between us—not after those stolen moments within the glass, not after he'd willed death and life from my forbidden veins.

"I wonder how Myla is doing?" I said quickly.

"Charles probably enjoys having another Winter quell there. It's nice to be around quells like your own." His gaze lingered on the shadow relic etched into my palm.

I didn't bring it up. I didn't have the energy to explain, nor did I want to hear Damien's sharp remarks about how harboring too many quells could surge me. I was a walking disaster, waiting to be stripped of everything once the bid came.

"I swear, if Bridger takes my father's title…" I curled my fingers into the dried grass, the heat of my frustration sparking at my fingertips.

"Your father needs an heir, Severyn," Damien said softly. "He's not quite as lucky to have two rivals like us."

And I wondered if things between us would have been different if I were called to Winter in another life.

But I couldn't live beneath someone, and I'd seen Damien's fantasy about him being the Serpent.

Archer. He still hadn't returned to the academy. And the ache in my gut was enough for me to need a bed.

"Where are you?"

I felt no ebony shadows running down our unsealed bond. No response as night soaked the sky.

Chapter 28

"Meet me at the combat fields." It was the day before the bid when Archer called back.

Damien and I approached the combat grounds, where Monty and Archer stood across the field. Their expressions were serious. Devoid of humor. Archer's eyes refused to meet mine, and I burned with questions I couldn't voice. Why had our rider bond gone cold for days? Why had he half-heartedly shadowed me during the trial?

I stopped in my tracks as the other four Serpents approached. Saani emerged within flames, Tydon through the wind. Jenessa's steps frosted the ground beneath her, while vines sprung up in Levisly's wake.

Damien steeled himself beside me. "Prepare yourself," he muttered. "Nothing like the day before the bid."

The six Serpents stood before us as the surviving students gathered. Winter's numbers had dwindled to ten. Robi's index finger was missing its tip—frostbite, I assumed. Chanvin refused to lift her gaze from the ground, even as Bridger loomed between them.

Had living in the Winter trails sucked the life from them?

Jenessa's voice broke the silence. "Stand with your Serpent, students. We're doing a round-up."

I stumbled into place beside Archer, glancing at him from the corner of my eye. He didn't acknowledge me, even as I pounded on the paper-thin walls of our bond, desperate for any response.

Malachi joined the ten Night students—a mix of second and third years. Only Antonia and Jace remained as first-years. Antonia's short silver hair was pinned back, with four gleaming swords strapped to her. Jace looked rugged, his hair shaved into scorned lines. He stood protectively beside Antonia, as if he'd made the same vow to Alaric as Archer had to Klaus.

I wondered how ruthless Archer was, that only two first-years remained under his command. Perhaps impressing him was harder for most students. And yet here I was, sleeping in his bed and tasting the remnants of his shadows on my tongue. I gnawed on the thought of him, dreamt of his hands on my body in every stolen moment of silence—

Archer shifted, his shoulders tense beneath the black suit that hugged his frame. His breathing was uneven, and I wanted nothing more than to twine my fingers with his, to feel him again after a week of silence.

I was starved for him, quenching my longing with untamed shadows that barely sufficed.

Saani's gaze lingered on me, unyielding, even as Damien stepped into place beside her. Knox had abandoned his exaggerated hobble, his supposed injury dismissed as a surface wound. Beside him, Everett stood shoulder-to-shoulder, their fingers brushing ever so slightly.

Saani cleared her throat. "There are students whose quells do not match their Serpent. Severyn Blanche, you will be placed under my mentorship. Everett Killian will move to Jenessa's Winter realm, and Malachi Herring will be under Tydon's watch."

My stomach dropped. I glanced at Malachi. "Does this mean we have to move rooms?" I asked Saani softly.

Saani's whip of fire scorched the grass. "Which room are you speaking of? You seem to switch beds often, including those of Serpents. I don't think it will be an issue for you."

Heat rushed to my cheeks. "Excuse me?"

Her eyes raked over me. "I don't take kindly to winks and pretty smiles, girl. Take your place behind me before I call in a favor to Malvoria and have you escorted out."

Humiliated, I moved behind Damien.

"There's an empty room beside mine," Damien whispered. "I'll help you move."

I nodded quickly. Malachi joined Tydon's Autumn group without hesitation. Everett followed Jenessa, his expression blank, as if still processing the shift.

Damien voiced my thoughts. "The day before the bid, and you're switching students around?"

Saani clicked her tongue. "Orders from the king himself. He believes students should be mentored by the Serpent of their chosen realms. Do you disagree?"

My throat dried. Archer finally met my gaze, his expression unreadable. His silence told me everything. Saani had already decided I was unfit to be an heir. My fate was in her hands now... and Damien's.

"Did you know?" I asked Archer.

"Yes."

"Saani is going to send me to Malvoria... Myla is gone."

"I won't allow it," he said softly.

Saani's whip cracked again. "The ship will arrive at noon tomorrow. If you're late, consider it a one-way ticket to Malvoria. Your attire has been chosen and placed in your dorm."

Charles's words echoed in my mind—the hidden threat to keep Damien in my good graces gnawed at my gut as I raised my shield. Could I trust him after everything he'd done and lied about?

Saani smiled at Monty, who nodded quickly. "Combat is canceled today. I suggest spending the afternoon projecting your quell. The king is eager to see what powers lie within the new students."

Damien walked with me, and I couldn't help but notice his slight nod towards Saani. He'd be just one door down from me, close enough to hear my thoughts anytime he wanted.

I shot a desperate glare at Archer, but he walked away before I could shout his name down our bond.

I followed Damien silently to the Summer dorms, where an empty room two doors down from his awaited me. "Does this happen often?" I asked when we were out of sight.

"I'm sure it will over the next few years. Our parents all came from various regions. Normally, the mark you got on your palm sorts you correctly."

Damien opened the door. "I figured it was your quell, but Knox hasn't shown any unexpected powers since the trial."

A few hours had passed. Aides had delivered attire for the bid tomorrow. The Summer dorms were hotter than the shadows of Night I'd called home. Every corner of the room seemed lit, even under the pressing sunset streaming through oval windows. A red gown lay on the bed, its flowing skirt embroidered with lace flowers. It reminded me of the one Archer had given me in Ravensla.

Damien caught my stare. "What do the gowns represent?" I asked.

"Sometimes, the king handpicks the attire. That gown is vintage, passed down for new students. The lace bodice shows it was created by a quell."

"What did Saani mean by projecting our quell?"

"We'll get a chance to show off our quells to the Serpents."

I glanced at the tapestries on the walls. "I probably shouldn't burn the Summer halls down my first night." I forced a nervous laugh, hoping he'd leave so I could find Archer.

He chuckled but didn't smile. "The walls are thin, Severyn. I'll know exactly when you visit those Serpents' beds." But Damien wasn't staring at the walls; his gaze fixed on the mirror nailed to the door. A faint smirk curved his lips. "Goodnight, Severyn."

As the door clicked shut, I sank onto the bed. Somewhere down the hall, another door closed softly. My heart thundered as I reached for the dagger strapped to my thigh.

In one swift motion, I hurled it at the mirror. The glass shattered, shards cascading to the floor in a glittering storm. Silence followed, broken only by the erratic rhythm of my breathing.

He was watching my every move.

I needed to find Archer. I bolted for the stairs but barely reached the fourth step when hands gripped my mouth, stifling my frozen scream as I was shoved against the wall—an elbow pressing into my chest, pinning me in place.

A silhouette emerged within the crawling shadows, blue eyes burning with wicked fury.

"Severyn," Archer whispered. "You shouldn't be out. Not tonight." His grip shifted to my wrist as he tried to pull me back towards my room.

"Archer?" I asked. "What's going on? You can tell me."

"There's too much to explain in one night. Please, stay in your dorm."

"I was worried about you," I said. "What was that back at the trial?"

A line creased his brow. "I have duties as a Serpent—ones I hope you'll never have to face."

"Why are you pushing me away?" My voice broke. I became a threat whenever he had more than five minutes alone with his thoughts.

His gaze locked with mine. "This shouldn't be happening. You staring at me like I'm your favorite person in the world. We can't exist, Severyn. When—if you win—they'll never allow it. Victor... he'd have to die before an alliance between Demetria and Ravensla could form."

"What is the worst that could happen, *Serpent*?" I spoke his title as if it was a poisonous bile in my mouth, burning away at my gums.

His lip curled back as he recoiled a step down the stairs. "I fall in love with you, and this becomes a hell of a lot harder."

I gripped the wall as if I'd forgotten how to stand. "And that's so horrible? You told me sometimes you must fight for your heart... sometimes your breath. Fight back."

"There are a million reasons why falling in love with you is wrong, and none matter right now. What matters is you are here and safe. The king ordered you to be out of my mentorship."

I shook my head. "I'm going to be sent to Malvoria."

"I won't let that happen, Severyn."

"What happened at the Capital?" I asked,

He pulled me inside my room, sucking a hefty breath in. "I told them I care about you, and the king wanted you out of my mentorship—made up some excuse and scorned me for spending time with a student."

"You feel something more for me. I know you do. We can fight this."

He stood there, maskless. A face of utter devastation. "Severyn—"

"Do not Severyn me, *Serpent*." I held his stare as if it were the only thing keeping me upright. "Tell me or tell me I am crazy for believing you feel something other than caring for me. Other than a promise you made to Klaus."

"I can't be anything other than what I am supposed to be. It's best if we don't take this any further."

Archer waited for my reply.

"Why are you pushing me away? I thought…"

His chin leveled, but those eyes continued to hold. "Because simple makes sense. Simple is not the desire to kiss you. It is not me going mad every mile I travel away from you. Because saying I care about you is easier than saying that you consume me, Severyn Blanche. That every thought is encased by you, and I am a terrible friend because my protection swayed. My promise is null because I do not care to protect you as a *friend* should." He looked out of breath as if it took everything to tell me the truth. "You do not want *this*, trust me. A life of sneaking around, a lust silenced to darkness."

The distance between us had slivered. I took his angled jaw between my needing fingers and kissed him. I kissed him like the world was on fire and we were the last people alive. I kissed him through the ash, and shadow choked through my tightened veins.

He had me against the stone wall within a second as his hands were welded to my hips. I could hardly breathe, but I used those sparse moments when the last folds of sunlight struck my lips to suck the air through my desperate lungs.

There was a clash of tongues as his mouth pressed into mine. Hands roped every inch, claiming my curves, the flesh that held me together.

He could be my lungs for all I cared.

He was already in control of my beating heart.

"*This* feels right," I murmured.

He took a complete step back, exasperated and pale. "Severyn," he began. "Something… is horribly wrong."

I gripped the bare stone wall.

He stood silently.

It took me a moment to understand, but I'd seen the same shakes in Estella and Charles.

"This complicates things," I said, arms slacked at my sides. "You've been warded."

His head shook slightly. "You are shielded, Severyn. It's a powerful one at that. The king has no idea what you are to him. He thinks you are his blood but not his granddaughter. Telling him will only place you in the light of vengeance and greed. I'm guessing *this* has something to do with it."

"Does he think you're a danger to me?"

"Not me. If the Night realm fails, our entire Continent is at risk. Whoever put the shield on you wants you… away from me."

I leaned against the wall. "I don't understand."

"You are shielded, Severyn. Someone put a shield on you during the days I was gone." He closed his eyes.

Telling the king the truth would mean his secrets would come crawling out. It had to be bold. It had to be tomorrow. No longer would this secret be kept. No longer would I live in the shadows of Summer. I'd do it for Estella. And maybe releasing this secret meant Archer could be shielded from me forever. But I'd kept silent during Callum's attack, and I had no choice but to let this secret scream.

I kept my place against the wall, resisting every desire to smooth over those frown lines on Archer's forehead.

Bound by life.

We were bound by *life,* and every bond endured throughout the decades within it.

He stepped back unwillingly as I said, "I need you to leave my room."

Archer left with a subtle nod—as if kissing me had wounded him more than any laceration.

That night seemed to draw on longer than usual, as if the moon heard my cries and decided to hover longer. Tomorrow would call for more than the truth to be spilled, but blood.

A Herring's blood will be spilled.

Had that been Knox? Had I saved the prophecy from becoming the truth? I needed to break this shield. I needed to tell the truth—but how much would that cost me? Was my life truly priceless when a secret buried under wards and shields could resurface, dragging everything into chaos?

Daylight pierced through the window, casting rays across the shards of the broken mirror. The chirping of birds filled the air, their melody a haunting contrast to my dread. I dragged myself out of bed, my limbs heavy, my thoughts heavier.

After a cold shower, three aides entered carrying a cart of supplies. One held the red dress, motioning for me to step into the lace black undergarments. My chest was pinned upright. Every strand of hair was twisted and pinned into place, and my skin shimmered under the light powder and glitter dusted over every limb.

"Is this necessary?" I asked as the male aide brushed a cool liquid over my eyelids.

"If you are to be a Serpent, you are expected to look like one," he replied curtly. "This gown has not seen the light of day in nearly forty decades."

I caught my reflection in the window. The gown clung to me like a second skin, velvet bones hugging my ribs and cascading into flowing lace. Diamonds stitched into the hem dragged lightly against the floor, catching the morning light. My hair framed my face in soft waves, my neval streak sweeping over my left eye.

Inky silver lined my lids, and deep copper shadowed beneath. My lips glowed like fresh blood, and my cheekbones were sharply defined.

The aides stepped back, nodding in approval before leaving. I strapped two daggers to my thighs, the only part of the dress thick enough to conceal them.

A soft knock sounded before Damien entered, his smug grin already in place. "Severyn Blanche, you clean up nicely. I never thought I'd see you without blood caked somewhere on you."

His black suit fit him perfectly, the low neckline revealing the scars on his muscled chest. His left eye bore a faint red mark where the glass had sliced him.

"You look good," I said, my shield snapping into place as his gaze flickered to the shards of glass on the floor. I knew he'd already pieced together the image of Archer in my room.

Damien's heel crushed a shard as he stepped closer. "Do I dare ask about the glass?" He smirked, brushing a finger over one of my hidden daggers. "You can't bring these, Severyn."

Before I could protest, he plucked the blades from their sheaths and hurled them into the wall, the clang of metal against stone ringing out.

"Am I not allowed protection?" I snapped as my heels clicked against the floor, my stride quickening to keep up with him.

"I won't let the Serpents take a bite out of you," he said simply.

We reached the docks, where the remaining students gathered in their realm groups. Malachi stood out in her burnt orange gown, the hem swirling around her as phantom wind followed her every step. Her gaze locked on me, and she rushed forward, her embrace warm and grounding.

"Sev, Damien, we're making bets on who the Serpents will bid on this year," Malachi said.

"Damien," I answered without hesitation.

Damien adjusted his suit with a confident smile. "Hardly. You won Skyfall."

Malachi grinned. "I got another letter from your mother this morning. She won almost unanimously during her bid in her second year."

Cormac, standing beside her, scoffed. "So did my father. That doesn't mean shit. The bid is just another way to pit us against each other. The lindworm will choose regardless of the votes."

Damien's expression darkened. "I've heard rumors. The Serpents already have the lindworm, and the final six from each realm will fight to the death for the Winter trial."

Cormac's gaze drifted to the horizon, his voice faltering. "The academy has done worse. I still can't wash off the blood from that last trial."

Malachi gripped his arm. "You were asked to slay, and you did. Their blood is not on you."

The ship loomed closer, its black hull glinting with algae and shells. A flock of dragons soared above, their shadows dancing on the waves. My stomach twisted with each passing moment.

Damien leaned down, his voice teasing. "Do you get seasick?"

"I've never been on a boat before," I admitted. The frozen lakes of North Colindale were my only experience with water. The ocean was a mystery, a realm of monsters Cully had warned me never to explore.

As the ship anchored, students began boarding, each grappling with the swaying ladder. Damien gestured for me to go first. I took a running leap, my fingers slipping briefly on the cold metal before I steadied myself. Damien followed close behind, his hand brushing my heel as I climbed.

Knox arrived next, leaping effortlessly onto the deck. His leather boots landed with a solid thud, and light rippled from his fingers as if it were a part of him. He nodded at me, his pale velvet tunic catching the breeze. For the first time, I saw the Day realm in him.

Monty followed, his tailored pearl suit accentuating the sharp lines of his frame. His serpent tattoo peeked from his thumb as his gaze lingered on me briefly. Then came Spring, with Levisly Bloom carried aboard by vines that curled around her like living ropes. Her strawberry blonde hair and yellow eyes glowed with an unsettling allure.

Winter's entrance was less dramatic, though Everett's face lit up when he spotted Knox beside me. For a moment, I forgot Everett was displaced like Malachi and me, forced into a realm that didn't quite fit.

Night was the last to board, Archer standing firm as he instructed his remaining students. I caught his silhouette, my mind betraying me with memories of his lips on mine, his shadows binding me in moments of stolen passion. But his back remained turned, and my shield wavered under Damien's knowing smirk.

"You're blushing, Severyn," Damien whispered.

Knox's eyes narrowed. "Is that the Serpent Saani mentioned? I thought she was joking." Anger flickered in his gaze. "Severyn, I never expected you to fuck your way to power." He trailed off, his voice dropping. "I should have known it was him protecting you during the trial."

"Nothing is going on between us," I hissed.

"Right," Knox scoffed. "You're just like Mother. She'd have done the same. Although you were her only child, she didn't tell her secrets too, so that should say something."

"You don't know what you're talking about." My voice was sharp, trembling with restrained anger.

Knox's jaw tightened. "Our mother deserved that title." He pointed at Damien. "His father ruined our family, and now you've got both brothers in love with you. You're bound to crash and burn, Severyn."

"Maybe I enjoy crashing and burning," I shot back.

Knox's voice lowered, venomous. "Just remember, power consumes our bloodline. It always has." He turned away, Everett at his side.

"Love is a rather strong word," Damien muttered. "Loving you seems like a lifetime of misery." His smile relaxed. "I pity whoever is bound to you for life."

I blinked a few times, jabbing him in the ribs. "You're a prick."

The humor dimmed in his eyes as he moved closer to me. "Your mother should have told you who her father was. Knowledge comes with trust. But being strong is nothing to fear, only when you lose yourself. There is a reason Knox was compelled to kill you. I don't think your mother's quell ever entirely was stripped. Her quell could have evolved into a compulsion."

No. I refused to believe my mother could be that cruel. I refused to believe she could kill me. My head whirled, but Damien held me upright as my heel jutted between a plank.

She never wrote back to me.

I gaped at Knox, who held Everett's hand near the iron balcony. Had he known? Had this been Mother's plan all along— to get Knox into the run for the king's title? I forced my boiling tears not to shed. I couldn't hold my shield any longer, and slowly, that cemented ash began to crumble, and my thoughts slipped out like a dam breaking over a waterfall.

"No more secrets," I said solemnly. "I forgive you."

Damien pulled me into his arms, his chin resting atop my head. "Friends," he whispered. "Until one of us takes our last breath. Although, since we are being honest, I knew who your grandfather was when I first read Knox's mind. And when I read yours, you didn't know anything. You were sheltered, cast away like me."

I wasn't a gripping book on his shelf as he turned the pages, uncovering this mystery like me. He knew all the lies I had been told the moment he met me. "You should have told me," I said.

"It's not really something you blurt out."

"What else do you know? Tell me."

He shook his head. "It's nothing."

I scoffed. "There's never just nothing."

We went to the balcony. Below, the ocean of black curled waves thrashed.

"I just wish things were different, Sev. I tried to make this easier between us…" his voice trailed off. "Forget I said anything."

Damien was in love with me. And I wasn't.

The mountains on the way were chipped into snakes and dragons, forming the mouth of a cave. Scales etched along the algae-flecked stone, rippling along the slashing waters.

The salted air burned my eyes, and the boat lurched under the cave. Darkness blanketed the rocking ship. Muggy breaths drew from my lungs in ragged attempts to find clean air during that moment of shadows. Bats squealed, shrieking as the boat groaned through the tight cave. Eyes of yellow beams blinked.

Daylight stole the shadow as I met Archer's gaze from across the ship.

Whatever we were could not exist or breathe in sunlight. I tightened that shield as my eyes locked on the horizon.

Damien pointed to a narrow island in the distance. "That is the Serpent estate."

Golden light broke through the sun as clouds of copper smoke hovered over the island. An aged brick building sprawled along the grounds with sphere-tipped fences guarding that mysterious island. An electrified current ravaged my veins as we went through a ward. I hunched over the steel, resting my cheek along the bar. Waves threw us right and left, nearly shoving me against Damien's hip.

A wild, silver-back wyvern broke through the cloud bank, crying a deadly noise as it got trapped in the shield. Ash and smoke curdled the flurried air. The wyvern swerved, wings burnt and cindered.

"I think—I think I'll be sick."

Damien patted my back, but I flailed my wrist, demanding he stop immediately.

Keeping my head crouched, a crash sounded from the waves, splashing the railing. I knew it was the wyvern's last screech as it drowned.

I steeled when a shadow crawled up my lungs on my next clipped breath. Through the gap in my elbow, I met Archer's gaze—his one finger angled loosely towards me. And those shadows were the one thing keeping me from hurling.

"You've been holding your shield for too long, Severyn. Let it down until we get to the estate, or you won't be able to hold it for the entire night." Damien gave me a look of concern. "I am… impressed with how you've managed to hold it this long. Whatever is on your mind can't further hurt me."

He looked like he wanted to say more, humor brimming in his slivered iris.

I cursed silently because Damien was right. I knew my body couldn't handle this sweltering heat racing through my veins, and those shadows could only tie me down for so long. I closed my eyes, and that shield slowly broke down, chip by chip, until I braced against the balcony.

Chapter 29

The captain threw a rusted anchor over the ledge. The mass of students swarmed towards the ladder. I stayed back, hand on my thumping chest.

Damien was silent—we both were. Antonia skimmed past me, eyes locked, half-parted lips bursting with giggles at my distress. "At least you know you'll have one bid."

I gritted my teeth. "Why do you hate me, Antonia?"

"If you believe I hate you, being a Serpent will ruin you," she said, strutting along the path toward Jace.

"Antonia, wait—"

She spun back on her heel, pinching the wedge of her shoe between a rock. "What?"

Alaric's last words hung on my dried tongue. "Nothing... good luck."

She rolled her eyes and walked forward.

I knew I needed to tell her. But I couldn't. He took a dagger for me and Antonia would never forgive me.

Whatever fear I had boiled to the surface. I needed to suffocate it, starve the flesh of my anxiety to skin and bone. I descended the wobbling ladder, taking in the lush, forested path leading to a castle. My heels sunk into the damp earth. Lanterns floated along the expansive property, jutting out from the mountainside, carved with those same scales I'd seen along the way.

It was muggy outside. The golden flecks of light bathing the land were gone, leaving behind dark swirled clouds, brimmed and ready to downpour. We crossed a bridge spanning the rapids below as we walked towards the black castle doors, armed with guards on either side.

"Shield, Severyn. Now," Damien hissed under his breath.

But the cool air stifled me to a weak simmer. A drop of rain fell onto my forehead. I tried—I tried everything to solidify my shield, but every thought spilled as if I'd held that molten protection for too long.

They are going to find me out. They will see right through me.

The guards assessed us as we entered the castle. We were led down a stone hall, and finally, a single spark of my quell ignited, following a rush of warmth through my veins. It was weak but enough to hold as we entered the bidding room.

Glass.

It was glass that caged us from the Serpents of Verdonia who stood on the other side, as if we were animals for their amusement. I met each of those hardened eyes, searching for Father's distinct mark.

Archer clustered himself between Victor and another Serpent I didn't recognize, with shifting embers dancing between them as if their quells were communing. Archer sipped a dark liquor, shadows crawling the lengths of his fingers, delicately tracing shaded shapes.

Serpents passed by the glass, grins curling their lips. I heard Bridger's muddled name as Lasar, a Serpent of the Frozen Valley of Neverin, pointed towards the Winter students.

We lined up in a single file, separated by realm, facing the glass wall. Damien released a jagged breath as the king walked in, and every vein in my blood iced, including my weak shield that evaporated into dust.

The king waved his hand, and the glass between us shattered into a million dazzling pieces, vanishing before a single shard touched the slick stone. I didn't dare look for Knox down the line of students. I couldn't risk a single eye turning to me.

A veil of scales draped the king's raised arm as he announced, "Welcome to the Serpent Bid." His wide grin sent fury rippling through my stifled breath.

He continued, "For first-year students, the Serpents will bid on a student to lead their house. If the academy finds a lindworm, the final six leading each sector will be put in a match for the final Winter trial. But first, the students will display their quells one by one. Each student will converse with the Serpent of their lands. As the Season goes, we shall start with Spring."

Levisly narrowed her slivered, yellow eyes as the Spring students took their stance.

I whispered to Damien, "You'll be put in a death match if they find one."

Damien leaned closer, eyes ahead. "Unless you steal the lead from me. Impress them, Sev. I don't mind a little competition."

First up was the short, blonde woman I'd seen kissing Archer's neck during our first night here. She struck her curled fingers in the air, and a lily sprouted from her veins. She traced her finger in the sky, and a vine slithered along the wall. I imagined the force of the vine could strangle. I imagined she'd used it on Archer that night as their lips tied as one.

Levisly nodded in assurance as the next student stepped forward. Her orange-rimmed eyes wavered silently on each Serpent. "My blood is poisonous, tears too. I don't figure there are any volunteers?" the student said.

The room stirred.

The king raised a brow, shooting a narrowed finger towards a third-year Winter male—Callum.

Fear struck his eyes.

"Your Majesty, I don't wish—wish to die," Callum cried.

The king pressed his lips together. "Pity. We need a volunteer."

Damien surveyed me, noticing my slight grin as guards dragged Callum down the line toward the Spring girl.

"You can't poison me. This is bullshit!"

His arms thrashed as the Spring student cocked her head, and a single tear, clear as a diamond, dripped down her cheek.

"It's only painful for a moment," she murmured, wiping the droplet with her thumb before brushing it over Callum's quivering lower lip. Her voice softened to a whisper, laden with regret. "...I am sorry."

His jaw erupted in a rash, his face ballooning, crimson ears ablaze as he doubled over, unleashing screams of agony. Skin blistered and melted like burnt leather over flames, contorting as bone threatened to protrude. Guards flanked him on either side, dragging Callum out of sight.

His screams echoed down the hall.

The Spring student bowed, arms flat as a devilish smile curled her lips. "Anyone else?"

He deserved it. That's what I told myself.

Most of the Serpents' faces turned grave, unmoved, as student after student performed their quell. The rest of Spring's quells varied from rain manipulation to flower spawning. One male could speak to plants. Damien was the first to perform for

Summer. He stepped forward, and two glass daggers formed in his hand. Damien flicked his wrist, and those glass shards from the wall appeared, hovering in the air, dazzling in a million fluttering orbs before dropping to the ground.

Victor clapped, and a few others joined in unison.

All eyes turned to me as Damien nudged me forward. Then my father sprang from his chair, and those golden eyes burned into me… and so would I.

I would burn.

One by one, I stole the flame from each candle and lantern with only a slight glance until the entire room was shrouded in darkness.

I waited a few seconds as the Serpents began to shuffle in their seats before I swept my gaze over the iron lanterns hung from the ceiling. A black flame shot from my palm, hissing before it formed into a ten-foot snake of ash. It slithered along the stone wall until I sucked it back in, taking a step back.

Victor was the first to speak, his fist slamming into the air. "She is of Forgotten blood. She wielded a snake," he hissed. "Kill her before she infects the minds of our students."

Outrage. I'd caused outrage as the king ordered silence. Damien dragged me back beside him. "Stay quiet," he hissed.

I didn't know what I did. My father looked broken, as if he still expected ice to ripple from me at any moment. He saw me at the trial, but I never used my flame. Did he know? Had Mother warned him?

Panic gripped me as the king raised his cane. "Silence. Any students found to harbor forbidden quells will be dealt with. Wielding the shape of a snake is hardly due for execution."

Execution. Every hair on my arm stood tall. My flame was gone, chilled with fear, as Victor kept his eyes peeled on me, one finger resting under his chin.

He knew I was in line to steal his throne. I'm sure it enraged him as Damien gripped my arm and saw nothing but himself standing beside my mother years before. Rivals. He hoped we were that, hoped Damien would be the one to end me as he knocked back his dark, swirling drink.

After Summer came Autumn, and Malachi was the second last to perform as she twirled her finger in the air, creating a whisper of screams within the wind that had nearly every student holding their ears in pain. She curled the wind back into her palm with a snap.

Whose screams were those? Had they mimicked the voices of the fallen students during the trials?

Winter was next. Everett appeared as confused as ever, especially when his quell was weak and could barely produce a single snowflake. He shook his head in frustration as he struck a light from each finger—a blinding light as I palmed my sight.

The king tapped his fingers on his cane. "It is rare to see a student harbor a quell from two different realms. Tell me, when did the Winter quell come in?" He gripped the arms of his throne, leaning forward a bit. His salted beard speckled, illuminating the wiry hair intricately braided along his jaw.

Everett cleared his throat. "During Skyfall. I have trained my entire life to lead Day. Monty was my leader for two years." He didn't outright confess his indifference towards being a Serpent of the frozen valleys, but anyone could understand the true weight of his words.

Myla wanted it. She wanted to become a Serpent as her late father was.

Bridger raised his frosted palms. Snow danced in the air, flurried as we breathed chills into our chests. The air clouded, and vapor rose, clinging around the lantern light like frozen moths. Father looked impressed, as did Lasar, who curled a finger under his chin.

Lasar muttered something to Father, and all I caught was his last words. "…the boy could be your heir."

The king waved a golden-ringed hand as Knox took his stance. And I believed for a moment that Father had no idea that neither of his children would ever be the heir to his title as a rope of light whipped out. The king tilted on the edge of his seat as if that neval streak in his hair would display a forbidden quell.

Daylight turned into an outpour of calm vibrations soothing the air. An unnatural emotion breached our bodies, slowing our racing hearts. The king flinched forward, enthralled in my brother's mental quell. And I wondered why Damien never mentioned his mind reading. Perhaps that quell was dangerous for the wielder in a room that held the most powerful humans on the Continent.

Father clutched his chest, his face paled. I knew he couldn't handle it anymore. Was it despair I saw in his wide, golden eyes?

Before Knox could suck the daylight back inside his palm, it was seized and consumed by shadows. Antonia waved her eyes over every lantern in the room. She gave a subtle wink to Archer, who nodded. Then, Jace opened his palm, and starlight struck each candlewick in a shimmer.

And I hadn't realized how strong Night was. They were light, dark, and heat in their own ways. The king clapped three times. "Powerful quells, students." He rubbed his hands together. "Picking only one will be difficult… now, I release the Serpents."

Father was the first to rise but the last to take a step towards us. Damien gripped my elbow. "You survived, good job," he whispered.

Lasar crept towards me with his white cloak dragging along the stone, snow crusting his fingers as he carried two goblets of wine.

"Severyn Blanche," he began, flaring his crooked nose as hollowed cheeks swallowed a gulp of red wine. I flinched as his bony hand rested on my shoulder. "I was sure you'd be a Winter." He passed me the wine glass, and I took a steady sip, rolling red legs dripping down the rim.

Father joined a few beats later, eyes wild, lashes frosted in snow. I couldn't handle disappointing him.

I met Lasar once at half the age I was, but I hid behind Charles the entire time. Now, I had nowhere to hide.

I smiled at Lasar. "I was placed in Winter, but it seems my mother, Fallon's Summer blood, called to me first." I made sure Father heard every word.

Father reached for me with a shaking hand. "Severyn, you remind me so much of your mother. The dress, your quell…"

He didn't look well. I shifted out of Lasar's grip and held my father upright. "Father, are you okay?"

Anger struck through those golden eyes. He never admitted his shields were shattering, and not once had he willingly allowed me to see his weakness, but as my false winter cloak shed, so would my father's and whatever he kept from me. "Yes, Severyn. It's difficult keeping my wards up this far from home."

I was—exposed enough to the outside world to hear the truth. "What are you shielding from?"

Father began to speak, but Lasar interrupted. "Tell me, Andri, did you ever recover from that barter with Victor from the bid all those years ago?" He shot a cold, cunning grin towards Father. "We all expected another barren land."

"What barter?" I asked. And Lasar sipped from his goblet, awaiting my father's response. And so, I asked it again. "What did you barter with Victor?"

"That is enough, Lasar," my father mumbled. "The barter is done. I called it off."

"It appears Summer doesn't take well to other Serpents not holding up to their end of the bargain." Lasar's eyes went towards my father's shaking hands before he turned on his heel and walked away from us.

I gripped my father's shoulder. "Father, tell me. Is—is it why you're sick?"

Golden eyes bore into me, pleading and confused. My father seldom displayed emotions other than a curt grin. "You. I bartered you, Severyn," he said in one defeated breath. "I could never fall through with it, not when it meant your life would never be your own."

Any sense of shield crumbled at that moment, molten barriers collapsing in my humming mind. I shook my head, scorching the edges of my shield. "*How* did you barter me?" I gripped the goblet between my fist, the glass heated, crackling near the stem.

"Those years when the coldness nearly took everything from us. I had to barter with Victor. He didn't want anything on my land, and I offered him *everything*. Diamonds, jewels, oil, but he only had one demand." Father flexed his hands, a whirl of ice falling on his boots. "He wanted revenge on Fallon. He told me he would warm our valley three months of the year. He placed the sun we know as a barter so our land would not starve. He wanted to marry you off to his heir. And yet… I still owe him something I cannot give him, Severyn." My father nearly collapsed as his mouth parted, uttering low sobs from his lungs.

"Victor wanted me to marry a Lynch. He wanted me to marry Archer Lynch." My entire body froze as if Father had stunned me with his frozen quell.

"I never told you because I would rather die knowing my realm was saved than have you marry someone you didn't love. I assumed another heir would claim, and they'd be stronger to hold the wards up." A tear clung to his wrinkled lower lid. "There is nothing Victor will take as a replacement. You were the impossible bargain. And… if his son does claim—he will force you to marry him."

There was still a son in line to claim his heir. Damien, but I couldn't dare wonder about that. Couldn't dare wonder if he knew, and that was his real reason for wanting to become close with me.

I felt nauseous.

"I thought it would be easier this way." Those were Damien's words. No. Damien knew. He fucking knew all along.

Love. This stemmed down to love. Father loved me enough and his realm to die for it. He couldn't live knowing I'd be married off, and now, Archer and I's lives were tied. I could not tell Father the truth. He'd made that barter, knowing he'd never fulfill it. But I wondered if Victor knew about Fallon's blood— if he could not tie his bloodline to the Herrings, he would force it upon his children.

But I couldn't stop the anger I felt.

"There must be something we can do." My voice broke. I broke. I reached for my father's chilled fingers. "How can I help?"

"Severyn, there is nothing you can do. Please, I never wanted you to suffer. Our realm has only gotten colder. It's only a matter of time before my shields break and Winter's vengeance is unleashed. If his son claims the throne… that is the only way for your home to survive."

"How long?"

"If Victor does not have an heir, then I win the bargain. If he does, then you must marry his son. When I called it off, the sun began to fade." Father shook his head, chin low. "I came for you and Knox, Sev. I came to see you win. I know you will become a great Serpent, Severyn. The Summer title called to you for a reason. Serpents run through your bloodline on all sides."

"What if I win? And I become Serpent of Ravensla? I can… undo it. I can gift you the sun." I'd crawl on my hands and knees to warm North Colindale if I could—

His eyes told me all I needed to know. "Time is my enemy, Severyn. Winter will always be in your blood—don't cry, my child." A shaking hand brushed the dampness of my cheek, crystallizing the droplet. "You are not a caged bird, so I never clipped your wings. I made that barter, knowing I would never give you away. I stole time…"

"Your title will die."

"And so, it shall." No sadness hid within his voice—only genuine care. Care for my well-being, care for me to prosper and bloom.

I couldn't save his title. I couldn't save my father. I could bleed my boiling veins dry along the snowy peaks and cry out to any god that would listen to make me a Winter, but the frozen ground would never call back to me. My blood would only burn, and even burning would not save him.

If Bridger became a Serpent, he might save the land. I had to let go of the North and relinquish it to the hands of a man who'd hurt me, who'd forced me to fail. And so, I laid my life down for Winter—laid that boiled hatred for Bridger to rest because it would happen anyway.

"I'll make you proud, Father. I promise on my life," I whispered into his sleeve. I closed my eyes. "You should bid on Bridger Thorne. He's from North Colindale."

Father raised his chin as a shadow approached from behind. I turned to see Monty's tight grin as he extended a hand towards me. "Come on, Andri, we would not want to take all of Severyn's time up."

Monty's eyes motioned for me to take his elbow, so I did. Not because I wanted to, but I wasn't about to piss off Monty with all that he knew. I gave one last subtle nod to my father before I was dragged through the crowd of Serpents.

"Monty, what do you want with me?" I hissed as his grip tightened around my wrist, leaving the imprint of his fingers.

"Let's see what you are, Severyn, without the protection of your Serpent. We both know about your Gemini bond. A dead dragon has risen. One way or another, I will rip the truth from you." His pale eyes pierced through me as if daylight could sear. "Don't fight it."

Flame against sunlight. But his power was stronger, nearly blinding as my eyes burned with every vein illuminated beneath my skin. He clutched my waist, and lashing ropes invaded my mind. I thought he'd stolen the light from my thoughts as he ripped back.

His lips were on my ear. "You are a hothead, Severyn, aren't you? Flame needs release, and I know what you need."

"Get away from me," I muttered as he held me in place. I felt a pierce in my shield, a hole he'd punctured with light.

He gripped my jaw. "The blood of a Herring will spill. Shall I spill your blood, Severyn?" He licked his lips, sloshing the remainder of the red wine down. "Gods, I love secrets."

I gasped for air as I healed that hole before his Serpent hooks could claw into me further and reveal my forbidden quell. I looked back to see Archer's eyes locked on mine, shifting through the crowd. And it wasn't flame keeping me together, but a steel shadow shielding me. Darkness bound the holes, refracting the light out.

Archer went to grab me. "Monty, release her."

"Archer—" There were a thousand words in my mind. A thousand words I wanted to say to him at this moment.

Monty grinned, dropping my arm. "She's yours for now."

I inhaled sharply as I clung to Archer. "My father will die if Victor doesn't drop his barter." I didn't care about Monty—or my own life. I needed to save my father.

His hand moved to my waist. His voice was quick and hoarse, as if the slight touch of me sent spasms of pain down his spine.

"My father won't listen to me, Severyn. What barter are you talking about?"

"Our fathers bartered us, and mine never held up his end. Victor mentioned it at dinner."

He looked down, then towards the king whom Monty was speaking to. As if the flickering flames had ears—I heard my name on his tongue.

The king rose from his throne, his golden serpent-shaped cane slamming into the onyx tile. "We have our first claim," the king said enthusiastically.

Nearly every Serpent's breath stilled as Monty stood near the front, glaring at me.

It all happened so fast. I stared at Archer as if desperation could save me from the king's next words, "We have our first claim! Monty Garcia has claimed Severyn Blanche to win a title this year."

Every eye turned to me like I'd grown horns and wings. Archer kept his hand around my waist. "No," he breathed.

Monty claimed me. Monty. Claimed. Me. My world dimmed as I saw Monty's cruel smile beside the king. Violent heat rose through my veins. I didn't have the breath to scream as an invisible tether yanked me towards Monty. Archer's grasp dropped unwillingly as Monty placed his hand where Archer's was.

His mouth was on my ear again. "You're mine for the night, princess."

I was in his arms. He forced my hands on his shoulders as we swayed. My mind was tethered to his control as I leaned against him, and even that false smile tasted like tears. I ground my teeth. "Why are you doing this?"

He held my chin to meet his pale gaze. "I'm not as cruel as you suspect me to be, Severyn." He spun me around, and I saw a flash of Archer's rage from across the room—helpless. He stood there helpless. "I want to be king, and you Herrings stand in my way. Now that you're mine for the night, I can't wait to drag whatever forbidden quell ripples through you. Klaus was quite the writer. Do you write, Severyn?"

I kept my jaw clenched to avoid trembling. A claim was greater than a bid. Archer had lied that night in Ravensla—I wasn't priceless. I was the heat of salvation and a secret worth a lifetime of lies. I was Monty's claim, his pet for the night.

"I'm not a Seeker," I hissed. "And if I was, I'd write your death. I'd write it a hundred times over."

The king cleared his throat. "What is your claim, Monty?"

Monty grinned at the crowd, keeping me close to his hip. "I claim that Severyn will take the title this year, and if my bid is correct, I want every Serpent in the run to claim the king's title to step down."

Monty didn't plan to kill me—not yet.

His words tinged my ears, hanging before I realized what his claim entailed. I kept my feet grounded, holding the flame pulsing at my fingertips. Monty craved power, a desire to be great—greater than his promised life. Knox caught my eye in the corner of the room beside the other Day students, appearing as taken back as the rest, as if he'd been hopeful that claim would bear his name.

A moment later, the king pounded his cane into the stone as if the room's silence was too still. "Shall we let the bidding begin? What do you offer, Monty, at such a steep claim? Unless Saani wishes to bid, only she can counter you," he asked, a voice full of curiosity.

Saani kept silent. That whip of flame was gone, hidden beneath her red cloak stark against the starlit lanterns.

Monty cocked his neck. "I did not mention whose title she would take, Your Majesty." Monty gripped me harder.

"Severyn is a Summer, and the only Serpent title she can claim is Victor's. I presume you mean his title, Garcia." The king's grin nearly faltered, quivering at the side.

Archer pushed through the crowd, and all those moments of denial shuddered. "Severyn is up against my title. She can wield darkness. To steal light is a Night quell, and to consume light falls under the shadow powers. I have a right to claim her."

My mind raced back and forth as the soft muttering began amongst the Serpents. My tongue froze, clenching my fingers on the ribs in my gown. I could only stare at Archer as the king waited for an explanation.

"Ciaran was born in Demetria, and she gave her a shadow quell the day of Skyfall. Severyn had the mark of Unknown on her first day. Severyn is a split—drawn to both shadows and flame. Severyn will become my heir, and I claim it. I claim her!"

It was me who shadowed Knox during that trial.

Monty loosened his grip. "There is no such thing. We are only called to one realm."

Victor's attention drifted to my palms. "Show us your shadow mark."

I didn't know how. Not with a hundred eyes staring at me. Not with the heat of Summer bearing into me and the coolness of the Frozen Valley Serpents breathing up my spine. I held my palm out, waiting for something, but my body was too warm to drown out the hum in my boiled veins. Even the lanterns didn't do so much as flicker.

Victor laughed under his breath. "I think we've seen enough of her outburst tonight. Monty has claimed Severyn unless he wishes to back out before he bids his stakes."

Archer was loud, and I thought the entire room rumbled as he stalked towards his father. "My stakes are that you drop your barter with Andri Blanche if Severyn wins, and in return, I shall give you back your piece of Summer. You have my word, Father."

The sole reason his mother was dead, what she fought for—he'd give up for me. There was nothing Victor would want more than his sunlight back. I swallowed my spit, bracing for this to be over. For another student to be where I stood.

Victor clicked his tongue, glancing at the shallow and lifeless figure that was my father. "You wish to barter, son?"

Archer nodded. "It's what you've always wanted."

"Fine," Victor said. "You have a deal."

I didn't sigh in relief. I didn't think of Damien and those empty promises that our fighting for the same title would never sever our friendship because we'd never shatter, never if I wasn't the heir to Ravensla.

The king seemed to enjoy this as if every year before was a mindless bid with no real stakes. As if a broken promise meant a greater lie had yet to unfold. He rubbed his bony fingers together, dismissing us. I kept beside Archer as the bid continued, and as expected, no other claims were made. But I'd caught the attention of every Serpent in the room as they approached me from a distance one by one.

Lasar made a bid on Bridger. Then, four more Serpents said his name. He was once again titled the leader as a metal brooch shaped like a snowflake was pinned to his chest. Damien beat that by five. Knox had also made an impression, but standing nearly seven feet tall with three swords would do that. Knox was pushed first in line to claim the Day Throne, and when Everett unpinned his circular relic and handed it to Knox, something between them changed as their hands grazed.

Most Serpents offered gold; some threw in the lure of rare jewels. Nothing quite matched Archer's loss—nothing that would tear the sun away from a land.

Since Brantlyn's death, Malachi consumed his ranking, claiming the lead to become an Autumn Serpent.

I was worth the sun. The warmth I had dreamt of during every Thaw, through every one of Winter's harsh breaths during the ice storms, had been me the entire time.

The remaining Serpents bid on Malachi, but most did so while staring at the king, as if that would keep them in his good graces. Father too. He had made his bid on her. And that was when I realized—he had no idea I was against three titles. He bid six diamonds, one for each realm, and all he wanted in return were seeds, even asking for some hellebores.

A violin played softly in the distance as gallons of wine were poured after the bid. Nearly every Serpent was drunk an hour later.

I downed three glasses after that interrogation, and my stomach churned as Malachi grabbed my wrist, pulling me into the flurry of the Serpents.

"Shit. You got claimed by two Serpents, girl. That is unheard of," she hissed in my ear. "You really are Fallon's daughter."

We were a blend of burnt orange and flame as we twirled under the starlit ceiling. I nodded—apprehensively, still uncertain what that even meant. "Now what? We dance after that?"

"We drink, we dance. We pretend for a night we are not all fighting for our lives and that tomorrow does not exist," she said.

The king kept his eyes on us. And I wondered if he knew it now—if he could see right through my shield and the screams in my mind telling him that I am his family.

And I spun until my stomach whirred on that red wine, grabbing Mal's elbow to steady myself. "Can we walk around the estate? Is that allowed?" I desperately wanted to escape this room.

She smiled quickly, eyes on the metal door behind us. "For the other students, no. For me, probably not, but let's do it anyway." She pulled me through the room, past a set of heavy metal doors, and into a hall that stretched on and on. A red and golden runner went down the entirety of the narrow room.

"It's… portraits," I said.

"This is the Serpent Gallery. Every Serpent who has ever claimed title has their portrait on here."

History. A hundred years of faces were loved, and some were lost. Others looked no older than me as they stood proud with grins. I found my grandfather's snow-white beard and round glasses staring back fifty-seven frames down. He had the same crinkled, golden eyes as Father and Charles, and I swore the glass frame was frosted with cracks.

A hundred years of title no longer rested on my shoulders. And it was bittersweet.

I shifted my eyes over Veravine Almera. And I couldn't help but notice the color of her eyes, how that striking green was a shade of every fern, every leaf… and how I saw my mother in those features. She had a neval streak—smudged and concealed through time and age. She wore a red dress. The exact one I was in, right down to the diamond straps and the stain on the bodice.

I was wearing Veravine's gown.

My lungs burned for air. "Malachi, I think that's—" The words didn't dare to empty from my trembling lip. Once spoken, I could never take them back in this unforgivable place.

Malachi understood. She saw what I saw, the eyes, the dress. She tilted her neck, listening—

"Veravine was born in Southern Ravensla. She was known for her beauty and charm. She met a boy at the academy, and they fell in love, but that boy had a future already planned for him, a marriage arranged with Autumn because to control the air meant you controlled the very life force of everyone. They met every few years, relinquished in the simple days when a title meant freedom. No one knew what happened to her. Some say the wife killed his mistress in a jealous rage. Victor claimed her title years later, even her home. There were a few rumors of a mudded blood, a daughter born, stolen by scavengers, and forced to live a life unknowing the power she held."

"How do you know all of this?"

"The wind does more than give us life—it hears everything, even those secrets hissed under breaths years before. Veravine's daughter lived a hard few years, never knowing who she really was." Malachi shrugged her shoulders. "I wonder if this was when she found out who she was. If she stared into the portrait of Veravine and saw her own reflection."

But Malachi stared at me as if I was finding my truth, the bare truth stripped to chipped paint and clouded glass. I was never destined for Winter—my lungs would forever bleed flame, and I was the burning heir.

Veravine was my grandmother, and she was beautiful.

I couldn't claim Archer's title when I knew where my blood was born. But no matter how I was pulled along in this life, I'd lose a piece of myself either way. My father's life for my own will. He had done everything to ensure I could walk my own path, never realizing I'd be the one to save him from his own barter.

"I don't believe this. I stayed in Ravensla, in Victor's home."

My mother lost her title to Victor. Ravensla was mine to reclaim. A scavenger must have found her as a little girl and sold her for the neval mark she bore. Victor claimed Veravine's title— my mother's rightful name as the Serpent of Ravensla.

Victor's barter with my father was revenge against Fallon because he knew he could control her. Or perhaps he knew how powerful their bloodline would be together. He knew whose daughter she was and hoped to lace his heritage with royalty, replacing his tattered tapestries with golden columns.

"Perhaps she led you there. Most secrets as powerful as this don't like to be kept."

I continued down the line of Serpents until I got to my father's. His hair was less grey, eyes less concerned, unseen by the horrors of the world. He was just a boy.

Blue eyes caught my stare. I went to Archer's portrait—to see a version of him who'd been the last to see Klaus alive as if Malachi's words of the wind absorbing the past would make him appear. As if I could hear his voice once more and tell him I would win it for him. And he'd already be standing beside me if love and hope could bring him back.

I imagined the portrait beside him to be Klaus—those freckles, though I could never recall how many, and the eyes that seemed too brown in the painting back on the wall at home. But there was no portrait, and I would never know the moments he existed while I was away. Those versions of him had ceased to exist.

Archer didn't smile. Instead, his expression was defeated— the face of a man who had disappointed his father and taken the Night title. He was a man who had to claim that name for himself before he even understood what it meant. He'd done everything right, yet it would never be enough.

I saw myself in those portraits, in the reflection of failure and resilience. And I knew I had no choice but to make that vision a reality. I would lay my life down for my home, just as Archer said made a great Serpent.

I'd save the boy and the man—my father—who had done everything right, as if fire could not melt ice but could instead mold it into something entirely new.

"Are the shadows true?" Malachi asked softly.

"It's true," I said, uncurling my fist and showing her the faded shadow relic on my palm. "I don't want to claim Archer's title, but I don't think I have a choice. I didn't know Ciaran and Naraic were born in Demetria." I drew out of my breath. "He keeps saving me."

Malachi looked over the wall of Serpents, thumbing the lace bodice of her dress. "Possibly. But you saved him first."

I didn't believe that was true. I hadn't saved him—I only prolonged his inevitable death. And everyone who knew about my forbidden quell was on that list. Malachi included.

I'd seen enough. "We should get back to the bid," I said, turning on my heel.

We were back in the hall that reeked of booze and sweat. Serpents communed with one other, speaking of warding and infrastructure. Bottles clanged together, and a glass of wine was already in my empty hand as a server whisked away in the flurry. Father spoke to Knox, patting him on the back. Archer talked to a Serpent of Autumn, a wide grin spread across his face.

Everyone had a place. I could speak endlessly of the frost that coated our windowsill and the howls of the ice beasts in the middle of the night. I had a million words to say, but none that made sense. I could not speak of the heat and how I'd seen every ray of sun. But perhaps that mark of the Unknown was for my heart—and so for the next hour, I spoke about ice whenever the conversation dulled.

Lasar seemed particularly interested. Even debated the best types of snow with me. Archer's voice brought me back to the present as I downed another drink.

"I never knew that was how snow formed," he said while grabbing the stem of my glass and finishing the last sip as red stained his lips.

Heat flashed in my cheeks for no reason. "There are different types of snow, and it all depends on the amount of water in it." He'd claimed me to win a title, and here I was speaking about the snow.

"Moisture," he mumbled. "Do you enjoy the cold, Severyn?"

It was all I knew. "No, not really."

Archer furrowed his dark brows. "Then the heat?"

I had to say yes. "It is better than cold."

"You'll have to visit the Night realm sometime. I think you'll find it the perfect temperature, Severyn." He played the act of not knowing more than my name well. Meanwhile, I debated dragging my nails down his chest and mounting the Serpent of Night.

The wine sloshed in my stomach with one look at the shadows dancing within his fingers.

"Take me."

"Is that a demand, Severyn?"

"It was a demand, Serpent." I'd spoken it aloud, and Lasar gave me a strange look.

Archer grinned back. "Someday."

Heat flushed my cheeks. *"Can we speak alone?"*

Archer nodded. *"Let's not be rude, Severyn. Your guests are still here."*

Father approached, resting a hand on my shoulder. "I love you, Severyn. I should have said it more." And his shoulders finally relaxed after all those wordless months he'd been weakened from warding. I knew he loved me. I knew he held on to see us become Serpents, even for us to live a life carved with our own daggers.

"I love you, Father." I promised again to make him proud.

That was all. I nodded and watched him leave, and a part of me thought I'd never see him again. The king kept glancing at us, and I swallowed hard when he stood from his golden throne, cane stomping into the stone as he walked closer.

He stopped before us, holding my hand between his. The hardness I'd seen in his stolen gaze was gone, shrouded by what I could only say was kindness. He blinked, and his eyes paled.

"Veravine would have loved to see you in that gown." His jaw clenched tight, a whisper hanging on his lips.

I didn't think I could speak. I believed my teeth were forced shut. "Thank you. I wish I could have met her."

The king hardened his eyes. "Our love was starved and brittle. It had never seen daylight. And yet, I have never found something so powerful before. Something that fed off secrets and lust, and I knew the poison between our touch, how I'd be willing to destroy my legacy for one more gaze into her eyes." He twisted off a silver bracelet and placed it in my hand. "It was Veravine's. She wore it every day. They say all things loved hold memories. Please take it. Unveil her words for me."

I curled my fingers around the metal band, and a simple purple seaglass pendant was looped around. "I don't know what to say." I wanted to ask why he saved me. He knew what I was to him. He knew of my forbidden quell. "Neval hair—is it truly powerful?"

"It seems to be." The king waved his cane in the air and was gone, leaving a shattering wall of brilliant dust behind.

He had no idea. He'd just sent Bribers on a hunt for anyone with this streak, knowing it could be a descendant of Veravine's—possibly his.

I ran my thumb over the band, meeting Archer's eyes. "He knows I am related to Veravine. He must assume—"

"You would be dead, Sev, if he didn't know. Forbidden quells are just that—forbidden. The bracelet he gave you is called a port, where a Serpent stores a memory." We walked through the silent hall, the night still rung in my ears as the violin strummed a few final chords.

"Do you have a port?" I asked.

"Not yet. Only when we die does that memory get released. For most, it is their wedding band, but Veravine wasn't married. Most Serpents use it for their wills."

I tightened the chain in my fist, the glass stone pressing into my palm. "How do I—open it?"

"Not here. Keep it safe, and only open it in a place you trust. You are holding the last piece of Veravine. Who knows what is in there."

The last piece of my grandmother. I put my fingers through the hoop that seemed to mend to the shape of my wrist. The silver was bright, catching the glow of the lanterns as we stepped along the flickered halls. We were alone at last. Archer leaned against the stone archway of the staircase.

"I suppose we shouldn't get any closer." I stared at his lips.

Archer shot a grin at me, his fingers stroking along the stone. "I think you'll find a Serpent claim to be more powerful than whatever shield someone placed on you."

"Archer, you didn't have to bid the light in your realm. Your mother… gave her life for it."

His eyes were a deep mix of piercing blue. He reached for my hand. "I was tired of a feud between my father. He would never have let up if I hadn't. And if I can save your father… I will."

I cupped his jaw, smoothing my palm over the afternoon shadow pricking below his chin. I pulled back quickly—afraid I'd hurt him. Afraid that shield would shock him when he gripped my wrist and held it above his heart.

"Why didn't you tell me Naraic and Ciaran were born in Demetria? That you thought I could be your heir?" I clenched my jaw, holding my wobbling knees upright.

"How could I take that away from you? You fell in love with Ravensla. It is still your claim, Severyn. And I would be cruel to take that away from you. We are bonded between Gemini dragons. Naraic's quell gave you flame, and Ciaran gave you shadows. The choice is yours."

"Not when my father's life is at risk. Archer, I don't know what to do. I need to win Serpent, and Summer seems like a lifetime of bartering." Tears brimmed my lids. They were not warm but chilled, as if a shadow had wrapped around us.

His thumb wiped my cheek. "Follow your heart, Severyn. If it is rushing canals you desire and the heat of the desert grazing your face, then you know your choice. I have many suitors who will take your place."

"Take me to Demetria. Take me there now," I whispered into his soft touch. "You claimed me. Now make use of it, Serpent."

His lips inched closer to mine. He curled his fingers around my waist, pinning me against the stone wall. "Someday, but for now, you are entirely mine, Severyn. Every breath you breathe is owed to me." His fingers slid under the slit of my gown and toward my thigh. "That includes every moan."

He traced the seam of my underwear. My gaze darted for anyone watching as a finger ran over the lace. My feverish body needed his touch, my thighs buzzing, heating as he circled the lacy strap with his thumb.

"Archer," I breathed as he caught the gasp with his mouth, devouring any thoughts. I reached for his buckle, smoothing my hands over the metal straps, but a shadow of rope bound my wrists together. "What if someone sees?"

I cried in protest as his finger slipped out.

He portaled us to a room. My head hit the cotton pillow as Archer's hands replaced the shadow binds. "Is this what you want? To silence our lust to darkness? For the moon to be our keeper."

I nodded. "This is what you want."

His fingers untied the corset backing, slipping the gown off my body as he exposed my breasts. "I cannot resist you," he said. Then his lips traced the contours of my hardened nipples, sucking each one until my head spun.

"You do a great job at distracting me. Knowing my body will listen," I whispered. "I asked you—to take me to Night."

I grabbed his jaw, bringing him to my lips. His tongue slid over my teeth, devouring every gasp as his hands traced along my inner thigh. "Widen. I want to feel you," he said. I obeyed and he edged a finger inside of me.

I closed my eyes and he grabbed my jaw. "No. I want to see the pleasure in your eyes." Then, another finger entered my wet opening, and my body lurched into his chest, riding him with delighted moans. "I said widen, Severyn."

"Yes." I said, spreading my thighs even more. The way his cock strained and hardened on me had me wanting to tear his clothes off. Everything about Archer felt forbidden, knowing I was promised to him in another life. My body, my name was his.

And I wondered if he knew about our father's bargain and he believed I was his.

"Your body does more than listen to me," he groaned, and I was unsure if the words were in my mind. "Allow yourself to relax. You are safe."

"What do you want to do to me?" I asked.

He stretched me even wider, leaning closer. "I want to fuck you until every part of you is bonded to me. When you smoked that birth-control suppressant, there was no way in hell I was allowing anyone to touch you after that."

"I don't have much experience," I admitted. "I don't want to ease into things."

He slipped his fingers out, brought them to his lips and sucked on them. "We will bond tonight and you will cum. We will ease into things, Severyn, because I do not want to scare you away."

"Please, touch me," I said. "I don't want to wait anymore."

Shadows crawled under my veins as starlight tinged my skin, our skin. Flame and smoke whirled as I clawed at his tunic, popping three buttons to slide my hands over his chest. I needed more as I struggled to lift his shirt off, running my lips down his neck. Thunder rumbled outside, shaking the glass windows as he kissed my pelvic bone, lowering, his tongue gliding over the sensitive area before circling my opening with devilish licks. I ran my hands down his bare back, gripping his clenched muscles as he tasted me.

"Archer, I need you… closer."

"You want me to fuck you because you wish for a bond to form, or do you *want* me?"

"Both."

He twined our palms together, relic to relic. Then, he placed me on my back, arching me into him as his legs locked my hips wide. "Be as loud as you want. I want my claim on you to be clear to every Serpent that you are mine."

My other hand traced the serpent on his neck. Closer. I needed him *fucking* closer.

"I am yours," I whispered, his body pressed into me, hips squared on top, hardening as he fiddled with his belt.

"Tell me you want this," he said. "I want your consent, Severyn. There is no going back once we tie our rider bond this way."

"Yes. I want our bond to be strong."

His cock was so hard it was pressing into my stomach. His knees spread my legs open, locking my spine to the woven sheets. "You're wet, Severyn. I think you want me more than just for a bond." He grinned at the dampness between them.

"Then fuck me or shall I make you beg for it?"

His thrusted two fingers inside of me again, before tasting it a third time. He didn't seem to like that answer as his gaze locked between my thighs. "Then why are you grinding against my hard cock?"

Shit. He was huge—and somehow between my horny grinding his bottoms had slipped down.

"I don't think I can fit you," I blurted out.

He laughed and leaned back, and it took everything in me not stare at his erection. "Sit on me and take it at your own pace."

I climbed his naked thighs, centering my wet entrance over his legs. He slid in and I arched my back, slowly taking more and more of him inside of me.

His strokes deepened as he lifted his hips with mine. I saw the depths of ebony within his eyes. Stars lined my vision with each breath and moan of my name on his tongue. It was slow and agonizing and I knew there was more of him when we both fell backwards and I moaned as another inch of him entered.

Suddenly, his hips were flesh with mine and I bit back my scream of pleasure. "There we go," he said, as if he could feel my climax rising.

His relic glowed with embers, while mine was outlined in shade. The blue of his iris was rimmed with a soft red. I kissed him again, licking the ash off his tongue. Then, a swirl of ebony consumed my mind.

And time seemed to stop. Each thrust of him inside of me sealed our bond. I swore I'd never felt pleasure, never breathed pure air without his breath choking down my lungs.

I dug my nails into my back. "Do *you* accept our bond?" I asked.

He moaned, "Yes," nipping at my lower lip again. "Nothing, Severyn, could keep you away from me. Not a shield, a ward, or distance." He kissed each rib, the underside of my breasts, as he slowed his swaying hips in tune with mine.

"Cum for me," he said. "I want to feel it through the bond."

He spread me wider, my knees braced on either side of the mattress. I was close, narrowing into that heated touch. "Archer," I moaned. "Don't hold back."

Without a second thought, he flipped me on my stomach, his chest against my spine. I braced against the headboard and stars swirled in my vision as I cried out in pleasure. He didn't hold back.

"Fuck, your arousal will be the death of me," he whispered.

That comment alone had my walls contracting around his hardness for a second time. "I want to feel you," I said. "I want you to finish in me."

His cock swelled at my words, twitching as he dove deeper, giving me all of him and more. I felt his warmth fill me until our arousal soaked the bed and we were both panting like wild beasts.

He rolled onto his side. *Shit*, even shadows swirled my thoughts.

His blue eyes, still ringed with ash, swayed to meet mine. "We could do that again until the sun rises. I know a trick that slows midnight," he snapped playfully, hoisting my bare legs over his chest, and the desire to have him back inside of me was overwhelming from how empty my body felt.

I swore there was never a more beautiful man to exist. I swore darkness didn't need light as his shadows touched my burning skin.

He didn't flinch from my cindering palms as I placed them on his cheeks. "Why doesn't my flame hurt you?"

He smiled. "I've never feared your burn, Severyn. Shadows and flame—they exist in both of us. We balance each other." He chuckled, the sound low and dark.

I stared at him, knowing moments like these—when we were alone—were rare. Knowing every power-hungry Serpent was walls away. After a beat, I let myself fall into his chest, listening to his heartbeat sync with mine.

"I lied when I said it was only about the bond."

"I know," he murmured. "We need to clean up." He rose, stepping out of the room before returning with a towel, gently wiping us down.

I wanted him again.

But his gaze flicked to the door. "I feel like a complete asshole, but I'm not staying tonight. I have business in Night. Things to take care of."

I knew what he meant. The bid with his father. He'd need to prepare for the sun to be stripped away, if I was to claim the title.

"Take me with you," I said. "I'll portal back myself—or have Naraic fly me."

"You've never attempted portaling, Severyn. Let alone the dangers of portaling through realms, which can be deadly. I can't ensure your safety through the shadows, and I'm not willing to risk it."

"I don't care. I want to see Night—show me Demetria, please." The words hung from my parted lips.

I thought he'd say no. But instead, he cupped my cheek with one hand, the other resting at the small of my back. Cool shadows crept beneath my skin, encasing my beating heart in a clenched fist of darkness.

"Stay still," he whispered in my ear. "Focus on our bond."

A flurry of shadow and starlight rippled around us. In his eyes, I glimpsed jagged mountains beneath a bright, cratered moon. Darkness unfurled over us, stretching for miles in a galaxy of blinking lights across the hills and peaks of the Night Realm.

Bats cried out above, circling through a swirl of yellow, orange, and blue—the last remnants of sunset. Moths hovered, their eye-patterned wings flickering around lanterns like tiny ghosts. And then I understood: night was not the terror I had always feared. It was not constant darkness, nor the screams of death beasts and night crawlers. It was every shade of night, from the soft glow of twilight to the deep hush of midnight.

A waterfall spilled like silver thread down the crystal mountains, winding through a valley where cabins lined narrow, cobblestone paths. The scene was alive, a harmony of shadow and light, fear and beauty.

Archer dropped his hand, and I was back at the estate where we had never left.

"It's beautiful," I whispered. "How long will you be gone?"

"Only a few days." He tucked a strand of hair behind my ear, his fingers lingering. "You can reach me through the bond. And if you're missing me... I'll feel it. Every bit of it." His grin curved crookedly, flicking briefly between my thighs.

He closed his eyes, resting his hand on the curve of my jawbone. "How strange the world works. Most do not find this."

I wondered what he meant by *this*, how the universe had conspired for us to find each other. Even though our bond had survived death and been reborn, we were together in this moment. I had been promised to him in a different life, knowing that being with him destroyed all my father had done to give me a life of my own. For us to find each other, a life had been lost—possibly two.

The universe cooed in satisfaction, but its greedy claws knew no bounds. Just as the king had described his love with Veravine, Archer's and mine could never exist in daylight.

He dressed swiftly, leaned in for a fleeting kiss on my knuckle, and vanished without a trace. No lingering shadow, just a sudden void that ripped away the coolness in my heart.

A yearning for him to stay lingered, but such desires were hollow—he had no obligation. My wish for him to stay was merely a surface-level craving. I yearned for Archer's company because it brought comfort, not out of necessity.

And falling for a rival was insanity. But falling for a Serpent? I knew it was naïve.

Chapter 30

The wind nipped at my cheeks as we docked at the academy.

The full bloom of autumn reigned, with shimmering golden leaves trailing across the mountainside. A warmth prickled my spine as I turned to face Saani's sharp brown eyes.

"Where do you think you're going, Severyn?" she asked, her voice sharp and commanding.

"Back to my dorm," I said.

"I'm rounding up Summer to go into the woods. It's time you all understood the dangers you face while guarding the borders. Clearly, Damien has no intention of training you any further in the forests."

Damien caught up to me, his hair windblown from the sail home. "What about our weapons?" he asked.

"There are daggers in the cabins. That's all you'll need, and your quells should protect you. The Serpent has claimed you, Blanche. That's a heavy promise for a first-year student." She clicked her tongue and headed towards the bright warmth of the Summer trail.

Damien groaned, cursing under his breath. "Did you get any sleep at the estate? Because I swear, rock is more comfortable than those beds."

I'd tossed and turned all night. The bond between Archer and me pulsed until it dimmed in the early hours of dawn. I tried not to let it get to me, but I knew he was home in Demetria.

"Same here," I muttered.

A brush of warmth consumed my skin as we entered the Summer trail and walked until we reached the long rope swaying over the rushing waters below. One by one, we crossed over. Damien let me go first. I gripped the zipline, heaving myself over. My muscles groaned in protest as I landed—muscles that hadn't had more than a few days to recover in months. I wasn't stretching nearly as much as I should have.

And the bond between Archer and me might have stolen a bit of my energy.

We passed by the broken bushes, just a mile from the lake where I'd found Klaus and Naraic. Damien noticed my lingering stare.

"Sev, have you ever thought if your quell could... resurrect him?"

I shuddered. "He's... bone. That's all that's left of him, Damien. If I tried, I think I'd create something far worse than any forbidden quell ever could."

Damien shuddered, too. "Is there a reason it worked with Naraic?"

"Naraic severed his bond with Klaus before he died and bonded with me. Klaus knew I'd come to the academy. It was only a matter of time after I got my letter."

I told him about Veravine and showed him the bracelet on my wrist. I didn't mention that barter between our fathers. I didn't know how to bring up the possibility that if he won, I would become his wife.

"It seems our families have known each other for decades. My father told me the past Serpent was killed by the Forgotten. I think you should open the port. My grandfather left his last words in his."

"On your mother's side?"

He nodded. "Archer has it now. My father would have smashed the ring if he'd gotten his hands on it."

I flinched. I could never imagine destroying a person's last words.

We neared the trail's end, where it forked into a campground. Saani flicked her wrist, and her whip struck the burnt logs, sparking a flame.

She pointed towards the end of the trail. "Daggers are near that tree. Suit up. We're going to spend the night in the woods."

Jutting from the bark were two dozen daggers. No sheaths, but I managed to prod three between the thickest parts of the leathers I'd changed into at the estate. Damien placed the end of a dagger between his teeth as he tightened his boots.

The twelve of us moved towards the forests. The sun crept between the gray clouds and across the horizon. Silence fell as the scurries of the woods grew louder. This felt like a death mission as howls tore along the branches.

"How many beasts does Summer have?" I asked Damien.

A student who resembled Saani locked eyes with me. Then, trilling passively, she said, "We learned this in week one. Summer has five predators. Rippers will tear your flesh off and wear it, so if you see a student who has gone mysteriously missing and glowing orbs, don't believe for one second it's them. Death dwellers are everywhere. But Summer has three other predators—cleavers, detors, and vermilds. My name is Bria, by the way. I am a second-year."

A tremor went down my spine. I'd have to do my research on those beasts. I smiled at Bria. "I've had my fair share of death dwellers," I said.

She shrugged. "You're the only Summer student who hasn't joined us in the forests on a regular basis."

"What do you mean?"

She nudged Damien. "You never told her? Gods, that nearly title sabotage."

Damien narrowed at Bria. "Why are you lying?"

She raised a brow at me. "You will have no chance of claiming the title if you don't enter the forests."

Why would Damien not invite me?

My fingers curled around the iron blade as Summer encased us in the heated sunset. The forest cried back, the squeals growing louder the farther we ventured in. The slim light of the setting sun guided us through the broken path. Palm trees wavered in the breeze, and vines crawled, wrapping along the branches.

Bria screamed as a vine coiled around her leg, slithering with a loud hiss. Before we could cut through the thick, curling vine, her yelps turned to chokes as it tightened around her throat. I sliced at the green veins of the vine, its circular mouth rimmed with razors. Blood spewed as the vine sank deeper.

I struck a flame against its body, withering the plant until it fell to the forest floor.

Bria clasped her neck, a circular welt forming from the suckers. Her tanned skin turned pale as her wild eyes surveyed the woods. Breathlessly, she kicked the dead, shriveled vine away. "Did I mention the vines can kill you?"

I'd felt those vines' pincers before. I knew their teeth left aching welts.

We kept going, the howling and cries growing closer, louder as dusk settled over the horizon. I glanced at Damien, whose dagger was out and ready to strike. I knew he could fight—we'd been spine to spine as the death dwellers surrounded us.

Then, Damien lunged at me, swiping at a glowing orb of fangs—I yelped, drawing my dagger as the creature fell to my feet.

"That is a ripper, Severyn," Damien said breathlessly. "Keep your quell at the ready."

I didn't know if he meant my forbidden one or the flames with the number of deadly creatures. We were all exhausted beyond deprivation. How was this—right? To send us into the woods after the bid.

I nodded at Damien graciously—then another ripper came for us, and I slashed through the iridescent body, speckling light radiating from the see-through figure. If fear hadn't held me, I would have called it beautiful. Two more—a third came from the trails. Sweat dripped from my chin. Exhaustion claimed my will to move as my knees buckled.

I craned towards Saani and the two lifeless bodies that bellowed below, a mask of stillness peeled over their fear-stricken faces. A ripper had gotten to them, tearing skin from the bone. I couldn't watch—not without nearly hurling my breakfast up. Damien raised two daggers above his head and slashed right through both, leaving a peeled-back cheekbone of a student.

It tried to rip their skin off.

Saani was killing us off.

A figure appeared from the woods. I raised my dagger as Klaus stood before me.

Klaus. It… resembled him.

"Severyn, you need to find him. Find him. Find him. Find him." His lips were delayed, puffed, and unnatural. His body slumped over as if submerged in water for too long. "Find him now. Find him."

A pruned finger reached for me.

A ripper had torn his skin off. I stood there numb, gripping the dagger as it came towards me.

Klaus. What had those beasts done to him? A ripper… found his body and *wore* him as an iridescent glimmer shone through his dull skin.

Kill it. Kill it. *Kill him*. It wasn't my brother.

His thrashing arms heaved forward. He smelled decayed and rotted. This wasn't Klaus. I knew it wasn't. Damien raised a dagger, and I scorched his hand back.

"No, don't kill him," I snapped.

Damien's features twisted. "That's not him, Severyn! A ripper claimed his body when he died. It's not him, Sev. He is dead."

The figure slashed into my arm, and I stifled my cry, "I need to be the one who does it."

Damien stared wildly at the dagger clenched in my fist. "Severyn, do it. Kill it."

I pierced the dagger through his heart.

A stream of clear fluid emptied from his body. His tears leaked a silvered brine as I tore my dagger out.

"Sev," Klaus cried. "Why did you—hurt me? Why did you claim my dragon? Why? *Why?*"

"It's mimicking him, Sev. Don't believe it." Damien slid the knife across his throat.

But not before the beast, compelling my brother, sputtered, "Archer is in danger."

I ran.

My legs barely held me up as I flew through the Summer forests. My eyes dampened with tears as trees and vines escaped my sight. Saani yelled for me, but I didn't care. Boots and hisses chased after me. I swung my dagger at the lunging claws.

Archer needed me. Archer was in danger. I got to the trail, and Damien rushed behind me, reaching for my shoulder.

"Severyn, what are you doing?"

"It's Archer. I haven't felt him all day. I'm leaving for Demetria."

"You'll be expelled and sent to Malvoria the second you step off this academy," he warned, pulling me back. "Don't risk your future for him."

I clenched my jaw. "I don't care. I'll be dead if I don't find him."

I thought Damien had just understood how powerful our bond was. He staggered back. "Emerich!" he yelled, caving his mouth with his hands.

"You aren't coming with me," I hissed low.

Emerich cried from above, and not even a minute later. His talons raised high before striking the ground. Naraic and Ciaran flew through the clouds. "Damien, I won't risk you getting expelled."

Damien ignored my curses as he mounted Emerich. "Archer is my brother, in case you forgot."

Naraic huffed a breath of ash, lowering his spiked spine for me to mount. Ciaran flew in circles above, releasing a cry through the sharp wind. I had heard that cry before—a cry of mourning.

I stared at Damien. "Night is three days of travel. I don't have that kind of time."

"I can portal us halfway once we get to Ravensla. You can portal us once we're in Heit, the western Summer realm."

"I have never portaled, Damien. I'll scorch you all!"

"You trusted me in the trial. I trust you, Severyn. You are more powerful than you think."

I climbed onto Naraic's back, grazing my hand over his scales.

"What's going on?" I demanded through the bond.

"The bond is down."

"Is he—dead?"

A pause. *"I don't know. Ciaran can't hear him."*

Ciaran cried from above like a wounded bird. The same noise Haziel made when Myla was taken to Malvoria. I nudged Naraic with my boot, and he took off.

Archer could be dead. The thought destroyed me. Destroyed any sense rattling my mind.

I had nothing to protect my body besides a few rusted daggers.

Which way was Demetria? I knew the capital was the other end of Verdonia, but was that west? Which way was west?

I swore Naraic was in control of my lungs at this point. We flew over the ocean, wings spread wide and fast. We hadn't flown like this since Skyfall. Ciaran stayed a few beats behind. The midnight sky loomed over, soaking us in nightfall. Not the stars I wanted, not the moon's glow I fasted to feel on my cheek.

"Naraic, can you hear him?"

Silence rang through our bond.

We made it to Ravensla at half the time, landing on the beach for a moment to catch our breath.

Damien closed his eyes, opening his palm. "I can't portal Naraic without the risk of slicing him, Sev. He can't come. I don't trust my quell, not after the last trial."

I glanced at Naraic and into his darkened eyes. The overhung shadows consumed the violet hues in them. "Tell Ciaran I will save Archer." It pained me to leave him, but I knew flying would take days.

Emerich bowed low.

Ravensla, stripped of the lights and glamour of the festival, appeared different without the flurry of visitors.

Naraic huffed as I climbed onto Emerich's back—and as those shadows ripped off my heart, the bond between Naraic and I swayed, fading as I gripped new scales.

Emerich clawed at the sand before taking off.

Damien yelled, "Hold onto me."

Naraic followed, not listening to my pleading demands to stay back. I gripped Damien's waist as he palmed the air, casting a flurry of glass and sand. I screamed as shards whirled, slicing into my hands and legs.

One sliced Naraic's neck scales as he dove at us, wild eyes pleading like I'd never seen before. I couldn't hear Naraic, and maybe that was for the best.

His talons shredded through the glass, stirring the shards in all directions. I opened my palm, twirling a rope of flame around Naraic's neck.

"I'm sorry, Naraic."

He growled, snapping his barred jaws like a wild beast, wings thrusting to break free. A white flash struck us as we traveled through the portal.

Fragments whirled, slicing me, slicing Damien. I screamed in agony. "Damien!"

Clipped mirrors and sand throttled the air.

Emerich hurled me off, crashing onto the unforgiving ground. Blurred vision, a brisk breeze, and cool dirt pressed against my cheek. Head throbbing from the impact, I rose to my bloody knees, tasting the metallic tang of blood on my bitten tongue.

"Damien!" I cried, staring into the shallows of the dark forest.

No answer.

I swung my gaze along the starlit woods, searching for him, for Emerich. But only wisped trees scorned the dirt path.

And then I saw the blood.

A bloodied body lay on the darkened dirt with a glass shard sliced through his neck.

Oh—*Oh*.

I ran, unsure how I hadn't collapsed from the sight. A deep gash trailed along Damien's neck, a shard sticking out of bloodied flesh. His hazel eyes shifted in every direction before latching onto me.

I crawled towards him on my hands and knees, bracing his cold cheeks. "Damien, you got struck," I cried. I was tired of crying.

"Severyn, take Emerich—find Archer."

"I'll save you," I said. "I can save you." Burning tears fell onto his forehead as I brushed the dirt off his chin.

"I'm not dead. Yet," he chuckled low and reached for my face. "Severyn—"

Yet. Damien would not die. "I'm not leaving you!"

"It's me or you, Severyn. One of us will end up in Malvoria or worse…" He shook his head and blood dripped from his lips. "It's easier this way."

He wasn't dead. I couldn't save him, not yet. But how long would yet last until he was choking on his blood? How many breaths did he have left in him?

"You're not fucking dying," I hissed. "Stop!"

A shaking hand reached for me as if I would be his last sense of peace. "I loved you since I saw you, Severyn, and I need you to know that. I need you to know that it kills me that I will never be him."

A trickle of blood dripped from his trembling lip. "I need you to know that—I love you as my last words. I don't care if you don't love me back, but… you… need to know it. If you bring me back, at least this voice has admitted it."

"Damien," I whispered as his hand tightened around me. "I'll save you." I crawled back towards Emerich, knowing I had two lives to save in moments. I reached for those algae-streaked scales—

"We were never rivals," he said, eyeing his pocket. "Take the letter… it's the one we received at the sanity trial… I only wish things would have been different between us."

I shakily reached for his torn pocket, gliding my chilled hands over a folded sheet of parchment. "You'll wake up. You have to."

I couldn't save everyone—it would kill me knowing how many times death had crept into me. And as Damien took his last breath, I stayed there for a moment, allowing the silence to take over.

One less. One less to the title.

I covered my ears as Emerich cried the most devastating howl I'd ever heard. He spread his wings wide, a green scale already hued gray as if the color had washed out within the moonlight.

"Damien," I cried. "I need you. I need you to stay, to wake up… I'm sorry."

But he was also Archer's brother, Kian's too. And I could never—never wish the pain I felt when Klaus passed on anyone.

For a moment, I thought how cruel I was to believe a title meant more than a life.

I pressed my hand on his cold cheek, and a tremor went through my body, and it took everything in me to keep my hand there against his stillness. I sobbed as I ran my hand over Emerich's scales. "Breathe. Breathe. Damien! Fight it."

But both bodies were too still. Had I done something wrong? I got to my shaking knees. "Damien, you need to live. You need to fucking live."

There'd been seven keys. With two more lives to save. Why was this not working? Was it because it was his quell, his glass?

I waited an hour, resting on his chest.

Damien was dead, and he wasn't coming back. I needed to leave.

I peeled myself off the cold ground, my body trembling. Blood smeared the inside of my mouth with every pounding beat of my heart.

Jagged peaks rimmed the land, and flocks of wild wyverns manically carved shapes into the clouds above. I was merely a mouse to them.

The wyverns swooped low, talons outstretched, ready to tear through my leathers. I struck a flame at the nearest beast's neck, but it wasn't enough. Both palms faced the cold air. The flame erupted from my scream, knocking me onto my backside.

"Enough! I've had enough!"

Three wyverns roared in response, releasing a storm of quilled spikes. I buried my face in my sleeve as the projectiles pierced my leather, biting into the flesh beneath.

I gritted my teeth and forced the remaining quell in my veins forward.

Then, a golden griffin descended from the night sky, talons ripping into oily scales. Her beak snapped at a wyvern's face, scattering its quills to the winds.

Setrephia.

Her feathers stretched wide as she hit the ground, crouching low enough for me to understand she wanted me to ride her.

She wanted to save me.

But where was Charles?

The remaining wyvern whirled and fled south. I climbed onto Setrephia, leaning into her soft feathers and avoiding the new healing scar near her left wing.

"Thank you," I whispered.

Her sharp eyes turned towards the mountains in the distance.

That's when I saw them—the masses, guards on foot, their armor gleaming under the moonlight as they marched towards the borders of Night. Something had attacked the walls, leaving rubble and broken stone scattered along the fences.

Archer wouldn't allow enemies to breach his wards.

Archer was dead. He had to be.

Why had Damien portaled us so far? The plan was to stop in Heit. He wasn't strong enough to transport us this distance.

Setrephia veered low, wings stirring dust and debris as the guards below pointed at the sky, their lips moving with shouted commands I couldn't hear. I was too weak to feel my quell, drained and chilled within the shadows of whatever ripple remained of Archer's wards.

The soldiers ran through the Night realm, swords drawn, while the civilians of Demetria screamed. Violet-caped figures darted into the alleys, seeking shelter.

Near the gates, I spotted him.

Charles.

He was leading the charge, his form steady as he directed others through the broken barriers. My grip tightened on Setrephia's feathers as we landed.

"Charles!" I screamed his name, over and over, flailing my hands.

His blank gaze flicked toward me, his eyes softening as they met Setrephia's. He gave her a subtle nod, acknowledging her presence.

In the pale moonlight, Charles looked different—his face dirt-smudged, his chin shadowed with grime. The three relics at his side glinted faintly, catching the silver glow.

Three cloaked figures emerged from the shadows, moving towards him. They whispered in his ear, their words too low for me to catch.

Charles's lips moved.

He mouthed my name.

I stepped back instinctively, my pulse hammering in my ears.

Before I could react, slender hands gripped my elbow, their hold as cold and unyielding as iron.

I turned to face Myla... her face was unrecognizable, and a new scar marred her temple.

I felt a pound on the bond. *"Severyn, Naraic says you took off?"*

"You're alive?" I called back.

"Myla, what—what's going on?"

Not a muscle quivered in her blank stare as if she had no idea who she was, who I was. Then, she dragged me toward Charles.

"Charles, what the hell is going on?" I demanded.

Archer yelled through our once-faded bond. *"Severyn, leave. Now!"*

Charles closed his eyes. "You should not be here, Severyn. Why the *hell* are you here?" A red-handled sword rested against his spine, rusted with blood. There's no denying the royal guard stood before me.

"Are you attacking—are you the threat?" I lifted my arm, forcing it out of Myla's grip.

Archer was in my eyes.

"I don't have a choice. Malvoria was—taken over." He eyed the cloaked figure behind him. "They—"

"Who are *they*?"

Charles winced through his teeth. "I can't say. I'm warded."

"The Forgotten ones?" I hissed.

Charles kept his jaw still. But the look he gave me, I knew it was that. His face contorted, his spine tremored. His golden eyes faded to white, and my brother was unrecognizable.

It was the same void that held Knox during the last trial.

The cloaked figure lowered his hand, peering at me. His voice was icy and hoarse. *"Severyn Blanche*, you should not be here."

"Severyn—" Archer called. *"Forgive me."*

I shuddered as though an invisible rope wrapped around my neck, dragging me closer to the three figures. From beneath the cloak of one, violet eyes pierced into me, her fingers curling in a sweeping motion. She glanced at the third figure.

"Fallon, she has already seen too much," she said.

Fallon—the third figure was Mother.

Though her cloak remained tightly drawn, the glimmer of those familiar, unyielding black eyes was unmistakable.

"Severyn, my dear daughter." Her voice was soft, dripping with honeyed venom. She stepped toward me, arms open as if for an embrace.

And it was true. Death always brought us together.

Hot tears streaked down my face. "Why are you attacking the realms? Archer has done nothing wrong!" I stepped back, keeping my distance as her arms slackened and dropped to her sides.

"I was stripped of my existence, Severyn," she said, her tone sharpening. "Stripped of everything. Those whose quells are deemed forbidden are slaughtered. This cannot continue."

The woman before me wasn't just a shadow of my mother. She was the wielder of death, the one whose name was a curse whispered in fear.

I tried to rattle the bond with Archer, to will enough strength through my fear to reach him, but my mind spun helplessly.

"What are you doing here?" I forced the question through gritted teeth.

She raised her hand, and the ground beneath us shifted and sank. A mound of dirt erupted, giving way to a twelve-foot snake that slithered into view. Its dark brown scales shimmered with pointed ridges, its massive form curling across the ground.

It struck without warning, its fangs glinting like daggers as it lunged. Pain shot through me as it pierced my leg.

"Your father will die, and I will be nothing but a titleless widow," she hissed.

"You—you can call snakes," I whispered hoarsely, staring at the ungodly creature before me.

"*I should have told you when you first found it,*" Archer said. And that's when I noticed its left eye was scarred.

I knew this snake.

The golden egg hidden in my room months ago had grown tenfold in size. It was not an ordinary snake, it was a lindworm. I had found the lindworm.

"You kept it—" My voice cracked through the bond. *"You knew."*

This was the lindworm that claimed me on Winter trails. It had chosen me to face it in battle, and Archer had known. He had known since that night when he found me in my bedroom.

My mother laughed—a sound so soft yet sickening.

"And you will kill it and claim a title, Severyn. The lindworm is the final trial. Kill the snake and become a Serpent. It has already chosen you, my dear."

Her words slithered over me like the beast itself.

"A certain Night leader will be punished if I release it. It's nearly treason to harbor one."

He lied.

He had kept it on his land all this time. Archer had lied.

I couldn't pierce through wyvern scales, let alone this beast. I couldn't kill the lindworm when my quell barely simmered in my veins. I was daggerless, defenseless, and my leathers were shredded.

A faint spark flickered in my trembling palm, yet the force was so weak I doubted it would ignite a wick.

The lindworm hissed and struck again, fangs sinking deeper into my already-wounded leg. Blood pooled beneath my shredded slacks, staining the earth red.

The blood of a Herring would spill tonight.

A faint shudder went down our bond as Archer spoke, *"You weren't ready."*

I sucked a breath of cool air down my lungs, dodging the second blow of fangs—barely. I've trained for this. I've trained for months.

Shadows crawled within me, suffocating my lungs with each draw. The flames in my palm faded into a liquid black rope. I struck the lindworm's broad frame, curling that black smoke around its wavering neck. Its scales sizzled, breaking free from my quell.

I screamed at my mother, cursing with each breath, "Why didn't you tell me what you were? For months, I've been uncovering your bloodline."

"Our bloodline, Severyn. We were never meant to be someone's shadow. It is time we take back what is ours. You'll be dead the second you return to the academy. They will strip you of your quell. Do you think you've kept it hidden?"

"I had no choice."

And I didn't. I didn't regret who I saved.

The snake struck me again on my palm, piercing into my flesh. I screamed in pain as I rose, trying to muster a spark again. "I will not die," I cried.

I only had the darkness to will. My flame relic was pierced.

"Wield the snake!" Mother screamed. "Tame it."

Bloody ash hissed through my clenched teeth. I raised my fist, just as my mother had done, and the snake followed.

Mother grinned under her concealed hood, those glassy eyes fixed on my every quiver. I raised my other fist, and the snake lifted its curious head, hissing.

And all those snakes I'd willed into my flame—they had been warnings, whispers of a power I could wield. A power I could claim, just as the Forgotten once had.

Victor wasn't far off.

"Claim it," Mother hissed. "You are my blood, child. Only mine."

Tears welled in my eyes. I blinked, turning around as I twisted both fists and heard the snap of the snake's torso, bones wrapping together. I fell to my knees, dragging my nails along the bloodied dirt.

A vibrant ray of light shattered from the mangled creature. Something hot clung to my spine, melting through my leathers. I screamed in agony, begging anyone to relieve the pain and torture.

Shreds of my leather tore off my back, and only my wrap covered my breasts as every fabric on me cindered in flames.

I was bare. Bloody. Half-alive and broken.

A Serpent born through deception, a false guard of the moon.

Not one person helped me. Not the guards sworn to their posts. Not Myla or Charles. Even my own mother watched diligently as my skin melted with each twist.

"It hurts," I sobbed. "Help me."

"Heir. You are my heir," Archer's faded voice whispered down our bond.

It was a pain like no other. Not grief, not a broken wrist. It was the pain of loss.

Charles's golden eyes stared from a distance. Disgust. Fear. Terror bore through his unmoving features. "What have you created?" he hissed.

"A Serpent was born," Mother hissed, "now it is time to claim what is rightfully ours." Her voice faded, but the sear in my spine intensified until I could no longer see or speak. My cheeks gritted against the rocks, eyes tracing the slender moon soaking me in light.

A blanket of soft silhouettes consumed me as my mind went dark.

Chapter 31

A cool towel was wrapped around my spine. Silk brushed my cheek and body. Groaning in pain, I saw Archer leaning against an unfamiliar stone wall.

"Archer," I whispered.

Archer clenched his jaw. "What were you thinking coming here? You could have died."

Everything in me that was still alive shattered. "I couldn't feel you anymore."

He took two steps closer, keeping the distance between us. "The Forgotten discovered I was harboring a lindworm. They planned to kill it… to take reign of a title. They knew I'd be at the bid."

"My mother—she's working with the Forgotten. She sent the snake after me—"

But he'd seen it through our bond.

Damien. Damien was dead. It was a crushing realization. How could I tell him that the blood soaked into the shredded leather wasn't mine?

No. No.

He kept his eyes low. "You're safe, and that's all that matters."

"You kept it."

"When I found the snake in your room, I knew it had chosen you, but I didn't think you were ready, and I was not… ready to lose you. But there is still a chance the mark might reject you—it's been three days, and you've had a fever ever since."

"Archer—" Tears welled in my eyes. "Damien got spliced. He's dead, and I could not save him."

His fingers curled around the air. "Damien went with you?"

I nodded. "Yes."

I didn't think shadows could break, but dark fragments chipped like flakes from his fingers. "I'll send a letter to Victor," he said.

A sheer silk blanket covered my bruised body. I was still in the Night realm—an eternal sunset blanketed the horizon as I gazed out the window.

"Am I a Serpent?" The question felt wrong—beyond wrong. I hardly knew how to shield or even control my quell.

Archer slowly nodded. "It's complicated, Severyn. You killed the lindworm in my realm… but the way it was done was unnatural and forced. It's normally a spectacle."

Night. I was the heir to Night.

"What about your barter with Victor? Will my father survive?" My mind raced in a million different directions.

"I'm not sure. The Forgotten broke through my wards along with the Malvoria guards." His face fell briefly. "You are a Serpent, Severyn. You are my heir."

"Who will be the heir to Ravensla?" I knotted my fingers in the silk blanket, barely holding on as every second thought drifted back to Damien.

You are a Serpent. Damien is dead. Archer is alive. Those three thoughts whirled in circles, over and over.

"There are still eleven Summer students alive. One will take the title, or the cycle will repeat next year. It could take years."

"You suspected I'd claim your title." It wasn't entirely a question. "You kept it for me, didn't you?"

Archer was silent for a moment. "Gemini dragons are rare, but they cannot be separated—not realms apart, like they once were decades before. That flame Naraic gave you was Veravine's, and then it was Klaus's, and now it is yours."

"I didn't have a choice," I said. "You said I had a choice!"

He closed his eyes briefly, and a look of defeat crossed his features. "When I was marked with stars that first day, I knew I could never change… I despised myself for what I was. Klaus was marked with the Unknown, but the headmaster placed him in Summer. When we found the dragons, we knew one of us had been placed in the wrong realm. Cain advocated for Klaus to be moved to Night, but Saani wouldn't let him leave. Klaus was a Seeker… he saw things—morbid predictions—and it consumed him. You would have been sent to Malvoria if I hadn't placed you under my mentorship."

"So, what, you die, and I claim your title?"

"I don't plan on dying anytime soon. You will work under me as my second in line, and I will train you. We will need to work on your shadows." His blue eyes dimmed.

I couldn't think of the after. Even tomorrow seemed terrifying… I was barely gripping the present.

"Damien—can you send someone to retrieve his body? They deserve a proper burial."

"It's customary for the parents of the students to hold the burial. It's out of my hands."

"He's dead, Archer. It's all my fault."

Archer's shoulder tensed. "No." He turned away. "It is not your fault."

"I'm sorry," I cried. "I can't handle this—"

He cut me off. "I know how it feels, Severyn. He is dead. People die."

I was okay with the world believing I was dead for a while, perhaps forever.

"Is Naraic here?" I asked.

Archer nodded. "He tried to stop you. His wings got sliced. He may never fly the same again." His voice choked.

"Why did our bond go cold? Even Ciaran couldn't hear you."

Archer pressed a thumb to his temple. "It was the shield, Severyn. Our bond never went cold. You just… couldn't hear me." He went toward me. "We need to clean your injuries. The lindworm bit you, and I've been pulling glass shards from you for the last day."

He reached for me, but I recoiled. "Archer, no—the shield."

"The shield died three days ago."

A shudder tore through me, a cry too soft to be heard. "Damien placed the shield—"

Archer nodded, the weight of his gaze steady. "Quells can manifest, grow stronger. Damien's ability was rare—he could shield minds, twist them to his will."

Naraic knew. And once again, I was left with the shattered fragments of myself, scattered along a path I no longer recognized. If I could call it greatness…

But I didn't feel great.

I wasn't worthy.

Archer's arms wrapped around me, gentle, almost reverent. I leaned into him as he carried me down the hall, his warmth grounding me as we entered a bathing room.

An aide had already drawn a steaming bath. Archer shrugged the blanket from my shoulders and eased me into the tub, my spine to him.

"Did you… take care of me?" I whispered.

"Always," he murmured. "I thought I was protecting you. Keeping distance was the only way I knew to keep you safe." His voice dropped, softer now. "How is your heart?"

I turned my face toward him, though the weight of his gaze stilled me. "How did you react when Klaus died?"

Silence stretched, his hand gentle as he ran a cloth over the mark on my spine, tracing beneath my ribs. "I despised the world."

I sobbed into the warmth of the water, a sharp pain radiating from the scar. I didn't want to say his name. "Damien was my friend, Archer. I cared about him."

His voice cracked. "I wish… I wish I knew the version of him you did."

Why did you have to die?
You asshole. Answer me.

But no answer came.

Archer's fingers brushed my cheek, lingering on the scar where Estella's stitch had once been. "Things that survive without light are the strongest. And the shadows of my realm will devour every last trace of weakness." He paused. "I'm sorry you're my heir, Severyn."

I stared at the rising steam, my thoughts too scattered to find clarity. "I need to understand this."

* * *

I spent the next week healing, and every night, Archer carried me to the tub and gently washed my injuries. By the eighth night, I was able to walk there myself, and Archer joined me, kneeling beside the tub with his hands resting under his chin.

The mark on my back worsened with each passing day, bloodied flakes of skin drifting to the surface of the sudsy water.

How Archer made me feel was something I'd only read about. The way his fingers grazed my skin was reserved for the pages of stories where a prince saves a damsel, but we weren't in those kinds of tales. We had saved each other in ways I couldn't even begin to explain. And I realized, deep in the ache of my bones, that I trusted him with everything—my life, my heart, even the parts of me I barely understood.

I searched for a savior in myself, but I never considered the shadow.

I leaned back against the bath, the flickering glow of a chandelier casting soft shadows across the room. Ravensla had become my second skin. I'd always wanted the sun's warmth, but I never imagined how beautiful the stars could be. The moon was softer, more comforting than the sun's harsh heat—and maybe that's why Archer kept this realm hidden from me. He knew that, once I saw it, once I breathed in the lavender-tinged air beneath this sky, I'd fall in love with the Night.

As we rode horseback through the crowded streets, I saw her—the woman I could have been. Veravine's portrait hung in the corner of my mind, a reminder of a title I could never truly claim. The thought of it made my stomach twist. Deep down, I knew it belonged to Damien, not me.

We walked through the Valley of Night, the stars above us shimmering like soft whispers. The distant hum of music felt like it belonged to this world, slow and seductive, guiding us along. I'd seen this image in Archer's eyes before, but he'd hidden it from me, masked its beauty until it seemed more like a distant dream than a reality.

I wore a backless gown, the night air cool against my mark, as Archer's hand slid into mine, fingers entwining. The broken remnants of the Malvoria army's destruction had faded, though I had seen his guards hauling away the last of the debris.

He grinned, nodding toward the crystalline peaks in the distance. "I wanted you to see this during the Winter Solstice. The snow-capped mountains—they're brilliant. Perhaps it will make it feel like home."

Winter was closer than I realized.

I turned to face him, my fingers brushing his jaw before I pulled him close, needing to feel the heat of him against me. Our breaths synced, his hand slipping around my waist, pulling me into him. A thunderstorm rumbled in the distance, and when our lips finally met, I moved onto his lap, my hands running down his arms, memorizing every muscle, every curve of him beneath the fabric.

"The shield... it's really gone?" I whispered against his lips.

"It's gone," he murmured, his voice low. "I can touch you however you please."

I clawed at his jacket, tugging it off, my hands skimming his shirt, tracing the hard planes of his chest. His lips traveled to my jaw, and I spread my legs wider across his thighs, grounding myself in the heat of him. His hand slid down the fabric of my gown—stars and moons—his fingers tracing the shapes, sending shivers up my spine as he slid under the dress, his touch teasing higher.

"Where do you wish to be touched, little heir?" He groaned against my neck. "No panties, Severyn? I didn't expect this indecency from you," he said. "I expect the heir to my throne to be modest."

"Not like you haven't stared at my breasts straight for two weeks."

He placed his lips on my skin, trailing them down my collarbone as he slowly pulled the thin straps of my dress down, his hands never wavering in their sure, hungry touch. His fingers cupped my breasts, and I couldn't stop the moan that escaped my trembling lips as my spine arched involuntarily.

"Oh, Severyn," he murmured, his breath warm. "I've dreamed of this... of you. Since the night I saw you, drenched in the water, so beautiful, so vulnerable."

I wrapped my legs around his waist, drawing him closer as he stood, lifting me effortlessly, and we traveled through the shadows.

He laid me gently on my back, the soft click of the door lock turning behind us. Shadows curled lazily around the canopy bed, wrapping us in their embrace. I needed him—his body, his lips, his touch. His lips traveled over every inch of my skin, even the palm where the lindworm had once attacked, and I needed him to feel it. My fingers tangled in his dark hair, tugging him closer as his teeth grazed my neck, sending a shiver down my spine.

With a breathless sigh, his hand moved to his shirt, undoing the buttons one by one, revealing the inky swirls of the serpent tattoo that marked his neck. I reached for it, my fingers tracing the shape of the snake.

He pulled my hand away, pinning my arms behind my head as he fell between my legs. "What do you enjoy when it comes to pleasure?" he asked.

"I don't... I never really thought about it."

He raised a brow. "Was that your first time at the estate?"

"No, it wasn't, but—" I felt embarrassed for some reason talking about past sexual experiences with Archer.

He yanked my hips closer. His fingers went under my dress, tracing shapes along my inner thigh. "I can figure it out pretty quickly, seeing as you are already dripping wet." His mouth found the nape of my neck, brushing his lips down my breasts once again. "I want you to be loud, Severyn. I want your moans to fill the sky of your new kingdom."

Two fingers dipped inside me, slowing in rhythm. His thumb teased my clit. I moaned through the pleasure, and he lifted my hips with his other hand, plunging his fingers deeper.

Stars swirled my vision, and ash coated the back of my hoarse throat. "I don't know how," I said. "How to be loud."

"Give all of yourself over," he said. "Allow yourself to relax."

I moaned, and he pulled his fingers out slightly. I went to reach, to claim back that pleasure as he teased my opening with a devilish grin.

"Keep going," I said, wriggling my hips closer to him, nearly grinding against his forearm.

"Louder," he growled. His mouth found my puckered nipples, slowly nipping, slowly sucking each one until they were raw with heat.

"Archer—I need you inside," I breathed. "Please."

"So demanding, little heir." He stroked over my core, and my body clenched at the sound of his breath filling the air. "Not until you cum once, maybe twice." He growled low into my ear, "Let me worship you like a seventh God."

The thought alone of Archer inside of me was enough to tip me over the edge. He kept going, knotting that desire, that pleasure, until my flame nearly branded his shoulder.

"It's… too sensitive," I cried.

"I can feel when you cum, and you haven't yet." Pleasure knotted in my core as he stroked his fingers deeper, and my cry pierced through his veil of shadows.

"That's it," he said. "Ride it out, little heir."

My hips ground into his fingers, lifting my knees up as stars exploded in my vision. "Oh, *my*— Archer."

He unbuckled his pants, one finger still buried under my dress, only leaving briefly as he slipped his pants below his ankles and threw them off the bed. My legs locked around his waist as he lined himself up, rocking my hips until he plunged inside of me.

"Fuck." He cursed. His hands glided through my hair, and I dug my nails into his skin, into his serpent mark clenching as he thrusted in me.

Our chests slammed against each other. His knee nudged my thighs to spread. *Shit*, that wasn't all of him.

Flashes streaked my vision. This wasn't fucking, this was something… *Oh Gods*. My knees buckled.

"I will show you what pleasure is, Severyn until you know how you like to be worshipped." He placed a hand on my knees, pushing them back. "We will ease into my pleasure, but you will always come first."

He cupped my face in his hands and kissed me hard. Kissed me as if it were his last breath… as if it were our last kiss. His rhythm slowed as our shadow relics were palm-to-palm. His heart raced in beat with mine, pulling out just before he finished.

"That was three," I said, breathlessly.

"I know."

He carried me to the shower, legs dangling over his arms. "I often forget how isolated you were in the north," he said. "You're so innocent, and I… just want you to know you can be comfortable around me. We can ease into other things."

"What other things?" I asked.

He turned the tap on cold, and I swore my skin sizzled as he carried me under the stream. "*Oh*, was I not good?"

"Fuck, no. Sev. If we make love, you will cum. I don't care if you must ride my fingers for an hour."

I wrapped my arms tighter around his neck. "I want all of it. You. I want you. I want to know what you like," I said.

"As long as you are wrapped around me. I will like it."

My thumb brushed the serpent on his neck. "How did you kill your lindworm?" I asked.

"After Skyfall. My grandfather led the six students of Night through every valley to find one. The snake appeared out of nowhere. Killed four of us before we could draw our swords."

The water streamed down our faces, now near ice temperature. "And the snake killed the fifth, leaving you to slay it?"

"Sometimes the lindworm draws from your weaknesses. The other student left standing turned on me, and it was like the lindworm had tied his life to him."

I shuddered. "You—your first blood was another Night student?"

"I'm not proud of it."

I furrowed a brow, leaning into him. "I—I guess our first blood is the most impressionable."

"Someday, it will get better. The guilt goes away." He leaned his forehead against mine. "A leader can't break."

"No one will know." I touched a tear on his cheek. "I'm sorry I couldn't save him." Maybe he figured I hadn't tried, that I'd left Damien to die. "My quell… it didn't work."

"I didn't want to ask."

"It's okay to grieve him. He had faults, but we all do. It's okay to be upset that your brother is dead."

Archer ran his fingers through his dark, drenched locks, still holding me in his arms. "He had issues. When my mother passed, it… ruined him. It ruined all of us, but his quell is a different kind of poison, and he wasn't strong enough to carry it."

And I wasn't strong enough to save him.

* * *

Another day had passed as I gazed at my reflection in the mirror. I arched my back, tracing my finger along the scaled mark of the serpent etched upon my skin.

We needed to fly to the capital to see the king and announce my title. Then, the rest of Verdonia would hear the Serpent of Night had an heir in the next Serpent Press article. I'd done everything right. I'd saved Father's wards from falling. I'd claimed Serpent. But I still felt as if my life were tethered to strings.

And I could feel the snaps, the fraying edges with every jerk of my fragile body.

An aide offered me three traditional Demetria gowns—one even worn by Archer's mother. Silks made of violets and ebony black, trimmed with a million diamonds, hand-sewn with lace.

I stared at the mound of fabrics, not daring to step toward either of them.

"You don't have to wear Demetria attire, Severyn. I would never force that upon you."

I shook my head. "They are beautiful. But this is all new to me. The last gown I was in was my grandmother's, and that made sense. This—this isn't me."

Archer leaned against the door, one hand on his temple. "We will have new gowns made for you. Whatever you like, whether silver, gold—hell, even fuchsia. I know this can be unsettling."

Amria, the aide, grinned. Young with a rounded face. I knew she'd never be called to the academy. It seemed some were meant for this, their fingers too nimble, their eyes too detailed for the life of a Serpent.

"Silver would look best on her skin tone. But I think Severyn is a Summer's night. Give me an hour—I will sew her something tailored to her body."

Archer hardened his eyes, waiting for my approval. "It's up to Severyn. Whatever she is comfortable with."

"That is very sweet of you, Amria. I would love for you to make me something."

Amria clapped her fingers as she wound thread, measuring my waist and every limb. Her fingers weaved through the air, gliding like ocean water over a log. Fabric and yarn spooled from her palms. She hummed a tune, closing her eyes while the gown was crafted before my eyes.

Archer motioned for me to follow him as we stepped into the library. Time didn't exist here, not when sunset was the brim of day and a midnight moon was the evening. I never knew so many stars could lay atop, plucked, and placed into the milky river of the violet galaxy. Books I'd never touched—not concealed behind wards were placed in rows and rows along the brick wall. A simple armchair, only for one, sat facing the large window.

Archer skimmed his fingers over the cover of a book. "Your scar should be healed by now, Severyn, and it still looks fresh and painful."

I cleared my throat. "Perhaps whatever magic is behind creating a Serpent doesn't find me worthy."

"Or you do not accept the Night as your realm," he replied calmly. "A Serpent is only as strong as their connection to their realm."

I tensed. "This realm is beautiful—"

"Beauty does not fulfill—it is a mask. I had the same reservations when I became Serpent of the Shadows. I understand, Severyn. I understand more than anyone. So, when we make it to the capital, I want you to ask the king if you can transfer your title to Summer. Given your mother's history and

Veravine, I think he'd consider it… it's only going to get darker here."

"Archer," I breathed.

Archer slumped into the wall, shoulders squared. "I don't want you to be my heir, Severyn."

A lantern's flame dimmed. "What?"

"I would never force you into anything." His voice was soft. "You can either leave before I fall in love with you or allow the inevitable to happen."

I lifted a finger. "Light is a mask. I will find beauty within this darkness—if a candle is my only source, I will find it in you."

Archer furrowed his brows, reaching for my hand slowly before curling it within his. "I think my mother knew you'd come. She stole the Summer's light, knowing you'd come soon enough. Klaus scribed it—I thought he was reciting the past, not knowing what my mother had done."

"What did he write?"

Archer stared at where Klaus's name was marked on his ribs. "He told me flame finds its shadow."

I wrapped my arms around his neck. "This is where I belong, Archer."

A soft knock sounded at the door as Amria stepped inside. Eyes wide and excited as her fingers clasped the iron door handle. "Severyn, your dress is ready."

Archer released my hand, not shying away from the wide grin on his mouth. "I'll wait here."

With a nod, I followed Amria into the dressing room. She instructed me to close my eyes, and I obeyed, feeling a strange disorientation as I stepped forward. The world blurred into nothingness, leaving only the sound of my breath and the soft scrape of fabric against the floor. Suddenly, I felt a gentle nudge on my elbow, halting my steps.

Amria's voice was a whisper, trembling with excitement. "You can look now."

I uncovered my eyes, and my breath caught in my throat.

The gown was a masterpiece. The lace shimmered like liquid fire, deep red at the bodice, cascading down in layers of twilight hues that melted into velvety blues, fading effortlessly into an ethereal lavender.

It was a sunset.

"Moonlight will follow you," Amria said softly, her eyes wide with awe as she watched my reaction. "The strings are crafted with nightcloth, one of the strongest threads in Verdonia."

I was speechless for a moment. The gown felt like it was made for someone else—someone more beautiful, more powerful. But I nodded, fighting the lump in my throat. "Amria, you're—" I stopped, struggling to find the words. "It's breathtaking."

A small smile tugged at her lips, her hands fluttering nervously as she adjusted the dress on the mannequin beside me. "I'll have the whole closet ready for you when you return, Severyn. I know the Serpent of the Night prefers simplicity, but every now and then, I sneak in a bit of color." She gestured to the violet buttons on a table.

I smiled, a warmth filling my chest. "Thank you, Amria. You've been more than generous."

Her smile faltered for a moment. "I haven't congratulated you properly yet." She paused, the words hanging between us. "I never thought a flame-wielder would claim his heir… but at least now, he doesn't have to worry about his realm while he's at the academy."

The weight of her words pressed on me. "He stays," I whispered, more to myself than her. I lifted my gaze, meeting her eyes with quiet resolve. "And I will stay."

Chapter 32

Archer and I left for the capital—a day's flight away, and most of it was over the shadows of the Night realm.

Archer suggested we take Ciaran while Naraic was still healing.

The darkness stretched on, but the stars followed—gliding like fireflies weaving through fields. I'd glimpsed Naraic earlier, a pearl dipped in oil from below, shining against the black sea.

We rode over the riptide, winding through valleys of crystalline mountains. At the edge of Verdonia, at the edge of everything, I remembered Damien's words—about a world without quells, where the restrictions of wards no longer separated Night from Day, where sunlight existed in seasons, not bartered for or brined.

And if I could be his calm for just a moment longer, I would.

I had dreamed of leaving the North my entire life—dreamed of darkness and daylight, of autumn leaves. Now, the world seemed vast, infinite, with every beat of Ciaran's heart echoing in my lungs. I thought I would be a Winter and make Father proud as snow danced between my fingers. And when fire boiled in my blood, I thought I'd make my estranged grandmother proud, too.

My mother's words about living in someone else's shadow made sense now. I would not live in anyone's shadow, but I would become one.

Archer guided Ciaran, his eyes accustomed to the dark, promising that in a few months, I'd see as clearly as daylight.

We'd sent a letter to the capital the night before our journey. No response had come, but Serpent Post worked differently. Archer had assured me the king had received our notice.

Night bent into light—a prism of stars above. We flew for twelve hours, then stopped to rest at a Serpent hostel on the capital's nomadic outskirts. Once, this small plot had belonged to Spring. I imagined lush mountainsides, not barren and withered, the trees alive with color. The hostel was a dilapidated bunker, its walls coated with a decade of dust and decay.

I curled into Archer's arms beneath the fractured, silver moonlight. The stiff mattress creaked beneath us as we shifted, but it was a bed—our bed to rest, for now.

"I promise the Capital is nicer. This place... well, it's terrible," he said, his mouth curling in distaste.

"I don't care." I nestled closer, threading my fingers through his.

He ran his fingers down my spine. "You're already better than most Serpents. I don't mind staying in these places. It is a reminder that nothing is permanent. I see the history of our land and what used to be."

I was silent for a moment. "This was a Forgotten attack?"

"Yes. Verdonia is slowly dying with each attack. Charles was under compulsion that night. One of the Forgotten, or nomads, holds a forbidden quell that can compel. This was only the beginning of their attacks on us."

"What do they want?"

"I thought it was to take over Verdonia, but knowing they could control the Malvoria army and wipe out half of our Continent, I am not sure anymore."

"My mother said she wanted to fight for the forbidden quells. I've been thinking, what if they are the rebellion, fighting for our humanity? What if they aren't the enemies?"

In the darkness, Archer shook his head. "Those kinds of words will get you killed, Severyn. There are no wards here. Even my shield is weak."

Archer was right. My eyes danced over the whirling dust caught within the shabby lantern above us, the tight space only large enough to fit one other person. My skin crawled, thinking of how it was stripped to nails and shredded curtains. A cracked skylight was above, a narrow square, just large enough to see the stars above.

Then, the night took me under its veil and through a dreamless state.

* * *

The capital was a monstrous city along the coast.

We flew in as close as possible, docking Ciaran on a hill. The capital was neutral land. Not bound with wards of Spring nor heat. The ground was hard, stiffened with a layer of ice.

The first frost of the year was always the coldest and most ravenous time, as if our bodies had never felt a chill in our bones before. Knox always hunted on the first sign of frost. The townspeople would gather, a silent weep to tame the wind. Ash rippled the sky, and the burning of logs continued for months.

I never understood the cruelty of the lands that claimed lives like Bridger's. I'd seen his ear, his fingers sewn together, but I never believed Winter was that harsh.

A year ago, I was reading by a fire. Now, I was trying to steady my flame as we entered the Capital.

Most of the king's circle were Griffins—people who were great but not quite Serpents. Those who survived three grueling years at the Serpent Academy. Guards stood at attention, swords drawn, as towering buildings rose from the dirt, touching the golden clouds. Scavengers lined the walls, their eyes hidden beneath tattered cloaks, their trinkets and knives clinking as they beckoned us, offering trades and bargains.

I shuddered, staying close to Archer as we passed through the gate leading to the white-stoned castle behind it. My dress clung to my body, tracing every curve.

One scavenger called after us, "What's your price for the neval? King pays well." He muttered something before slumping forward.

Archer pulled me closer. "Where do most scavengers come from?" I asked. "They are without quells."

"Across Verdonia," he said. "The lands like the one we stayed in last night. Those people had nowhere else to go. Most of those lands became nomadic long ago. My grandfather took many from the Spring land into Demetria. Some children have shown quells since. Amria's family were refugees. The aftermath of a barren land is always tragic."

"That's devastating. Amria is from a barren land?"

Archer nodded toward the guards. "Amria is the first in her bloodline to have a quell after surviving a barren land. She was only seven when she came to our land."

My heart pounded as we ascended the final steps to the king's estate. Wild griffins soared above, their armor gleaming. I remembered the feel of those claws during Skyfall, grateful for the leathers Archer had given me.

The guards escorted us through dark halls. A haunting melody echoed. I wrapped my flaming shield tightly around my mind.

A dragon, frozen in liquid metal, was carved into the throne. The king sat, one leg crossed, tapping his fingers along the chair.

"Severyn and Archer," he rasped, his voice thick with age. "I didn't expect you so soon." His gaze sharpened on Archer's hand gripping my elbow, how I leaned into him.

Did he see Veravine between us? The lust he could never contain?

I felt the leather of my new jacket—one Amria had made for me—press against my back. The serpent's tail slid down my ribs.

Archer bowed, his head low. "Sir, Severyn has killed the lindworm. She is my heir."

The king clicked his tongue, eyes narrowing toward the arched doorway behind us. "Show your mark, Severyn Blanche." He rose, his eyes cold and piercing.

I closed my eyes and slipped off my jacket. Amria had sewn a diamond strand along the spine. The gown clung to my body, cinching at my waist before flowing out at the hem. I turned, revealing the serpent mark on my back. My breath trembled as the cool air touched the still-healing skin.

The king's breath caught—half fear, half disbelief. He flicked his wrist, and in an instant, he stood beside me. His hand hovered above the mark, his touch a sting of invisible light.

"That mark is rejecting her. Once we strip her of her quell, she won't survive."

I yanked the jacket back onto my shoulders and spun to face him. "Strip me of my quell? What do you mean?"

Then, the door creaked open. Charles stepped through, his eyes as hard as steel. Charles. Why was he here?

He glanced at me, frost dusting his lashes, a new silver badge pinned to his suit. "Severyn Blanche, you harbor a forbidden quell. Under Prospect Five of the Tome of Verdonia." His voice trembled slightly as he read the ancient text. "Forbidden quells are punishable by death or stripping."

Archer seethed. "How many of your siblings will you kill, Charles? You're a traitor to your blood."

My heart rattled. "You killed Klaus?"

Charles met my gaze, his expression calm, almost detached. "I had no choice, Severyn. He died with honor."

"Tell her, Charles," Archer spat. "Tell her how you stripped him mid-flight during Skyfall."

Charles exhaled sharply, silver medals gleaming in the lantern light—one for bravery, two for nobility, and a fourth, with my name replaced by a silver badge. Rage surged through me, my fingers starting to smoke. Archer didn't cool me with shadows. He let me burn.

"Monty Garcia provided this information. My hands are tied, sister," Charles said, his tone clipped. "I must strip you of your quell. If you survive, Malvoria will take care of you."

Archer slammed his fist into the ceramic column. "You'll kill her if you do that. She's healing!"

"There's no other way, Serpent," Charles muttered, his words heavy with duty. "I must do my duty as the lead guard of Malvoria. Severyn is a threat to our continent. And you," he sneered, "are in no position to speak. Harboring a lindworm is treason. Perhaps I'll deal with you both."

This wasn't the king's decision. He'd spared me before, knowing I'd saved Knox. But with Malvoria's wards breached, I knew I stood no chance.

Charles's gaze faltered as he reached for me, and I sank to my knees, searching his face for any trace of tenderness, any hint of mercy.

"Charles! You're my brother. You're supposed to protect me."

"This is me protecting you from yourself," he said, his voice cold, almost pitying.

Suddenly, Veravine's port rattled on my wrist. A voice echoed through the chambers.

The swallows of songbirds tore through the muggy Ravensla air that morning. I watched her from afar, her beauty as she ran through the streets. She'd once given me this bracelet as a gift, my heart nearly shattering as she embraced me. It wasn't made of fine material—just a simple silver chain with a glass pendant. I kept it, crying as the relentless moon watched me every night.

I knew she was mine—her diamond-shaped face, the strand of blonde curling against her jaw. I'd ensure her safety, and that Lynwood would care for her if she ever needed anything. I never wanted this life for Fallon—a life of hiding, of mystery. She was better off never knowing the truth. They'd kill her if they found out whose daughter she was.

I watched her roam the streets. The knots in her hair were always untied weekly. Did she feel unloved? A life spent searching for a place in a cruel world. And was I cruel for letting her dwell on those thoughts, on the idea that she might never know her worth?

Her children were cursed with quells, tainted by Forgotten blood. But death was no punishment. The blood of the misjudged would rise. Weakness would find strength, sprung through the shallows of flame and shadow.

They'd come for me. But they didn't kill me because my heart pounded for a man of power. They killed me because they believed I didn't love them back. But I smiled as my blood ran red—the same color as theirs.

As my last breaths filled the night air, they came for vengeance, and I stared at her slender fingers as her quell broke through my body. If only I had told her how much I loved her, would she have killed me? Would the king still have stolen her eyes?

And on my last breath, I whispered, "You will rise, Fallon."

"What was that?" I gasped. "Who was that?"

Charles struck me again with his relic of ice, its power seeming to drain not just my strength, but my very essence. Frost settled on my lashes and coated my vocal cords, and I was pulled lower, sinking to my knees on the cold stone before the king's throne.

No one else seemed to hear it. Not Charles, not the king, not Archer. No one had heard Veravine's voice.

Charles lowered his trembling hands. "You have no forbidden quell, Severyn. I don't understand," he murmured. "Monty said you resurrected two students and a dragon."

The king narrowed his eyes. "Perhaps it wasn't Naraic. In my old age, I see things... it must be the songbirds. They're quite loud."

Songbirds. The king had heard her port… but how?

I peeked between my hands, bracing for pain, for death—but neither came. Had I used all those keys? Could Damien be alive? Archer would have told me.

"What now?" My voice was thin, drained.

Charles glanced at the king, then back at me. "You have one week, Severyn. One week until I take you to Malvoria."

Archer growled, "She is my heir. She will not leave my side."

What Charles said next felt like a blow to the chest. "A false heir, Serpent. Severyn has no shadow blood in her. That mark will kill her before the lack of sunlight does. A ruler cannot love their second in line. I hope whatever crush lingers between you dies before her titling service. I'll deal with you later."

"Then, fucking kill me. Take me to the prisons and see how well that goes when every realm has its stars stolen."

Archer stared ahead, his gaze empty, as if he understood the lust between us was forbidden. He couldn't protect me anymore.

Charles stiffened. "That's the risk of treason, Mr. Lynch. If anyone finds out you made her your heir, the Continent's trust will be shattered. You defied the Serpent Academy by keeping that snake for her."

"You know damn well why I kept that snake," Archer hissed at Charles. "Now, let's leave. Severyn is my heir and there is not a damn thing you can do about it."

The silence that followed was suffocating. The weight of my name crushed me. It was no longer about survival. It was about what I would lose before the end. My soul? My family? Or my place in a world that had already cast me aside?

I wasn't surviving anymore. I was just waiting for the inevitable.

I was a severed heir, torn between shadow, flame, and my home of ice.

Epilogue

Archer Lynch

Severyn once asked me if we truly find ourselves when we become a Serpent. I wish I had all the answers for her. Most days, I wish it had been Klaus who survived. I once heard a story about Gemini dragons and the strange, hidden words spoken by a golden-eyed man. He claimed they were a curse. He said our bloodlines are *bound* by this curse—doomed to merge as either flame or shadow.

Klaus was not Naraic's first rider, nor the first of his bloodline. Another had ridden him before—a flame wielder whose eyes haunted more than the dust in my family home.

This bond between Severyn and me feels like every bond between Ciaran and Naraic. Every friendship, every burst of laughter. We were meant to find each other, just as Klaus and I had been meant to. And every single rider of Naraic's has died. It would be me next... I would make sure of it.

I miss Klaus. I grieve in silence because I kept his last letter, the one he asked me to deliver to his father after his death. I held onto it even when *she* burned everything else he had written.

I made a promise to Klaus in those final weeks, when he would stay awake until the sunlight crept through his window, scribbling endlessly. He wrote about everything and nothing, and I forced myself not to read any of it. I didn't want to know how it would end. I didn't want to know how I'd find his sister, how my vow of protection would falter, or how hard the fall would be when I looked into her emerald eyes and felt pain, grief, and anger all at once. I didn't want to know how much I would hurt her.

I didn't want it to be her. I didn't want to hate and love the same person in the span of a few months.

I knew about our father's barter. I knew I'd never truly have her. But I also knew I couldn't bear to lose something I would desperately yearn for. I lived with her name in my mind for two years, waiting for the day she would learn mine. Maybe keeping that lindworm was my way of protecting her. Because when Klaus wrote that Damien would claim my father's title, I knew I had no choice but to make her my heir so she would not become *his* wife.

AUTHOR'S NOTE

Thank you so much for reading *Burning Heir*. I hope you enjoyed the story as much as I loved writing it. Stay tuned for *Severed Heir*, where Severyn begins her journey as an heir and uncovers even more dangerous secrets.

This series will span five books across three timelines at the Serpent Academy. Severyn's story will unfold as a trilogy, while Fallon and Veravine will each have their own standalone novels. When I started writing this series, I wanted to create a softer heroine—someone shy, thoughtful, and led by her heart. I hope you'll continue to love watching Severyn grow as much as I do while writing her.

If you enjoyed this book, I would truly appreciate if you would consider giving a review on **Amazon** or **Goodreads**. Readers want to hear your thoughts!

If you want access to exclusive book content and updates, please consider subscribing to my free newsletter at **www.Kelseyforster.com** I am mostly active on **TikTok**, where I will share updates about my series. I love chatting with fellow readers and adding to my endless TBR!

Thank you once again for giving *Burning Heir* a chance.

Acknowledgments

This book would not have been possible without the unwavering support of my husband, who was the first to hear my pitches and endless ideas for plot twists. My two cats deserve a mention for keeping me company during the countless hours I spent writing and, of course, my dog, Zelda.

I'm also deeply grateful to my family for believing in me and for the endless supply of books they gifted me during my childhood, sparking my dream to become an author.

When I began writing *Burning Heir*, it was a trial project titled *The Serpent Title*. Through numerous revisions, the story transformed into what it is now, and I fell in love with the idea of a magical academy. I hope you've fallen in love with it too.

And finally, thank you, readers. Your support and imagination bring these stories to life.

What's next? Severyn's journey continues as she navigates her faltered heirship, encounters unexpected faces, and uncovers more secrets and dangerous bargains.

Don't worry, this is a happily ever after… ♥

Soul Splinter

Kelsey Forster

In the depths of Scarlett's mind lies a world she never knew existed—a realm where dreams bleed into reality, and destinies intertwine. Scarlett, an ordinary eighteen-year-old, awakens to find herself living through the eyes of the powerful, angel-blooded Violetta Blackwell. In her dreams, she encounters a captivating stranger. This power comes at a cost that may demand even her very existence if she is not strong enough to harbor Violetta's soul and avoid getting attacked by the beasts that roam this forgotten world. With each leap between lives and her love for Ember in one—will she be able to live up to her past life and the prophecy Violetta swore to fulfill?

Prepare to lose yourself in a world where dreams and reality merge and the power of love and the weight of choice collide. Can Scarlett defy the odds, shape her destiny, and uncover the truth within her fractured soul?